Ian McFadyen was born in Liverpool and has enjoyed a successful career in marketing. He lives in Hertfordshire with his wife, his three children and his retired greyhound. *Frozen to Death* is his third novel featuring DI Steve Carmichael, following *Little White Lies* (Book Guild, 2008) and *Lillia's Diary* (Book Guild, 2009).

Northamptonshire

DISCARDED

Libraries

D0544346

**By the same author:**

*Little White Lies*, Book Guild Publishing, 2008

*Little White Lies* (large print edition), Magna Large Print Books, 2010

*Lillia's Diary*, Book Guild Publishing, 2009

# FROZEN TO DEATH

Ian McFadyen

Book Guild Publishing
Sussex, England

First published in Great Britain in 2010 by
The Book Guild Ltd
Pavilion View
19 New Road
Brighton
BN1 1UF

Copyright © Ian McFadyen 2010

The right of Ian McFadyen to be identified as the author of this
work has been asserted by him in accordance with the Copyright,
Designs and Patents Act 1988.

All rights reserved. No part of this publication may be reproduced,
transmitted, or stored in a retrieval system, in any form or by any
means, without permission in writing from the publisher, nor be
otherwise circulated in any form of binding or cover other than
that in which it is published and without a similar condition being
imposed on the subsequent purchaser.

All characters in this publication are fictitious and any
resemblance to real people, alive or dead, is purely coincidental.

Typesetting in Baskerville by
Nat-Type, Cheshire

Printed in Great Britain by
CPI Antony Rowe

A catalogue record for this book is available from
The British Library.

ISBN 978 1 84624 519 0

*This book is dedicated to the memory of Donald and Doreen, my parents, and to Chris, Emma, Jamie and Lauren, the four people I care about the most.*

# Chapter 1

**Saturday 24<sup>th</sup> January**

Gerard Poole was slightly built with angular features and a mop of silvery grey hair which sat Beatle-like on the top of his thin, gaunt head. In his younger days Gerry, as he was commonly known, had been an impulsive and decisive man. However, with the passing of time and more latterly with the death of his beloved wife, Lesley, the now retired 58-year-old had become almost unrecognisable from the impetuous, thrusting executive who had carved out a successful career for himself in sales and marketing in the UK motor trade. His once flamboyant nature had abandoned him completely and he now struck a very sad and lonely figure as he shuffled almost invisibly around the neighbourhood.

He had been wrestling over one particular dilemma and, whilst the decision he needed to make, on the face of it, should not have been that difficult, nevertheless he had dithered badly for the best part of two months, seemingly incapable of resolving his conundrum.

Now that he was faced with a final deadline, he knew he could prevaricate no longer. For almost an hour he sat in the quiet isolation of his front room making up his mind. As he mulled over what to do, he could feel his heart pounding and the palms of his hands felt clammy. At long last, having considered the only two scenarios available to him, he made a decision. He opted to take the route that was financially in his own best interests, even though he knew deep down that Lesley would not have approved.

He gazed with glum wistfulness at her picture in the ornate silver frame that rested on the piano, took a deep breath and picked up the phone to make the all- important call.

# *Chapter 2*

**Monday 26<sup>th</sup> January**

As the rain came down on the small, sleepy Lancashire hamlet of Newbridge, the young cleaner made her way to her regular Monday appointment at the secluded house. As the rainfall grew heavier she quickened her step. Dodging the puddles and trying her hardest to avoid the regular tidal waves thrown up by discourteous drivers, she finally made it to the house. The young woman quickly opened the front door and once inside removed her wet coat, kicked off her soaking shoes and took out of the bag she was carrying a clean blue apron and pair of comfortable flat shoes.

\* \* \* \*

Half a mile away, DC Rachel Dalton wearily sat up in bed clutching a handful of soft paper tissues. Her head ached and her throat was swollen and sore. She had managed only a few hours' sleep the night before and she still felt very weak and tired.

'I will be back to see you at lunchtime!' said her boyfriend Gregor in his thick Eastern European accent, as he gently kissed her forehead. 'I have left more paper handkerchiefs down here by the bed and don't forget to finish the hot lemon drink I have made for you.' As he mentioned the drink he moved his eyes in the direction of the bedside cabinet where the steaming mug he had prepared for her was resting.

'Thank you,' replied Rachel in a pathetic squeaky voice. 'You have been a real star.'

Gregor kissed her forehead again, passed her the remote control for the small TV that was perched at the opposite side of the room and left for work.

Rachel waited until the sound of Gregor's ancient Skoda had disappeared before she turned on the TV.

'It's either *Jeremy Kyle* or *The Lovelace Show*,' she muttered to herself. She ultimately elected to watch *The Lovelace Show*. At least they occasionally have some reasonably normal people, she thought, although the next ten minutes viewing did little to support that opinion.

'After the break,' proclaimed Caroline Lovelace with her upper-class diction, 'we will be meeting a man who claims his wife is cheating on him with at least three other people, one of them his own brother.'

Rachel must have dozed off because when she awoke the local weather report was just finishing.

'So in summary,' announced the pretty young weathergirl, 'for these last few days of January we will have more rain, I'm afraid, but enjoy it while you can because the long-term forecast for the middle and end of February is that we will have severe arctic conditions which look like remaining with us for a sustained period. I am Tamara Searle and I'll be back with another weather update in an hour.'

'Thank you, Tamara,' said the smiling Caroline Lovelace. 'It looks like we will all need our thermals in a week or so. Anyway, enough of the weather let's have those all-important lie detector test results.'

Rachel could not bear to watch anymore. She pressed the red button on the remote and fell back against her pillow.

\* \* \* \*

As her routine dictated, the young cleaner's first task was to tidy the kitchen and vacuum the downstairs rooms. This took her no more than thirty minutes. Having completed these rooms she then made her way to the master bedroom. At first she did not notice anything amiss. However, as she walked around the bed she discovered a sight which took her by surprise and made her immediately reach in her pocket for her mobile phone.

# Chapter 3

**Monday 2ⁿᵈ February**

Carmichael had always loathed the month of February and since moving north this hatred had only been reinforced. The cold, soggy Lancashire winters certainly did not agree with him and by the time the month of February had arrived he was sick and tired of the weather and the associated colds and sniffles that he seemed to encounter with just about everyone he met.

'When will we get some warm bright weather?' he moaned as he pulled open the bedroom curtains and gazed despondently at the heavy rain as it slanted across the sky.

'June, I think!' replied Penny from beneath the warm duvet.

'I wouldn't mind if it snowed or was frosty,' Carmichael continued. 'At least then we would get some variety, but all we seem to get here from October to March is rain and when it's not raining it's either windy or just damp and miserable.'

'Well, actually the weather report on the radio yesterday did say that we may be in for some arctic conditions towards the end of this week which could stay with us for two to three weeks,' said Penny in an effort to appease her ill-tempered husband.

'At least that would be something different,' Carmichael replied grumpily, 'but to be honest I wouldn't hold much store in what they say. They only get the next day's weather right about half the time, which is amazing given that it rains here about ninety per cent of the time, so it's not exactly difficult.'

Penny realised that there was no point in her trying to cheer him up; he was clearly in a bad mood, which she put down to him not having any interesting cases to work on at the moment.

'What are you up to today?' she asked, hoping to at least get the conversation onto another subject.

'Cooper and I have to go down to Hookham Cross this morning,' he replied with little enthusiasm. 'There have been a number of incidents of livestock being stolen from a couple of the farms down there, so we need to talk with the farmers.'

'Isn't that a job for the uniformed guys?' Penny asked with an air of surprise.

'Yes,' sighed Carmichael gloomily, 'under normal circumstances that would be true, but at the moment we are so short-staffed at the station, with all the colds and flu that are going around, that we need to do it; otherwise it will be weeks before it's looked at.'

'Is it really that bad?' enquired Penny.

'Yes, it's dreadful,' replied Carmichael. 'Yesterday we must have been down to just half the normal number of staff. Even Rachel's off. She's been off now for a week and doesn't look likely to be back for at least a few more days yet.'

'What about the others in your team?' Penny asked.

'Well, Marc Watson seems OK and so does Paul Cooper, so we are not so bad in my team. However, the uniform guys have really been decimated.'

'Well, you better not bring it home with you,' remarked Penny. 'We don't want to catch anything here. I'm not sure I can cope with you or any of the children being laid up for any length of time.'

'Don't worry!' Carmichael replied. 'We southerners are

made of much stronger stuff. It will take a bit more than a cold to put *me* out of action.'

If only that were true, thought Penny, whose painful memories of her husband's previous bouts of 'man flu' were still very vivid in her mind.

*     *     *     *

Carmichael left the house at about 7.25 a.m., which gave him more than adequate time to travel the fifteen winding country miles to Hookham Cross.

It was only after he had departed that Penny, Robbie and Natalie got up and slowly descended to the kitchen for breakfast.

As Penny entered the kitchen she could hear the unmistakeable sound of her son's voice. 'Big deal!' shouted Robbie as he seized the last carton of milk from the fridge and, not realising that his mother had entered the room, took a huge swig.

'Mum,' whined Natalie. 'Did you see what Robbie just did?'

Penny shook her head slowly in disbelief and despair. 'Robbie, that's revolting,' she said. 'As that's the last carton we have, you can go over to the shop before you go to school and get another one.'

Robbie put the empty carton in the bin and held his hand out to his mother for some money. 'I don't know why you're so concerned,' he snapped at his little sister. 'You don't even drink that milk; you have that disgusting goat's muck.'

Penny took out her purse from the drawer of the Welsh dresser and gave her son a two-pound coin. Robbie snatched it out of her hand and with little sign of any remorse marched down the hall and out of the house, slamming the front door behind him.

'Morning, dear,' said Penny to her daughter as soon as they were alone. 'Has there been any post today?'

Natalie, with her mouth full of cornflakes and her head in the *Daily Mail,* pointed to the end of the table where a small pile of letters had been plonked by her brother a few minutes earlier.

'This one looks like it's from Jemma!' exclaimed Penny, who quickly ripped open the letter with the Leeds postmark.

* * * *

At a little after 9 a.m. a narrowboat called *Safe Haven* glided silently through the heavy rain into the quiet village of Moulton Bank. This was the first time that Sidney Sydes, the dishevelled pilot of the vessel, had been to the sleepy Lancashire village and his arrival was certainly not a chance visit.

* * * *

Carmichael's experiences that morning did little to improve his foul mood. He was not a great lover of farms. He hated the smell of manure, and the rain and cold wind made him, not for the first time, question the wisdom of leaving his familiar surroundings in London.

The two farms he visited that morning were next-door neighbours. The first farm was owned by Harry Jackson, a dour, tall, skinny man in his mid-fifties, with a weathered and wrinkled, red face that had probably not smiled in the last twenty years. According to Jackson, he had lost six good young heifers in two separate incidents in the previous three weeks. As Harry Jackson led Carmichael and Cooper across his field to the spot where he believed the thefts had taken place, the cold wind picked up speed, driving the rain hard into their faces.

'It was along this stretch that they got in the first time,' he said in a broad Lancashire accent. 'You can see where I've had to rebuild it.'

'And you think this was all done in broad daylight?' Cooper asked.

'Yes,' replied Jackson. 'At this time of the year we always bring them in at night.'

'And the second incident?' asked Carmichael. 'Where did they break through then?'

'Down the hill a-ways,' replied Jackson, pointing further down the field. 'Stony Lane runs along the field here for about a half mile, so they have a fair way to break through the fence.'

'Wouldn't they have had difficulty herding the cattle out of the field and into their lorry?' Carmichael asked.

'If they were used to working with cattle I wouldn't have thought so,' replied Jackson.

'I see,' replied Carmichael.

The second farm the officers visited belonged to a younger, sturdily built man called Melvyn Hitchcock. He was in his thirties and to Carmichael's relief was a much more friendly man than Harry Jackson. He had also lost livestock to the rustlers. However, in his case this had all happened in one go, when ten of his dairy cows had been stolen.

'It looks like a similar MO to Mr Jackson,' said Cooper as the three men studied the mended fence where the thieves had made their entry.

'But in this case we got some very good tyre tracks,' said Carmichael. 'So hopefully this will help us locate the perpetrators.'

'I sincerely hope so,' said Hitchcock. 'It's hard enough to make ends meet as a livestock farmer these days without having to cope with losses incurred by theft too.'

After spending almost three hours traipsing around dirty farmyards in the rain, Carmichael finally clambered back into his car just before midday. Soaked to the skin and with the tell-tale signs of his mornings activities caked on his shoes and trouser bottoms, he decided to go home and change his clothes before going on to Kirkwood Police Station. Cooper, on the other hand, needed no such detour. Being a local man and having started his police career as a beat bobby in a rural area, he was well used to being around farmyards and, unlike his boss, he had arrived that morning appropriately attired, wearing his wellingtons and canvas waterproof over-trousers.

'I'll see you back at the station then,' Cooper said as he pulled away from Hitchcock's farm.

'Yes,' replied Carmichael, who felt very uncomfortable as he sat in his car in his wet and stinking clothes. 'You start writing up the reports; I'll join you in about an hour.'

\*　\*　\*　\*

After tying up his narrowboat, Sidney Sydes made a call on his mobile.

'Hello, it's Sid here,' he said to the person on the other end. 'I'm currently in a small village called Moulton Bank. I plan to moor up here for a few days. I'll call you again on Thursday.'

The person on the end of the line had little chance to enter into any dialogue, as Sidney ended the call as soon as he had finished his sentence.

\*　\*　\*　\*

When Carmichael arrived home he found the house empty. Not wishing to contaminate anything, he removed his shoes and gingerly went upstairs to the bathroom where he threw off his clothes and jumped under the shower. Once he had showered, he hastily changed into a new suit and fresh shirt, before descending the stairs carrying his smelly suit and shirt screwed up in a ball and held as far away from his body as possible. On reaching the bottom he made his way down the hall and into the kitchen where he stuffed his suit into a black bin bag, which he then abandoned with his shirt on the floor next to the washing machine.

As he headed towards the door, he noticed the opened letter from Jemma on the kitchen table. Another letter addressed to him lay next to it and the handwriting caught his eye. It was in a hand that he did not recognise, but it grabbed his attention as it was very neat and precise and looked as though it had been written with great care. He picked up both letters and put them into his jacket pocket before leaving the house for Kirkwood Police Station.

Carmichael was oblivious to the sniggers in the main office as he walked towards his desk. Cooper had naively told Marc Watson about the mess the boss was in and the fact that he had gone home to change, and Watson, being Watson, had made it his business to spread this bit of news to everyone he came into contact with. So as soon as Carmichael arrived it became the cue for the rank and file to nudge each other and make infantile comments under their breath.

Fortunately for them, Carmichael did not pick up on any of this juvenile banter, and as soon as he was safely inside his office he shut the door behind him and started to read the letter from his daughter Jemma at Leeds University. Jemma was now in her second term and to Steve and Penny's delight appeared to be settling in really well. Her weekly letters were always very upbeat about all the new friends she was making and usually listed in some detail the various great bands she had been able to see at the Student Union. At least that is what Carmichael assumed they were, not really having any idea who or what the likes of The Ting Tings were. This letter was no different to previous ones; however, to cap everything off and to his utter astonishment, Jemma finished by claiming that she had found herself a part-time job to earn some money. Having spent the past two years trying to encourage his eldest daughter to get a weekend job to earn a little pocket money, with absolutely no success, Carmichael could not believe that she had now decided off her own back that she needed to work. In her letter she did not say what the work involved but Carmichael did not mind this minor oversight. Feeling suitably impressed with her, he set her letter down and opened the other one.

* * * *

To Penny's delight, her husband's mood when he returned home that evening was much improved from when he had left that morning. 'Did you read Jemma's letter?' he asked excitedly. 'It would appear that she's finally got herself a job. After eighteen years, at last she will start to realise that money is hard to earn and she may even start to value it a bit more.'

Penny was not so optimistic, but she did not want to curb her husband's enthusiasm.

'Yes, it's great news,' she replied. 'I suspect the simple truth is that she has realised that to get every last bit of socialising in she needs to be able to fund her excesses, but it's good that she is showing some initiative, not that she said what she was actually doing.'

Carmichael laughed. 'Yes, I'm sure she won't be saving anything, but at least this will help to prevent her student debt getting too far out of control.'

'I wouldn't go as far as that,' replied Penny. 'But it's certainly going to help her. Anyway, changing the subject, what on earth did you get up to this morning? That suit you so carefully screwed up and left in a bin bag by the washing machine stank the place out. I've had to tie up the bag and put it in the garage. I also had to spray air freshener everywhere when I came in – the whole house smelt like a pig farm.'

'Cattle farm, to be precise,' replied Carmichael guiltily. 'I'm sorry about that, I was in a rush and didn't have time to take it to the dry cleaners. I spent all morning in farmyards and they were not that well kept.'

'You need to dress appropriately if you're going to wander around farms, my dear,' laughed Penny. 'Wellingtons rather than brogues are what you need; and a suit is totally the wrong thing to wear!'

'Yes, I realise that now,' he replied. 'Anyway, changing the subject again, guess where we've been invited?'

'I've no idea,' replied Penny. 'Maybe the West Lancashire livestock show. Are we being asked to judge the best bull in show?'

'No,' replied Carmichael sternly. 'We've been asked to a Valentine's night dinner party by Caroline Lovelace a week on Saturday at her house.'

He handed to Penny the letter he had opened up that afternoon in the office.

Penny carefully read the invitation before passing it back to her husband. 'My word, we *are* honoured.'

# Chapter 4

Caroline Lovelace was the local celebrity in Moulton Bank. At just forty years of age she was an accomplished journalist and celebrated TV reporter. Latterly she had become particularly well known for hosting the highly popular daytime TV programme *The Lovelace Show*, which was on every weekday and specialised in investigating and resolving relationship issues, Caroline's self-professed forte.

Her arrival in the village, a little over three years earlier, was the cause of much conversation at the time and, although she and her family were now firmly established in the area, she continued to be the main source of gossip within the community. In keeping with their lofty status, Caroline had bought just about the grandest house in the village, which was located at the end of a quiet private lane at the top of the Common.

Carmichael and Penny were not avid viewers of *The Lovelace Show*, nevertheless they were very flattered to be invited to one of her famous dinner parties, which were certainly a sought-after prize in the village.

In the days that led up to the dinner party, Penny decided that it might be a good idea for her and Steve to watch a few of Caroline's shows, just in case the conversation should meander in that direction. Carmichael was not one hundred per cent happy with the plan as he was uncomfortable with the idea of appearing to be a mere sycophant to the 'great lady', however, he reluctantly agreed. He knew that Penny was right and, no matter how much he tried, he could not imagine the possibility of the dinner table *conversazione* avoiding Ms Lovelace's day job. He certainly did not want to look foolish should he be required to pass comment on the subject of one of her shows.

'I suppose you'll need a new outfit?' he asked, although he knew full well the answer.

'I think a new outfit, new handbag and a visit to the hairdresser's are the minimum required,' Penny replied with enthusiastic delight.

\* \* \* \*

Caroline Lovelace had invited ten people to her 'Valentine's Evening' dinner party. In addition to Carmichael and Penny, she had invited two other couples and four single guests, two males and two females. As usual, the RSVPs did not take long to arrive, which Caroline and her husband, Roy, personally checked.

\* \* \* \*

Sidney Sydes' stay in Moulton Bank was not as short as he had planned. When he tried to start up the engine of his narrowboat on the Thursday morning, a loud bang accompanied by a thick black fog and a burning smell indicated to him that he had a problem. After several hours of banging and tinkering, he came to the conclusion that the engine needed repairs that were far beyond his capabilities.

He picked up his mobile and called the same number he had called twice weekly for the last three years. 'It's Sid here,' he said moodily. 'I'm going to be staying here in Moulton Bank for at least another week. The engine's buggered and it will take me a while to get someone out here to sort it out.'

'Do you need any assistance from us?' came the reply from the well-spoken man at the end of the phone.

'No,' replied Sydes firmly. 'I can handle this. I just want to make sure you know why I'm going to be here for a bit longer than I had planned.'

'OK,' replied the voice at the end of the phone. 'If you change your mind call me again.'

Sidney did not bother to reply. He pushed the red button on his mobile to end the call.

\* \* \* \*

When the day of the dinner party arrived, Penny and Carmichael donned their finest threads and armed with a fine bottle of red wine expertly selected by Carmichael from the village wine merchant, the couple set off in a taxi to the Lovelace residence.

It had been a cold day and the ground was already icy, but as they made their way towards the house it started to snow.

'Here it comes,' commented the driver. 'They reckon that this snow could be quite severe and it could linger for weeks.'

'Really?' replied Penny who remembered the conversation she and her husband had had the week before. 'Did you hear that, Steve? We could be in for a cold spell. Didn't I tell you?'

\* \* \* \*

Rachel Dalton's flu had finally receded and she felt able to return to work. She could not remember ever being off school or work for more than a couple of days in her life, so to have been laid up in bed for three weeks was a sure sign of how nasty the current bout of flu was. Feeling guilty about being absent from work for so long, she had volunteered to be the token member of CID on duty at Kirkwood Station that weekend and had arrived at the station at about 8 a.m.

Apart from a few minor interruptions her day was relatively quiet. So much so that she managed to catch up with all her outstanding paperwork by the time she was ready to call it a day at around 6 p.m. It was just at that time when she received a call from the desk sergeant.

'What!' she exclaimed in frustration. 'Can't it wait, 'til the morning?'

Having been advised in no uncertain terms by the duty sergeant that the matter in hand could not wait, she made her way down to the custody suite to greet the two Asian-looking men accused of cattle rustling. They had been apprehended by a couple of village bobbies as they made their way on foot down a remote country lane, about 200 yards from where a broken-down white transit van laden with two traumatised cows had been abandoned.

\*     \*     \*     \*

When Caroline Lovelace opened her front door to greet Carmichael and Penny, the first thought that came into Carmichael's mind was that she was a throwback to the early twentieth century and the days of the British Empire. He could easily envisage their hostess holding court in India, with a myriad of servants following her instructions to the letter and pandering to her every wish. Although clearly confident and articulate, and certainly still a very fine-looking woman for her age, her posture, the way that she talked to people and the general air that pervaded her, smacked of someone who saw herself as a class above the mere mortals whom she had deigned to invite that evening. Having said all that, Carmichael did find her a fascinating and not unlikable individual, and when he found his name card placed directly to the hostess's left-hand side at the dinner table he felt very honoured.

As always, Caroline had carefully selected her dinner

guests that evening with three main criteria in mind: first, that the balance between males and females was equal; secondly that there was a good mixture of single people and married couples; and thirdly that as far as practically possible her guests would be unacquainted with each other.

'Before we start dinner,' Caroline announced, 'I would like to spend a few moments introducing all my guests, as I'm not sure you will all have met each other before. Starting at the far end of the table we have my wonderful husband Roy, who you all probably know is not only a renowned barrister but as from the last General Election became MP for the borough of Mid-Lancashire.'

The overweight, middle-aged man at the opposite end of the table smiled broadly and nodded to the rest of the guests.

'To my husband's left we have Emma Cashman and to *her* left her husband Declan. Roy and I have known Declan and Emma for many years. Emma is well known for her sterling work with a plethora of charities. She's also the proprietor of The Helpful Angels, who have provided the catering staff this evening. Declan, her charming husband, is a very successful local property developer.'

A frumpy-looking lady in the plain dress smiled gently down the table. Her smug husband, who was much more expensively dressed, made no attempt to engage the rest of the guests, preferring instead to continue to take small sips of red wine.

'To my husband's right I have pleasure in introducing Dr Sarah and Mr McIntyre,' continued Caroline. 'Sarah is an eminent child psychologist and has written many books on child development. She has also been very helpful to me and my team on *The Lovelace Show*. You may have seen her on the show. Euen, her husband, is the headmaster of Kirkwood Academy, the new school opened three years ago by Tony Blair.'

At this juncture the very smartly dressed couple in their

mid-thirties to Roy's right, peered down the table and in harmony, grinned and gave a friendly wave.

'My next guest is a very old and dear friend of mine,' continued the hostess. 'To the right of Euen we have Sally Crabtree.'

The very thin and pale woman in a bright-green outfit smiled politely at the rest of the dinner guests. 'Sally and I were at university together. However, our career paths have taken very different directions. Isn't that correct, Sally?' Caroline asked.

'Absolutely,' replied Sally.

'For those of you who don't know,' continued Caroline, 'Sally is now a highly renowned sculptor. Her bronzes are highly sought after and very valuable.'

Sally Crabtree smiled down the table in the Carmichaels' direction, patently enjoying her host's flattering introduction.

'Sitting opposite Sally we have Tamara Searle, who I suspect needs no introduction, being the face of the region's weather reports most mornings.'

The familiar face of the region's weathergirl smiled generously and as she did she acknowledged the rest of the guests with a slight nod of her head. Tamara was a tall, elegant woman in her mid-twenties, with bright blue eyes that shone like priceless sapphires. Carmichael had seen her many times on TV and had always thought that she was very attractive, but he had to conclude that TV did not do her justice at all; in the flesh she was infinitely more eye-catching. His admiration was clearly shared by the other males scattered around the table, who simultaneously smiled in her general direction like love-struck schoolboys.

'The lucky man sat to the left of the lovely Tamara', continued Caroline, 'is Dr Alan Wilson, who is again a friend of my husband's and works as a GP in Liverpool.'

This was the cue for the bearded doctor to take his turn to smile up and down the table.

'Sitting to Sally's right we should have had Gerard Poole. Gerry is the widower of Roy's sister, who sadly passed away last year. However, unfortunately he has yet to arrive, hence the spare place.' At that juncture Caroline looked down the table directly at her husband, with more than a hint of frustration.

'I'll try to reach him again on his mobile shortly, my dear,' Roy said, in an effort to reassure his wife. 'I'm sure he'll be here presently.'

Caroline put on what Carmichael took to be a forced smile. He sensed that she was not happy that one of the guests had not arrived as summoned.

'And last, but certainly not least,' commented Caroline as she turned her gaze to Carmichael and Penny. 'We have Penny and Steve Carmichael.'

Carmichael took this as his prompt to say hello and to wave to the rest of the diners.

'Penny is a local Moulton Bank lady and also a mother,' continued Caroline. 'She has three children and also works in the local primary school here in Moulton Bank. And as for her husband, Steve, to my left, I understand that he is originally from the London area but has been a police inspector here in Lancashire for the last three years.' Both Carmichael and Penny were taken aback by the quality of Caroline's research.

With that Caroline sat down and, as conversations started around the table, the door to the dining room opened and four pretty young girls dressed in matching white blouses and tight black pencil skirts arrived with the first course.

\*     \*     \*     \*

Initially the two cattle rustlers refused to comment. They would not even provide the custody sergeant or Rachel Dalton with their names, although it was clear by their accents that they were from Lancashire. However, once their legal representative had arrived they agreed to furnish Rachel with a little information, but refused to admit their guilt.

It was nearly 9 p.m. when Rachel finally managed to escape from Kirkwood Police Station. By the time she left she had managed to establish that the two men who were in custody were brothers called Vivek and Billy Gupta. They were from the Rochdale area some thirty miles away and both had minor criminal records, although no serious convictions.

'Can you let Inspector Carmichael know we have them in custody?' Rachel asked the duty sergeant as she left. 'He may want to interview them himself in the morning as he was personally involved in this enquiry.'

The duty sergeant nodded acceptance and told Rachel to have a nice evening.

\* \* \* \*

There must have been at least four separate conversations being conducted at any specific time during dinner. As such Caroline Lovelace's dining room was a very noisy place that evening. Most of Carmichael's conversations were with Caroline, although occasionally Dr Wilson would chip in too. Penny, on the other hand, was able to join in several conversations, including those involving Tamara Searle, whom she found to be very vocal. Penny surmised that Tamara was a lady with great ambitions.

'How did you get to be a weathergirl?' Penny asked.

'Well, I was working as a researcher for the BBC, but when I heard Sunrise Productions were looking for someone to present the morning weather I just applied.'

'So you have no qualifications or experience in the subject?' Penny enquired with surprise. 'I thought that you would have to have a degree in geography or something like that.'

'Good God, no!' replied Tamara with a giggle. 'I have a

degree in Media Studies from Lincoln University, but I have no formal training in meteorology. That's all done for me by other people far cleverer than I. I just read it out and try and look like I know what I'm talking about.'

'And may I just say you always look absolutely stunning, my dear,' interjected Declan Cashman, his eyes fixed on the beautiful young woman.

'Why thank you!' replied Tamara, who unashamedly lapped up the compliment.

'So where do you see your career going from here, Miss Searle?' asked Dr Wilson.

'I want to get into some real TV journalism,' she replied. 'I'm hoping that Caroline can help me there.'

'I'm sure she will be more than happy to help you as much as she can,' commented Roy Lovelace.

Penny had been monitoring Declan Cashman and Roy Lovelace quite closely over dinner. She had concluded that the two men were from similar moulds. It was obvious that they both found Tamara very attractive, and she could also not help noticing them eyeing up a couple of the young waitresses. Although Penny could not make out exactly what was said, she had observed Declan whisper something to one of the girls, making her look very embarrassed. On another occasion she was sure that Roy Lovelace put his arm around the waist of one of the other waitresses, which was so unwelcome that from then on the poor girl tried as hard as she could to only wait on people towards Penny's end of the table.

'So what made you decide to invite a humble police inspector and his wife to your dinner party?' Carmichael finally managed to ask his hostess.

Caroline considered the question for a few moments. 'To be honest with you, Inspector,' she replied loftily, 'it was your wife I wished to meet. I am considering sending Chelsea, our youngest child, to the local school here and I wanted to talk to her about the school.'

Carmichael was crestfallen at being there only as his wife's partner, but he tried hard to mask his disappointment.

'I'm sure Penny will be more than happy to answer any questions you have,' he said. 'but it's normally the headmistress parents go to for such things.'

'I know,' replied Caroline, 'but I always discover that the people who are at the coal face are the people who really know what's going on. In my work I usually find that those people in power are very adept at making things sound much better than they really are. I am hoping that Penny will give me an honest appraisal of the school, warts and all.'

'I'm sure she will,' replied Carmichael.

At that moment Carmichael's mobile started to vibrate in his pocket.

'Please excuse me,' he said as he rose from the dinner table. 'I really do have to take this call.'

'It's true what they say then,' commented Caroline. 'That a policeman is never off duty.'

Penny smiled at her hostess. 'Never!' she said with feeling.

Carmichael made his way out of the dining room and once in the hallway took the call.

As the desk sergeant updated Carmichael on the apprehension of the rustlers earlier that evening, he noticed that at the far end of the corridor one of the waitresses was in a distressed state and was being comforted by another. At first neither of the waitresses noticed him. However, once they did the distraught waitress rushed off in the direction of the toilet. Her friend did not follow; she smiled at Carmichael and sheepishly made off in the opposite direction.

'I don't particularly need to be in on the interviews tomorrow,' Carmichael said to the duty sergeant. 'Make sure, though, that either Cooper or Rachel are present, and ask them to keep me informed by phone on what happens.'

He ended the call and made his way back towards the dining room. Carmichael's mind was preoccupied with the conversation he had just had on the phone and he was not looking where he was heading. As a result he almost collided with Tamara Searle, who was coming down the corridor towards him.

'I'm sorry!' Carmichael said, as he sidestepped Tamara. 'I was miles away.'

Tamara smiled sweetly at him. 'Please don't apologise. It was my fault entirely,' she replied. As the weathergirl sauntered down the corridor, Carmichael could not help thinking what a gorgeous-looking woman she was.

\*　\*　\*　\*

As the evening progressed the snowfall grew heavier and the air temperature dropped to well below freezing.

Despite having the wood burner on all day, Sidney Sydes could not seem to get his narrowboat warm. He sat close to the burner in several layers of clothing, but still he shivered. Even the numerous mugs of hot tea he had drunk that evening seemed to do little to help him. At last he decided that his best course of action was to try and get some sleep. He figured that once under the blankets he might be able to retain some warmth.

Before turning in he put a large pile of logs on the burner and took one last peep out of the window across the canal and out into the countryside. The snow was now coming down so thick that it was impossible for him to see more than a few yards. The canal had frozen over and through the blizzard he could see that there was already a thin layer of snow starting to form on the top of the ice.

In the undergrowth, roughly a hundred yards down the towpath from where *Safe Haven* was moored, the body of Gerry Poole was rapidly becoming covered. By the time Sidney Sydes fell asleep, the frozen corpse was completely hidden under a blanket of thick freshly fallen snow.

*   *   *   *

Carmichael had ordered their taxi for 11.30, but when it finally arrived it was 11.50. He and Penny thanked their hosts for a lovely evening and bundled themselves into the back seat.

'I'm sorry I'm late. The roads are treacherous tonight!' announced the taxi driver. 'It's taken me about twenty minutes longer than normal to get up here and I've passed dozens of cars that have been abandoned in the snow along the way.'

'Well, I have it on good authority, from a lady who knows, that this is going to be with us for some time yet,' said Penny, referring to a conversation she had had earlier with Tamara Searle.

'Well, after I've dropped you two off that's it for me tonight,' replied the driver. 'This weather is deadly.'

# Chapter 5

When Penny threw back the curtains on Sunday morning, the snow lay deep on the ground, like a thick white duvet. The sky was now bright blue with no trace of a cloud to be seen. In the east over Ambient Hill she could see the gleaming winter sun, which hung low in the sky. Its piercing rays of light bounced up from the whitened ground below and made her tired eyes squint and blink.

'It must be years since we have had so much snow,' she said with childlike glee, as she rubbed her eyes.

Carmichael gently stirred. 'Wow, that's bright!' he moaned, as the reflected sunlight reached his eyes. 'How much snow is there?'

'I'd say about a couple of feet,' Penny replied.

'Thank God it's Sunday,' Carmichael responded. 'At least we don't have to go to work today.'

'I doubt you would make it anyway,' said Penny. 'The cars on the main road out there look like they're finding it hard going, so I would imagine that most of the back roads to Kirkwood station will be impassable.'

Carmichael clambered out of bed, yawned, scratched his stomach and ambled over to join his wife at the window. 'Bloody hell,' he remarked. 'You weren't kidding, were you! It must be at least two feet thick. It's probably even deeper in some places.'

As it was now approaching 9 o'clock, they could see some people out there, struggling to make their way on foot and those who were in cars looked to be faring even worse.

'I think we should give church a miss today,' Carmichael yawned. 'I think it will be almost impossible to get a car up Ambient Hill, and I'm not keen on trying to get there on foot in these conditions.'

Penny nodded her agreement.

\* \* \* \*

Despite the poor road conditions, Rachel Dalton and Paul Cooper had both managed to make their way to Kirkwood Police Station that morning. Living as she did considerably closer, Rachel arrived first, followed about twenty minutes later by Cooper in his beaten-up but trusty Rover.

'Before we do the interviews can you give me a quick update on these cattle rustlers?' he asked Rachel.

\* \* \* \*

Sidney Sydes woke up still feeling cold, but was relieved to find that he did not feel nearly as rough as he had the night before.

His first instinct was to check the burner. To his relief it was still alight, but only just as it was very low on firewood. He opened up the tin box where he stored the kindling. Apart from a few small sticks it was empty. 'Bugger,' he muttered out loud. 'That's all I need.'

\* \* \* \*

'So, Mr Gupta,' said Cooper, to the younger brother. 'What were you and Vivek doing in Moulton Bank?'

Billy Gupta did not even attempt to make eye contact with

Cooper. He just continued to fix his gaze at the coffee cup in front of him.

'To be honest,' continued Cooper. 'It's no skin off my nose if you remain silent. Although it would make it much simpler for all of us if you told us the truth; all you're doing is making matters worse for yourself.'

Billy Gupta didn't flinch; he just kept staring at the cup in front of him.

'Do you know what I think?' interjected Rachel. 'I think that you and Vivek were stealing livestock to order, and some disreputable butcher or dodgy abattoir owner was in it with you, wasn't he?'

'I don't know what you're talking about!' Billy Gupta replied cockily in his broad Rochdale accent.

'At one of the crime scenes we got some really good tyre tracks and I will wager a month's pay these tracks will match the transit van with the broken axle, the one you and your brother were fleeing from last night,' continued Cooper. 'You and I both know that we have more than enough evidence to convict you both. So if you're smart you'll cooperate. At least then you may be given a reduced sentence by the court.'

Billy still did not baulk at what was being said. 'No comment,' he replied arrogantly.

'OK, it's your choice,' sighed the exasperated Cooper. 'Interview with Billy Gupta terminated at eleven forty-five.'

Rachel Dalton turned off the tape and the two officers left the interview room.

'Let's see if big brother is more forthcoming,' Cooper said, as they crossed the hallway and made their way towards the other interview room.

Less than fifteen minutes later, at just on twelve noon, Cooper and Dalton emerged from their short meeting with Vivek Gupta.

'At least he's a bit less conceited than his little brother,'

Cooper commented. 'And I would not be surprised if, given a bit more time to stew, he doesn't try and do a deal of some sort with us. But I can't see us having any breakthrough with either of them today so let's keep them in for another night and then the boss can decide what we do with them in the morning.'

'Agreed,' replied Dalton, who had just about had enough of the brothers Gupta.

\*　\*　\*　\*

It was also twelve noon when Penny took the call from Caroline Lovelace.

'Can I speak to your husband?' she asked in a tone that was more like an order than a question.

# Chapter 6

It took Carmichael over forty minutes to drive the five miles down Bentley Way, the twisting country lane that connected Moulton Bank and Newbridge. The abandoned silver Jaguar XF that Caroline Lovelace had talked about on their call was parked against the brick wall of the tunnel which ran under the Leeds to Liverpool canal, just as she had stated. Marc Watson, who Carmichael had called directly after he had put the phone down to Caroline, was already on the scene.

'Afternoon, sir,' he said as Carmichael wound down the window. 'It's pretty much as you said. The car is locked and doesn't look like it's been involved in any accident, but there's no sign of the driver.'

Carmichael parked his car about three metres beyond the abandoned car and walked back to where Watson was standing.

'It's not easy to say how long it's been here,' continued Watson. 'Being left under the bridge it's been sheltered from the snow, so it's hard to know whether it was left here before it started snowing last night or not.'

'OK,' replied Carmichael. 'My guess is that it was. It's got no evidence of being exposed to the heavy snowfalls from yesterday evening and it was so cold last night that I suspect there would still be some snow on it had it been parked after the snow started to fall.'

'So what do you think it's doing here?' asked Watson.

'Well, under normal circumstances I would say it was just stolen and abandoned,' explained Carmichael, 'but the owner was supposed to be at a dinner party last night that I attended and he didn't show. I've not met him, but I'm told by his sister-in-law that this is totally out of character and she is concerned that something may have happened to him. Also if it was stolen it's unlikely to have been locked before it was abandoned.'

'So who told you the car was here?' Watson asked.

'It was the sister-in-law,' replied Carmichael. 'Apparently she was so worried about him that she and her husband decided to drive to his house in Newbridge this morning. She maintains that they spotted the car on the way, which is when she called me on her mobile.'

'So where are they now?' asked the slightly confused Watson.

'Good question!' replied Carmichael. 'I did ask her to remain here.'

As he spoke his mobile rang.

'Hello, Inspector,' announced the familiar voice of Caroline Lovelace. 'Have you arrived at Gerry's car yet?'

'Yes I have,' replied Carmichael. 'Where are you?'

'Oh, Roy and I decided to carry on to Gerry's house,' she replied. 'We are there now but of course he's not here. And when we arrived the snow on the drive hadn't been disturbed, so it's clear that no one has been here for at least the last eighteen hours or so.'

'I'm sure there's a perfectly logical explanation,' replied Carmichael, trying his best not to worry Caroline. 'We'll have a look around the area and I'll call you later.'

'Thank you so much,' said Caroline. 'Roy and I are most grateful to you for being so helpful. I am sure you're right and that there's a completely reasonable answer to this puzzle, but we're both very concerned as it's so out of character for Gerry to go missing like this.'

Carmichael put the phone back in the pocket of his new waterproof over-trousers. A recent purchase made for him by Penny.

'Let's have a quick look around to see if we can find any clue to where the owner has gone,' said Carmichael.

'I suggest we look along the canal bank first,' suggested Watson, as he pointed up the snow-covered steep stairway that led up to the waterway.

Carmichael nodded and then followed Watson up the slippery flight of steps.

Once they were safely at the top they found themselves on a relatively wide towpath. It was covered in a sparkling, thick layer of untouched snow.

'Clearly nobody has walked down here since the snow took hold,' remarked Carmichael.

Watson carefully walked over to the edge of the canal, which was still completely frozen over. 'If he's in here we'll struggle to find him until it thaws,' he observed.

Carmichael nodded. 'You're right but we don't even know if he's around here,' he said as he shivered in the icy cold wind. 'For all we know it could all be quite innocent. He could have just met someone under the bridge and gone off in another car.'

'That would make sense. It would explain why he parked up under the bridge,' added Watson. 'And unless he's been on Mars these last few weeks, he must have known that the snow was on its way. Warnings have been on the news and in the papers for ages now.'

'You're right, Marc,' Carmichael sighed. 'We have no reason to believe that he's come to any harm and if he *is* up here it would take an army of officers to find him under all this snow and ice.'

'Shall we call it a day and get back?' Watson asked, hoping the boss would say yes.

It was then that Carmichael saw the small plume of grey

smoke coming from the chimney of a long green barge moored about two hundred metres down the towpath.

'Let's just go and talk with the owner of that narrowboat,' he said. 'You never know, he may have seen something that will shed some light on this mystery.'

That was not what Watson wanted to hear. However, he reluctantly nodded to signal his agreement with Carmichael's idea and the two officers trudged along the footpath towards Sidney Sydes' boat. Carmichael arrived first. He clambered carefully onto the deck at the stern of the boat and knocked loudly on the wooden door.

'Hello!' he shouted. 'It's the police. Is anyone at home?'

Sidney Sydes considered lying low and staying quiet, but once he heard the second policeman ask his colleague whether he should take a look through the windows, Sidney decided he would have to open the hatch.

'Can I help you?' he asked grumpily, his head protruding out of the now open doorway.

'Sorry to trouble you, sir' replied Carmichael. 'My name is Inspector Carmichael and this is my colleague Sergeant Watson. We are looking for the owner of a car that was left under the bridge down the towpath probably sometime yesterday.'

As he spoke Carmichael brandished his warrant card to confirm his identity.

Sidney shook his head. 'I'm sorry, officers; I don't think I can help you. I've not seen anyone since this snow fell.'

Noticing that there were only a few footprints in the snow around the barge, it was clear to Carmichael that hardly anybody had passed that way in the last twelve to eighteen hours.

'Have you ventured out much today?' Carmichael asked.

'As you can see,' said Sidney pointing at the treadmarks he'd made earlier, 'I've been out, but I didn't venture far and as soon as I had collected enough wood to keep the burner going, I came back.'

Carmichael had no reason to doubt what he was being told. 'Thanks for your time,' he said. 'I didn't get your name, sir?'

Sidney paused for a moment, but eventually responded. 'It's Sidney Sydes.'

'Well, Mr Sydes,' continued Carmichael, 'we won't trouble you any further and we'll let you get back inside, out of the cold.'

'Thank you,' replied Sidney, who in next to no time had disappeared back into the boat, shut the hatch and slid across the large bolt that kept the door locked from the outside world.

'What now?' Watson asked.

'We should get ourselves off home,' replied Carmichael. 'If Mr Poole is still missing in the morning we may need to get into his house, but I don't see there's much we can do today, especially as he's not been missing that long.'

Watson nodded his agreement. 'What about his car?' he asked.

Carmichael shrugged his shoulders. 'It's not causing an obstruction and is parked legally. It's taxed and looks roadworthy, so we have no reason to remove it at this stage.'

As he watched Carmichael and Watson tentatively make their way back down the towpath, Sidney Sydes picked up his mobile.

'It's me – Sidney,' he said. 'I've just had a visit from the local police. They said that they were looking for someone who had apparently abandoned their car under a bridge not far from where I'm moored. I just thought you should know.'

# Chapter 7

**Monday 16<sup>th</sup> February**

By the time 10 o'clock arrived, Chief Inspector Hewitt was in a foul mood. Not only had he incurred a minor shunt in his shiny new Mercedes on the way to work, he had also received two phone calls, both of which related to Steve Carmichael. Neither was particularly complimentary.

'Ask Inspector Carmichael to come up and see me at once!' he instructed Angela, his faithful and long-suffering secretary. 'Make sure he comes up straight away, no excuses!'

Angela was not surprised when her boss didn't wait for her reply before slamming down the receiver. Having worked for Chief Inspector Hewitt for eight years, she was well used to his abrupt and discourteous manner when he was annoyed. She took it all in her stride and carried out his order.

When Carmichael arrived some ten minutes later, Hewitt was still pacing up and down his office in a very agitated state.

'You wanted to see me?' said Carmichael.

'Yes,' Hewitt barked back at him. 'I've just had Roy Lovelace, our local MP, on the phone complaining that you didn't carry out a proper search for his missing brother-in-law yesterday.'

'What!' exclaimed Carmichael.

'He maintained that, despite their obvious concern and the fact that they had found his abandoned car, you did little to try and locate the missing man.'

Carmichael could feel his temperature rising. 'That's absolute rubbish,' he replied forcefully. 'Watson and I, on our day off, went to the location of the missing man's car. We spent about an hour in the surrounding area and talked to the only person there. We could find nothing. As the man has only just been reported missing I decided that we would not take any further action, but clearly if he doesn't turn up today at work or at home we will have to use more resources to try and find him.'

Hewitt seemed to be reasonably happy with what he was being told. So much so that he stopped pacing the floor and sat down in his chair. 'So when was he reported missing?' he asked in a much calmer tone.

Carmichael took a few moments to give his boss a full report. 'We questioned a barge owner,' he said in conclusion. 'He hadn't seen anything that could help us so we called it a day.'

'I see,' said Hewitt. 'So you're going to resume the investigation today?'

'Of course,' replied Carmichael. 'But my guess is that he has just met up with someone and left his car or, more likely, it's simply broken down and he's left it because the weather was so bad.'

'And you don't think the man on the barge can be of any help?' Hewitt asked.

'No,' replied Carmichael with a shake of his head. 'He seemed a bit strange but I'm sure he knows nothing that will help us in any of this.'

'OK,' replied Hewitt, who decided not to mention the nature of the other call he had received that morning. 'But please make sure you get on to this without any delay. Roy Lovelace is not just our local MP, as if that was not enough, he's also on various police committees and he is very well connected with the Chief Super. I don't want him telling the Chief that we're dragging our heels. So even if there's nothing in this, please be seen to be doing everything you can to get this resolved.'

Carmichael could not stand the thought of having to treat this particular case as a priority just because it concerned a relative of the local MP. However, he knew that he had little choice, so elected to say nothing more on the matter.

'Is that all?' he asked.

'Yes, thank you, Inspector,' replied Hewitt.

Carmichael turned to leave but was stopped in his tracks by another question from Hewitt. 'You say you were a dinner guest at the Lovelace's house?' he asked without any attempt to hide his astonishment.

'Yes,' replied Carmichael. 'To be honest we don't know the Lovelaces at all, but then out of the blue we get this invitation to go to dinner. They're known for occasionally inviting local people to their parties, but even knowing this we were quite surprised.'

'I see,' replied Hewitt. 'So you think that maybe being a senior police inspector meant that you got an invite?'

'As it happens, no,' continued Carmichael. 'It transpired that Mrs Lovelace, that's Caroline Lovelace, actually invited us so she could talk to Penny about the local primary school. It appears that Mrs Lovelace is thinking of sending her daughter there.'

'I see,' said Hewitt again. 'And did your wife give the school a rave review?'

Carmichael pondered the question for a moment as he hadn't asked Penny about her conversation with Caroline Lovelace. It had completely slipped his mind.

'I'm sure she did,' he replied.

Hewitt, for the first time that morning, managed to crack a faint smile. 'That will be all, Steve,' he said. 'But make sure you and your team get behind finding this Gerry Poole character.'

For a second time, Carmichael turned to leave the office.

However, again he turned once more to face his superior. The station that morning had been full of gossip about the Chief's scratched car and he could not resist the chance of embarrassing Hewitt. 'I see you had a bit of a prang in the car this morning,' added Carmichael somewhat mischievously. 'Did you skid in the snow?'

'No,' replied Hewitt curtly. 'It was some damn idiot in the car in front who braked quickly without any warning. I had to take evasive action and clipped the wheel arch of a parked lorry.'

'Oh, that's terribly bad luck,' replied Carmichael, who was finding it really hard not to smile. 'It's amazing what damage a small collision like that can do to a car, isn't it? And I suspect the lorry didn't have a scratch either.'

'No it didn't,' Hewitt replied through gritted teeth, while at the same time shooting out a withering look in Carmichael's direction.

\* \* \* \*

'OK, team, gather round,' Carmichael bellowed when he arrived back downstairs.

'We have a lot to get through this morning, so listen up!'

Within twenty minutes Cooper, Watson and Dalton were all busily carrying out their instructions. Cooper and Watson were despatched by Carmichael to the missing man's house. Their immediate task was to gain entry and try to ascertain when he was last there and find clues as to the reason for his disappearance. They had further been instructed to get the dog handlers on standby to search the area around Gerry Poole's abandoned car.

Rachel Dalton was asked to contact the solicitors of the two men she had interviewed on Saturday evening. 'They've been in custody for almost forty hours, so I think it's high time we got them charged and in front of a magistrate,'

Carmichael proclaimed. 'But before we do I want to speak to them and give them their final opportunity to unburden themselves of their guilt. I'm sure they will just be foot soldiers. It's the people they're selling on to who are probably the ones making a killing out of all this.'

While Rachel Dalton made the call, Carmichael quickly called Caroline Lovelace's number which he had wisely saved and added to his mobile's contact list after she had called him the day before.

'Is that Caroline?' he asked when the call was answered.

'Sorry, no,' came back the reply. 'This is Amanda Buchannan, Mrs Lovelace's PA. Mrs Lovelace is currently on air.'

Carmichael looked at his watch. 'Of course,' he replied. 'I should have realised that she would be working. Can you possibly just ask her to call Inspector Carmichael? She has my number.'

'I hope it's nothing serious,' enquired the PA.

'No, it's nothing for you or her to worry about,' Carmichael said reassuringly. 'When she has finished recording if she could call me; that would be greatly appreciated.'

'I'll make sure she gets the message, Inspector,' said Amanda Buchannan. 'I'll tell her as soon as she comes off air.'

'Thank you,' Carmichael replied.

\*     \*     \*     \*

When Cooper and Watson arrived at Gerry Poole's house it was almost 11.30.

They made their way through the snow keeping to the footsteps that the Lovelace's must have made the day before.

Cooper peered through the large front window into what looked to be Mr Poole's lounge. 'It all looks deserted,' he announced. 'It's very tidy, too!'

'This is a joke,' Watson grumbled. 'If this was my brother-in-law or yours there's no way we would get this sort of attention. But just because his relatives are in the media and an MP, we have to jump through hoops. He's probably off with some woman somewhere or, knowing his type, more likely some toy boy.'

Cooper stared back at his colleague. 'That's crass even by your standards. For God's sake, Marc, we know absolutely nothing about this man other than he's missing. I agree that the attention here is a little over the top, but I have no idea how you can come up with a theory of him being on some gay jaunt.'

Watson was cold and fed up. He realised Cooper was right but wasn't about to admit this or make any form of apology. 'I guess we need to try and gain entry?' he mumbled.

'Let's just knock first,' replied Cooper. 'We are going to look really foolish if we break in and he's in the house.'

The two officers made their way to the front door and rang the doorbell.

After waiting for about twenty seconds Watson looked at Cooper and in his most condescending voice said, 'Are you satisfied? Do I now have your permission to break in.'

Before Cooper had a chance to reply, the door opened.

'Can I help you, gentlemen?' asked the young woman who answered the door.

\* \* \* \*

'The time is eleven thirty-four,' said Carmichael into the recorder. 'Inspector Carmichael and DC Dalton conducting an interview with Billy Gupta at Kirkwood Police Station. Mr Gupta's solicitor, Mr Fry, is in attendance.'

To conduct the interview Carmichael had removed his jacket and rolled up his shirt sleeves. He leaned forward over the desk with his elbows on the table and his head resting in

41

his cupped hands. 'OK, Billy,' he said gently, 'you've had a good deal of time to consider your predicament. Are you now willing to be more cooperative?'

Billy Gupta leaned back on his chair. 'No comment,' he said cockily.

'You do realise that we are going to charge you with the theft of livestock, and my guess is that you and your brother, if you maintain your silence, will probably get a custodial sentence. That would be a first for you, wouldn't it, Billy?'

'No comment,' Gupta responded.

'That would be a real shame, Billy,' continued Carmichael, 'given that my guess is that you and your brother probably only got twenty or thirty pounds per animal. Not much really when you consider that the people you were stealing for would be getting the animals slaughtered somewhere and selling on the meat at ten times your cut. Are you going to go to prison for them and allow them to get off scot-free?'

'No comment,' replied Billy in a slow and deliberate way.

'OK,' replied Carmichael. 'I'll give your big brother the same chance I've given you. If he's smarter than you then maybe he can help you both. If not, then my guess is that you will both be found guilty and will almost certainly spend a few months, maybe a few years, inside.'

Carmichael waited for a few moments to see if Billy looked likely to change his position. After no more than fifteen seconds he realised that this was not about to happen. Looking at the clock on the wall, Carmichael spoke for a second time directly into the recorder. 'Interview ended at eleven forty,' he said before turning off the recorder and standing up.

'My suggestion to you, Mr Fry, is that you have a word with your client and advise him that he is looking at a custodial sentence. If he wants to avoid that, he might want to reconsider and cooperate with us.'

Carmichael and Dalton left the interview room.

* * * *

Neither Cooper nor Watson had anticipated that there would be anyone at home when they had rung the doorbell. What neither of them knew was that on every Monday and every Thursday a cleaner from The Helpful Angels cleaning and catering company came to Gerry Poole's house to tidy up. It was not always the same person who was asked to do the cleaning for Mr Poole and on this occasion it was Melanie Dreyfuss.

Watson and Cooper made themselves comfortable on the lounge sofa. The slightly nervous young cleaner sat opposite them on a large but very old and worn armchair.

* * * *

'OK, Rachel, let's see if Vivek Gupta is going to be a bit more cooperative than his little brother was,' said Carmichael as he entered the interview room.

As neither Rachel nor Cooper had been able to get the pair to talk, she doubted that her boss would fare any better, but thought it was worth a try.

Although he was quite a few years older than his brother, Vivek was nowhere near as conceited, a trait which Carmichael detected immediately he entered the room by the way the elder brother was sitting upright in the chair, rather than adopting the brash slouch of his brother.

'The time is eleven fifty,' said Carmichael into the recorder. 'My name is Inspector Carmichael and with DC Dalton we will be conducting an interview with Vivek Gupta at Kirkwood Police Station. Mr Vivek Gupta's solicitor, Mr Fry, is also in attendance.'

Carmichael removed his jacket, placed it over the back of his chair and stared in Vivek's direction. 'You're the elder brother?' he asked.

43

'Yes,' replied Vivek in his broad Lancashire accent. 'I'm twenty-six. Billy is nineteen.'

'That explains it!' said Carmichael.

'Explains what?' Vivek asked.

'Explains why he's acting so unconcerned,' replied Carmichael. 'It's the ignorance of his youth. As I'm sure your solicitor will be able to confirm to you when you talk later, Billy is being totally uncooperative and seems hell bent on going down. Even though I have made him aware that if he cooperates he may get a more lenient sentence.'

Vivek looked very edgy. He glanced at his brief. 'Is this true?'

Mr Fry leaned over and whispered something to his client.

Vivek Gupta slumped back into his chair. 'Look, Inspector,' he said. 'I would like some time to talk with my solicitor in private before we carry on with this interview. Is that all right with you?'

Carmichael looked at his watch. 'I'll give you thirty minutes,' he said, 'then I am going to resume the interview and decide whether we charge you both or not. But at the moment it looks like you and your brother will be heading for the magistrates' court very soon.'

Carmichael switched off the tape recorder and he and Rachel left the interview room.

'What do you think that was all about?' Rachel asked.

'I don't know,' replied Carmichael. 'I'm hoping that he's using the time to find out from his brief how he goes about limiting the charge we bring against him and his brother. If that's right, we may get a confession from him and some names of the people behind this.

'I see,' replied Rachel. 'And if that happens, would we agree?'

'Absolutely,' replied Carmichael. 'If we can get Vivek to hold his hands up and also give us the names of the people who are really benefiting from this, I'm happy to do a deal of some sort.'

*　*　*　*

Melanie Dreyfuss was a young woman in her early twenties. She was slightly built and had a pale but pretty face. Her most striking feature, however, was her long ginger hair. When she was working she kept it tied back, but its vibrant colour had always allowed those who met her to recall her instantly, which had not always been to her advantage. Marc Watson and Paul Cooper would be no exceptions to this rule.

'So let me get this straight,' said Watson. 'Your agency sends cleaners to this house every Monday and every Thursday to tidy up and do some light cleaning.'

'That's correct,' Melanie replied.

'And although you have been here quite a few times, this is the first day that you have been asked to clean Mr Poole's house for about three or four weeks.'

'Yes,' replied Melanie. 'It's normally Clare Sands who does Mr Poole, but she didn't turn up today so Mrs Cashman asked me to come instead.'

'Mrs Cashman?' enquired Cooper.

'She's the boss at The Helpful Angels, which is where we work,' Melanie confirmed.

'That's a strange name to call a cleaning agency,' said Cooper.

Melanie shuffled in her chair a little uncomfortably.

'All of us employed at The Angels have police records,' said Melanie. 'Just for minor offences, mind you. Mrs Cashman takes us on and, if things work out, she then helps us find permanent jobs and gives us references and that.'

'I see,' replied Watson. 'So what was your offence?'

'Mainly shoplifting,' said Melanie. 'A few other things too, but mainly it was the shoplifting.'

'And your friend Clare, who normally cleans here?' asked Cooper.

'I don't know,' replied Melanie. 'I suspect the same as me, but I'm not sure. We don't really talk about the past once we're in the programme.'

'So it's a programme?' said Cooper with an air of surprise. 'I've never heard of it before.'

'You probably wouldn't as most of us are from places outside the area, so when we come here we don't bump into people we knew before.'

'Like shopkeepers who you've stolen from?' said Watson with a smile. 'I'm pretty sure they would probably not be that keen on you tidying up in their houses after you have been caught stealing from them in their shops.'

Melanie just shrugged her shoulders. 'We all make mistakes and, as Mrs Cashman says, we are all entitled to try and change our lives. I can tell you that I'm never going back to my old ways, but without this programme, and people like Mrs Cashman who believe in me, I would have found it really hard to get out of the type of life I was living.'

Cooper nodded. 'Yes, we all should be given a second chance,' he said with genuine warmth.

Watson glanced at his colleague with a look of total disbelief. 'Anyway, enough of you and your rehabilitation programme,' he said. 'We're here trying to locate Mr Poole. He appears to have gone missing and has not been seen for several days. When you arrived here how was the place. Did it look like someone had been living here recently?'

Melanie thought for a moment. 'Mr Poole is normally very tidy anyway,' she said. 'The house looks pretty much like it did when Clare left it on Thursday, I expect. I didn't need to make the bed at all as it hasn't been slept in. I put a few cups in the dishwasher and turned that on and I have vacuumed the carpet, but to be honest I was just about to go when you rang the bell. I only got here about forty minutes ago and I'm already done. Normally a house like this takes about two hours.'

'What about his laundry?' Cooper asked.

'We don't touch laundry,' replied Melanie firmly. 'We just do tidying and change the sheets on the beds.'

The two officers looked at each other. 'OK, Melanie,' said Cooper. 'Thanks for all your help. We don't need to keep you anymore, but we will need your full address and contact number in case we want to talk to you again.'

'And also the number of the agency you work for,' interrupted Watson.

'While you give all that information to my colleague I'll just have a quick look around,' continued Cooper, much to the annoyance of Watson, who, having been made up to the rank of sergeant before Cooper, still saw himself as the senior of the duo. Cooper was oblivious to this as he did not hang around to witness his colleague's expression of incredulity. No sooner had Cooper finished his sentence he was up off the sofa and out of the room to search for clues.

\* \* \* \*

Inspector Carmichael and Rachel Dalton arrived back outside the interview room precisely twenty-nine minutes after they had left.

'Let's keep our word,' said Carmichael as he watched the second hand on his wristwatch slowly tick around for one more minute. 'Thirty minutes exactly,' he exclaimed. 'So let's see what Mr Gupta has to say for himself.'

Carmichael didn't bother to knock; he just turned the handle and marched in.

'OK, gentlemen, are you now ready?' he asked as he leaned over to turn on the recorder.

'Before you do that,' announced Mr Fry, 'my client and I

would like to speak with you about the charge you will be bringing against his brother should he decide to be more forthcoming with you.'

Carmichael turned and gave Rachel a wry knowing smile. 'As I have made it clear to both of your clients, Mr Fry,' he said with an air of smug satisfaction, 'it is not Billy and Vivek that I'm interested in. It's the people who planned all this and who are making the money out of this activity that we are most keen to arrest. Clearly your clients will be charged, but if Vivek is totally open and honest with us, and if as a result we are able to apprehend the real criminals behind this, then I'm sure we could arrange for Billy to face a much lesser charge, like maybe aiding and abetting the crime ... And of course his cooperation will be something we will bring to the court's attention.'

Vivek nodded towards his solicitor.

'That would be acceptable to us,' replied Mr Fry.

* * * *

It was just about 12.30 p.m. when Watson and Cooper left Gerry Poole's house with Melanie Dreyfuss.

'Is that everything?' Melanie asked as she locked the door behind them.

'Actually,' said Cooper. 'You can leave the key with us. We may need to come back here at some stage.'

Melanie was unsure whether the agency would be happy with her handing over her key to Poole's front door. For a few seconds she held it tight in her clenched fist.

'Oh, what the hell,' she said. 'It ain't for me to say you can't have it.'

With that she gave it to Cooper.

'Thank you,' said Cooper. 'Do you need a lift anywhere?'

'No thanks,' replied Melanie. 'My next house is just around the corner so I can walk.'

The two officers clambered into Coopers beaten-up car and watched the pretty young woman walk down the road.

'You know I bet she'd scrub up to be a right little cracker,' Watson announced, his eyes transfixed on her pert bottom as it disappeared further into the distance.

'Really,' sighed Cooper. 'You like redheads, do you?'

'Not particularly,' Watson replied, his eyes still focused on Melanie's rear. 'It's women in service that turn me on. You know, having to do for you.'

'Good God!' exclaimed Cooper. 'Don't tell me. I bet you have fantasies about being a rich Victorian aristocrat who has his wicked way with the servants.'

'Doesn't every red-blooded man?' replied Watson.

Cooper shook his head and pulled out a screwed-up shirt in a clear plastic bag, which he had previously kept hidden under his jacket. 'Come on, m'Lord. It's time we got back to the station and got the sniffer dogs to try and track down Mr Poole. And you never know, if they're quick you could be back at Watson Towers by mid-afternoon before her ladyship finishes her fine embroidery. You could have your wicked way with at least three or four of the servants and still be dressed and ready for tea.'

'I think you'll find we aristos call it dinner,' Watson replied with no hint of shame.

# Chapter 8

With the weather conditions being so bad, and the forecast threatening even more snow for the day and for the rest of the week, all the local schools in that part of Lancashire were shut that Monday. So Penny's day started quite peacefully. By the time she got up, Steve had already left the house and Natalie was already up and dressed and in the garden working on the enormous snowman that she had started the day before. Robbie was still dead to the world in his bed.

Penny could not remember the last time she had been able to get up after 9 a.m., have a long shower and eat her cornflakes and toast without being disturbed by one of the children, or by Steve panicking because he was late and couldn't find a clean shirt.

'I could get used to this,' she mumbled to herself as she tuned in the radio to listen to the presenter's familiar chirpy background nonsense.

Penny even managed to get through about two-thirds of the morning paper before she was eventually interrupted.

'Hi, Mum, it's me,' came the recognisable voice of Jemma down the phone line. 'Is the weather bad by you too?'

'Yes it is,' replied Penny. 'We must have several feet of snow here and they're saying we'll get more later today and during the rest of this week.'

'Is Dad there?' Jemma asked.

'No, he's at work,' replied Penny, surprised that her

daughter expected her father to be in at that time on a Monday morning.

'Did you want to talk to him?' Penny asked.

'Well, not really,' replied Jemma. 'But I do have a bit of a problem that I think I need him to know about.'

'Oh yes,' said Penny, who was now starting to fear that some bad news was about to be coming her way. 'What's the matter?'

'Promise you won't get angry,' said Jemma, who was by now sounding very sheepish. 'It's just that I was arrested last night.'

'What!' exclaimed Penny, 'whatever for?'

It was twenty minutes before Penny finally hung up the phone. The last thing she said to her eldest daughter being, 'For goodness' sake, don't tell your father. He'll go apoplectic if he finds out. Let me think about it and I'll decide what we do.'

\* \* \* \*

By the time Cooper and Watson had arrived back at Kirkwood Police Station, Steve Carmichael and Rachel Dalton had managed to extract from Vivek Gupta a very detailed statement.

'It's a much cleverer scam than I had expected,' said Carmichael. 'You have to admire the person who thought this one up.'

'Yes,' replied Rachel. 'So what's our next move?'

'I'll speak to Chief Inspector Hewitt,' he responded. 'I think we should plan to arrest all four of the people Vivek has implicated at the same time, but as that will take a fair amount of resources we may not be able to do it this afternoon. However, I'll speak with Hewitt and push for his support. In the meantime you need to chase up the service providers and find out who these two have been calling on

51

their mobiles. If we can support Vivek's statement with proof of calls being made we should be home and dry on this case.'

At that moment Carmichael caught sight of Cooper and Watson through his office window.

'Any joy?' he shouted.

'Yes,' replied Watson, who shortly after entered Carmichael's office. 'We met Poole's cleaner and she maintains that he had not been in the house for at least the last four nights.'

'She's not his usual cleaner though,' added Cooper, who was also now in Carmichael's office. 'Apparently the normal cleaner is off sick.'

'So how do you know it hasn't been used for that length of time?' Rachel asked.

'Because the cleaner thinks the house is just too tidy and Thursday was the last time the house was cleaned,' responded Watson. 'And she thinks his bed hasn't been slept in since then either.'

'But maybe he just made his own bed,' replied Rachel. 'I don't see finding the bed being made is a sure-fire sign he's not been there.'

Cooper and Watson looked at each other. 'You could be right,' said Cooper, 'but looking around the house we did get the impression that Mr Poole hadn't been there much if at all since the last cleaner was there.'

'So from what you're saying it does suggest that he's been missing now for about four or five days,' announced Carmichael. 'In which case we need to start searching more thoroughly for him and we should start near where we found his car.'

'Yes,' replied Cooper. 'We thought that and we've already asked for the sniffer dog to be down there at two today. Hopefully a good whiff of this will help it locate the missing man.'

With that Cooper held up the plastic bag containing the

shirt that he had taken from the linen basket at Gerry Poole's house.

'Good work, guys,' said Carmichael, looking at his watch. 'I need to go and see Chief Inspector Hewitt, but I'd like to join you at two. Rachel, you bring the others up to speed on your cattle rustling case. I'll go and see Hewitt to see if we can get our four suspects arrested later today.'

On that note Carmichael left his office and headed down the corridor to see Hewitt.

\* \* \* \*

'Great result, Inspector!' exclaimed Hewitt. 'But I'm not sure it's going to be possible to arrest them today. With two of them being out of our jurisdiction I would imagine that it will be at the earliest tomorrow morning before we can apprehend all four men.'

'But as we've had the Guptas in custody for nearly two days now we'll need to charge them or release them soon,' said Carmichael. 'I suspect the fact that they have not delivered Saturday night's cargo will have alerted the rest of the gang that we may be on to them and they will no doubt want to find out from the Guptas what is going on. So I was hoping that we could make the other arrests today.'

Hewitt thought for a moment. 'I don't see there's a big issue here. Charge them both now but keep them locked up in the cells for another night. I think we can do this based upon it being our opinion that if they are released they will abscond. But you're right: we can't hold them for too much longer so we'll need to get them in front of a magistrate in the morning.'

Carmichael nodded. 'That sounds OK to me,' he replied.

'So how are you progressing in trying to find Roy Lovelace's brother-in-law?' asked Hewitt.

'We've established that he's not been at home for four or

five days,' replied Carmichael. 'We still have no reason to believe there's any foul play here, but as he's so well connected we're going to get the sniffer dog out this afternoon to try and pick up his scent from around where his car was abandoned.'

'Excellent,' replied Hewitt, who was clearly relieved that he would have some positive news to convey to the MP, should he get another call.

'I'll keep you posted,' said Carmichael as he left the Chief's office.

* * * *

When Carmichael had first joined the Met he had looked into being a dog handler himself, as he thought the work would be quite interesting and rewarding. He never pursued this avenue as he could not really see himself being tied to a dog for every living hour, which, he discovered, was what was needed and, more importantly, he couldn't find anyone at a senior level within the force who had previously been a dog handler. At that time he was still very ambitious and he did not want to find himself in a role that would hamper his long-term chances of promotion, so he abandoned any thoughts of following that particular path. Nevertheless, Carmichael still admired the way police dogs were so well trained and he was always impressed when he saw them in action, whether it be in pursuit of a criminal or, as in this case, trying to locate a missing person.

Carmichael had instructed Rachel and Cooper to remain behind at the station to make sure that the Guptas were charged and they each understood their respective charges and also why they were being retained in the cells for another night. The officers were also tasked with making arrangements for the prisoners to be seen by the local magistrate in Kirkwood in the morning. With this now all in hand,

Carmichael joined Watson at Gerry Poole's abandoned car where they met PC Ben Redwood and his dog, Conker.

PC Redwood removed the shirt from its plastic bag and held it down for Conker to get a good scent. The dog sniffed the shirt for about twenty seconds before his handler let him off the leash and shouted, 'Go find, Conker.'

The dog needed no more encouragement. He first sniffed around the car for a few moments before heading across the snow and up the steep banking that led up to the canal.

Carmichael looked across at Watson. 'This looks promising,' he said.

The three police officers hurried up the bank after the dog which was already making its way down the towpath towards the place where Sidney Sydes' boat was moored.

'Looks like he's got a good scent,' announced Redwood, who reached the top of the banking first.

'Great,' said Watson who was just a few paces behind.

By the time all three officers had got to the top of the banking, Conker was already stationary twenty yards down the path. He was barking loudly and, as he barked, he was also gently moving away the thick snow which was covering the body of Gerry Poole.

'I think he's found something, sir,' said Redwood.

From inside his narrowboat Sidney Sydes watched as the three offices made their way as quickly as they could down the snow-laden towpath. He continued to watch as the men bent down and gently removed the snow which had shrouded Poole's body.

'He's cold as ice,' Watson observed. 'Do you think he's been here for long?'

'I've no idea,' replied Carmichael. 'We'll have to let Dr Stock and his team advise us. However, it does look like he was here before it started to snow as there's no snow underneath him.'

'So that would make the latest he got here to be early

evening on Saturday,' said Watson. 'As I recall it was about six or seven when it started to snow.'

Carmichael nodded. 'Yes, I think it was about then,' he confirmed.

By the time the SOCOs arrived in their white suits, some thirty minutes later, it had started to snow again.

'I can't see any obvious signs of assault here,' said Dr Stock. 'Do you know who he is?'

'We think it's a man called Gerry Poole,' replied Carmichael. 'I'll try to get the body formally identified this evening, but I don't expect it will be anyone other than him.'

It would be another hour before the body was eventually taken away, by Dr Stock and his team.

'If you can get someone to the path lab tonight to do the formal identification, I should be able to let you know the cause of death in the morning,' the pathologist told Carmichael as he made his way along the canal towpath.

'Thank you,' replied Carmichael. 'I'll do my best.'

The two officers watched as Dr Stock gingerly walked away down the canal bank. In his white overalls and white Wellington boots, it was not too long before he was lost from sight in the increasingly worsening snowstorm.

'What now?' Watson asked when Stock had finally disappeared.

'I'll try to reach the Lovelaces to see if they can do the ID,' Carmichael replied. 'But before I do that, why don't we have another talk with the guy on that narrowboat? I can't believe he saw nothing.'

As Carmichael and Watson tentatively walked up the towpath to speak with Sidney Sydes for a second time, the snowfall became even heavier. Carmichael looked up to the sky.

'It look's like it's here to stay for a while. It could even be getting worse,' he said. 'So on second thoughts let's get ourselves back to the car. My guess is that if we hang around here for much longer we could end up getting snowed in.

Let's see what Stock has to say in the morning about the cause of death. If it's suspicious then we should come back and interview our boatman again, but for now let's call it a day here.'

Watson did not argue with his boss's decision.

Sidney watched the two officers walk towards his boat, saw them stop in their tracks, before turning around and beating a retreat. As the two figures disappeared into the distance, he decided that it was time for him to make a couple of important calls on his mobile phone.

# Chapter 9

Penny's thoughts were never too far from the conversation that she'd had with Jemma that morning.

How on earth her daughter could have got herself into a position whereby she had been arrested and charged with possessing drugs was beyond her. She trusted Jemma completely, so she was in no doubt that what Jemma had told her was true, but this still didn't help her to understand how she could have got herself into such a mess. What sort of bar was she working in? she asked herself. And more worryingly, what should she tell Steve?

Penny had still not managed to formulate a plan of action when Steve called.

'Oh, hi darling,' she said, trying hard to sound as normal as she could. 'Have you had a good day?'

'Actually yes,' replied Carmichael. 'We've made great headway with the cattle rustlers. It was actually a big scam that included the two farmers, an abattoir owner in Rochdale and a butcher who didn't seem to mind where his meat was coming from. We're hoping to make more arrests tomorrow.'

'That's great,' replied Penny with as much enthusiasm as she could muster. 'What about finding that missing relative of Caroline Lovelace?'

'That's why I'm calling,' Carmichael replied. 'We think we've found him. He's dead, I'm afraid, but I need to get one of the Lovelaces to do a formal identification this evening, so I may be quite late home.'

'That's fine,' said Penny, who was pleased to be getting more time to try and work out what to do about Jemma. 'I'll save you some tea.'

\* \* \* \*

Including the message he had left with her PA that morning, Carmichael had left two further messages for Caroline to call him back before she finally found time to contact him.

'Inspector Carmichael,' she said in her haughty upper-class tone. 'I'm frightfully sorry to have taken so long to get back to you. All hell has broken loose here today. Did you see the show?'

'No I didn't,' replied Carmichael. 'However, we think that we may have found your brother-in-law.'

'Is he all right?' Caroline asked hesitantly.

Carmichael took a deep breath. 'I'm afraid if the person we have found is Mr Poole, he's dead.'

'Oh my God!' exclaimed Caroline. 'I suspected that might be the case. Where was he?'

'He was found just off the canal bridleway, near where his car had been abandoned,' Carmichael replied.

'And how did he die?' continued Caroline.

'If it's all the same to you, Mrs Lovelace, I'd first like to ask you and your husband to come to the pathology lab in Kirkwood to identify the body. I am sure it's Mr Poole, but until that is confirmed I'd rather not go into any more details with you, and a positive identification will also allow the pathologist to start the post-mortem.'

'I understand,' replied Caroline. 'When do you want to do the identification?'

'It would be very helpful if you could do that this evening,' said Carmichael. 'I could have a car collect you as soon as you're ready.'

There was a slight pause before Caroline replied. 'My

husband is busy this evening, so it will just be me. I'm now at home, so if you want to send a car now that's fine.'

'Thank you,' Carmichael replied. 'I'll get a car to you straight away. And I'll meet you at the pathology lab when you arrive.'

\*    \*    \*    \*

It was forty-five minutes later when the police car carrying Caroline Lovelace arrived at the lab. Steve Carmichael and Rachel Dalton were already waiting inside and Stock's team had laid out the body for the identification.

'Hello, Mrs Lovelace,' Carmichael said as she entered the room. 'This is DC Rachel Dalton.'

Rachel smiled softly and put out a hand.

Caroline shook her hand gently. 'I'd rather just get this done and dusted if it's all the same to you,' she said in a manner which made Carmichael think that she was not that close to her brother-in-law.

'Of course,' Carmichael replied. 'Follow me.'

Carmichael walked through into the small anti-room where the body lay covered from head to toe in a thick white sheet. Caroline followed closely behind and Rachel Dalton, a further two paces back, completed the trio.

Carmichael slowly pulled back the sheet to reveal the face of the dead man.

Caroline nodded. 'Yes, this is Gerry,' she said with only the slightest hint of emotion.

'Would you like to be alone with Gerry,' Rachel asked.

'Good God no,' replied Caroline in horror. 'We were related but we weren't close. I'm naturally very sorry he's dead, but to be honest our relationship was never that strong.'

'I see,' replied Rachel.

'I'll get the driver to take you home then,' said

Carmichael, who ushered the two ladies out of the room before replacing the sheet over the face of Gerry Poole.

*   *   *   *

It was after 8.30 p.m. when Carmichael eventually arrived home.

'What's the weather like now?' Penny shouted down the hall when she heard the door close.

'It's still snowing but it's eased quite a bit,' he replied.

Penny emerged from the kitchen and joined him in the hall.

'They say that tomorrow and on Wednesday it will get very cold, minus eight or nine at night and about freezing during the day,' she announced. 'But they also said it would probably stop snowing by midnight tonight and we shouldn't see any more snow then until later in the week.'

'It's hard to believe that there could be any more left to come down,' replied Carmichael as he removed his thick woollen overcoat.

'I've saved you some tea,' said Penny. 'Do you want it now?'

'Let me just get out of these clothes and have a shower first,' said Carmichael. 'I'll be ten minutes.'

Penny gave her husband a kiss and walked back into the kitchen.

*   *   *   *

Melanie Dreyfuss had been trying all day to contact Clare Sands. She had left a couple of messages on her mobile and had texted her several times. When it got to 8.45 p.m. without any reply she decided to go around to her flat to speak to her in person. Clare only lived about a mile away so Melanie decided to walk. It had just about stopped snowing when she set out, but it was now very dark and the air was so cold that she could feel her breath freezing as it made contact with the knitted scarf that she wore over her chin. The walk took her longer than normal, as she was forever having to stop to try and avoid the slush thrown up from passing cars. Although the gritter lorries had been out in force spreading salt on the roads, the pavements were all still covered in snow and with the temperature now falling below freezing they were already very slippery.

When she eventually arrived at the first-storey flat she could see that the lights were on so she assumed that Clare or one of her two flatmates were at home.

It was Clare herself who answered the door. 'Oh it's you,' she said as if she was expecting someone else.

'Why haven't you returned my calls or my text message?' Melanie asked.

'Quick, come in,' replied Clare.

Melanie followed her friend up the steep stairway that led to the lounge diner.

'You're not sick at all,' she observed. 'If Mrs Cashman finds out you've thrown a sickie you'll be off the programme.'

'That is the least of my worries,' replied Clare. 'I'm in real trouble.'

\*     \*     \*     \*

Penny waited for Carmichael to finish his tea before starting to put her plan into action.

'As the school's certainly not going to open this week,' she said, 'I thought I'd take a trip over to Leeds tomorrow to see Jemma.'

'You're not thinking of driving, are you?' Carmichael said. 'The M62 will be pretty hairy in this weather.'

'Good God, no,' replied Penny. 'I'd get the train from Kirkwood. I've checked and they run hourly and they only take about an hour and a half. I could get there for say ten in the morning and be back by seven in the evening.'

'Why though?' Carmichael asked. 'Is she all right?'

'Well, I did speak to her this morning and she seemed really down,' said Penny. 'I think she is finding the work a bit hard, so I thought I'd cheer her up and maybe take her shopping.'

Carmichael shrugged his shoulders. 'Yes, it's fine with me, but what about the other two? I can't take time off to look after them.'

'Robbie's eighteen!' exclaimed Penny. 'He can look after himself for a day.'

'Yes, but Natalie's not and I can't see her brother being too keen to look after her?' Carmichael replied.

'I've thought of that,' said Penny. 'I'll drop her off at the stables. I've already spoken with Hannah De Vere and she's happy to keep her until either you or I collect her in the evening. As long as she's with Lucy and the other horses she'll be fine. Hannah even said she would give her some tea.'

'It all sounds a done deal to me,' replied Carmichael as he gave his wife a hug. 'Yes, you go then.'

Penny felt really bad about lying to her husband, but she knew it was for the best.

\*   \*   \*   \*

Tamara Searle had set her sights on being a TV journalist ever since her first year at Lincoln University. Although she had already achieved more fame than any of her university peers, she was still driven by ambition. She envied the status and notoriety of people like Caroline Lovelace and she was determined to achieve her goal as quickly as she could and at pretty much any price. Her dream was to uncover a scoop of some sort which would instantly catapult her into the limelight and in so doing move her career to the next level. Little did she realise when she accepted Caroline's kind invitation to the dinner party that Saturday evening that the opportunity she so intensely coveted would fall into her lap so easily.

All through Sunday Tamara had contemplated what her next step should be. By Monday morning she was still undecided. However, by lunchtime she had made her mind up and that afternoon she made her move.

# Chapter 10

The four men implicated by Vivek Gupta were picked up separately at 8.30 a.m. Cooper and two uniformed officers from Kirkwood Police Station made the arrest of Harry Jackson, while Watson and two uniformed officers picked up Melvyn Hitchcock from the neighbouring farm. The Greater Manchester Police completed the quartet of detentions when they descended on Colin Southwaite, the assistant manager of a small abattoir, and at the same time, in the centre of the city, they also apprehended Frank Bradshaw, the proprietor of one of the largest livestock auctioneers in the North West.

'Fantastic!' exclaimed Carmichael when the news of the four successful arrests arrived back at Kirkwood Police Station. 'Jackson and Hitchcock should arrive here within the next thirty minutes. We'll get them interviewed first, then we'll do the two from Manchester later this morning once they've arrived.'

Rachel Dalton clenched her fist with elation. 'What a result,' she said. 'Can I be in on the interviews?'

'Of course,' replied Carmichael with a self-satisfied smile on his face. 'In fact, I think I'll leave the interviews for you, Watson and Cooper to conduct. I'm sure you'll cope fine without me.'

'Great,' replied Rachel, who was very surprised that the

boss didn't want to take control as was normally his wont. 'What are you going to do?'

'I'm going to see Dr Stock,' said Carmichael. 'I'm keen to find out how Gerry Poole died and I may also pay a visit to Caroline Lovelace. With her being such a high-profile celebrity and her husband being such an important public figure, at least in Hewitt's eyes, I think it would be wise for me to be seen to be giving that particular case due importance.'

'Do you expect Stock to conclude that Poole's death was suspicious?' Rachel asked.

'I've no idea,' replied Carmichael. 'However, I am intrigued to find out what happened to him and I really would like to know what he was doing down the canal towpath.'

'I suspect he was meeting someone,' said Rachel. 'Well, that's assuming he died where he was found. He could have been just dumped there.'

'Who knows?' Carmichael remarked. 'But I suspect Dr Stock will be able to guide us once he's concluded his autopsy.'

\*　\*　\*　\*

Dr Stock was very busy that morning. The cold weather had brought with it quite a few sudden deaths and his workload that day was far greater than he had experienced for some considerable time. He had three autopsies that he needed to perform before lunchtime. In addition to Gerry Poole he also had the bodies of two elderly women to examine. He chose to start with Gerry Poole.

\*　\*　\*　\*

Confident that his three trusty lieutenants were more than capable of conducting the interviews with the four detainees, Carmichael made his way out of the Police Station and into

66

the car park, which was situated in full view of Chief Inspector Hewitt's office. Hewitt watched as Carmichael climbed into his car and drove out of the main gate.

'I understand,' he said as he turned to face the sharply dressed man who was sitting facing him on the opposite side of his desk. 'As I've already told you, Inspector, I don't intend to share the details of our conversation with him at this time. But I'll keep close to the Gerry Poole case and, should the need arise, I'll take the appropriate steps to ensure Carmichael doesn't compromise your operation.'

'Thank you,' replied Hewitt's visitor, who rose from the chair as he spoke. 'I'm pleased that we can count on you, sir.'

\* \* \* \*

Before going to see Dr Stock, Carmichael thought it would be a good idea to pay a visit to Poole's house so he could see for himself where the dead man had lived. He had taken the front door key that the cleaner had given to Cooper the day before, so he could let himself in. He also thought if there was time after his meeting with Stock, he might return to the canal towpath where Poole's body had been found.

It took just twenty minutes for Carmichael to reach Gerry Poole's cottage. It was situated at the end of a row and was quite sheltered from the prying eyes of neighbours due to some very tall hedges on three sides and a substantial wall between the front gardens. To the right of Poole's cottage were large open fields.

Carmichael parked his car on the driveway and carefully made his way along the slippery path which led up to the front door. Once inside, Carmichael walked through into the cosy lounge, which was neat and tidy, but also cram-packed with small pieces of furniture and with ornaments and photographs on every flat space. Carmichael opened a few drawers and started to rummage through the contents. Up until that point Carmichael had not really considered what Gerry Poole was like when he was alive, however, being there in his house gave Carmichael a much better feel for the man.

After spending thirty minutes in the lounge reading some of the letters and documents that Poole had secreted in various drawers, Carmichael walked through into the large kitchen at the back of the cottage. The room was set out and equipped as Carmichael would have imagined most top chefs would kit out their own kitchens. In addition the large walk-in larder was well stocked with sauces, spices and all manner of tins, from tomatoes to peaches.

Carmichael took a peek under the lid of Poole's huge cabinet freezer. He was intrigued at not only how well the freezer was stocked, but also how neatly the packets of frozen products had been laid out. Penny's freezer at home was probably only half the size of Poole's but he rarely ventured into that *black hole*, as he could never find anything. In Poole's freezer everything seemed easy to locate, even though it lacked much variety. 'The poor guy must have existed on a diet of burgers, chips and curry meals,' Carmichael mumbled to himself before putting the lid down. Having seen how full the freezer was, it was therefore a big surprise to Carmichael when he opened up Poole's large fridge to find it almost empty. There were no perishables to be found; no milk, no salad and no cheese. In fact as hard as he looked he could not find any fruit or vegetables anywhere else in the house, which Carmichael found quite strange.

Carmichael glanced at his watch. It was now 10.30 a.m. and he had already been in the house for forty-five minutes. He decided that he needed to get over and see Dr Stock. However, before he left, Carmichael looked into the two bedrooms and gave the bathroom a quick once-over. All were spotless and all looked as if they had not been used for some time.

His final task before he left the house was to check the bins. These were located at the rear of the house. There were two bins, both of the same size, but one was black and the other was brown. Carmichael assumed that these were colour-coded in the same way his bins were at home, with the black one for household waste and the brown one for garden waste. However, he couldn't confirm that because when he peered into the brown bin it was completely empty, as was the black bin.

*    *    *    *

Penny's train arrived at Leeds City station at 10.45 a.m. She had never been to her daughter's rented house before so she was not sure how much the taxi would cost. However, Penny knew that Headingley was not that far out of town, so she did not expect the ride to be too long or too expensive.

She clambered into the back seat of the first in a long line of taxis that waited patiently outside the station entrance.

'Grantby Grove in Headingley, please,' Penny said to the driver in the black woollen hat.

'No problem,' he replied chirpily. 'Have you there in no time.'

As the taxi pulled out of the station and headed off towards Jemma's flat, Penny eased herself back into the seat and started to send her daughter a text message.

*    *    *    *

On his way to see Stock, Carmichael put a call through to Marc Watson.

'Hi, Marc, it's Carmichael,' he said. 'How's it all going?'

'Not too bad,' replied Watson. 'We've just finished interviewing Jackson and Hitchcock. Jackson's not saying anything and denying any involvement, but Hitchcock's really

69

panicking. He's holding his hands up and is more than willing to implicate Vivek Gupta, Bradshaw and Jackson in the scam. He doesn't appear to have had any contact with Billy Gupta or with Southwaite, but he's more than willing to incriminate the other three if it's going to help him get a lesser charge.'

'Great news,' replied Carmichael. 'With Vivek Gupta and now Hitchcock being so cooperative we will have a great chance to convict all six of them. But it's Bradshaw and to a lesser extent Southwaite that will have been making the most out of all this and I suspect we'll find that these are not the only farmers being sucked into the scam. So it's those two I really want to nail.'

'They've both arrived now so we plan to start interviewing them next,' said Watson. 'Southwaite is happy to just let the duty solicitor attend so we'll be interviewing him first. Bradshaw is insisting his brief attends and he's yet to arrive, so we may have to wait until after lunch before we start on him.'

'Typical,' replied Carmichael. 'It just supports my theory that he's the main man. In my experience only major criminals ever ask for their own brief to attend. The rest of us would certainly not even have a lawyer.'

'We couldn't afford one either,' interjected Watson.

'Too right,' concurred Carmichael. 'OK, I'll let you get back. I'm on my way to see Stock. Depending upon what he has to say, I may either head off to speak with Caroline Lovelace or just head back to the office. Whatever the outcome, I'll certainly be back by the middle of the afternoon. So tell the others to make sure they're available at four p.m. so we can have a full debrief.'

'OK, sir,' replied Watson.

* * * *

The taxi pulled up outside 16 Grantby Grove at precisely 11.20 a.m. Jemma was waiting on the curb side shivering from the cold. Penny paid the driver and walked over to where her sobbing daughter was standing. 'You stupid girl,' she said. 'Come on, let's get inside and you can tell me all about it.'

* * * *

Carmichael arrived at Dr Stock's path lab at 11.30 a.m. He hated seeing dead bodies so morgues and pathology labs were places he would circumvent if at all possible. However, on this occasion, his desire to understand more about the circumstances of Gerry Poole's death outweighed his discomfort at being around the recently departed.

Dr Stock knew Carmichael was uncomfortable around corpses and found it very amusing. 'Morning Inspector,' he boomed as Carmichael made his way towards him down the brightly lit corridor. 'Have I got some interesting news for you!'

'What's that?' enquired Carmichael, his face contorted as his nostrils got the full impact of the detergents Stock's assistants had liberally spread on the table where, thirty minutes earlier, Stock had gruesomely dissected one of his silent specimens.

'The cause of death was a heart attack,' replied Stock as Carmichael reached where he was standing. 'There's nothing suspicious at all in that respect. His arteries had narrowed a fair amount, probably through a combination of poor diet and a lack of exercise...'

'Well, he certainly liked junk food,' muttered Carmichael to himself, as he cast his mind back to the freezer contents at Poole's cottage. This news was a disappointment to Carmichael, who had hoped Stock would tell him that Poole's death had been caused by some sort of foul play. 'Do you think the cold had brought it on?' he asked.

71

Stock shook his head. 'No, I've no reason to say that.'

'So when did Gerry Poole die?' Carmichael asked.

'Well, that's where it does get interesting,' replied Stock. 'The when and the where are not as straightforward.'

'What do you mean?' Carmichael asked.

'Well, I know it's been very cold these last three or four days,' continued Stock. 'And it's probably been cold enough to freeze a body if it was left out there. However, when something freezes it tends to do it from the outside in. So if we take our Mr Poole and make the assumption that he died while walking where we found him, you would expect that his skin and hair would all freeze first and then only later would he start to freeze further down into his body.'

'Yes,' replied Carmichael. 'But as I recall that's how we found him. His hair was clearly frozen and I suspected that he would be pretty much frozen through.'

'Well, that's the thing,' replied Stock. 'His outer skin was frozen, but the freezing process had not penetrated that far into his body. I'd say roughly a centimetre down at the most. However, his heart, lungs and most of his other internal organs and intestines were quite frozen.'

'I don't get it,' said Carmichael. 'What does that mean?'

'I'm not totally sure,' replied Stock. 'I plan to speak with colleagues who've more experience than me in examining frozen corpses, but I suspect that our Mr Poole was either frozen from the inside out, like a microwave in reverse, or that he was frozen completely and was actually partially thawed then dumped and it was so cold that he started to refreeze.'

'So you're saying that he died, was frozen, defrosted, dumped on the canal towpath and then was starting to freeze again when we found him,' said Carmichael in amazement.

Stock nodded. 'Yes, that's exactly my theory.'

'So when did he die?' Carmichael asked.

'It depends upon how long he was frozen,' replied Stock

rather flippantly. 'However, I'd say that it was not more than two weeks but certainly more than six or seven days.'

'Why do you say that?' Carmichael asked, deep frown-lines etched across his forehead.

'Well, the snow started to fall late on Saturday evening. He was certainly put on the ground before it snowed, so that means Saturday afternoon or early evening at the latest. He was thawed out to a degree when he was put there and that would take at least a day, probably more like two days, and it would have taken about two days to freeze him in the first place.'

Carmichael did the maths in his head. 'OK,' he replied. 'So it's minimum last Tuesday. However, if he was frozen, how do you know his death was no more than two weeks ago?'

'That's simple,' replied Stock with a grin as he held up a small scrap of paper. 'This VAT receipt for petrol that I found in his trouser pocket was dated Tuesday 3rd February. Unless this was planted by someone or he was wearing someone else's clothes, it suggests to me that he was still alive then.'

# Chapter 11

Jemma's remorse at being arrested was all too evident to Penny. However, this did little to lessen the anger and disappointment that Penny felt, emotions that were only surpassed by her fear about the sort of punishment her daughter could face, and worse still what sort of reaction Steve would have if he found out.

'Start from the beginning,' Penny said calmly. 'What were you doing in that club anyway?'

Jemma took a deep breath and wiped the tears from her eyes with the back of her hand. 'It was my friend Lizzie's twentieth birthday,' she said in a shaky voice. 'I'd been working behind the bar at a club called Jaspers that night; it's where I've been working for the past few weeks. Anyway I wasn't able to meet her and the others until my shift ended at eleven. By the time I got to the Student Union bar it was about half past. The Union bar had a band on but their bar was closing at twelve, so I quickly got a drink for me and for Lizzie. We drank our drinks and then decided to go back to the club as it was going to be open until about two.'

'So far that sounds fine,' replied Penny. 'But have you any idea how the package got to be in your pocket when the police searched you?'

Jemma shook her head. 'I've no idea,' she said. 'It was certainly not there when I left the Student Union bar. I know that because it was cold so I had my hands in my pockets while we walked back to the club. It could only have been put there when I was back in the club.'

'How long after you had arrived was it that the police carried out their raid?' Penny asked.

'It was almost straight away,' replied Jemma. 'I was in the corridor just inside the door. I'd not even taken off my coat when the officers told us to line up against the wall and the sniffer dog was brought in.'

'And the dog came up to you straight away?' Penny asked.

'Yes,' said Jemma. 'The dog singled me out and I was arrested.'

'Was anyone else arrested?' Penny asked.

'Yes,' replied Jemma. 'They found a similar amount on another girl who works in the club. She was also in the corridor and she was arrested too. They also found a bigger amount behind the fire extinguisher, which the police are saying either I or the other girl hid when we saw that the club was being raided.'

'And this other girl,' continued Penny, 'does she work behind the bar with you at Jaspers?'

Jemma's chin dropped down against her chest and she lost eye contact with her mother. 'No,' she said quietly. 'She is one of the dancers.'

'Dancers?' enquired Penny. 'Are you telling me that this club you're working in is a lap-dancing bar?'

Jemma's silence answered her mother's question.

*   *   *   *

Carmichael sat in his car for a few moments to consider his next move. He gazed at the clock on the dashboard, which flashed out a time of 12.27 in a bright red light. He initially considered going back to Kirkwood Station to help with the interviews of Southwaite and Bradshaw. However, he was confident that the team would be more than capable of wrapping up that case and, although he was keen to conclude the enquiry, he was far more interested in the Gerry Poole case. He decided to call Caroline Lovelace to try and set up a meeting with her to inform her of Stock's preliminary conclusions and also try and understand a little bit more about Gerry Poole. He dialled her mobile number.

After three rings his call was answered, and to his surprise it was not the PA whose voice he heard on the end of the line.

'Caroline Lovelace speaking.'

'Oh good afternoon, Caroline,' said Carmichael. 'It's Inspector Carmichael here. I was wondering if you were free this afternoon. I'd like to meet with you to bring you up to speed with the enquiry into your brother-in-law's death.'

'Good afternoon,' replied Caroline. 'As it happens I'm planning to meet up with Roy at a quiet little restaurant we know for some lunch, in about half an hour's time. Why don't you join us there?'

'That would be ideal,' said Carmichael. 'What's the name of the restaurant?'

'It's called The Fisheries,' said Caroline. 'It's located on the village green in Newbridge.'

'I know where you mean,' replied Carmichael. 'I'll meet you both there.'

Carmichael had been to The Fisheries several times, as it was one of Penny's favourite local restaurants.

* * * *

In Carmichael's absence, Cooper and Watson had pulled rank on Rachel Dalton and decided to conduct the interviews of Southwaite and Bradshaw without their female colleague, leaving her, to her annoyance, to start writing up the reports on the two interviews they had conducted that morning.

Bradshaw's brief had still not arrived, so they had started their interviews with Colin Southwaite.

The assistant manager of the abattoir was a tall, wiry man with sharp chiselled features and a slight stoop. Although he was only in his mid-thirties, he was not a very healthy specimen and his dress sense was such that he could quite easily have been mistaken for a man some ten years older.

Watson and Cooper had spent nearly an hour with him before he started to open up to them. It was when Marc Watson informed him that Vivek Gupta and Melvyn Hitchcock were already cooperating, that Southwaite also decided to be more forthcoming.

'If I hold my hands up and give you a full statement on all I did, will that help me when it comes to court?' asked Southwaite in a very shaky voice.

'As long as you leave nothing out,' replied Watson. 'Then I can assure you that your cooperation will be made very clear when this comes to trial. That usually means the judge will give you a lighter sentence, though we can't give you any cast-iron guarantees.'

Southwaite looked pathetically at his solicitor, who nodded to him to indicate that he should take this course of action.

'Very well,' replied the crestfallen detainee, 'I'd like to be alone now with my solicitor to write my statement, if that's OK with you.'

Watson and Cooper suspended the interview and left the room.

'Result,' whispered the elated Watson as the two officers walked away down the corridor.

\*　　\*　　\*　　\*

As the name suggested, The Fisheries was a restaurant that specialised in seafood. It was located in the village of Newbridge, which was only a few miles away from

Carmichael's house in Moulton Bank. Penny and Carmichael had eaten there on a number of occasions and, although it was a pretty expensive place to dine, in Carmichael's opinion the food was just as good as some of the trendy eateries that he and Penny had visited in London.

It took Carmichael forty minutes to travel from Dr Stock's path lab to the restaurant, and by the time he arrived, Roy and Caroline Lovelace were already sitting at the table. 'Hello, Inspector. Do come and join us,' Caroline said in her now familiar haughty tone.

Carmichael removed his overcoat, handed it to the waiter and made his way over to where the Lovelaces were sitting.

'We haven't ordered yet,' said Roy as he stood up and offered Carmichael his hand to shake. 'I don't know whether you've eaten here before but I can highly recommend the mussels.'

'Oh Roy,' interrupted Caroline. 'I'm sure the Inspector is capable of ordering his own meal.'

Carmichael smiled and shook first Roy's hand and then, more gently, Caroline's.

'It's good of you both to see me at such short notice,' he said, as he sat down in his chair and unfolded the large white napkin. 'I've just come from the pathology lab where I received a preliminary report regarding your brother-in-law's death.'

At that point the waiter arrived and handed out menus to the three diners.

'How did the poor boy die?' asked Roy, even though Carmichael could see that his main focus of attention was on the content of the menu rather than his question.

'It was natural causes. A massive heart attack,' replied Carmichael.

'Oh dear,' replied Caroline. 'He was only in his fifties. What a dreadful waste.'

Carmichael nodded. 'Yes, I agree,' he said.

Roy Lovelace's eyes did not move from the menu. 'Weird really,' he said. 'There's poor old Gerry, who was always so wafer thin, pegging out with a heart attack, while there's me, who I admit could do with losing a few pounds, as healthy as anything. It just shows that you can't always rely on those know-it-all doctors telling you that eating carefully and staying thin will prolong your life.'

'So was Gerry careful with what he ate?' Carmichael asked.

'Not especially,' replied Caroline. 'Lesley, his wife, and Roy's sister, was a great cook and loved entertaining. She would always cook from fresh ingredients, so when she was alive I expect he would have eaten very well and probably a very healthy diet, but I think once she died his diet did suffer.'

'I see,' replied Carmichael. 'So the kitchen in the cottage was really Mrs Poole's domain?'

'Definitely,' replied Roy, who finally put down the menu. 'Gerry was a complete dunce in the kitchen. In fact, generally pretty useless about the house altogether, I suspect.'

'So do you think he just died while he was walking along the canal bank?' Caroline asked, trying hard to steer the conversation away into another direction.

Carmichael did not want to share too much of Dr Stock's theory with the Lovelaces so was guarded in his answer. 'We just don't know,' he replied carefully. 'But clearly that's what it looks like. It seems that for some reason he decided to park his car under the bridge and take a walk down the bank. It would then appear that he died while he was walking.'

'What a tragedy!' Caroline announced.

'So when was this?' asked Roy. 'And what was he doing walking down there?'

'We're not sure on either count,' replied Carmichael. 'It was certainly before Saturday evening but it could have been any time after 3rd February.'

'Why do you say that?' Caroline asked.

79

'Well, he had a fuel receipt in his possession with that date on it,' replied Carmichael. 'So we know it was after then. And he was already dead before it started to snow on Saturday evening, so it's clear that he died before then.'

'Well, we knew that,' snapped Roy. 'If he'd have been alive on Saturday evening he'd have been at our dinner party.'

'Quite correct,' replied Carmichael.

The conversation paused for a few moments while the three diners studied the menus. It was Caroline who put her menu down first.

'So what's the process now?' she asked.

'We have a few unanswered questions to tidy up,' said Carmichael, who having also made his choice rested the menu in front of him. 'But there will have to be an inquest.'

'Of course,' replied Caroline.

'I would like to get some information on Gerry Poole from you if I may,' said Carmichael.

Roy Lovelace placed his forearms down on the table and looked up. 'Fire away,' he said. 'We'll help you as much as we can.'

'I'd just like to know what sort of man he was, get some insight into how he earned a living and what sort of health he was in,' Carmichael said.

'Gerry was a quiet man,' replied Caroline, 'even more so after Lesley died.'

'He kept himself to himself,' continued Roy. 'He used to work in the motor industry for a French company. He was their UK Sales Director, I think. But just before Lesley died he retired. Well, to be more specific he took early retirement after being made redundant.'

'I see,' replied Carmichael. 'And as I seem to recall from reading in the papers at the time, your sister died in a car accident when they were on holiday in France.'

'Yes,' replied Caroline, who gently rested her hand on her

husband's. 'When Gerry lost his job they decided to take a few months out and drive around France. By all accounts they were having a wonderful time, when one evening they were hit head on by another car which was overtaking on a bad bend. Lesley died instantly, but Gerry survived with hardly a scratch.'

'I'm so sorry,' said Carmichael, who could see from the expression on his face that the memory of his sister's death was still raw with Roy. 'What about Mr Poole's health?'

'He did suffer with high blood pressure,' replied Caroline. 'I remember Lesley telling me this when he was made redundant. She was actually very pleased when he lost his job as she was convinced that the work he did had contributed to it.'

It was at that moment that the waiter arrived. 'Are you ready to order?' he asked, taking out a small notepad from his pocket.

* * * *

Penny tried to call Carmichael on his mobile, but he wasn't picking up. She was not looking forward to his reaction when he found out that his eldest daughter had not only been arrested for possessing cannabis, but was also being employed in a lap-dancing bar.

'Come on,' she said to her daughter. 'Get your coat. I want to speak with the arresting officers. I want to find out whether they plan to charge you. If you're telling me the truth, then I don't see them having any grounds to charge you. Even if they don't believe that the drugs were planted, the quantity you had will probably be classed as only enough for personal use, so I don't think they will press charges.'

Jemma grabbed her coat and followed her mother out of the house. 'I promise you, Mum – I'm not lying about the drugs and you have to believe me that all I do at Jaspers is serve drinks from behind the bar.'

* * * *

Carmichael took another mouthful of delicious crab ravioli. 'When was the last time you saw or spoke with Gerry?' he asked.

'It would have been about two weeks ago, I think,' replied Roy vaguely. 'I'm not really sure though.'

'Well, I think the last time I spoke with him was when I mentioned about the party,' said Caroline. 'That would have been when he called us the week before last.'

'That's right,' agreed Roy. 'It was the Thursday evening as I remember.'

'So would that have been Thursday 5th February?' Carmichael asked.

'Yes,' replied Roy. 'I think it was. He called me from his house at about seven in the evening. We'd been working on some business together and he wanted to check that everything had gone through. It was then that I suggested he joined us at the dinner party on the fourteenth.'

'And presumably he accepted your invitation?' Carmichael asked.

'Yes,' said Caroline with a sideways look towards her husband. 'But that did leave me in a bit of a quandary.'

'Why was that?' Carmichael asked.

'Well, it's stupid really,' she replied. 'But I like to have even numbers and up until Roy invited Gerry we had invited eight guests, four males and four females. With Gerry now coming I felt I needed to invite another guest and to balance the numbers it needed to be a single lady.'

'I see,' replied Carmichael, although he did not really see this as being such a big deal.

'So who was the last guest you invited?' he asked.

'Tamara Searle,' Caroline replied. 'She works with me so it was quite easy to get her to join us at the last minute.'

'I see,' replied Carmichael. 'But when was it that you last *saw* Gerry?'

Roy shrugged his shoulders. 'I don't know,' he replied. 'I suspect it was the week before. We were selling off some land that was inherited by Lesley and me when my father passed away. After Lesley died, her half share reverted to Gerry. We had been offered a good price for it and Gerry needed the cash, so he asked me if I would agree to the sale. To be honest I was not keen at first, but in the end I agreed and we signed the papers on the Thursday. I think it was on 29th January.'

'What I still can't understand is,' announced Caroline as she sipped on her glass of Chardonnay, 'what he was doing along the canal towpath?'

'I would have thought that was an easy one to answer,' snapped Roy. 'He was probably meeting up with that young tart he seemed so obsessed with.'

'Sorry,' replied Carmichael, his interest levels having been dramatically heightened on hearing this latest piece of information, 'Gerry had a girlfriend? Who was it?'

'Roy!' exclaimed Caroline. 'We have absolutely no evidence that he was meeting Clare Sands. I've told you before that, although he might have had a thing for her, she was not interested in him and I don't think for one minute that she would have agreed to a meeting with him.'

'Clare Sands?' asked Carmichael. 'Who's she?'

'She's the bloody cleaner,' Roy snapped. 'She's about thirty years younger than him, she's an ex-offender and in my view she was after his money, actually my sister's money.'

'Now, now, Roy!' Caroline said in a raised voice. 'That's enough of that. Clare is doing well on the programme and how you've got it into your head that she had designs on Gerry's money … Anyway, I suspect that he had nothing much other than a little inheritance and the money he was going to get from the land you both sold. Clare will have had nothing to do with his death. I'd stake my life on it.'

'I am sure you're right,' Carmichael said. 'However, you can understand that I will need to talk with Miss Sands, just to make sure she's not implicated. Do you know where she lives?'

'No,' replied Caroline, who was clearly exasperated with her husband. 'But Emma Cashman will know. She works for Emma at The Angels.'

'I take it that would be The Helpful Angels?' remarked Carmichael. 'Can you tell me a bit more about them?'

'It's a company that Emma and I set up a few years ago to help girls who were trapped in a life of crime,' said Caroline. 'I am on the management board but it's Emma that manages the business on a day-to-day basis. We supply cleaners and catering staff. Clare is one of our best employees. She was one of our waitresses on Saturday as it happens. We always use The Angels for our dinner parties.'

'She was also Gerry's cleaner,' Roy Lovelace interjected.

'I see,' said Carmichael for the third time that lunchtime. 'And where might I find The Angels offices?'

'I'll write down the number for you,' replied Caroline as she reached into her handbag for a pen and some paper.

\*　\*　\*　\*

Penny and Jemma had been kept waiting in the small interview room for thirty anxious minutes before the door eventually opened.

'Good morning,' said the young, smartly dressed plain-clothed officer in a broad Welsh accent. 'My name is DC Evans. I'm the investigating officer for your daughter's case.'

Evans walked over to where Penny and Jemma were sitting, rested the small file he had been carrying on the table and offered his hand.

Penny stood up, took hold of his outstretched hand and shook it vigorously.

'Good afternoon, Constable Evans,' she replied. 'I'm Penny Carmichael, Jemma's mother.'

'Please sit down,' said Evans in a very quiet but controlled way. 'I assume you're here to understand what the situation is regarding your daughter's case?'

'Yes,' replied Penny. 'I'm sure you can appreciate that we're both very anxious about the whole situation.'

'I can understand that,' replied Evans, with a warm smile.

He then opened up the file in front of him and took out the statement that Jemma had made on the night of her arrest. 'As I am sure you are aware,' continued Evans, 'your daughter was found with a small amount of cannabis on her person on the evening of Saturday 14th February. In her statement she maintains that it wasn't hers and she claims that it had been planted on her.'

'That's correct,' Penny concurred.

'Although we can't categorically say whether or not your daughter is telling the truth here, after careful consideration we've decided that, on this occasion, we won't be taking the case any further with Jemma.'

Penny's delight at hearing this news was etched across her face for all to see. 'Thank you,' she said with a huge sigh of relief. 'You can't believe how thankful we are to you for this.'

Evans smiled again. 'Our view is that even if the drugs were Jemma's, the quantity was so small that it would not be in the public interest to press charges. However, you both need to understand that the records of the arrest will remain on our files.'

Penny nodded. 'We understand.'

Evans stood up and again offered out his hand.

'Thank you again,' replied Penny as she clasped onto the officer's hand.

Once her mother had finished, Jemma also shook the

hand of DC Evans, but with much less verve. 'Yes, thank you,' she said quietly.

'My suggestion to you, Jemma,' said Evans, 'is to consider very carefully who you socialise with, especially if you continue to work at that particular club. And if you take my advice, I'd also seriously think about whether Jaspers is a good place to work.'

'I'm just a barmaid,' snapped Jemma, quickly releasing the officer's hand. 'I'm not one of the dancers and as long as it's not a criminal offence to work there I don't see what's wrong.'

'So you will still be working there?' Evans asked.

'We're not sure about that,' said Penny with a sideways look of disapproval in her daughter's direction. 'We'll be discussing that later.'

'There's nothing to discuss,' replied Jemma firmly. 'I accept that I had drugs on me, but they were planted. I don't take drugs and I don't intend to take drugs. I'm not a lap dancer, I don't intend to take up that particular occupation, but I need to earn some money while I'm at university and the pay at the club is as good as it gets here without doing anything illegal, so I'm not about to quit.'

'Then we may be seeing a bit more of each other in the future,' continued Evans. 'We tend to raid Jaspers quite regularly and we rarely come away without some good reason to arrest someone or other.'

# Chapter 12

By the time 4 p.m. arrived, Cooper and Watson had completed the interviews with Southwaite and Bradshaw and were waiting patiently for Carmichael's arrival in the briefing room. Although they remained largely silent, they each wore the sort of self-satisfied grins that are normally only found on the faces of those who know they have achieved something remarkable. Rachel Dalton completed the trio but, having been excluded from the interviews of Southwaite and Bradshaw, her demeanour was nowhere near as triumphant as her smug male colleagues.

'Afternoon, team,' announced Carmichael as he bounced into the room. 'Can I assume from the look of contentment on your face, Marc, that all went well with the interviews?'

'Absolutely, sir,' replied Marc. 'Although Billy Gupta, Harry Jackson and Frank Bradshaw are all refusing to cooperate with us, the assistance and subsequent statements we have from Vivek Gupta, Melvyn Hitchcock and now Colin Southwaite should be more than enough to nail all six of them.'

'Excellent,' said Carmichael, who couldn't help but notice that Rachel Dalton was nowhere near as excited as her colleagues. 'So why the glum face then, Rachel?'

'It's nothing,' she replied with a faint forced smile. 'I suspect I'm just tired.'

'So was the scam just as Vivek Gupta told us?' Carmichael asked.

'It's even more cunning than we thought,' replied Cooper.

'Tell me more,' said Carmichael as he sat down on the desk facing his team.

'Well,' replied Watson, 'not only were the farmers in on it and claiming on the insurance, but between them and Frank Bradshaw, who is clearly the driving force behind it all, they were falsely inflating the prices of the stolen animals so they could maximise the insurance value.'

'I think you'll have to run it past me slowly,' said Carmichael.

'Well, it appears to have worked like this,' said Cooper calmly. 'At the beginning Bradshaw got together with Jackson. Jackson would buy some cattle at Bradshaw's auction. He would pay way beyond the market price for the animals and using the invoice would insure the beasts at prices well above their true value. Bradshaw would at this point get a good commission on the deal.'

'OK,' replied Carmichael. 'But to get a higher price, surely he would have to get another person to bid against Jackson?'

'Yes, sir,' that's correct. 'Initially this was Vivek Gupta. However, after a few auctions Jackson and Bradshaw felt it may raise suspicions if Gupta was always the one Jackson was bidding against. This is when Melvyn Hitchcock was brought into the scam.'

'Makes sense so far,' said Carmichael.

'Once the cattle had been brought home and insured, then the Guptas would steal them out of Jackson's field and take them at night to Southwaite's abattoir. He would kill and prepare them and sell on the meat at knock-down prices to restaurants and butchers in the Manchester area who were willing to ask few questions, as long as they got a reduced price.'

'But surely there must be pretty tightly controlled rules about tracing meat in abattoirs?' Carmichael asked. 'How did they get around those?'

'Simply by just using the abattoir as a processing area,' replied Watson. 'The cattle would go in at night, be processed and would be out the next morning before the morning shift came on. The abattoir doesn't operate at night so Southwaite and the Guptas, who were his accomplices, would just have to make sure the slaughtering and processing was all done before the morning shift came in. According to Southwaite this was easily possible as long as they only processed a few per night. The Guptas would bring in the live cattle at about ten in the evening and leave at about five the next morning with the processed meat, which they would then deliver to the restaurants and butchers' during the next day.'

'So the cattle were already processed and in the marketplace before they were even reported as being stolen,' continued Watson.

'Crafty buggers!' said Carmichael, who was secretly quite impressed with the scam. 'But hang on a moment. When Jackson and later Hitchcock reported the thefts they were usually for more than two cows. If they could only process two at a time in the abattoir where did they keep the others?'

Cooper and Watson glanced at each other before Cooper explained. 'They never took more than two at a time from the farm,' he said with a smile. 'It's just that Jackson and Hitchcock only reported the thefts once there was a relatively large amount missing. In fact, by the time the farmers had alerted us to the thefts it's fair to say that all the animals had been taken, processed and despatched to the various dodgy buyers.'

'And in the main already consumed,' added Watson.

Carmichael folded his arms and contemplated what he was being told for a few moments. 'So they would make money on the inflated commission on the initial sale, the insurance and then on the sales of the meat,' he said.

'Yes,' replied Cooper. 'But once Hitchcock was involved,

too, they even sold each other cattle at the auction. We have one example of Jackson buying for one thousand five hundred pounds a cow that Hitchcock had bought only two weeks earlier for eight hundred pounds.'

'They must have made thousands out of this,' remarked Rachel, who was slowly coming out of her bad humour.

'My guess is that between them they pocketed at least twenty thousand pounds,' said Cooper. 'And although Southwaite is absolutely adamant that he has only processed the cows that were reported stolen from either Jackson and Hitchcock, I'd bet that Bradshaw is pocketing some extra commission from doing other dodgy deals, though maybe with other partners.'

'I agree,' said Watson. 'Apart from Billy Gupta, who's a minor player, the others are in this up to their necks, but it's clearly Bradshaw who's the mastermind behind it all.'

'Well, all I can say is great work, team,' said Carmichael. 'This is certainly a massive result. But for goodness sake make sure that you tie up all the loose ends so that when this comes to court we make sure that nobody gets off the hook.'

'What about the ones who have cooperated with us?' asked Rachel. 'Surely we need to honour our commitments to them to let the courts know they assisted our enquiries?'

'Absolutely,' replied Carmichael. 'We'll certainly need to do that for Vivek Gupta, Melvyn Hitchcock and Colin Southwaite, but it's for the judge to decide what allowances he makes at sentencing. We should make it clear they cooperated, but that's as far as we go. The rest is down to the courts to decide.'

'How did your meeting go with Dr Stock?' Watson asked.

'Interesting,' replied Carmichael. 'The cause of death was a heart attack, but there are further questions that need answering.'

'Such as?' enquired Rachel.

'Let's leave the Gerry Poole death until tomorrow

morning,' replied Carmichael who was conscious of the time and still wanted to do one more thing before he called it a day. 'I suspect that you three will need to spend time writing up your notes from this afternoon's interviews and getting all the paperwork completed so that the case is ready to be put in front of the CPS. It's still only four fifteen so you should have enough time to get that all sorted before the day's out. We can get together at eight-thirty tomorrow morning. I'll brief you on the Poole case then.'

\*   \*   \*   \*

Penny had spent her final two hours in Leeds trying desperately to persuade her daughter to quit her job at the lap-dancing club, but with absolutely no success.

'Look, Mum,' said Jemma as her mother finally clambered into the taxi that would take her back to the train station. 'I'm not going to pack in the job just because you think it's a seedy place. I know it's a bit sleazy and I am not so gullible as to think that some other things don't go on there, but I don't intend to get involved. I'll just do my shift behind the bar, collect my money and then get on with being a student. So don't worry about me.'

Penny shook her head in dismay. 'Just take care,' she said. 'And promise me that you'll keep your clothes on and stay on the right side of the bar.'

'Mother!' exclaimed Jemma with a look of horror. 'How could you even think I'd do anything like that.'

\*   \*   \*   \*

Carmichael's last act that day was to return to the canal towpath where they had found Gerry Poole's body the day before. The temperature was still around freezing but the wind from the north had now started to pick up, which made it feel much colder. The light was starting to fade as Carmichael made his way carefully up the slippery steps that led to the canal bank. Once he had reached the top, the strong beam of his torch guided him as he tentatively walked along the towpath. The large hollow in the snow made it easy for him to locate the spot where the body was found. He stopped for a brief moment before heading off further down the towpath towards the twinkling lights of Sidney Sydes' narrowboat.

\*    \*    \*    \*

At the age of thirty-three, Sidney Sydes had shocked everyone who knew him by opting out of the world of business. For nearly ten years he had enjoyed a successful career as a senior brand manager in what the marketing men call a fast-moving consumer goods environment, which in normal speak meant that he had been responsible for launching and managing a range of air-fresheners for a large global conglomerate. The official line was that the pressure of life in the cut-throat world of household products, coupled with the fierce internal competition for brand management roles within his firm, had pushed Sidney almost to the point of a nervous breakdown. So one sunny day, four years earlier without any warning, Sydes quit his job. Having no family ties he was able to sell his flash sports car and highly desirable riverside apartment in Manchester and take up a new life travelling the waterways of the UK on his thirty-foot narrowboat, *Safe Haven*. Although this sudden decision surprised his friends and colleagues, they had accepted the rationale behind his spectacular lifestyle change. They had no way of knowing the real reason for his dramatic actions.

With the exception of his cat Hazel he now had no friends, which is exactly how he liked it. And not having a fixed address he enjoyed the fact that he was no longer to be found registered on the electoral role, that he was no longer registered with a doctor and that he no longer had any active record with HM Revenue and Customs. In all respects, from the point of view of the state he no longer existed, which was just what he wanted. In fact, apart from the need to occasionally draw cash from his telephone bank account and to use the address of a trusted old friend to receive debit card replacements when they were required, Sidney Sydes lived completely outside the rest of the community. With the savings he had amassed while he was working, bolstered by the sizeable sum of money he received from the sale of his apartment and car, he calculated that he could live in reasonable comfort on his boat for at least the next thirty years. Given the amount of cigarettes he smoked each day, this was way beyond his life expectancy and was something he had taken into account when he'd decided to quit his job and spend the rest of his days as a nautical hermit.

\*   \*   \*   \*

Carmichael didn't consider Sidney to be a suspect in the death of Gerry Poole, but he could not bring himself to believe that a body could have been dumped just a hundred yards from Sydes' boat without him noticing.

Since he had met Sydes, Carmichael had a 'gut-feel' that something was not right about this man. He wanted to talk with Sydes again, if only to dismiss this initial negative perception as a simple error of judgement on his part.

Carmichael carefully clambered across the small wooden bridge that straddled the gap between the towpath and Sidney's barge. He knocked loudly on the green wooden door at the stern of the vessel.

Carmichael could hear footsteps from inside the boat.

'Who is it?' enquired Sydes.

'It's Inspector Carmichael. We met briefly on Sunday.'

Sydes slid open the hatch and unlocked the door. 'You'd better come in out of the cold,' he said as he ushered Carmichael below.

Once Carmichael was inside, Sydes slid back the hatch and pushed the door shut.

'Still bloody cold out there,' he said.

To Carmichael's surprise the narrowboat was more spacious than he had expected.

'I saw that you found your missing man,' continued Sydes as he gestured to Carmichael to sit down. 'I assume from all the activity yesterday that the body they found was his.'

'Yes,' replied Carmichael. 'Unfortunately it was.'

'If you don't mind me asking,' continued Sydes, 'how did he die?'

'Natural causes,' replied Carmichael. 'However, to complete our investigations we're talking to anyone who may have seen him in the last few moments before he died. I was wondering whether you remember seeing anything suspicious down where we found the body at the back end of last week?'

Sydes considered the question for a few moments. 'No,' he replied eventually, with a faint shake of his head. 'As I told you, I can't recall seeing anyone down that towpath. Until your people all arrived yesterday, I don't remember seeing anyone down there since at least Thursday last week.'

'I see,' replied Carmichael.

'Is that everything?' Sydes asked in a way that clearly suggested to Carmichael that he wanted to cut short the discussion.

'Yes,' replied Carmichael. 'I think I've taken up enough of your time already.'

Sydes walked back over to the door of the barge, pushed it open and slid back the hatch once more.

'So how long have you been living on a barge, Mr Sydes?'

Carmichael asked as he sauntered slowly towards the open door.

'About four years now,' replied Sydes. 'I was in marketing before, but had a bit of a breakdown. I have no family, so one day I just sold up and have been living on this thing ever since.'

'It must be great in the summer,' said Carmichael as he arrived at the door.

'Yes, summer is the best time,' replied Sydes. 'But it gets really busy. Not so much on this stretch of waterway I expect, but on some other stretches it's really manic in August.'

'So you've been all over?' asked Carmichael with genuine interest.

'Well, not all over, but I've spent a good deal of time in and around the Midlands. There's a lot of waterway down there and some nice places to moor up for a week or two.'

'So how long have you been in Moulton Bank?' Carmichael asked.

'Just over two weeks now,' replied Sydes. 'And once the ice starts to clear I will move on down towards Liverpool. I've never been there so that will be good.'

Carmichael smiled and carefully exited the boat. 'Thank you for your time,' he said.

'Not at all,' replied Sydes, as he started to shut the hatch.

Sidney Sydes watched intently as Carmichael carefully trudged away from the narrowboat. He then picked up his mobile and dialled the usual number.

# Chapter 13

It was almost 7 p.m. by the time Penny arrived at Moulton Bank train station. As she climbed out of the clammy and crowded carriage, the cold air smacked her hard in the face and she could feel almost immediately that icicles were forming on the top of the woollen scarf she had wrapped tightly around her chin. She made her way gingerly down the slight incline that took her from the station platform to the main road, where she hoped her husband's car would be waiting. Steve's car was on the opposite side of the road parked up in front of the village post office. The level crossing barriers had not yet been opened to let the traffic pass, which made it easy for Penny to cross the road. However, the mixture of the car exhaust fumes and the cold damp air made it impossible for Carmichael to recognise his wife until she was almost at the car.

'I think it's colder now than it's been all week,' remarked Penny as she opened the car door and clambered in.

'Yes,' replied Carmichael. 'They say it's going to be minus five tonight.'

'It feels like that now,' she said as she slammed the car door shut.

'How was your trip?' Carmichael enquired.

'Not too bad,' replied Penny. 'But I'm glad I don't have to get the train every day. It's so jam-packed with people. I got a seat but there were people who'd been squashed in so tightly that you could hardly breathe. There was a rather portly ginger-haired man opposite me who I thought was going to collapse. Poor chap was so hot. He must have lost about ten pounds in sweat.'

'Sounds delightful,' replied Carmichael. 'Anyway, how's Jemma doing?'

Penny had fully expected Steve to ask a question like this and for the last two hours she had been pondering what her answer should be.

'She's fine,' replied Penny carefully. 'But there's something you need to know.'

Carmichael turned his head slightly so he could see the expression on his wife's face. 'Oh yes,' he said. 'And what's that?'

'Well, don't get mad, but she did have a bit of a run-in over the weekend with the police in Leeds,' said Penny. 'It was a total misunderstanding and no charges are going to be brought against her, but I think you need to know.'

'What!' exclaimed Carmichael. 'What happened?'

'Well,' replied Penny, who was trying as hard as she could to remain calm. 'It would appear that she was in the club where she works and the place was raided by the police. They found a very small quantity of cannabis in her coat pocket and she was arrested. I've spoken to her and she swears to me that it was planted on her and I believe her. The police are not bringing charges so it's not going to go any further, but I thought you needed to know.'

'Cannabis!' exclaimed Carmichael. 'Jemma was caught in possession of cannabis!'

'Yes,' replied Penny. 'But it wasn't hers. She is sure that someone slipped it into her pocket when they saw the police dog coming in. She's really upset about it all and she's worried that you'll take it badly. She's adamant that it was not hers and I believe her.'

'Well, I hope you told her that she needs to pack in that job and find herself another bar to work behind,' said Carmichael in a raised voice.

'I did,' replied Penny. 'But she's twenty now and old enough to make her own mind up, so it's up to her.'

Carmichael's BMW arrived back at their house a few minutes later with its driver still fuming over the news he had just received.

# Chapter 14

**Wednesday 18<sup>th</sup> February**

As the day started, the residents of Moulton Bank slowly began to rise. From 6 a.m. the blare of engines running and the unmistakable sound of scrapers could be heard as the drivers of the village slowly removed the thick layer of ice that had been deposited the night before. From 7 a.m. the cacophony had become much louder as more people rose from their beds and joined the grumbling cold throng of car windscreen scourers. When dawn finally broke and the first rays of light burst out from behind Ambient Hill, the bleary eyed dog walkers emerged from their homes, all wrapped up to keep warm from the icy cold.

One of the first of thes was a woman in her fifties. She carefully led her dog onto the Common, a large expanse of grass that had occupied the centre of the village for as long as anyone could remember. As she crunched her way over the frosty grass, she could see an object in the distance. At first she couldn't make out what it was, but as she got nearer the outline gained greater clarity. At a distance of thirty feet it looked like a statue of some sort, which she assumed to be the result of some drunken outing the evening before. It was only when she got within a few yards that she realised to her horror, that the object was not a statue, but the frozen naked body of Tamara Searle.

\*   \*   \*   \*

Carmichael had not slept at all well the night before. The news of Jemma being arrested had been a bolt from the blue to him and as hard as he tried he could not get it out of his mind. By 6.30 a.m. he had managed to snatch only a few very short periods of slumber, maybe twenty minutes each in duration. Penny, on the other hand, had gone to sleep as soon as her head hit the pillow, where it had remained unmoved for the last seven hours. Although her snoring was not as loud as usual, the very fact that his wife seemed so capable of sleeping soundly, given their daughter had been arrested for the possession of drugs, only made Carmichael more restless and angry.

'Bugger this!' Carmichael finally exclaimed as he threw back the cover and clambered out of bed.

Even Carmichael's sudden movement could not wake Penny, who remained still and to Carmichael's further annoyance continued to emanate her persistent metronomic snore.

Once shaved, showered and dressed, Carmichael collected the newspaper from the doormat and walked down the hall and into the kitchen.

He poured himself a large bowl of cornflakes and placed two slices of brown bread in the toaster. With his attention mainly focused on the front page of the paper, which sensationally predicted more heavy snow to come, Carmichael walked over to the fridge and opened the door.

'Oh bugger!' he found himself saying for a second time that morning, as he discovered that there was only a minute drop of milk in the bottom of the carton.

Carmichael took out the milk from the fridge and poured the contents onto the mountain of flakes in his bowl. There would be no milk for his coffee that particular morning. As he started to crunch away at the predominantly dry cereal in his breakfast bowl, he read deeper into the headline story:

The latest forecasts are warning of more snow for the next two weeks. The worst affected areas are predicted to be in the lowlands of Scotland, the Lake District, Lancashire and North Wales, where up to two feet of snow could fall within the next 48 hours. Severe disruption is likely to road and rail services and the advice from the Met Office to the public is to keep a close eye on the latest forecasts in your area before venturing out and to only travel by car if your journey is essential.

'What the hell does "essential" mean?' he mumbled, just as the smell of burning toast hit his nostrils.

'Bugger!' he shouted for the third time that morning, and it was still only just after 7 a.m.

As Carmichael juggled the hot and blackened pieces of toast, the fire detector in the hallway started to emit its piercing high-pitch shriek, followed quickly afterwards by the detector which he had positioned on the ceiling at the top of the stairs.

By the time Carmichael had managed to open up the fire detector in the hallway and remove its battery, he was surprised to notice that the upstairs detector had also fallen silent. He soon realised that this was due to a similar intervention by Penny, who slowly descended the stairs clutching the rectangular battery in her hand.

'What on earth are you doing?' she whispered. 'It sounds like all hell is breaking loose down here.'

'The toaster must be broken,' he replied. 'It's burnt the bread to a cinder.'

Penny walked over to the offending appliance and turned the dial 90 degrees.

'It was set on the highest setting,' she said as if she was addressing a simpleton. 'The last person to use it probably made some toast from a frozen loaf of bread. You need to check the setting before you start to use it.'

Carmichael shrugged his shoulders and continued to eat his cornflakes.

'It's not been a good day so far,' he said. 'I hardly slept last night due to that daughter of ours; there's no milk so I'm eating almost dry cereal; I have none left for coffee and the bloody toast is burnt. The paper says we are going to get more snow and the sun's not even properly up yet.'

'Just sit down and read your paper,' replied Penny. 'I'll make you some more toast.'

'I'm going to call Jemma later,' said Carmichael as his wife placed two slices of bread into the toaster.

'OK,' replied Penny. 'But please don't be angry with her. She is very upset about the whole affair and she's worried that you'll be cross with her.'

'I'll be calm, don't worry,' he assured her.

Carmichael had only just finished his toast when the call came through from the police station. 'I'll be right there,' he replied to the officer down the phone. 'Get Watson, Cooper and Dalton to meet me there.'

'What's up?' asked Penny.

'They've found a body on the Common,' he replied. 'I'm going to have to dash.'

Within a couple of minutes Carmichael had put on his shoes and overcoat and was making his way on foot to the Common, a matter of just five minutes' walk from the front door of his home.

Two uniformed officers had already set up a ten-metre cordon around the body of Tamara Searle by the time Carmichael arrived. As he approached, Carmichael could see that they were doing a good job in keeping back the small group of people who had come out to see what was happening. As he strode out across the snowy grass, he could see a third uniformed officer crouched by the passenger seat of a parked police car talking to a distraught lady who was sitting down, ashen-faced but still clutching tightly onto the lead of a tiny dog that she had been walking.

'Morning, guys,' Carmichael said as he ducked under the police tape. 'What have we got here?'

'It's that young weathergirl from the telly,' replied one of the excited PCs.

Carmichael squatted down next to the cold naked body of Tamara Searle. Over the years Carmichael had seen many dead bodies, but never before had he witnessed one like this. Bizarrely, the body of Tamara Searle was sat upright with her hands clasped around her legs and with her head and long brown hair resting gently on her knees. It was as if she had been deliberately posed by a fastidious photographer for some arty promotional campaign. He got as close to the corpse as he could without making any contact.

'Has anybody touched the body?' he shouted back at the PCs.

'No,' came back the reply. 'She was just like that when we came. It's weird, isn't it?'

When Carmichael had met Tamara Searle at the Lovelace's Valentine's party, she had come across as a beautiful and bubbly person but she now just looked like a cold, fragile, porcelain figurine.

It took no more than twenty minutes for Carmichael to be joined first by Rachel Dalton and Marc Watson, who turned up together, then Dr Stock who arrived with a team of three all dressed in their unmistakeable white overalls.

'What do you make of this one?' Carmichael asked Stock.

'Very unusual,' replied Stock, without bothering to turn back to face Carmichael. 'I can't see any signs of bruising or anything else that would suggest how she died.'

'I doubt she just stripped off and sat down here to die,' commented Watson. 'She must have been dumped here.'

Stock continued to examine the body closely. 'I will need

to get her back to the mortuary. Until I do a full autopsy it's impossible to say the cause of death.'

'Have you any idea when she died?' Carmichael asked.

'Not precisely,' replied Stock. 'But less than forty-eight hours ago that's for certain.'

'Why do you say that?' Carmichael enquired.

'Because I saw her live on TV on Monday morning giving the weather report.'

'Do you think this one is linked to the death of Gerry Poole?' asked Rachel.

'I'm not sure,' replied Carmichael. 'It's certainly a strange coincidence to discover two frozen bodies in the space of two to three days, but we know that the first death was of natural causes so I'm not sure we can truly say that they're connected.'

Stock nodded. 'Perhaps,' he said, 'but it's looking like Poole's death might not be quite as natural after all. I asked a colleague from Liverpool University to take a look at him. He has a lot of experience in autopsies on frozen corpses, as he spent many years as a lecturer in Montreal. He's certain that Poole died and was frozen afterwards. He believes that his death could have occurred anything up to four weeks before we found the body.'

'So someone put him in a freezer?' said Rachel.

'Yes, that's his considered opinion,' replied Stock.

\*   \*   \*   \*

Twenty minutes later Carmichael, Watson and Rachel clambered into Watson's car.

'Drop me off at my house, Marc,' Carmichael said. 'I'll pick up my car and then we can head off to Kirkwood Station. Once we're there we can get that briefing session started; we've quite a bit to do now we have two suspicious deaths to investigate.'

As Watson started the car, Carmichael's mobile began to ring.

'Hello, Carmichael speaking,' he said.

'Hello, sir, it's Cooper,' replied the weak voice at the end of the line. 'I'm sorry, sir, but I won't be in today, I've got a terrible headache and all my muscles are aching. I think I'm coming down with this flu bug.'

Carmichael normally had little time for people who were ill, but as this was the first occasion that Cooper had ever been ill in the two and a half years he had been at Kirkwood, and as the flu epidemic was now widespread at the police station, for once he was reasonably understanding. 'OK, Paul, just rest up and get back to work as soon as you're feeling better,' he said in a sympathetic tone.

By the time the call had ended they had reached Carmichael's house.

'That was Cooper,' he announced as he opened the car door. 'He's got this flu bug so he won't be in for a while.'

'I thought he didn't look well yesterday,' said Rachel.

'Well, that means we three are going to have to work extra hard if we're going to get to the bottom of these deaths. I'll see you both back in the briefing room in one hour.'

With that he climbed out of the car and walked over to his ice-covered BMW.

# Chapter 15

On his way to Kirkwood Police Station, Carmichael pondered what the team's next steps should be. He could see three links between the two suspicious deaths. First, and most obviously, the two bodies were both frozen, but in the current weather conditions he concluded that this was not so surprising. Secondly, both were well known to Caroline Lovelace and, thirdly, they had both been invited to her last dinner party. He decided that after the briefing he would get himself over to the studio of *The Lovelace Show* as he was sure Caroline must know something that would help with their enquiries. She might even be the killer, he mused, though it seemed far-fetched.

He was almost at the station when he received a call from Hewitt.

'Where are you, Inspector?' Hewitt enquired abruptly.

'Actually I'm just a few minutes away,' replied Carmichael.

'Well, when you get here I need to talk with you,' continued Hewitt. 'Get yourself up here straight away, as soon as you arrive.'

Hewitt did not elaborate and without any further comment ended the call.

'That's all I bloody need,' said Carmichael under his breath.

\* \* \* \*

Penny was not convinced that Steve would remember to call Jemma that day, now he had a murder to solve, but she was worried that when he eventually did he would not be as understanding as he had implied earlier that morning. After some deliberation she decided it would be wise to send her daughter a text message, just to forewarn her of her father's impending call:

> Hi darling, it's Mum. I spoke with Dad about what happened and he was a bit shocked but did not take it too badly. He said he would call you later. XX

When Jemma read the text her heart sank. She knew that her dad would not be pleased, but on balance was happier with the prospect of him talking to her over the phone, rather than having to discuss her arrest with him face to face.

*    *    *    *

'Shut the door,' ordered Hewitt when Carmichael entered his office. 'I need to talk to you about your ongoing enquiry.'

'Which one?' Carmichael asked as he closed the door behind him.

'The investigation into the death of Gerard Poole,' replied Hewitt.

'That's progressing well,' replied Carmichael as he sat down opposite his boss. 'We're now pretty sure that he died some time before his body was found and that he had been kept in a deep freeze. According to Dr Stock, he died of a heart attack, but I'm not ruling out the possibility that his heart attack was brought on by being locked in a freezer.'

Hewitt looked shocked by what he was hearing. 'So where does Sidney Sydes come into all this?' he enquired.

'Why do you ask?' replied Carmichael, who was very

surprised that his boss was asking him again about the narrowboat pilot.

Hewitt did not respond immediately, but from his body language Carmichael could see that his boss was clearly agitated.

'So do you think that Sidney Sydes is connected to the death of Gerry Poole?' asked Hewitt, who was trying to maintain a degree of composure.

'I don't know,' replied Carmichael, who was now becoming very suspicious about the reason for Hewitt's interest in Sydes. 'He was the nearest person to where the body was found. He would have had a clear view of all the people who passed by along the towpath, so naturally I have been keen to talk with him. However, he's not been very helpful and, although he's not exactly my prime suspect, I do feel that he may be hiding something from me.'

Hewitt stood up and walked slowly to the window. He gazed out over the station car park as if he was considering what to say next.

'What's your reason for asking about Sydes?' Carmichael asked.

Hewitt continued to stare out of his window. 'I am not at liberty to share all the details with you, Inspector, but you need to take it from me that Sydes is not connected with your mystery death. As such I am ordering you to exclude him from any aspect of your investigation. You need to leave him alone.'

Carmichael could not believe what he was hearing. Even during his days in the Met, he could never recall being instructed by a senior officer to refrain from interviewing a potential witness.

'Why are you so sure he's not connected?' asked Carmichael. 'And what reason is there for me having to leave him out of my investigation?'

Hewitt turned around to face Carmichael. 'I can't say any

more, Inspector. You have your instructions and I expect you to follow them to the letter. You must carry out your enquiry without harassing Sidney Sydes any further.'

Carmichael could feel his temperature rising. However, he tried hard not to let his anger show. 'As you wish,' he said as he rose from his chair. 'As I said before, I'm pretty sure he's not connected with it anyway and now we've found a second body my hunch is, if the deaths are linked, the person we are looking for is not Sidney Sydes.'

'A second body!' exclaimed Hewitt. 'I was not aware that we had another body.'

'It was discovered this morning,' replied Carmichael. 'It's a young woman called Tamara Searle. She's a weather presenter on local TV. I've just come from the crime scene now. We're not yet sure how she died, but she was found naked and frozen in the middle of some common land in Moulton Bank. Her death looks very suspicious.'

'I see,' replied Hewitt. 'So do you feel the two deaths are linked in any way?'

'I've no idea,' replied Carmichael. 'But my gut feeling tells me they are and I intend to follow that instinct until I discover the truth.'

'And where does that intuition tell you to start looking?' asked Hewitt.

'I'm not sure,' replied Carmichael as he made his way towards the door. 'However, I will probably start with anyone who has access to a large freezer. I suspect that will rule out Sidney Sydes. I doubt there's room on that boat of his for an appliance big enough to hide a body.'

\* \* \* \*

Marc Watson and Rachel Dalton were already in the incident room when Carmichael arrived.

'That bloody man,' he growled as he slammed the door

shut behind him. 'He's only told me that Sydes is off limits to us.'

'What!' exclaimed Watson. 'Why?'

'He wouldn't say,' replied Carmichael. 'But I bet it's because of some deal he's done with one of his Masonic chums somewhere.'

'Maybe he's under surveillance from the drug squad or some other division,' suggested Rachel.

'Who knows?' said Carmichael his frustration apparent for all to see. 'All I know is that Hewitt is insistent on us leaving him alone.'

'And do we obey him?' asked Watson.

Carmichael thought for a while. 'I recall him telling me not to harass him and to leave him alone, but I don't recall him saying that we can't do a bit more digging into his background. I'd like to know a bit more about this man before we just exclude him.'

Watson and Dalton glanced quickly at each other.

'So who do you want to do that?' Watson asked.

'Rachel, I'd like you to take on that task,' replied Carmichael. 'But be careful. I don't want Hewitt to know what we are doing. Just get some background on him. I'd really like to know where he's from and what the big mystery is with him.'

'OK,' said Rachel, although she was not sure where to start.

'Anyway,' announced Carmichael. 'That's not the most pressing job for us to be getting on with. We have two suspicious deaths to solve.'

'What do you want us to do?' asked Rachel

'Well, as both were well known to Caroline Lovelace, and as they had both been invited to her dinner party last Friday, I think our first task should be to interview Caroline Lovelace and also the people at the TV studio where she and Tamara Searle work,' replied Carmichael. 'That's what I will be doing as soon as we have finished here.'

'And what about us?' asked Watson.

'I want you and a few plain-clothed officers to get yourselves down to the streets around the Common where Tamara's body was found. I can't believe she would have gone there naked and just sat down in the cold and died. I'm sure the good Dr Stock's autopsy will show that she was already dead by the time she got there and was moved there by someone. If that's the case, I can't believe for one moment that whoever did that was able to do so without witnesses. Your job is to find those witnesses.'

'Right you are, sir,' replied Watson. 'I'll get started.'

With that, Watson grabbed his coat and headed for the door.

'Call me this evening, Marc,' said Carmichael. 'I want an update from you on how you get on.'

Watson nodded and left the incident room.

'What about me?' Rachel asked eagerly.

'In addition to digging into Sydes' background, I want you to find out a bit more about Tamara Searle's movements in the last three or four days. We'll also need to get her body formally identified, so you will need to find her next of kin.'

'OK,' said Rachel. 'But I'm not sure where to start as there was no clothing found at the scene and I've no idea where she lived.'

Carmichael smiled. 'Get your coat. You and I are off to the TV studio. I want to see what Mrs Lovelace and the rest of those luvvies have to say about Tamara's death. While I'm doing that you can talk to Ms Searle's colleagues. They should be able to help you get started.'

# Chapter 16

The TV studio building was nothing like Carmichael had imagined. Rather than being the imposing brand-new structure with gleaming glass offices that he was expecting, Sunrise Productions was tucked away down a small side street with a solitary security guard on the gate.

Carmichael wound down his window and presented his identity card for the guard to check. 'We're here to interview Caroline Lovelace,' he announced.

The guard studied his identity for a few moments. 'If you proceed to reception they'll sort you out with a visitor's pass,' he told them before waving them on.

Once inside, the site appeared to consist of a large number of ancient, small, single-storey garages that looked to Carmichael like they had been constructed in the 1950s and which were badly in need of a coat of fresh paint.

Carmichael parked his car in front of the reception building. 'Seems like a good place for us to start,' he said with a smile.

Unlike the façade, the inside of the reception area was much more what Carmichael had anticipated a TV studio to look like. The reception desk was staffed by two very good-looking, well-groomed young women in their late twenties. To the left of the reception desk were situated two large, comfortable-looking, red sofas. To the right of the desk was a set of double doors which Carmichael assumed would lead into the various production offices, and all around the walls were glossy colour photographs of stars, past and present. In pride of place behind the reception desk were three larger photographs, the middle one of which was of Caroline Lovelace, whose smile beamed eerily out in the direction of every visitor arriving there.

'Good morning,' Carmichael said as he presented his identity card once more. 'My colleague and I need to talk with Caroline Lovelace and whoever heads up the team responsible for the weather reports.'

The young women behind the counter studied Carmichael's identity card. She then handed Carmichael two large visitor's passes suspended from bright blue cords. 'If you would both be kind enough to wear your visitor's passes at all times when on the site, that would be appreciated.'

'Thank you,' said Carmichael as he placed his around his neck.

The receptionist smiled and pointed at the sofas. 'If you'd care to take a seat, I'll see if I can get Ms Lovelace's PA to come down and also see if Mr Yerbovic from the weather department is free.'

'Thank you,' replied Carmichael, who handed Rachel her pass before walking with his colleague to the red sofas.

'When they come down you go off with this Mr Yerbovic,' he whispered. 'But don't mention anything about Tamara being dead until you absolutely have to.'

'OK,' replied Rachel. 'I'll see what I can glean from him first.'

'I'll do the same with Caroline Lovelace,' continued Carmichael.

With that Carmichael and Rachel Dalton each sat down on one of the sofas and waited for the arrival of their respective interviewees.

\* \* \* \*

By the time Marc Watson arrived back at the Common, Tamara Searle's body had been removed. The police cordon was still in place around the site where the body had been found and there were three SOCOs dressed in white overalls combing for clues within the cordoned area. Outside the cordon the rest of the Common had pretty much returned to normality.

Watson strode briskly across the frozen snow towards the two police officers who were stationed like sentries, guarding the crime scene.

'Has anyone started the house-to-house yet?' he asked when he arrived at the place where the two officers were standing.

'Not yet, Sergeant,' replied one of the officers. 'We were told to wait here until the SOCOs were finished.'

'Well, there's nobody around now, so you can both make a start,' replied Watson. 'Before the day's over I want all of the adjoining households to have been questioned and I want statements from each of them. We need to know what they saw or heard yesterday evening, last night and earlier this morning.'

The two officers left their posts and started to walk together down to the road.

'Split up,' Watson shouted at them. 'You don't need to do the interviews together. You'll get them over much quicker if you do half the houses each.' On that note Watson shook his head and turned to see what the SOCOs were doing. 'Have you found anything interesting?' he asked the nearest one.

'Actually, yes,' came back the reply. 'Some footprints which may belong to someone involved in her death and a woman's purse.'

Watson could feel the adrenalin starting to rush through his body.

'Does the purse belong to the dead woman?' he asked.

'No,' came back the reply. 'It's only got a couple of things in it. Some coins, that are worth no more than a few pounds in total, a train ticket to Manchester with yesterday's date on it and a NatWest debit card.'

'What name is on the card?' Watson enquired.

'It's someone called Melanie Dreyfuss,' replied the SOCO.

\*   \*   \*   \*

Tony Yerbovic burst into the reception of Sunrise Productions like a tornado. He was a tall imposing man in his mid-forties, with a mop of undulating black hair, which waved from left to right as he made his way towards Steve Carmichael and Rachel Dalton.

'Good morning,' he boomed. 'My name's Tony. I'm head of news and weather here. I understand you want to talk to me.'

'Yes,' replied Rachel, who had immediately scrambled to her feet when Tony Yerbovic had mentioned his position. 'I'm DC Dalton from Kirkwood Police Station. I'd like a few minutes of your time if I may?'

Tony Yerbovic held out his mammoth right paw. 'Of course,' he replied with a broad smile.

Tentatively Rachel reciprocated, her tiny hand suddenly becoming engulfed in Yerbovic's firm grip. Once in that hold, her arm was soon shaken by his vigorous greeting. 'Is your colleague not joining us?' he asked, pointing in Carmichael's direction.

'No,' replied Rachel apologetically, her hand now free from his vicelike grasp. 'Inspector Carmichael has another person to see.'

'So I just get a DC and someone else gets the Inspector,' Yerbovic replied with a mischievous grin. 'Lucky I'm not a sensitive soul. I promise I won't take offence.'

Rachel smiled back and then followed Tony through the double doors.

As they disappeared from sight, Carmichael could hear

Yerbovic inviting Rachel to call in at the coffee bar en route to his office. 'They do a great cappuccino here,' was the last part of their conversation that Carmichael could make out before the double doors closed behind them.

As Carmichael waited patiently for Caroline Lovelace to arrive, his mobile rang.

'It's Stock here. I thought I'd call you to let you have an initial summary of my findings.'

'Thanks,' replied Carmichael, who stood up and made his way to the corner of the reception as far away from the receptionists as he could.

'This one was asphyxiated,' continued Stock. 'Looking at the state of her body she could not have been killed more than thirty-six hours before we found her.'

'So that would mean she died on either Monday evening or Tuesday,' confirmed Carmichael.

'Yes,' replied Stock. 'However, looking at the contents of her stomach, my guess is that it was on Monday evening, after having a light meal of pasta and chicken.'

'But couldn't the fact that she was frozen mean she was killed earlier?' asked Carmichael.

'No,' replied Stock firmly. 'Unlike the first body, this one wasn't already frozen when it was left on the Common. She was only partly frozen and I'm certain that was just caused by her being left naked overnight in such an exposed position, in such cold temperatures.'

'So you think she was killed two days ago and then dumped on the Common yesterday evening?' Carmichael enquired.

'Yes,' replied Stock. 'However, I wouldn't say she'd been dumped. The way she had been positioned looked more like a careful and deliberate pose, wouldn't you agree?'

'I'm going to have to go,' said Carmichael as from the corner of his eye he could see the figure of a woman by reception, who looked like she was waiting for him. 'Thanks for the update. I'll call you later.'

Carmichael ended the call, placed his mobile in the deep pocket of his warm overcoat and walked over to where the woman was patiently waiting.

'Inspector Carmichael, my name's Amanda Buchannan. I'm Caroline's PA. We did talk briefly on the phone on Monday.'

'Yes, we did,' replied Carmichael, who recalled the trouble he had endured trying to get hold of Ms Lovelace two days earlier. 'I hope she is available to see me.'

'Caroline is fully aware that you want to see her, but she's on air for the next fifteen minutes. If you follow me I'll take you up to the studio. She will see you straight after her show finishes.'

Carmichael nodded his agreement and followed the slightly built PA through the double doors.

\*   \*   \*   \*

Marc Watson decided that his main priority was to talk with Melanie Dreyfuss. He left the two uniformed officers to complete their house-to-house enquiries and headed off towards Much Maddock, the small village on the outskirts of Kirkwood where The Helpful Angels' offices were located. He was excited at the prospect of meeting Melanie once again.

\*   \*   \*   \*

Rachel followed Yerbovic into his office. She placed her paper coffee cup down on the table, removed her coat, flung it over the back of her chair and sat down.

'What can I do for you?' Yerbovic asked from behind his untidy desk.

'I'd like to talk to you about Tamara Searle,' Rachel said, trying hard not to give too much away too early.

'Is she in trouble?' enquired Yerbovic, who was now not as cheerful as he had been when they first met.

'No, she's not in any trouble,' replied Rachel deliberately. 'But I need you to provide me with some information about her.'

'Of course,' responded Yerbovic. 'I will help you as much as I can.'

'First of all,' continued Rachel, 'can you tell me the last time you saw her.'

Tony Yerbovic considered hard before replying. 'It would be on Monday afternoon. She finished here as usual at about three in the afternoon and must have left the studio shortly afterwards.'

'So she wasn't in yesterday?' enquired Rachel.

'No,' replied Yerbovic, who was now looking very anxious. 'Has anything happened to her?'

Rachel thought hard before replying. 'I'm really sorry to tell you, but earlier today we found the body of a young woman and, although it has yet to be identified, we are fairly sure it is Tamara Searle.'

Yerbovic slumped back into his chair. The colour drained from his face as he took on board the dreadful news. 'How did she die?' he asked.

'I'm sure you can appreciate,' continued Rachel, 'I can't share too much information with you until we have a formal identification of the body. However, we are treating the death as suspicious so we would really appreciate all the help you can give us.'

Yerbovic's large left hand fidgeted nervously through his tangled jet-black hair. 'Of course,' he said. 'I'll help you all I can.'

\*　　\*　　\*　　\*

Carmichael waited patiently at the back of Studio 5 where Caroline Lovelace was just concluding her morning show.

118

'Tomorrow we will have a very special guest on the sofa,' she announced to the applause of the crew behind the camera. 'I'm delighted to say that it is the one and only Damien Mortimer, the famous author of *The Silent Partner*, which has taken the literary world by storm. If you have any questions for Damien, please text me at lovelace three four five six seven or email me at caroline at sunrisemorning dot com forward slash hot guest. Have a lovely day, but remember to wrap up warm. I'll see you again on Sunrise TV tomorrow morning.'

Caroline Lovelace remained motionless on her sofa as the closing music started to play. Her fake smile was as perfect as the day she created it some six years earlier.

After a few seconds a voice to Carmichael's left shouted, 'That's it. Thank you everybody. Great show!'

No sooner had these words been uttered than Caroline stood up and, with a huge look of irritation on her face, marched over to where the man was standing.

'Freddie, 'she shouted angrily. 'We need to talk. The show was an absolute shambles today. You have got to get the camera changes slicker and, as for that bloody stand-in for Tamara, she was hopeless.'

It was at about that point that Caroline first spied Steve Carmichael waiting at the back of the studio. 'We'll talk later, Freddie,' she said with her plastic smile now back on her face. 'I need to spend some moments with this gentleman first, but we need to talk before the end of the day.'

Freddie said nothing, but from the look on his face it was clear to Carmichael that this was not the first time he had received a tongue-lashing from Caroline.

'Good morning, Inspector,' Caroline said as she pushed forward her right cheek for him to kiss. 'I was told you needed to speak with me urgently, but I expected you to be in my dressing room rather than in the studio.' As she uttered

119

these words it was obvious to Carmichael that she was now scolding her PA for bringing him into her studio. A message that Amanda received loud and clear, judging from her embarrassed expression and the way her normally pale cheeks started to turn crimson.

'Yes,' Carmichael said as he uncomfortably obliged and greeted Caroline with a faint peck on either cheek. 'I would appreciate a few minutes with you in private, if that's possible.'

'Of course,' replied Caroline. 'We'll go up to my dressing room.'

With that she marched towards a door at the opposite end of the studio. 'Follow me.'

\*    \*    \*    \*

Tony Yerbovic was very helpful. He brought up the studio's HR department file for Tamara Searle on his PC and supplied Rachel with a disk containing all Tamara's personnel details and records.

'I just can't believe it,' he said as he passed over the shiny, silver disk. 'She was such a great presenter, very clever, hard working, never late or absent and she had that rare ability to bond with her audience. No matter what their age or background, she seemed to connect with everyone.'

'So when she didn't turn up for work yesterday, what did you think?' Rachel asked.

'We were all very shocked,' replied Yerbovic. 'Especially given that she seemed to have been absolutely fine the day before. However, this flu bug is nasty and it does seem to strike very quickly, so I didn't think that anything was amiss. To be honest it was so late when we received her text, all we could think of was getting someone in at short notice to cover for her.'

'A text!' repeated Rachel, with some astonishment in her voice. 'Is it normal for people to text in sick?'

'Actually, no,' replied Yerbovic, 'I was going to talk to her about that.'

'Do you still have the text message?' Rachel asked.

'Probably,' replied Yerbovic, who took out his mobile from his pocket and started to pore through his text messages.

Rachel waited patiently as Yerbovic interrogated his mobile's inbox. 'Here it is,' he said as he held it out for Rachel to see.

Rachel read the message and took a note of the time it was sent. 'I'm afraid I'll need to take your phone as evidence,' she said.

'Is that really necessary?' enquired Yerbovic. 'I rely on this.'

'I'm sorry,' replied Rachel. 'I'll try to get it back to you as soon as I can, but we do need to make sure the message is taken off and kept available in case it's needed later as evidence.'

Yerbovic accepted what he was being told and gently handed over his phone to Rachel.

'Is there anything else?' Yerbovic asked

'I've just two or three further questions for you,' replied Rachel. 'First, who was Tamara closest to at work?'

'She was popular with most people,' replied Yerbovic. 'She didn't have any specific special friends here to my knowledge, but she was a great admirer of Caroline Lovelace. I think Tamara had ambitions to follow in Caroline's footsteps. God knows why. Also, I think she was quite chummy with Amanda Buchannan, Caroline's PA. I think they were at school or university together.'

'I see,' said Rachel. 'Also, do you know if Tamara was in a relationship with anyone?'

Yerbovic shook his head. 'I don't think so but it wouldn't surprise me. She was very popular and a really beautiful woman, so I'm sure she was not without her admirers.'

Rachel stood up and started to put on her coat. 'You have

been very helpful, Mr Yerbovic,' she said. 'I do have one final question for you, though. Can you tell me who her next of kin would be?'

'It will be in her HR file so it should be on the disk I've just given you, but let me check,' he replied as he started to tap into her HR file on line. 'Looking at her data, she gave her mother as her next of kin when she was taken on, but I know her mother died about a year ago, so I'm not sure who her next of kin would be now.'

'Not to worry,' replied Rachel as she held out her hand.

To Rachel's relief, the handshake she received from Yerbovic as they parted was nowhere near as brutal as the one she had received when they had met thirty minutes earlier in reception.

'There's no need to take me back to reception,' Rachel told him. 'I think I can remember the way.'

# Chapter 17

It was just before noon when Marc Watson's car pulled up outside the small terraced house in Much Maddock where The Helpful Angels bureau was located. Watson marched through the front door into the small office and held up his identity card to the young girl behind the desk.

'Good morning,' he said in a loud authoritative voice. 'Is Melanie Dreyfuss available?'

The young woman looked closely at his identity card. 'No,' she replied glibly. 'She will still be doing her calls, I suspect.'

'I see,' replied Watson. 'And where would I be able to find her at this time on a Wednesday?'

The young girl shrugged her shoulders. 'I don't know,' she said without bothering to look up. 'You'd have to ask Mrs Cashman.'

'And where would I find her?' asked Watson, who was starting to get annoyed by the young woman's apathy.

'I'm here,' replied a voice from the older woman who emerged from the open doorway at the back of the office.

'I take it that you're the manager here?' enquired Watson.

'I'm the proprietor. My name's Emma Cashman.'

'Then maybe you will be able to help me locate one of your employees,' continued Watson. 'I urgently need to talk with Melanie Dreyfuss.'

'Charlotte, why don't you take your lunch break now,' Mrs Cashman said to the young woman.

With that the young woman put on her coat, picked up her

handbag and walked out of the bureau. Mrs Cashman waited until Charlotte had shut the door behind her before turning her gaze back in Watson's direction.

'Is Melanie in any trouble?' she enquired.

'No,' replied Watson. 'However, I do need to talk with her urgently, so if you could tell me where I could find her that would be much appreciated.'

'Is it in connection with poor Mr Poole's death?' she asked.

'Yes, that's correct,' replied Watson, who assumed that Melanie would have already mentioned to her boss that she had been interviewed by him and Cooper a few days earlier. 'I just need to get some more clarity on a few things she mentioned when I last saw her.'

'Well,' replied Mrs Cashman, who picked up a file which contained all her employees' work schedules. 'Let me see.'

Emma Cashman took a few moments to study Melanie's timetable for the day.

'That's right,' she said presently. 'She will be about halfway through Mrs Prentice's house. She should have started at eleven and it usually takes her about two hours.'

'And where would I find Mrs Prentice's house?' Watson asked.

'Six Medway Court in Newbridge,' replied Mrs Cashman. 'It's a small group of flats just off the High Street. If you head towards Moulton Bank, it's located on the left-hand side just after you pass the butcher's shop.'

'Thank you,' replied Watson. 'You've been most helpful.'

Emma Cashman watched Watson clamber back into his car and head off towards Newbridge. Once he was out of sight, she picked up the phone and dialled Melanie's mobile number. Melanie was vacuuming Mrs Prentice's living room carpet, so she did not hear her mobile ring at first. However, after a few moments she realised that she had a call coming through. She turned off the vacuum cleaner and picked up her mobile.

'It's Emma Cashman,' said the familiar voice. 'I've just had a police officer here at the bureau. He wanted to speak to you urgently.'

'What about?' asked Melanie.

'I don't know exactly,' replied Mrs Cashman. 'He said it was just to clarify a few things from your discussion with him on Monday. I told him where you are and he's on his way now. I expect he will be with you in about fifteen minutes.'

'OK,' replied Melanie uncomfortably. 'I can't think what more I can tell him though.'

'I hope you're not keeping anything from me, Melanie,' continued Mrs Cashman. 'I won't be very happy if I find you were less than honest with me.'

*   *   *   *

Carmichael expected that Caroline Lovelace's dressing room would be fairly large and, in keeping with her image, a pretty lavish place. However, his expectations fell well short of the mark. The room was at least twice as big as he had imagined and with two large sofas and a thick shag-pile carpet it wouldn't have been out of place in 1940s Hollywood.

'This is very nice,' Carmichael said, trying hard not to go overboard.

'Yes, I like it,' replied Caroline with her normal air of superiority. 'In my job, one must have a relaxing place to retire to after a hectic morning in the studio. I find that I can unwind much quicker after an hour or so here. Particularly if the show was a disaster like this morning.'

Carmichael elected not to ask her why the show had not gone well. He didn't want to waste any time being sidetracked away from his true purpose.

'I'd like to ask you some more questions about your brother-in-law,' he said as he sat down on one of the sofas. 'Can you tell me if he had any enemies?' Carmichael asked.

'Enemies?' exclaimed Caroline. 'I thought you said he died of natural causes?'

'Yes, I did,' Carmichael replied. 'However, there are one or two things that we are still not one hundred per cent happy with regarding his death. So if you would be so kind as to answer my question.'

'Well no, not to my knowledge,' said Caroline. 'But as I said to you before, Inspector, my husband knew him much better than I. It was his sister he was married to.'

'I fully understand,' replied Carmichael. 'What about other friends and associates?'

'Again, I'm probably not the right person to ask,' replied Caroline. 'I don't recall him mentioning anyone in particular. I'm not being much help, am I?'

'No, that's fine,' replied Carmichael with a smile. 'As you say it may be better if I speak with your husband about Gerry's other relationships.'

'I do hope this hasn't been a wasted journey for you, Inspector,' Caroline continued. 'But I do feel that Roy will be much more able to help you than I.'

Believing that the interview was now at an end, Caroline stood up and made as if to guide her guest to the door. However, Carmichael remained rooted to the sofa.

'If it's not too much trouble,' he said. 'I'd like to ask you some more questions, but this time about one of the other guests at your dinner party the other night.'

'Certainly,' replied Caroline, who sat down again. 'Which one are you referring to?'

'Tamara Searle,' confirmed Carmichael, who studied closely the expression on Caroline's face as he mentioned the dead woman's name.

* * * *

126

It didn't take Watson long to find Medway Court where Mrs Prentice lived. He rang the doorbell and waited. After a few moments without any reply he rang the bell again. After a further few moments he decided to use the door knocker. Watson rapped the knocker as loudly as he could, four times. This did the trick. Within a few seconds a tiny elderly lady with thinning white hair and a very pronounced stoop opened the door. 'Can I help you, young man?' she asked.

Watson showed the old lady his identity card and gave her his best reassuring smile. 'I would like to talk to Melanie Dreyfuss,' he said gently. 'I understand she's here.'

'Melanie?' replied the old lady. 'You've just missed her, young man. She left about five minutes ago.'

\* \* \* \*

Caroline's face had not revealed anything to Carmichael when he had mentioned Tamara Searle.

'What precisely do you want to know about Tamara?' asked Caroline.

'How long have you known her?' Carmichael asked.

'About three years,' replied Caroline. 'She was an assistant on the weather for about a year and has been in front of the camera for the last two.'

'And what do you think of her as a person and as a weather presenter?' Carmichael asked.

'She's very ambitious, very outgoing and confident. She's very attractive and I've no doubt that we'll see her career blossoming in the next few years,' said Caroline. 'But why do you want to know about Tamara?'

'Does she have any specific friends, or indeed is there anyone you know who dislikes her?' continued Carmichael.

Caroline considered these questions for a moment.

'In this business, Inspector, we all make enemies. It's impossible to be liked by everyone. And if you're young,

127

attractive, talented and ambitious you will certainly have your fair share of both friends and foes. If you're asking if Tamara has any specific friends or enemies, I could not say for certain. Sometimes in this business it's hard to tell one from the other.'

'I see,' replied Carmichael. 'What do you think of her?'

'I really like her,' replied Caroline without hesitation. 'She reminds me of myself at her age. She is absolutely determined to succeed and nothing or nobody will get in her way. She'll probably make it too.'

Carmichael paused for a while. He was considering what his next question should be when his attention was drawn to one of the items in a glass cabinet mounted on the wall.

'What's that?' he asked, pointing at the small, black sculpture.

'Do you mean my TV award?' replied Caroline, who mistakenly thought Carmichael was talking about the large crystal object which sat next to it.

'No, the statue next to it,' replied Carmichael.

'Oh that's an original Crabtree,' replied Caroline. 'Sally gave it to me for my fortieth birthday. It's beautiful, isn't it?'

'Yes,' replied Carmichael, who had been attracted to it as it was an exact image of the pose in which they had discovered Tamara's body earlier in the day. 'May I see it?'

'Of course,' replied Caroline, who immediately went over to the cabinet and removed the statue. 'It's exquisite and, being one of only fifty she produced, it's now very valuable.'

Carmichael studied the statue carefully. 'You said it was made by Sally Crabtree,' he continued. 'Would that be the Sally Crabtree that was at your dinner party on Saturday?'

'Yes, that's right,' replied Caroline.

Carmichael studied the small sculpture carefully. It was beautifully crafted and, for its size, very heavy. But it was the pose that interested him, identical to the pose in which poor Tamara had been found.

Carmichael turned back to face Caroline Lovelace. He was keen to gauge her reaction when he made his next statement. 'I'm afraid I've some bad news,' he said calmly. 'We found a body earlier today on some common ground in Moulton Bank. The body was in exactly this position when we found it. We are certain that it is the body of Tamara Searle. I'm afraid she's been murdered.'

Once more Carmichael studied carefully the expression on Caroline Lovelace's face as he delivered this shattering information. This time Caroline's reaction suggested to him that she was very shaken by the news. Her body slumped back into the sofa, as if she herself had been hit hard and her right hand came up and clung onto her forehead.

Carmichael concluded that she was either genuinely shocked to learn of Tamara's death, or that she was a first-rate actress.

\* \* \* \*

Mrs Prentice peered out from behind the net curtains. As soon as Watson's car had disappeared from view, she returned to the kitchen at the back of the house where she had left Melanie Dreyfuss.

'He's gone,' she said. 'Now are you sure that you're not in any trouble?'

'Positive, Mrs Prentice,' she replied with relief. 'It's very complicated, but I promise you that I've done nothing wrong.'

'Well, if you've nothing to hide I don't know why you're so frightened to talk to the police,' said the old lady.

'I will, I promise,' she replied. 'I just need to talk with someone else first.'

\* \* \* \*

While Rachel waited for Carmichael in the reception, she made two calls on her mobile. The first was to a friend she had met on a police training course six months earlier.

'That's brilliant,' she said as she ended the call. 'Remember, though, that you need to keep this confidential; we've had specific orders not to harass this man, so you need to be very careful when you do the search.'

Her second call was to Watson.

'How's the house-to-house going?' she enquired.

'OK, I suspect,' replied Watson. 'I had to leave that to the local plods; I'm chasing a really hot lead on Tamara's death.'

'What's that?' Rachel asked.

'I'll tell you later,' he replied. 'But I need a few more hours to find someone first. Tell the boss that I'll call him this evening as planned. I'll brief him then.'

\* \* \* \*

Melanie wanted to be certain that the coast was clear before she left Mrs Prentice's house. As soon as she had received the call from Mrs Cashman, she had been sure that the police's latest interest in her was not a good sign. She had had a string of bad experiences with the police and, although the two officers she had met on Monday seemed pretty reasonable, her instinct still told her that she needed to avoid them.

She decided to wait for fifteen or twenty minutes before leaving the house to not only be sure that Watson was miles away, but also to allow herself some time to consider what she should do. She heard Mrs Prentice turn on her TV in the next room and, as Mrs Prentice was hard of hearing, the volume was loud enough for Melanie to hear clearly every word. Although her thoughts were elsewhere, Melanie could not avoid the noise from the TV set distracting her. Feeling agitated and annoyed, she got up and burst into the lounge with every intention of ordering Mrs Prentice to turn down the sound. As she entered the room Melanie was stopped in her tracks by a photograph of Tamara Searle on TV and the reporter's claim that a body, believed to be that of Tamara Searle, had been found that morning. As soon as the report was over, Melanie decided it was time to leave. She thanked Mrs Prentice for covering for her, assured the old lady again that she was not in any trouble and rushed out of the house. Once outside, Melanie ran as fast as she could in the direction of the nearest bus stop.

# Chapter 18

When Carmichael finally emerged into the reception at Sunrise Productions he found Rachel sitting patiently alone on one of the big red sofas.

'How did it go?' Rachel asked as she struggled to get up from the soft upholstery.

'Let's just say it was very interesting,' he replied. 'Let's talk in the car.'

The two officers made their exit out into the bitter cold of the studio car park. 'It look's like we may be getting even more snow!' exclaimed Rachel as she climbed into the passenger seat.

'That's all we need,' replied Carmichael with dismay. 'This must be the worst weather we've had in years.'

Rachel nodded. 'I won't need to go to France to ski this year. Ambient Hill will be perfectly fine.'

Carmichael smiled. 'So what did Mr Yerbovic have to say for himself?' he asked.

'He was really nice and ever so helpful,' replied Rachel. 'He was very shocked about the news of Tamara's death and it's clear he liked her.'

'Do you think he could be involved at all?' asked Carmichael.

'No,' replied Rachel, without giving it any thought whatsoever. 'I can't see him having a motive and by his reaction when I told him I'm sure he didn't know she had been killed.'

'So did he tell you anything that might help us?' enquired Carmichael.

'Well, he gave me a disk with all Tamara's details on it,' said Rachel. 'Also, he told me that to his knowledge she had no living relatives. According to Mr Yerbovic, she didn't have a current boyfriend either. One thing, though: she went to school or college with Caroline Lovelace's PA.'

'Amanda Buchannan,' replied Carmichael. 'I'll follow up on that when I'm back here tomorrow.'

'Tomorrow?' questioned Rachel.

'Yes, after Caroline got over the initial shock of Tamara being dead,' announced Carmichael, 'her broadcasting instincts kicked in and she has invited me to appear on her show tomorrow to do a live appeal for information about Tamara's death.'

'Really?' exclaimed Rachel. 'That should be an experience.'

In truth, Carmichael had not been totally sure that his acceptance of Caroline's offer was a wise decision. However, he did feel that it would be as good an opportunity as he would get to talk directly to the public and it was also a good excuse for him to build a stronger relationship with Caroline Lovelace who, he was convinced, knew more than she had been saying so far.

'Did you find out anything else?' he asked.

'Just one thing,' replied Rachel. 'According to Yerbovic, Tamara was rarely sick, yet bizarrely she texted in sick yesterday morning.'

'Texted!' repeated Carmichael. 'That *is* strange. It could well be that someone else sent it. You need to follow that up.'

'It's already in hand,' replied Rachel as she held up Yerbovic's mobile.

'Well done,' said Carmichael.

'So did your interview with Caroline Lovelace reveal anything of interest?' Rachel asked.

'Not really,' he replied. 'However, there's definitely a connection between that dinner party she invited me to on Saturday and the two deaths. Both people were invited and a third guest, a lady called Sally Crabtree, had given Caroline a sculpture she made which looks identical to the pose that Tamara was in when we found her.'

'Sally Crabtree?' enquired Rachel.

'Yes, that's right, replied Carmichael. 'Do you know her?'

'Yes, she's a great sculptor,' continued Rachel. 'My father has some of her work, which is now quite valuable, I'm told.'

'Valuable or not,' commented Carmichael, 'I'm convinced that the one I saw clearly inspired whoever put Tamara in that pose, so Sally Crabtree will be one of the next people we need to talk to.'

*   *   *   *

After drawing a blank at Mrs Prentice's house, Watson had driven over to the address that Melanie had given him two days earlier. When his heavy-handed hammering on her door received no response, he decided to try her on her mobile.

The phone rang several times before Melanie picked it up. She had forgotten that she had given the police her mobile number, so it had not occurred to her that it might be them calling.

'Hi, Mel speaking,' she said from the top deck of the noisy bus.

'Melanie,' said Watson, who was shocked that she had picked up. 'It's Sergeant Watson here from Lancashire Police. Where are you? I need to talk to you.'

Melanie considered hanging up but figured that if she did it would just make the situation worse. 'Oh hello,' she replied nervously. 'How are you, Sergeant?'

'I'm fine,' he replied, 'but we need to talk. Where are you?'

'I'm a bit busy now,' continued Melanie. 'Could we maybe meet up tomorrow or Friday?'

'Today would be better,' continued Watson. 'It's really important.'

'OK,' replied Melanie. 'I could meet you this evening if you want but I can't see you much before six o'clock as I'm going to be busy until then.'

'OK, but where?' asked Watson.

'How about The Red Lion in Newbridge?' she replied.

'That's fine,' said Watson. 'I'll see you at six.'

*     *     *     *

'I wonder how Marc's getting on?' remarked Carmichael as he and Rachel headed back towards Kirkwood Police Station.

'I forgot to tell you,' she replied. 'I spoke to him before. He's left two PCs to do the house-to-house calls, as he's on to a hot lead.'

'What sort of hot lead?' said Carmichael, whose immediate thought was that Watson was just trying to get out of doing the house-to-house enquiries.

'I'm not sure,' replied Rachel. 'He wouldn't say, but he did say he would call you this evening to bring you up to speed.'

'Did he really?' said Carmichael. 'I hope it *is* a hot lead because if anyone in the houses surrounding the Common did see or hear anything the sooner we know the better. In my experience most cases like this are solved by information from eyewitnesses.'

Rachel could see that the boss was not impressed, so chose not to keep the conversation alive.

*     *     *     *

Within two hours of Rachel calling her friend and asking him to check if Sydney Sydes had a criminal record, DC Dan White from the West Yorkshire Police was asked to report to his superior.

About an hour later, Chief Inspector Hewitt received a call advising him that he, Inspector Carmichael and DC Dalton should make themselves available for a meeting with officers from Special Branch, at 5.30 p.m. that evening, at Kirkwood Station.

\* \* \* \*

At 4.00 p.m. Sidney Sydes quietly made his getaway from Moulton Bank in the back of an unmarked white van. As soon as he had received the call advising him that his cover was blown, he had quickly gathered up his most precious belongings and stuffed them into two large canvas bags. With Hazel the cat securely imprisoned in her cat box next to him, he was rapidly driven out of the village and by the time Carmichael and Dalton arrived in Hewitt's office, Sydney Sydes was already out of the county.

# Chapter 19

Steve Carmichael and Rachel Dalton arrived at Chief Inspector Hewitt's office at 5.25 p.m. The door was closed, but from the muffled voices inside Carmichael deduced that the officers from Special Branch were already there and were almost certainly briefing Hewitt.

Dead on 5.30 p.m. Angela called through to Hewitt to advise him that Carmichael and Rachel were waiting.

'Send them in,' replied the voice of Hewitt out of the tiny speaker on Angela's handset.

'Good luck,' Angela said to the pair before ushering them to the door.

Once they were inside, Angela retreated and closed the door behind her.

Already seated inside Hewitt's office were two plain-clothed officers; one looked like he was in his late forties and the other was a little younger. Neither stood up or made any attempt to greet Carmichael or Dalton.

'Please take a seat,' Hewitt announced, pointing to the only two unoccupied chairs in the room.

Once they were both seated, Hewitt cleared his throat before continuing. 'First of all let me do the introductions,' he said in his most pompous voice. 'This is Inspector Ryan and Sergeant McFall. They are from Special Branch.'

Hewitt was just about to launch into some form of monologue when he was firmly interrupted by Ryan, the elder of the two officers. 'If you don't mind, Chief Inspector,

I think it's probably appropriate for me to take over from here,' he said.

Carmichael had crossed swords with officers from Special Branch on a number of occasions during his time in the Met. Rarely had he enjoyed the experience and his impression of the type of people who seemed to be attracted to that department was not favourable. It was the superior, self-important air they exuded which he disliked the most. Ryan and McFall did little to alter this perception.

'We're not happy, Inspector,' opened up Ryan, who stared aggressively at Carmichael. 'We're not happy at all. Having been instructed by Chief Inspector Hewitt on at least two occasions, you and DC Dalton have persisted in pursuing Sidney Sydes as a suspect in your enquiries. The upshot being that a major covert programme we have been managing for nearly twenty years has been severely compromised.'

'I don't understand what you're talking about,' replied Carmichael in a calm voice. 'Our interest in Sydes has always been purely to get some background information relating to the suspicious death of a man who was found close to where his boat was berthed. He has never been charged and, to be frank with you, was not a major suspect. I fail to see how this interest would compromise any unconnected programme that you may be running.'

'Don't try to be clever with us,' Ryan said in a raised voice. 'You were instructed on two separate occasions by Chief Inspector Hewitt to leave Sydes alone and, for whatever reason, you chose to ignore those specific instructions.'

Carmichael looked in the direction of his boss expecting him to intervene but, although Hewitt looked very uncomfortable, he chose to say nothing. 'Well, I think you need to get your facts correct before you start making wild accusations, Inspector Ryan,' Carmichael continued. 'First, as I'm sure Chief Inspector Hewitt will confirm, we only discussed Sydes briefly a few times. Until this meeting, I had no inkling that you or anyone else were working on another operation involving Sydes. It's true that this morning Chief Inspector Hewitt did ask me not to harass Sydes, an instruction I've adhered to.'

Ryan glanced over to Hewitt, who was now feeling even more uncomfortable. 'What the Inspector is saying is correct,' Hewitt spluttered. 'I didn't divulge the full nature of the operation with Sydes to Inspector Carmichael, as I felt that the fewer people who knew about the situation the better. However, Inspector Carmichael, I think I was clear that Sydes should be excluded from your investigations, so I was very unhappy to find that, earlier today, DC Dalton asked an officer from another constabulary to check Sydes out on the police records.'

'That may be my fault,' interjected Rachel. 'Inspector Carmichael did ask me to do some digging on Sydes, but that was a few days ago. I was unable to do this at the time, what with us being so rushed off our feet owing to the amount of people being off with flu. I only realised my oversight earlier today and I asked Dan White, a friend in West Yorkshire, to help me. I didn't realise that we were not meant to pursue Sydes anymore. If I'd have known, I'd certainly not have asked him.'

Ryan and McFall looked at each other. 'Do you expect us to believe that?' McFall sneered.

'Are you calling my officers liars?' announced Hewitt, who didn't totally believe what Rachel had said either, but seized on her words as a means of possibly extricating all of them from what had been, until that point, a major embarrassment to him. 'I think it's plain for all to see that neither Inspector Carmichael nor DC Dalton have done anything that warrants any further action. I think their account of the facts here is clear, and as far as I can ascertain, this has all been due to an unfortunate set of circumstances.'

McFall was clearly angered by what he was hearing. 'Twenty years of work establishing a cover for Sydes have been blown out of the water because of your team's incompetent meddling and you expect us to just accept this cock-and-bull story … ?'

At that point Ryan put his arm across his colleague to stop him from saying anything more. 'I have to say that I share Sergeant McFall's scepticism and our report will indicate that we feel the operation has been severely and needlessly compromised due to the clumsy and unnecessary involvement of Sidney Sydes in your minor local enquiry.'

'I disagree,' said Hewitt forcefully. 'A suspicious death is not a minor enquiry.'

'With respect, sir,' continued Ryan, who looked directly at Hewitt as he spoke. 'If you had fully updated Inspector Carmichael in the first instance, I think we could have averted this disaster and DC Dalton, although I expect your motives here are honourable, I don't believe that your explanation is the whole story.'

'Now just hold on there,' said Carmichael angrily. 'What you two gentlemen think or choose to disbelieve is not our concern. If your operation has been compromised as a result of our actions, I apologise. However, without being made party to the facts, I'm not sure what we could have done differently.'

Without uttering another word, Ryan stood up. 'Come on, Andy,' he said to McFall, 'let's get out of here; we've got better things to do. The damage is already done and we need to put our energies into getting Sydes a new identity.'

Ryan and McFall left Hewitt's office without bothering to exchange any normal niceties and, to demonstrate his annoyance, the sergeant deliberately slammed shut the door behind them as they departed.

Hewitt waited until he was sure that the two special branch officers were well out of earshot. 'I hope you're both telling the truth,' he said sternly. 'Your involvement with Sydes has really upset the applecart.'

'Clearly so,' Carmichael said. 'So can you please tell us what's going on here? What the hell is this secretive operation all about?'

Hewitt sat back in his chair and considered whether he should be open with Carmichael and Dalton.

'OK,' he said after a few seconds of thought. 'However, what I'm about to tell you is confidential and you can't repeat any of it to anyone.'

Carmichael and Dalton both nodded their agreement and then listened intently as Hewitt told them the full story.

\* \* \* \*

At 6.00 p.m. precisely, Marc Watson entered The Red Lion in Newbridge. The pub, which had been built in the 1700s, had originally been an old coaching house on the main road north from London to the Scottish border. The building's façade was largely the original front and, inside, the public house retained many of its original beams and whitewashed stone walls. However, in the last year, The Red Lion had changed hands and the new owners had spent a great deal of money renovating the place, gearing it to cater more for diners, much to the consternation of the traditional locals. Now there was only one small area where the locals could gather for a pint and to hear the latest gossip.

Six p.m. on a Wednesday evening was not the busiest time of the week at The Red Lion, so when Watson entered the bar area he was one of only three people there, the other two being a couple of farm labourers who had popped in for a quick one after they had finished work for the day.

'Can I get you anything?' asked the middle-aged barmaid.

'A diet Coke and a packet of salt and vinegar crisps, please,' replied Watson.

'Take a seat,' said the barmaid, pointing at the dozen or so empty tables. 'I'll bring them over to you.'

Watson made his way to the furthest table from the bar. He wanted to make sure that he and Melanie Dreyfuss wouldn't be overheard, and he thought his choice of table would be far enough away to avoid any eavesdropping by the locals.

\* \* \* \*

It was 6.15 p.m. when Carmichael and Dalton left Hewitt's office.

'That was a turn-up for the books,' Carmichael remarked. 'It doesn't mean he's totally innocent, but he'll be long gone by now and, as these people are experts at establishing new identities for their witnesses, we'll never see him again. We'll have to hope that Sidney Sydes, or rather Patrick Dawson, was telling us the truth.'

'Do you really think he'll already have gone?' Rachel asked.

'It's a certainty,' replied Carmichael. 'He was probably already being transported away when we were in the meeting.'

'So what do we do now?' Rachel asked.

Carmichael glanced out of the window. 'It looks like it's starting to snow again,' he said. 'I suggest we get off home while we can. I'm due to be back at Sunrise Production studio at ten thirty in the morning but I want to have a briefing here with you and Marc before I go. Can you get here for six in the morning?'

'I suppose so,' replied Rachel.

'Good,' replied Carmichael. 'I'll call Marc and tell him to be here too. We can go through both cases then and take it from there.'

'Right you are, sir,' said Rachel with a smile. 'I'll see you in the morning.'

Rachel Dalton marched off down the corridor.

'By the way, thanks,' shouted Carmichael as she walked towards the locker room.

Rachel turned back to face him. 'What for?' she asked with a smile.

'For helping me out of the proverbial back there in Hewitt's office,' he replied.

'No problem,' remarked Rachel with an even broader grin. 'It was my pleasure.'

\* \* \* \*

By 6.20 p.m., Marc Watson had finished his drink and, with the empty packet of crisps in front of him, he was starting to resign himself to the fact that he had been stood up by Melanie Dreyfuss when his mobile phone rang.

'Hello, Marc Watson,' he whispered down the line.

'Marc, it's Carmichael,' came back the reply. 'Where are you and what's this lead you're working on?'

'Bear with me a moment,' Watson remarked as he walked briskly towards the exit so he could talk with his boss without being overheard.

Once he was safely ensconced in the entrance hall of The Red Lion, Watson resumed the conversation.

'I'm in a pub in Newbridge,' he whispered. 'One of the SOCOs at the crime scene found Melanie Dreyfuss's purse.'

'Who's Melanie Dreyfuss?' Carmichael asked.

'She's the cleaner that Cooper and I interviewed the other day at Poole's house,' Watson replied. 'I've been trying to find her all afternoon. I went to the office of the Helpful Angels agency where she works, I went to the house she was supposed to be cleaning and I went to her flat, but as yet I've not been able to find her. I did speak to her on her phone and she said she would meet me here at the pub at six, but she's not arrived. I'm certain she's involved in both deaths in some way.'

'OK,' replied Carmichael. 'Stay for another ten minutes or so and see whether she shows. If not, why don't you try her flat again? Then, if you have still drawn a blank, call it a day.'

'OK,' said Watson.

'If anything develops, though, you should call me,' continued Carmichael.

'I will,' replied Watson.

'Last thing before you go,' said Carmichael. 'I need you and Rachel to be in the office by six in the morning. We need to have a detailed briefing session and I need to be away by eight thirty.'

'OK,' replied Watson who then trudged back to his seat inside The Red Lion.

\* \* \* \*

Carmichael sat back in his comfortable chair and gazed out of his office window into the dark February night. Although not yet heavy, he could see the snow was still falling and decided it would be sensible to start his journey home before it got too bad. He picked up his coat and gloves and headed towards the door.

# Chapter 20

Penny heard about the death of Tamara Searle on the early evening news bulletin, so she fully expected Carmichael to be late home. In the circumstances she also thought it highly unlikely that he would have found the time to have spoken to Jemma, as he had threatened to do that morning. So she was very surprised when at 7.15 p.m. her husband burst through the front door, his hair covered in wet glistening snowflakes.

'I wasn't expecting you back so soon,' Penny announced as she greeted him in the hallway with a peck on his cheek. 'I heard about poor Tamara Searle. I assume you're on that case?'

Carmichael removed his coat and brushed the wet snowflakes from his head. 'Yes, it's mine,' he replied. 'And to be honest it's been a sod of a day. I could murder a stiff drink.'

'You go and sit down. I'll pour you a glass of wine,' said Penny as she walked back towards the kitchen.

'A can of beer would be better,' replied Carmichael.

'Have you eaten much today?' Penny shouted through from the kitchen.

'No,' Carmichael replied, as he slumped down on the living room sofa. 'I'm not that hungry, though.'

Within a few minutes Penny joined him on the couch. 'Here you go,' she said as she handed him a can of beer. 'It's been a bad one, then?'

'The worst,' replied Carmichael. 'You just won't believe what a rotten day I've had.'

'Try me,' said Penny.

'Well, in addition to us still not solving the first suspicious death, I now have Tamara Seale's death to investigate and that was certainly murder. In addition to that, Rachel Dalton and I came within a whisker of being charged with disobeying orders and revealing the identity of a man who, for the last twenty years has been on a witness protection scheme. If that wasn't all, Watson has spent the day on a wild goose chase looking for a young woman he's certain is implicated in both deaths, when he should have been coordinating the house-to-house enquiries around the Common and, just when I need him most, Cooper has taken to his bed, the latest victim of this flu epidemic.'

'I see,' said Penny. 'So what's this about the man on the witness protection scheme?'

'It's a bloke called Sydes,' replied Carmichael. 'Well, actually his real name is Patrick Dawson. You may remember the story. About twenty years ago he testified against his two elder brothers who had robbed and murdered a neighbour. The brothers got life and in return for his evidence little Patrick was given a new identity and has been watched over by Special Branch ever since. It would appear that Dawson, or rather Sydes, was a bright lad and for years he was a very successful brand manager responsible for a range of air-fresheners. He made a mint, but then one day by pure coincidence he was introduced to someone who he had known in his previous life. They are fairly sure that this person didn't recognise him, but this spooked Sydes so much that he quit his job and has been spending the last few years as a virtual hermit on a narrowboat on the canals of the UK.'

'So how do you and Rachel Dalton come in to all this?' Penny asked.

'Well,' replied Carmichael, 'unfortunately for Sydes he just happened to decide to come to Moulton Bank and stay here for a while. And to his further misfortune, he just happened to

146

have parked his boat about twenty yards from where we found Poole's body. So of course we've been talking with him about what he might have seen. This spooked him and he then tells his Special Branch chums, who in turn ask Hewitt to get us to lay off him. But in true Hewitt style he elects to warn us off him, but didn't tell us why. So country bumpkin Inspector Plod here and my side kick DC Dalton just plough on with the investigation and then, surprise surprise, Special Branch get wind of what we're doing. So at five thirty tonight, two of their finest arrive in Hewitt's office to try and tear a strip off us.'

'I see,' replied Penny. 'So are you in trouble?'

'Due to some quick thinking by Rachel Dalton we managed to avoid being too badly mauled,' Carmichael continued. 'But if it had not been for her nimble footwork, yours truly would have been in a real mess. And that pompous burke Hewitt was not about to help us. That was quite clear.'

'So what did Rachel say?' Penny asked.

'In short she lied to help me out of a really tight spot,' he replied. 'She was quite impressive actually.'

'And this man Sydes?' said Penny. 'Where is he now?'

'He's probably Frank Smith and living in Kent for all I know,' replied Carmichael with a smirk. 'And good luck to him.'

'So what are you going to do next?' Penny asked.

'Have another beer,' replied Carmichael. 'Then have a shower and after that try to work out my next move.'

Penny gave her husband a kiss. 'Are you sure you don't want anything to eat?' she asked.

'No thanks,' Carmichael said with a smile. 'I'm fine, really.'

Penny snuggled up next to her husband as they sat on the sofa. 'Have you any strong clues as to who killed Tamara Searle?' she enquired.

'We are following up a few things,' he replied. 'Nothing earth-shattering. Actually, the name Helpful Angels keeps reoccurring. Marc mentioned it earlier to me and I'm sure there's a link between the agency and the two deaths.'

'Wasn't that the name of the caterers that did Caroline Lovelace's party on Saturday?' replied Penny.

'That's right,' said Carmichael, who was impressed by his wife's sharp memory. 'It was run by that Emma Cashman woman.'

'Yes,' said Penny. 'The one with the lecherous husband.'

'What do you mean?' replied Carmichael.

'Well, I might be wrong,' replied Penny, 'but Declan Cashman and Roy Lovelace were both ogling Tamara Searle all night and I am sure one of them said something to one of those waitresses that upset her. She looked really distressed and as far as I could see she didn't come near them afterwards.'

'Was that the blonde one or the ginger one?' Carmichael asked.

'The fair-haired one,' Penny confirmed. 'Why do you ask?'

'I saw them both that evening when I was taking that call on my mobile. They were in the hall and the blonde one did look very unhappy,' replied Carmichael.

'Do you think that is important?' Penny asked.

'I don't know,' Carmichael responded. 'But with The Helpful Angels doing the catering for Caroline Lovelace and being the cleaners for Gerry Poole, it looks like there are many links between the two deaths and too many coincidences in my mind for the deaths not to be connected to at least one person who was at the party on Saturday night.'

'Sounds like you're making some progress, dear,' Penny remarked with a smile. 'So it's not been all bad news today, then?'

'No, I suppose not,' Carmichael concurred. 'And actually there's one thing I wanted to tell you.'

Penny's hopes lifted for a moment as she hoped her

husband was now about to tell her that he had spoken with Jemma and that all was well between them.

'You might want to tape the Caroline Lovelace show tomorrow,' he announced, which caught Penny off guard.

'Why do you want me to do that?' She asked with amazement. 'You told me you never wanted to see that show again.'

'I know,' he replied. 'But that was before I knew I was going to be on it.'

# Chapter 21

**Thursday 19<sup>th</sup> February**

Carmichael's alarm went off at 5.10 a.m. Within seconds his left hand had thumped down on the top of the clock to silence the high-pitched shriek. Wiping the sleep from his eyes, Carmichael picked up the timepiece and examined the face. He found it difficult to believe that it was already time to get up. Having confirmed his worst fears, he turned on the bedside light and clambered out of bed. Trying hard not to disturb his wife, he attempted to tiptoe to the window to see what the weather was like. However, unfortunately, being still very sleepy, he failed miserably in his effort to keep quiet. His leaden feet seemed to hit every squeaking floorboard and any chance of Penny remaining sound asleep was shattered when Carmichael loudly yelled out a couple of choice obscenities, having stubbed his little toe on the metal leg of the bed frame.

'What time is it?' exclaimed Penny. She had surprisingly slumbered through the alarm and the sudden bright light from the bedside lamp, but had sat bolt upright on hearing her husband's deafening cry of pain.

'Ten past five,' replied Carmichael as he tumbled back onto the bed clutching his toe. 'I think I've broken my bloody toe.'

'Really,' replied Penny blandly, as she lay back down again and wrapped herself in the thick warm duvet.

To Carmichael's relief the severity of the pain subsided fairly quickly, so much so that within the space of a minute he felt well enough to finally look out of the window. Fortunately the snowfall had not been too heavy, so with a bit of luck his journey to Kirkwood Station would not be too much of a problem.

He grabbed his best suit, his favourite tie and the white shirt that Penny had ironed for him the night before and headed out of the bedroom door.

'Good luck!' muttered Penny from under the duvet. 'I hope it all goes well on *The Lovelace Show.*'

'Thanks,' whispered Carmichael as he limped down the hall to the bathroom and a warm shower.

\*　\*　\*　\*

At 6 a.m. sharp Carmichael entered the incident room that he and the team had set up at the station. To his surprise Rachel Dalton was already there.

'Morning, sir,' chirped Rachel, who had been there for thirty minutes already and had used that time to fix photographs of the two dead people on the noticeboard and start writing some of the key known facts relating to both cases.

'Glad to see you're already hard at it,' said Carmichael, who was very impressed. 'Where's Watson?'

'Here I am,' replied Watson who emerged through the door clutching a red plastic tray upon which sat three steaming coffee mugs.

'Fantastic,' said Carmichael, who had spent too long in the shower and had not had time to make himself a drink before leaving home. 'Let's get cracking then.'

With coffees in hand, the three officers all stared at the photographs of Gerry Poole and Tamara Searle.

'I've made a start,' said Rachel, pointing to the various

151

statements she had written next to Gerry Poole's photos and the three lines she had written against the photos of Tamara Searle.

'OK, let's go through them first and add to them anything else we know,' said Carmichael.

Within the space of twenty minutes the three officers had compiled the following lists of facts for the two cases:

Gerry Poole:

1. Died of a heart attack.
2. Didn't die where he was found.
3. Dumped on the canal towpath before the first snow fell (approx 6 p.m. on Sat 14th Feb).
4. Petrol receipt found on body dated 3rd Feb.
5. Thurs 5th Feb – the last time the Lovelaces remember talking to Gerry.

Tamara Searle:

1. Time of death still to be established, but between last known sighting by Mr Yerbovic at 3 p.m. on Mon 16th Feb and early hours of Wed 18th Feb.
2. Text message sent into work saying she was sick on Tues morning.
3. Tamara was a friend of Caroline Lovelace's PA, Amanda Buchannan.
4. Body found in the pose similar to a Sally Crabtree sculpture.
5. Purse of Melanie Dreyfuss found by body.
6. Melanie Dreyfuss avoiding the police.

'That's a decent start,' announced Carmichael. 'We now need to start putting down some hypotheses for each death.'

Within a further thirty minutes they had amassed the following lists of suppositions:

Gerry Poole's Death:

1. Placed in a freezer after death?
2. Placed in the freezer while still alive?
3. Body brought to canal in own car?
4. Linked to someone at the dinner party on 14th.

Tamara Searle's Death:

1. Linked to someone at the dinner party.
2. Murdered elsewhere then moved to the Common.
3. Melanie Dreyfuss involved in placing the body on the Common?
4. The pose that Tamara's body was placed in was deliberately mimicking the sculpture by Sally Crabtree?
5. The text sent to Tony Yerbovic not sent by Tamara, so whoever killed Tamara knew her boss's mobile number?
6. The text to Tony Yerbovic was sent <u>after</u> Tamara had been murdered?

'So what do we do next?' Watson asked.

Carmichael took a few moments to consider his options.

'I think our immediate priorities for today are to get the autopsy report on Tamara Searle from Dr Stock. We also need to finish the house-to-house enquiries. These are your tasks for this morning, Marc.'

'What about Melanie Dreyfuss?' Marc enquired in amazement. 'Surely finding her has to take precedence over anything else?'

'It is important,' replied Carmichael firmly. 'However, I

want you to focus all your energies this morning on the autopsy and the house-to-house. I want a detailed update from you on both at one o'clock this afternoon. Are you clear on what I'm saying, Marc?'

'If that's what you want,' replied Watson, with more than a hint of frustration in his voice.

'It is, Marc,' continued Carmichael. 'I'm convinced that both the autopsy and the house-to-house will yield some further clues on Tamara's death. If you get through all that I'd also like you to start checking out the receipt found in Gerry Poole's pocket. Find out if there's any way of tracing it back to the person who bought it. If the garage has any cameras, see if you can get the tapes for 3rd February.'

It was clear to Carmichael that Watson was still unhappy with his morning's assignment, but he was not in the slightest bit concerned. His experience told him that eyewitnesses and forensic reports were key to solving murders and, although he shared Watson's opinion that Melanie Dreyfuss was involved in some way, he didn't want his most experienced officer chasing around the county trying to find someone who was clearly not keen on being found. In Carmichael's view, Watson's talents at this juncture were best employed on looking at evidence that was available rather than hunting for clues that were likely to remain hidden.

'What about me?' Rachel asked.

'You're going to be busy too, Rachel,' Carmichael replied. 'First of all I want you to get over to Tamara's house. I want to know more about her. Her friends, boyfriends, habits, hobbies and most importantly I want to know if she was killed there. Find her mobile too and get it to forensics with that one you took from Yerbovic. I want to know who else Tamara called or texted recently.'

'Fine, sir,' replied Rachel, believing that this was the extent of her duties that morning.

'You need to also spend some time going through

Tamara's file on that disk Tony Yerbovic gave you,' continued Carmichael. 'Again, I want you to report back here at one and I expect a full update from you then.'

'OK,' replied Rachel.

'What about you, sir?' enquired Watson.

'I'm going to try and get some public response from the interview on *The Lovelace Show*,' replied Carmichael, trying hard to make it sound as though appearing on national TV was a run-of-the-mill chore for him. 'While I'm there I'm going to try and talk some more to Caroline Lovelace about her party guests last Saturday. I'm convinced that at least one of the people there that night who are still breathing knows what's going on.'

'Yourself and Mrs Carmichael excepted,' piped up Watson with a hint of sarcasm in his voice.

Carmichael ignored Watson's flippant comment. 'My guess is that there's more than an evens chance that Tamara's murderer was at that party. So I want to find out from Caroline why she chose the people she did, including the caterers. I'm also keen to talk with Amanda Buchannan. If she was Tamara's friend, as Yerbovic says, she should be able to give us some more on Tamara's background.'

*  *  *  *

At seven o'clock Caroline Lovelace burst through the front doors of Sunrise Productions.

'Morning, ladies,' she proclaimed in the direction of the two receptionists, before she disappeared through the double doors and out of sight. As usual Caroline was greeted by Amanda Buchannan even before she had managed to get to her office.

'The running order for today is here, Caroline,' announced Amanda rather meekly as she handed over a bound A4 booklet. 'Do you want to speak to Freddie about anything?'

'No, not this morning,' replied Caroline abruptly. 'I need to get to make-up and I could murder a skinny latte and a plain croissant.'

'Debbie's already waiting for you,' replied Amanda, who as always had made sure that make-up wouldn't keep her boss waiting. 'I'll bring your coffee and croissant to you there.'

As they were talking they continued to walk at a brisk pace down the corridor.

'On second thoughts,' announced Caroline. 'I do need to speak with Freddie. Ask him to join me in my dressing room in ten minutes. No, make it twenty; I think Debbie has quite a bit to do on me this morning. Tell him I want to discuss the interview with Inspector Carmichael. I want to make sure his camera angles are all set up properly. The public need to see how genuinely concerned we all are here about poor Tamara, so he needs to make sure they get a good shot of my reactions when we're talking.'

At that juncture Caroline swung a hard left and headed off towards make-up. Amanda, however, remained stationary. For the next few moments she watched intently as her boss vanished into the distance.

'Cow!' Amanda muttered under her breath when she was absolutely sure she could not be overheard.

\* \* \* \*

The briefing had finished much earlier than Carmichael had anticipated and with Rachel and Watson now out of the room, Carmichael took a few moments to look at the photographs of Poole and Tamara Searle that Rachel had fastened to the Perspex noticeboard. Carmichael was certain in his mind that the two deaths were linked and, although he had not said so, he was also sure that Marc Watson was right to stress the need to make contact with Melanie Dreyfuss. He gazed at his watch. It was still only seven fifteen. Grabbing his coat, Carmichael headed for the door. He was confident that he could make one unscheduled visit and still manage to be at the TV studio in plenty of time.

* * * *

Watson and Dalton had gone straight from the incident room to the station canteen and were munching away on bacon sandwiches when Carmichael's BMW exited the car park.

'I think he's got this one all wrong,' Watson announced without bothering to swallow.

'How's that?' Rachel asked, trying hard not to stare at the contents of her colleague's mouth.

'Well,' replied Watson. 'First off, he should be getting Hewitt to give us more resources. With Paul Cooper off sick we are woefully under-resourced. Then we should be out there looking for Melanie Dreyfuss, not spending our time doing desk research and house-to-house. The wooden tops should be doing that.'

Watson took another huge bite from his sandwich. 'Secondly, we should be pulling in that Sydes guy. He's got to have seen something. I mean let's get real here; his boat is just twenty or thirty yards away from where we found the body.'

Rachel put her head down and said nothing. She had given her word to Hewitt and the officers from Special Branch that she wouldn't mention to a soul what they had told her about Sydes. She knew all too well that they had got off lightly and had no intention of giving Special Branch any reason to return.

'Then lastly,' continued Watson, who by now was in full flow and oblivious to Rachel's awkwardness, 'why does Carmichael get the TV assignment? If we have to do all this donkey work how come he gets the cushy number?'

157

'Privilege of rank, I suppose,' replied Rachel, who didn't want to get drawn into the debate any further. 'I need to get on; I've got a lot to get through before the briefing at one.'

Rachel stood up, collected her mug and plate and headed off in the direction of the door. En route she carefully placed her dirty crockery on top of the trolley located by the exit.

Watson remained in the canteen. He was still hungry and wanted a second bacon sandwich.

\* \* \* \*

Carmichael's BMW arrived at The Helpful Angels offices in Much Maddock at 8 a.m. precisely. He parked outside the front door and cautiously tiptoed through the dirty, slushy snow that had collected at the kerbside, trying hard not to get his shoes and suit trousers too wet.

Once inside the tatty front office he wiped his feet on the tired-looking doormat and walked up to the front desk.

'I'd like to speak with Mrs Cashman,' he said to the young woman behind the desk.

The receptionist eyed Carmichael up and down for a few moments before walking over to the door situated at the rear of the office. Once there she stopped in the doorway and bellowed into the back. 'Mrs Cashman, there's someone here to see you. I think it's another copper.'

She then returned to her desk and, without a second glance at Carmichael, continued with the admin task that she had been doing when he arrived.

Emma Cashman appeared in the office in a matter of moments. Carmichael had not paid too much attention to her when he had first seen her at the party, probably as, compared to Tamara Searle, Sarah McIntyre and Caroline Lovelace, Emma Cashman had seemed quite frumpy. However, away from the glitz of the party and now dressed more casually in

158

jeans and a tightly fitting sweater, Emma Cashman looked far more attractive than Carmichael had remembered.

'Oh, good morning,' she said when she realised who it was. 'You're Inspector Carmichael from Caroline's party, aren't you? Steve Carmichael, isn't it?'

'That's correct,' replied Carmichael, who was impressed that she remembered him. 'Do you have a few minutes for us to talk alone?'

'Certainly,' replied Emma Cashman. 'Come through.'

As she spoke she gestured towards the back room. Carmichael walked into the room, followed closely by Emma Cashman, who closed the door behind them.

'Would you like a cup of tea?' Emma asked.

'If you don't mind, I won't,' replied Carmichael as he was keen to make sure he arrived at Sunrise Productions with plenty of time to spare before he went on air.

'Please take a seat,' said Emma, pointing to a worn brown settee, which apart from a small desk and chair, was the only seat available.

Carmichael sat down as instructed.

'I'm investigating the deaths of Gerry Poole and Tamara Searle and I was hoping that you could help me with both of these enquiries,' he said.

'I'll do my best,' replied Emma sincerely. 'However, I didn't know Tamara Searle at all. I only met her for the first time on Saturday at the party. I knew Gerry Poole a little through Roy and he had done some business with my husband, but again I wasn't a close friend of his.'

'But I understood that Mr Poole was one of your company's customers,' remarked Carmichael.

'Indeed he was,' replied Emma with no sign of emotion. 'We have cleaned his house for two days a week for over a year now. However, he never really had the need to come here at all. He paid his bills every month by direct debit and, apart from when he signed the contract a year ago, I don't think he's been here at all. Certainly I've not been to his house since I gave it the initial once-over when we agreed the price.'

'I see and out of interest how much did you charge him?' asked Carmichael.

'Including VAT we charged him a weekly fee of £82.25,' replied Emma.

Carmichael was impressed that she knew the price without having to check.

'I assume that, although you didn't see Gerry very much, your cleaners will have met him fairly regularly?' Carmichael enquired.

'Well, yes, they would meet him now and then I suspect,' replied Emma.' However, I think he would normally go out when he knew they were coming.'

'So what did you think of him?' asked Carmichael.

'He seemed quite sad,' replied Emma. 'I didn't know him well before his wife died so I can't say for sure, but he did strike me as someone who had taken her loss badly. He seemed lonely.'

'I see,' replied Carmichael. 'How did your cleaners take to him?'

Emma considered hard before answering the question. 'They didn't mention him much to me,' she said. 'However, I think they liked him well enough.'

'Did he have the same cleaner every time?' Carmichael asked.

'We try and do that where we can,' replied Emma. 'It's more efficient that way.'

'So who was Mr Poole's usual cleaner?' Carmichael probed.

'That was Clare Sands,' replied Emma. 'If she was away on holiday or off sick Melanie Dreyfuss would more than likely pick up her jobs, which in Clare's case is regrettably quite often.'

160

'I see,' replied Carmichael, as he pondered his next question.

'So would anyone else from your agency have cleaned Mr Poole's house in the last year other than Clare or Melanie?' Carmichael asked.

'I'd have to check my records,' replied Emma. 'However, I doubt it. Although Clare is not averse to taking days off sick, Melanie is very reliable, so I'm sure it would have been one or the other.'

'I see,' said Carmichael again. 'I'd very much like to speak to both Clare and Melanie. Do you know where they are at the moment?'

For the first time since they started to talk, Emma Cashman looked a little rattled. 'Well actually,' she said nervously, 'having said that Melanie is very reliable, I am a bit concerned about her. One of your colleagues was in here yesterday looking for her and since then she seems to have disappeared.'

'What do you mean?' asked Carmichael.

'Well, after she finished at Mrs Prentice's house yesterday she seems to have just vanished,' continued Emma uneasily. 'She didn't do her last job which is really not like her and I've not heard from her. I've tried her quite a few times on her mobile, last night and again this morning, but she's not replying. I even went round to her flat last night I was so worried, but her flatmates said they didn't know where she was.'

'What about the other girls that work here?' Carmichael asked. 'Is there anyone that she's particularly close to?'

'Well there's only really Clare Sands,' replied Emma.

'So doesn't Clare know where she is?' enquired Carmichael.

At this point Emma Cashman raised her eyes to the heavens. 'Well, *her* whereabouts are even more of a mystery. I've not seen that little madam since Monday. Mind you, that's not unusual. She's prone to go AWOL, so it's not that much of a shock but Melanie's normally totally reliable.'

'Do you think they could have gone off somewhere together?' Carmichael asked.

Emma shrugged her shoulders. 'I really don't know.'

'Tell me a bit about your agency?' Carmichael asked.

'It's a business I started about five years ago,' replied Emma. 'It employs only women and provides cleaners and waitresses for private parties. I only employ women who are from deprived backgrounds and, to be frank, only those who've been on the wrong side of the law.'

'So do I take it that if I were to check, Clare and Melanie would both have criminal records?' said Carmichael.

'Yes,' replied Emma. 'Nothing too serious, though.'

'But what exactly?' asked Carmichael.

'Well, in Melanie's case it was just shoplifting,' replied Emma.

'And Clare Sands?' enquired Carmichael.

'Well, a little bit more serious in her case,' Emma replied.

'Specifically what?' asked Carmichael, who could see that Emma Cashman was not keen to be precise at all.

'Well, some shoplifting. A little bit of petty vandalism. One minor assault and a few instances of possession of illegal substances,' replied Emma.

With the mention of drugs, Carmichael's thoughts quickly shifted to his daughter Jemma and he promised himself that he would call her as soon as he had finished interviewing Emma Cashman.

Carmichael looked at his watch. It was nearly 8.30. He expected that it would take forty to fifty minutes to get to Sunrise Productions from Much Maddock, so he decided it was time to start winding down the interview.

'Unfortunately, I need to get off,' he said as he stood up from the settee. 'Here's my card. Call me if you hear anything from either Clare or Melanie. I'll report that they're missing when I get back to the station and ask the uniformed officers to keep an eye out for them.'

162

'That would be very kind of you,' replied Emma.

Carmichael walked towards the door. Before he got there he turned to face Emma. 'Actually it would be helpful if you could give me some photos of the girls,' he said, 'or a brief description.'

'No problem,' replied Emma as she opened up one of the drawers of her metal filing cabinet. 'Here you go,' she said eventually as she passed Carmichael a small passport photo of each of the girls.

Carmichael looked intently at the photos. 'Aren't these two of the girls that were waitressing at Caroline Lovelace's party on Saturday?' he asked.

'Yes,' replied Emma. 'Clare is the blonde one and Melanie the redhead.'

Carmichael shook Emma Cashman's hand and walked over to the door.

'I appreciate your openness,' he said with a warm smile. 'I'll be in touch again, but please make sure you call me if you hear from either of them.'

# Chapter 22

Jemma Carmichael had been anxiously waiting for her father to call for the past twenty-four hours. Every time her mobile rang her temperature would suddenly rise and her hands would start to feel damp with nervous perspiration. She loved her dad and for as long as she could remember he was always the one person she most wanted to please. Whether it was through doing well at her school exams or at swimming, a sport she had excelled in when in her early teens, Jemma always wanted him to feel proud of her.

In spite of the attempt her mother had made in her text message to reassure her, Jemma knew that her father would be furious with her for being arrested. Although his anger did concern her, it was the thought that he would be ashamed of her that really troubled Jemma. When she eventually saw his number flash through on her mobile she could feel her heart start to race.

'Hi, Dad,' she said nervously. 'Are you really angry with me?'

Carmichael had made the call from the car on the way to the TV studio.

'Yes, I am,' he replied, although he tried hard not to sound too agitated. 'What on earth happened?'

Jemma could feel her heart beating loudly and could sense that her breathing was becoming more difficult. 'They were planted on me, Dad,' she replied. 'They weren't mine; I don't take drugs.'

'I don't think for one moment they were,' responded Carmichael as calmly as he could. 'What I do find strange and very worrying is that you would place yourself in a position where someone could plant them on you in the first place. I don't want to know the details, but what I do want is for you to promise me that you will be more careful which clubs you go to and also the friends you make at Leeds. I've come across drugs through all my working life and nine times out of ten it's down to who people mix with and the environment in which they find themselves. In many cases people can't chose where they live, but you can! If you know that there are people who take drugs and you know the places these people frequent you need to avoid them.'

Jemma knew full well that he was right and realised that she should quit her job at Jaspers, even though she really needed the money.

'I know,' she replied. 'I'll make sure I do.'

'That's good, Jemma,' Carmichael said with a sigh of relief. 'So other than getting arrested, what have you been up to?'

With the air now clear, Jemma was able to finally relax and spent the next ten minutes talking about her course and the various things she had been doing since they had last spoken.

'Look, I'm going to have to go,' said Carmichael as his car pulled into the car park at Sunrise Productions. 'Have you any lectures this morning?'

'No,' replied Jemma. 'My first one today is at two o'clock.'

'Then you might want to tune into *The Lovelace Show* in about an hour's time,' he said smugly. 'You may recognise someone?'

'Who?' shrieked Jemma.

'Me, of course,' replied Carmichael. 'I'm doing an interview to try and generate some response from the public about a case I'm working on.'

'What case is that?' Jemma asked excitedly.

'It's into the death of Tamara Searle,' replied Carmichael. 'She was the show's daytime weathergirl.'

'She's the really pretty one,' commented Jemma. 'I didn't know she had died.'

Carmichael's car glided into the only vacant space in the studio's car park.

'Look, I'm going to have to go,' he said. 'I'll speak to you at the weekend.'

\* \* \* \*

Rachel Dalton had wasted no time in getting on with the assignments that Carmichael had given her. As soon as she had left Watson in the canteen, she headed straight to Tamara Searle's house, which was a small, newly renovated, detached dwelling located in open countryside just ten miles from Kirkwood Police Station. Over the past twenty-four hours a small team of SOCOs had spent time searching Tamara's house, so by the time Rachel arrived they were quite advanced in their painstakingly detailed investigations.

'Have you found anything significant?' she asked the first SOCO she clapped eyes on.

'Nothing special,' he replied without bothering to stop dusting for prints on the handle of Tamara's deep freezer. 'Actually it's hardly yielded anything at all.'

'Is there any sign of her mobile, any credit cards or her purse?' continued Rachel.

'No,' he replied again. 'I would suppose that she may have taken them with her to wherever she was killed. There's no sign of any front door key or car keys either, so again I suspect she had these on her when she died.'

'Why are you dusting the freezer for prints?' she asked.

'Instructions from Dr Stock,' replied the officer with a shrug of his shoulders. 'I assume it's relevant.'

Rachel decided to leave the SOCO to his own devices. 'I'll

just have a snoop around,' she said before heading for the living room.

Although Tamara's home was quite small, it was in good decorative order and it was patently obvious that either she or the previous owners had spent a great deal of time and money giving the house a comfortable and welcoming atmosphere.

In spite of its relaxing ambience, what struck Rachel was the absence of the sort of clutter that she would have expected to find in a young woman's house. There were very few photographs or magazines on show. In fact, she could not find any of the items that visitors would expect to find if they were to make a search of her flat. No teddies, no frivolous or silly ornaments and knick-knacks, and there were no reminders of Tamara's past, or any clues to her interests outside work. The cupboard drawers had all the necessary items to make the house function, like bottle openers and even candles, which Rachel presumed were for use in case of a power cut, however, nowhere could she find anything that gave away any hint of Tamara's private life, her hobbies or interests.

Even Tamara's large walk-in wardrobe in the bedroom gave away few clues. It was reasonably full, but what surprised Rachel Dalton the most was that the entire contents were what Rachel considered to be just power clothes. Very expensive and in immaculate order, but nowhere could Rachel find anything casual that Tamara could have worn. There were no sweat shirts, no jeans, no sports tops, no jogging trousers, no Lycra, no baggy T-shirts, no training shoes and, although Rachel checked all of Tamara's drawers and even looked under her pillow, she couldn't find anything that looked like it was suitable to be worn in bed. 'Maybe she slept in the nude?' Rachel thought.

As she peered into the last of her bedroom drawers, the SOCO entered the room.

'It's very tidy, isn't it?' he said. 'It's almost like she didn't live here.'

'That's what I was thinking,' replied Rachel. 'Apart from a few items of food in the cupboard, a few bits in the freezer, her designer work clothes, her make-up and her toothbrush in the bathroom, you'd have thought she didn't live here at all.'

'I agree,' replied the officer with a slight nod of his head. 'I'd say it's either that or more likely someone's given this place an incredibly thorough spring clean.'

\* \* \* \*

At 10.30 precisely Penny, Robbie and Natalie Carmichael were sat in the living room of their house in Moulton Bank waiting patiently for Carmichael to appear on screen. On the other side of the Pennines, at 16 Grantby Grove in Headingley, Jemma Carmichael and two of her housemates did the same.

The video piece about Romanian travellers building a camp on the village green in a small town in Surrey ended and the camera panned in on Caroline Lovelace's head and shoulders.

Stern-faced, Caroline looked directly into the camera for five seconds before saying anything. Then in a controlled voice, she started to read the carefully scripted words on the autocue.

'Early yesterday morning the body of our dear friend and colleague Tamara Searle was discovered in a small public area in the village of Moulton Bank, here in Lancashire. As you can imagine, the whole team at Sunrise are shocked and devastated by the untimely death of such a beautiful, wonderfully talented and much-loved friend. The circumstances of her death are still under investigation, but we believe it's only right for us to devote some time today to try

168

and help the officers of Lancashire Police, who are conducting the investigation into Tamara's death.'

Caroline paused again and, in line with her specific directions, the camera then panned in closer onto her face, which looked pained and pale, as she intended. 'I am joined today on the sofa by Chief Inspector Carmichael, who is heading up the investigation into Tamara's death.' The camera slowly panned out to show a shot of Caroline and Carmichael, who were sitting within inches of each other.

'I need to correct you first,' said Carmichael. 'I'm just Inspector not Chief Inspector.'

'Thank you for pointing that out,' replied Caroline, who as she spoke became the only face in frame, due to the director switching to camera two which was instructed to remain focused on Caroline. 'I'm terribly sorry.'

'It's not important,' said Carmichael with a slight smile, with him and Caroline now both in shot. 'However, I thought it best to clarify my rank.'

'Absolutely. It's important we get these details right,' replied Caroline, again into camera two. 'Now I am sure there are aspects of this case which you're unwilling to disclose at this stage, Inspector Carmichael, however, can you please tell us how Tamara died and what progress you're making in solving her murder?'

'Certainly,' replied Carmichael, who took a deep breath and launched into the opening line that he had rehearsed in his head on his journey to the studio that morning. 'As you correctly said, Caroline, the body of Tamara Searle was discovered yesterday morning on the Common in Moulton Bank by a lady walking her dog. At the moment we are not at liberty to reveal how and when she died, but we are treating her death as suspicious. We would ask any member of the public who was on or around the Common on the evening of Tuesday 17th February or the early hours of 18th February, that's yesterday morning, and who saw anything suspicious, or anything that you feel may help us in our investigations, to come forward and talk to us. Anything you tell us will be treated in the strictest of confidence.'

The director switched to camera two, which showed a puzzled but solemn-looking Caroline Lovelace. 'So are you saying, Inspector, that you don't know whether the death was murder?'

'No, I am not saying that,' replied Carmichael. 'However, at this stage it's not something that we're happy to share with the public.'

Caroline appeared confused with this response. 'But surely it's obvious that her death was not due to natural causes; otherwise you wouldn't be here.'

'Obviously in cases like these there are things that we are unable to reveal,' he replied in a calm but firm tone. 'At this stage all we are prepared to say is that Tamara's death is very suspicious. I am really appreciative of Sunrise Productions for allowing me to come on air today and talk to your viewers and make this appeal for information that may help us, but equally I am sure you and your viewers will understand why I can't be too candid about all the details of this case.'

Again the director switched to camera two and, as if it had been rehearsed, Caroline stared intently into the lens. 'I am sure that all our viewers fully understand your position, Inspector Carmichael,' she said in an authoritative and decidedly demeaning way. 'However, I'm also sure that you will understand that Tamara was our friend and colleague, and to us she's not just a case, as you have said on at least two occasions – Tamara was our friend.'

Carmichael could sense his temperature rise. He had not expected his hostess to be so aggressive and could feel small droplets of perspiration forming on his temples.

'I can assure you and your viewers that we are doing

everything we can to get to the bottom of Tamara's murder,' he said.

Caroline pounced on his words, preventing him from finishing his sentence. 'So it was murder?' she said with no attempt to mask her hostile glee.

The director now chose to get the camera to pan in on Carmichael's face, which by now was showing signs of the strain that his interrogator was causing him. With the back of his hand, he wiped the beads of sweat that had gathered on his forehead and were slowly starting to trickle down towards his eyes. 'As I said before, we are doing everything we can to get to the bottom of this...' He was about to say case, but quickly corrected himself. '... of Tamara's death, but we need your help. Please contact either myself or one of my colleagues at Kirkwood Police Station if you have any information that might help us.'

The director again switched to camera two and the close-up of Caroline's wounded expression. 'Thank you, Inspector,' she said. 'I am sure that our wonderful viewers, if they know anything, will be on the phone. Now we will go over to Paul Hart at Westminster for the latest on the resignation of yet another Cabinet minister.'

The lights on top of the two cameras facing Steve Carmichael and Caroline Lovelace went out and within a split second Caroline stood up and marched across the studio. 'Freddie,' she shouted. 'You'll have to do something with that damn autocue. I couldn't keep up, it was going too damn fast.'

Carmichael remained sitting on the sofa for a moment, still dazed by the unexpected hostility he had just experienced.

It was Amanda Buchannan who came over to his aid, with a small plastic cup of water in one hand and a tissue in the other.

'It does get really hot under these lights, doesn't it,' she

171

remarked with what Carmichael took as a very genuine attempt on her part to put him at ease.

'Yes, it does,' replied Carmichael as his trembling hand grasped the cup.

Carmichael took a sip of the cold water and started to mop his now soaking brow with the tissue. 'I would like us to have a word in private, if that's OK with you?' he said.

'Me?' Amanda replied with unadulterated surprise. 'About what?'

'About your friendship with Tamara,' he replied. 'I understand you went to school together?'

'It was university actually,' replied Amanda.

'Can we go somewhere private?' Carmichael asked.

'Yes, there are some small meeting rooms just down the corridor,' said Amanda. 'We can go there if you like.'

\* \* \* \*

'What a nasty cow!' shouted Jemma as she switched off the TV in her digs. 'She was really rotten to Dad.'

Meanwhile, back in Moulton Bank the reaction of her mother was similar to hers.

'How dare she!' snapped Penny, who was close to tears. 'She deliberately tried to make your dad look a fool there.'

'Don't worry, Mum,' said Robbie, as he put his arm around her back to comfort her. 'Dad will sort her out now they're off air.'

\* \* \* \*

The small meeting room that Amanda Buchannan had mentioned was aptly named. It could not have measured much more than five feet square and, after allowing for the door to open, it left just enough room for three chairs and a very tiny, low-level table. By the time they were seated,

Carmichael had managed to regain his poise. Nevertheless he was still feeling hot, so in an effort to help cool himself down he opened the window a few inches.

'I want to know about your relationship with Tamara?' he asked Amanda.

'Relationship?' repeated Amanda nervously. 'What do you mean?'

'Well, you were friends from university,' Carmichael clarified. 'I assume that you also socialised with Tamara now that you worked together?'

'Not really,' replied Amanda. 'We were actually not that close at uni, but we were sort of friends and when we both graduated we found ourselves working here. It was a complete coincidence.'

'What courses did you both do?' Carmichael asked.

'Tamara did Media Studies,' replied Amanda. 'I actually did a Restoration course.'

'What's that about?' asked the perplexed policeman.

'Restoring works of art, pottery, ancient artefacts and all manner of things,' Amanda responded with a faint smile.

'So how did you end up here as Caroline Lovelace's PA?' Carmichael enquired, with even more bewilderment in his voice.

'It's a long story,' said Amanda with a wistful sigh. 'But I was struggling to find a good job when I graduated and, as I've a fair amount of debt as a result of having a good time at university, my aunty pulled some strings here and got me this position. It's not going to be for ever, but it does pay OK.'

'So what influence does your aunty have?' enquired Carmichael.

'She's a long-term friend of Caroline's,' replied Amanda. 'Actually they were also at university together, many moons ago.'

'And your aunt's name is…?' Carmichael asked.

'Sally Crabtree,' replied Amanda. 'You may have heard of her. She's a well-known sculptor.'

Carmichael could hardly believe his ears, yet another link between Caroline's party and his enquiries.

'I am familiar with her,' he responded with a faint smile. 'I'm not an expert on her work, but she's someone I know.'

'Do you mind if we close that window?' asked Amanda, who had spent the last few minutes with her arms folded and, in an effort to keep warm, had been fiercely rubbing her arms to generate some heat.

'Of course,' replied Carmichael, who gallantly pulled the window shut.

'So you didn't socialise much with Tamara?' continued Carmichael.

'Not really,' replied Amanda. 'We were on good terms but we didn't ever go out together on girlie nights if that's what you mean.'

'Did Tamara have any close friends to your knowledge?' he enquired.

Amanda shook her head. 'Not to my knowledge,' she replied. 'She was really ambitious so I don't expect she had much time for friends.'

'What about boyfriends?' Carmichael asked.

'Again I wouldn't know,' Amanda replied. 'We really weren't that close.'

Carmichael leaned back in his chair. 'OK,' he said. 'Thanks for your time, you can go now and see to her ladyship.'

Amanda stood up and smiled down at Carmichael. 'Caroline can be quite ruthless when she wants,' she said. 'I thought you did really well in the circumstances. But for some reason she was out to put you down today. Strange, really, as I never thought she was that close to Tamara. In fact, I always got the impression that Caroline disliked Tamara, but maybe I got that wrong.'

# Chapter 23

Chief Inspector Hewitt had not been having a good week. He had already received complaints from Roy Lovelace, the influential local MP, about Carmichael's handling of Gerry Poole's disappearance. There was the embarrassing episode with Special Branch regarding Carmichael's interest in Sidney Sydes and Sydes' cover subsequently being blown. Also, his car was still being repaired after his accident, which greatly annoyed him, and, to cap all that, he was now starting to feel like he was coming down with the flu virus that had decimated the team at Kirkwood Police Station. So when he was asked to take another call from Roy Lovelace he feared the worst.

'Norman,' boomed Lovelace down the phone. 'Did you see that bloody inspector of yours on Caroline's show this morning?'

Hewitt, of course, was well aware that Carmichael was appearing on *The Lovelace Show*, but he had not had the chance to tune in, so he was unaware of the way he had come across. 'No, Mr Lovelace,' he replied timidly. 'I was quite busy this morning so I was unable to watch the programme. Was there a problem?'

'I'd say there was a big problem,' Lovelace shouted down the phone. 'The man's an arse. He looked completely out of his depth. Caroline asked him a few simple questions and he came over as if he had no idea what he was doing. You'd have thought, after he'd been brought to task regarding the

175

casual way he investigated poor Gerry's disappearance, that he would have been more on the ball this time. I've really grave doubts about him being the right person to lead this inquiry.'

Having not seen Carmichael's performance, Hewitt felt quite vulnerable, but to his credit he took a firm stand. 'I appreciate your call, Mr Lovelace, and obviously I will look at a recording of your wife's show from earlier today, however, I want you to know that Inspector Carmichael has my full support. He is a very able and experienced officer and I've no intention of replacing him on either the investigation into your brother-in-law's death or the death of Tamara Searle. I will, as always, stay close to both cases, however, as I said before, Inspector Carmichael has my full support.'

'I think you may have cause to regret your loyalty to Carmichael,' Lovelace bellowed. 'Of course it's your decision, Norman, but don't say I didn't warn you when the brown stuff hits the fan on this one, as a result of Carmichael's incompetence.'

Hewitt had no opportunity to respond. As soon as Roy Lovelace finished his sentence, he rudely and abruptly hung up.

Hewitt replaced the phone and rested his head in his hands. 'For God's sake, please don't mess this one up, Carmichael,' he mumbled to himself, before picking up the receiver again and asking Angela to bring him in a couple of paracetamol tablets to ease his splitting headache.

\* \* \* \*

When Carmichael arrived back at the CID incident room at Kirkwood Station, Watson and Dalton were already there, waiting to update their boss on the progress they had made that morning. To Carmichael's great delight, they were joined by Paul Cooper, who if truth were known was not yet

176

fully recovered, but who, having seen his boss struggling so badly on TV that morning and feeling a little better than he had done the day before, had decided that he needed to get back to work to help out the team.

'Paul,' exclaimed Carmichael. 'It's good to see you back. Are you feeling OK now?'

'I'm not a hundred per cent better,' replied Cooper in a very nasal voice. 'However, I'm feeling much better than I did.'

Watson leaned over and whispered to Rachel. 'What was it, two to three weeks for you and just a couple of days for Cooper? Who says women are the stronger sex?'

Rachel ignored his comments. She had no intention of getting into a petty argument with Watson about the relative strengths of men and women. She had been down this road before with him and knew that she would only end up getting angry and the debate would almost certainly descend into the usual farcical discussion.

'Well, it's excellent to have you back,' said Carmichael, who was oblivious to Watson's jibe at Rachel and was relieved that the heavy workload could now be shared by four people rather than just three. 'Let's get going then. Marc, you start.'

'We've completed the house-to-house enquiries,' replied Watson, 'but so far it's amazing, nobody seems to have seen or heard anything out of the ordinary at all.'

'What!' exclaimed Carmichael. 'Out of all those houses not one person saw anything that was worth following up?'

'That's right,' replied Watson glumly. 'Absolutely nothing.'

Carmichael was not convinced that Watson and the PCs he had seconded to help him with the house-to-house enquiries had done a thorough job, but decided to press on and find out what else Watson had uncovered in the course of the morning. 'What about the autopsy report on Tamara Searle from Dr Stock?' he asked. 'Also were you able to check out the receipt found in Gerry Poole's pocket?'

'Here's where it gets intriguing,' replied Watson. 'First, Stock's report is quite revealing. He is certain that Tamara died on Monday. She was asphyxiated. There's also evidence that she had been struck on the head before she died and there are rope marks around her wrists and her ankles that suggest she was tied up before she was killed.'

'Interesting,' remarked Carmichael. 'So does Stock believe she died somewhere else and was then just dumped on the Common?'

'Yes,' replied Watson. 'He's certain that Tamara had already been dead for up to thirty hours before she was abandoned on the Common.'

'Was there anything else that the SOCOs found at the scene?' Carmichael enquired excitedly.

'Just the purse belonging to Melanie Dreyfuss,' he replied as he handed over to Carmichael a plastic bag containing a small red purse and the few items found inside it. Carmichael tipped out the bag's contents onto the desk. A debit card in the name of Melanie Dreyfuss, a day return train ticket to Manchester dated 17th February, a twenty-pound note, four pound coins and some loose change.

'I've checked with the bank and they have confirmed that Melanie withdrew fifty pounds from the cash point at their branch in Moulton Bank on Monday evening at nine forty five,' said Watson. 'She then appears to have walked across the road to the railway station and bought a return ticket to Manchester for the next day. I've spoken to the woman who served her in the ticket office and she confirms that a young woman of Melanie's build and age did buy the ticket.'

'She can positively identify her?' Carmichael asked.

'Well, not a hundred per cent, as Melanie was wrapped up in a large coat and had her hood up,' replied Watson 'but I've seen the CCTV tape from that evening and, although it's not fantastic, it does look like Melanie.'

'Good work,' replied Carmichael. 'I wonder why she was planning to go to Manchester on Tuesday.'

'I've no idea,' he replied. 'And if she did, then she would have had to have bought another ticket because this one hasn't been used.'

'What about the receipt that was found in Gerry Poole's pocket?' Carmichael asked.

'I'm certain it was planted,' replied Watson emphatically.

'Why do you say that?' Carmichael asked.

'Because it was for diesel and Poole's car runs on unleaded,' replied Watson smugly.

'So did you have time to check out whether the garage has a CCTV tape we could look at for 3rd February?' Carmichael enquired.

'Not yet, boss,' replied Watson. 'I just haven't had time to get over there yet.'

'That's fine,' replied Carmichael. 'One of us can follow that up either this afternoon or tomorrow.'

'How have you got on this morning?' asked Carmichael as he turned his gaze to Rachel.

'The first thing I did this morning was go to Tamara's house,' said Rachel.

'I think that was the second thing you did,' interrupted Carmichael. 'I think the first thing you two did was have a sandwich in the canteen.'

Rachel blushed, she had not realised that Carmichael had seen her and Watson in the canteen that morning. 'Well, after we had some breakfast I went to Tamara's house,' continued Rachel. 'It was weird. It was as if she didn't live there. It was just like a show house. It had her smart working outfits but apart from that there was nothing there that suggested it was her home.'

'Were there any clues to give us a better insight into who her friends were or if she had a boyfriend?' Carmichael asked.

179

'No,' replied Rachel with an air of disappointment in her voice. 'In fact, there were no clues about anything like that, or what sort of habits she had, or if she had any hobbies. If she was killed there then whoever killed her did a great job of making the place almost sterile afterwards.'

'Maybe it was Melanie,' interjected Watson. 'After all she is a cleaner by profession.'

'Maybe,' replied Carmichael. 'But I suspect most people can clean a house thoroughly if they have the time.'

'We could not find her mobile,' continued Rachel. 'In fact, we couldn't find *any* of her personal things. No casual clothes, no underwear, no money, no credit cards, nothing!'

'That *is* strange,' remarked Cooper just before he sneezed into his handkerchief.

'What about the text Yerbovic received on Tuesday saying she wouldn't be in work?' asked Carmichael. 'Did you have any joy in tracing that message?'

'Yes we did,' replied Rachel. 'It came from Tamara's phone and was sent at nine twenty-three in the morning.'

'Do we know who else Tamara called or texted recently?' Carmichael asked.

'Not yet,' replied Rachel. 'However, the phone company have promised to send over the activity report from Tamara's mobile for the last month this afternoon.'

'Good work, Rachel,' said Carmichael. 'Did you find time to go through Tamara's file on that disk Tony Yerbovic gave you?'

'Yes,' replied Rachel. 'I've got a printout here.'

Rachel handed Carmichael a small folder which contained all Tamara's details from Sunrise Productions.

'Is there anything of interest?' Carmichael asked.

'Not really,' replied Rachel. 'But what was interesting was that one of her references was Sally Crabtree, the sculptor.

'Really?' replied Carmichael. 'She appears to have been responsible for a couple of people getting work at Sunrise. I found out today that she is Amanda Buchannan's aunt, and that she got her the job there, too. Sally Crabtree's an old university friend of Caroline's and as she was also at the party last Saturday, I think that we need to talk with her as a matter of priority.'

'That's about everything from me,' said Rachel.

'How was your day, sir?' asked Watson.

'Well, I met with Emma Cashman earlier today,' he replied. 'It would appear that Melanie and a young woman called Clare Sands have both gone missing. What makes this relevant is that both were employed to serve dinner at Caroline's party and they were also the two cleaners she used at Gerry Poole's house.'

'It looks like every avenue on the Gerry Poole and the Tamara Searle deaths seems to lead us to either Caroline Lovelace's party or to The Helpful Angels,' remarked Cooper.

'Yes,' agreed Carmichael. 'The answer is linked to one or both of them, I'm certain.'

'What about the TV interview?' asked Watson. 'How did that go?'

'Not well,' conceded Carmichael. 'Caroline was very aggressive and, to be honest, I wasn't comfortable. To cut a long story short, I didn't take advantage of what was a good opportunity to get some information from the general public.'

'So what happened?' asked Watson, who was suddenly intrigued.

'I saw it, sir,' interjected Cooper. 'She really just went off on one. I got the impression that she was trying to make the viewers think she was distraught about Tamara, but in my view all she did was ruin the opportunity to ask for information and, to be honest, she made a fool of herself, I thought.'

Carmichael smiled. 'I appreciate your support, Paul,' he said, 'and I agree to a point, but I have to hold my hands up and confess that I didn't manage it very well either. It was not my greatest hour.'

'Did you manage to talk more with Caroline Lovelace once you came off air?' Rachel asked.

'No,' replied Carmichael. 'I was in no mood to talk to her just then. I will hold fire on that for a day or so. I did, however, talk with Amanda Buchannan as I said before. She tried hard to play down any friendship between her and Tamara. I don't know if I buy that though, especially after Aunty Sally appears to have had a strong hand in both their appointments. I think we need to look into their relationship a bit further.'

'So what is our immediate plan of action?' asked Cooper.

Carmichael considered this question carefully. 'We've lots of areas we still need to explore,' he replied. 'Let's update our lists, then we can decide what needs to be tackled first and who needs to do what.'

Rachel rushed over to the charts they had created that morning and grabbed hold of a marker pen. 'Fire away then,' she said with enthusiasm. 'I'll act as scribe.'

It took them a little over thirty minutes to update the information, at which point Carmichael remarked, 'Let's review what we've got.'

The four officers spent the next few minutes reviewing the four lists:

Gerry Poole Facts:
1. Died of a heart attack.
2. Didn't die where he was found.
3. Had been dumped on the canal towpath before the first snow fell (approx 6 p.m. on Sat 14th Feb).
4. Petrol receipt found on body dated 3rd Feb.
5. Thurs 5th Feb the last time the Lovelaces remember talking to Gerry.
6. Receipt was for diesel – Poole's car ran on unleaded.

Tamara Searle Facts:
1. Death occurred on Mon 16th Feb.
2. Died by asphyxiation.
3. Had been struck on the head and bound and tied before she died.
4. Last known sighting was with Yerbovic at 3 p.m. on Mon 16<sup>th</sup> Feb.
5. Text message sent into work saying she was sick on Tues morning (known to be sent on Tamara's phone).
6. Tamara was a friend of Caroline Lovelace's PA, Amanda Buchannan (from time at uni).
7. Body found in pose similar to a Sally Crabtree sculpture.
8. Purse of Melanie Dreyfuss found by body.
9. Tamara recommended to Sunrise by Sally Crabtree.
10. Melanie Dreyfuss's debit card last used on Mon evening at 9.45 p.m.
11. Melanie bought a return ticket for Manchester on Mon evening. Ticket valid for Tuesday but not used.
12. Tamara's house was void of personal possessions.
13. Amanda Buchannan is Sally Crabtree's niece.
14. Melanie Dreyfuss and Clare Sands both missing.

Gerry Poole's Death Suppositions:
1. Gerry Poole placed in a freezer after death?
2. Gerry Poole placed in the freezer while still alive?
3. Gerry Poole's body brought to the canal in his own car?
4. Gerry Poole's death linked to someone at the dinner party on 14<sup>th</sup>?
5. The receipt found on Gerry Poole was planted?

Tamara Searle's Death Suppositions:
1. Tamara Searle's death also linked to someone at the dinner party?

2. Tamara murdered elsewhere then moved to the Common?

3. Melanie Dreyfuss involved in placing the body on the Common?

4. The pose that Tamara's body was placed in was deliberately mimicking the sculpture by Sally Crabtree?

5. The text to Tony Yerbovic was not sent by Tamara, meaning whoever killed Tamara knew her boss's mobile number?

6. The text to Tony Yerbovic was probably sent after Tamara had been murdered?

7. Tamara's death is linked to Gerry Poole's death?

8. Melanie Dreyfuss is involved with both murders?

9. Clare Sand's disappearance is also linked to the two murders?

'Well,' announced Watson. 'I still think we need to find Melanie Dreyfuss. In my view she is our number-one suspect for both deaths.'

'You could be right,' conceded Carmichael. 'However, at the moment I will just agree that we need to find her. I don't think we can say she's our killer.'

'Can I take on that task?' asked Watson.

'OK,' Carmichael replied. 'However, you need to look for Clare Sands, too. I think they are probably equally involved in all this.'

Watson nodded his agreement.

'What about that bloke on the narrowboat?' asked Cooper. 'He doesn't get a mention.'

'I agree,' said Watson. 'I think Sydes needs another pull.'

Carmichael shuffled uncomfortably from one foot to the other.

'Look,' he said. 'What I am about to tell you is absolutely confidential.'

Cooper and Watson listened intently as their boss explained the full story about Sidney Sydes' past and the visitation from Special Branch.

When he had finished the two sergeants looked amazed.

'I see,' said Watson. 'But how does that make him innocent?'

'It doesn't,' agreed Carmichael. 'However, at this point in time we need to rule him out as he's now probably at the other end of the country with a new name and a new identity. It will be almost impossible to interview him again unless we have absolute proof that he's implicated.'

'And let's face it, we're miles from that now,' conceded Watson. 'So we just ignore him, I guess.'

Carmichael nodded. 'I'm afraid that's what it means,' he said wistfully.

'What do you want me to do, sir?' asked Rachel, who wanted to get the discussion back on track.

'Well, Rachel,' said Carmichael. 'I want you to check out Tamara's calls and texts when you get the summary from the phone company. In the meantime get on to Lincoln University and find out as much as you can about Tamara and Amanda. See if you can locate some past students that knew them or some of their lecturers. I want to know just how friendly they were. I'd also like you to get a copy of the CCTV tape of Melanie at the train station on Monday evening and try and get it enlarged so we can verify it was definitely her. Then get down to the petrol station and see if they have any tapes of the person they gave that receipt to.'

Rachel nodded. 'That's all fine with me, sir.'

'What about me?' asked Cooper.

'I want you to find Tamara's clothes and personal possessions. Yours is the hardest task but the most important. I want you to try and work out where she was killed and where the killer has dumped her things. My guess is that she was killed locally, so I think it's a fair bet to say that the killer will

185

have dumped the clothing locally, too. Also, with the exception of Sally Crabtree, get around everybody that we have not yet interviewed who was at the party I attended on Saturday. I'll give you a list of the people in a minute. Find out what they know about the two dead people and establish where they all were on Monday evening and on Tuesday.'

'That's fine with me,' replied Cooper, who was still struggling with his flu symptoms.

'What are you focusing on, sir?' asked Rachel.

'I am going to visit Sally Crabtree,' he said with a smile. 'Then, if I can, I might get myself over to see Caroline Lovelace again. I've quite a bit of unfinished business with her.'

## Chapter 24

Melanie Dreyfuss was an attractive young woman with an explosion of fiery red curly hair which blasted out from a pale, but cute, doll-like face. Although she was only in her early twenties, she had already more life experience than most people twice her age and as a result Melanie had become streetwise and totally independent. If the need arose, she was more than a match for pretty much any unfortunate foe that foolishly crossed her. In that respect she was the epitome of the stereotype redhead. In spite of this strong, self-sufficient streak, Melanie was also more than capable of showing compassion and affection, but only to those people close to her whom she trusted, which in reality could be easily counted on just one of Melanie's tiny hands. One such trusted friend was Clare Sands, whom she had met when they both were signed up on The Helpful Angels programme a few years earlier.

Melanie was worried about Clare and had been trying to contact her for the past twenty-four hours, but she had drawn a blank. Even though she had left numerous voice messages and texts, Clare hadn't bothered to reply. Based upon what Clare had said to her on Monday evening, Melanie had expected her friend to go to ground, but she had thought Clare would have still remained in contact with her.

Melanie was very concerned. She had no idea what the police knew or what they wanted to talk with her about, but her instinct, built up from a number of previous altercations with the police, told her to lie low. She felt sure that she was now somehow implicated, not only in the death of Gerry Poole but also in all probability in the murder of Tamara Searle too.

If it had not been for Mrs Prentice, Melanie would have been in real trouble. She knew that Mrs Prentice had a soft spot for her and that she wouldn't kick her out, but, following Carmichael's appearance on *The Lovelace Show* that morning, even Mrs Prentice's loyalty appeared to be on the wane.

'Melanie, my dear,' Mrs Prentice said to her new young lodger. 'If you have done nothing wrong, I don't see why you can't talk to the police.'

'It's complicated,' replied Melanie as reassuringly as she could. 'I can't explain; when I'm ready I will, but I need to do a few things first.'

Mrs Prentice was not convinced that Melanie was being honest with her.

'You know you can stay here as long as you want,' she told her. 'But I'm not happy with the way you're behaving, Melanie. I really think you should reconsider and talk to the police.'

Melanie put a comforting arm around the frail old lady. 'It will all be fine, I promise,' she said as sincerely as she could. 'You just have to trust me.'

\*　\*　\*　\*

Sally Crabtree's grand Edwardian house was situated midway between Moulton Bank and Newbridge. Her more modern studio was located in a large extension to the side which stretched back beyond the rear of her isolated detached home. Although visually the annex made an unsightly addition to her house, it was very functional and it afforded Sally Crabtree all the space she needed to carry out her work without having to commute from her home to a private studio, as she had once had to endure.

Sally heard Carmichael's car pulled up on the long gravel drive and had already opened the front door before Carmichael had a chance to knock.

'Good afternoon, Mrs Crabtree,' remarked Carmichael. 'I'd like to ask you a few questions if I may?'

'It's actually Ms Crabtree,' she replied calmly. 'I never married, but please just call me Sally.'

Carmichael stretched out his hand. 'Nice to see you again, Sally,' he said with a smile.

'Please come in out of the cold, Inspector,' continued Sally. 'Mandy called me earlier and said you might be paying me a visit.'

Carmichael entered the house. 'When you say Mandy, you mean Amanda Buchannan, your niece?'

'Yes,' responded Sally. 'She's my sister's girl. We've always called her Mandy; it was Caroline who insisted on calling her Amanda, as I am sure you can imagine.'

Carmichael smiled. 'I see,' he said.

'Would you like some tea or coffee?' Sally asked.

'Coffee would be excellent,' replied Carmichael, who was keen to spend as much time as he could with Sally Crabtree and taking coffee in these circumstances was always a good excuse for him to linger for slightly longer. Besides which, he was actually gasping for a warm drink.

'Go through into the studio,' she instructed as she pointed in the direction of a large oak door. 'Make yourself comfortable. I'll just be two ticks.'

Carmichael did as he was told.

The studio was spacious with gleaming whitewashed walls. It had a sloping ceiling with two large Velux windows letting in plenty of natural light, so even in the depths of that February afternoon, the whole area looked bright and airy. Carmichael walked over to the far corner of the studio,

189

where Sally had placed two large orange sofas and a bulky oak coffee table. He felt this would be an ideal place to have their drinks and to conduct his interview. He sat down and gazed around the studio. It was very large, almost twenty foot square with three large wooden benches, each crammed full of various artworks in a variety of states of development. There were drawings and sketches, small plasticine or clay models and half-finished three-dimensional structures made from all sorts of materials, but among the myriad of objects he could make out only a few pieces of work that looked completely finished.

Sally Crabtree took little more than five minutes to make their coffees. When she entered the studio she was carrying the two mugs on a tray with a large plate of chocolate digestives.

'I think Napoleon said that an army marches on its stomach,' she said with a smile. 'Well, I can tell you I've been sculpting for the last twenty years and it's all down to McVities chocolate digestives.'

Carmichael laughed heartily. 'What is it with women and chocolate?' he remarked. 'I've a wife and two daughters and they are all chocolate addicts.'

Sally Crabtree laid the tray down on the table and handed Carmichael his coffee.

'Please help yourself to sugar,' she said, pointing to the small sugar bowl, 'and of course please have a biscuit.' With that she picked up a chocolate digestive and dunked it in her coffee cup.

Carmichael declined the biscuit but shovelled two heaped spoons of sugar into his coffee mug.

'I saw you on Caroline's show this morning,' Sally announced. 'Do I sense there's some friction between Caroline and you?'

Sally's comment caught Carmichael totally off guard.

'No,' he replied. 'Mind you, I can understand why you would say that. Is she always like that?'

Sally smiled and took a sip of her coffee before replying. 'I've known Caroline for many years,' she said. 'She is a good friend of mine, but she's not always someone I like.'

'How do you mean?' Carmichael enquired.

'Well,' replied Sally. 'She can be ruthless, cruel and totally unscrupulous when she has a mind to be. Having said all that, she can also be charming and kind too.'

'A paradox then,' observed Carmichael.

'Oh yes,' replied Sally. 'She is a proper Gemini. Delightful and engaging one minute and the next she can be merciless and conniving. I suspect that this morning she was in one of her more devious moods. I wouldn't take it personally.'

'So how long have you known Caroline Lovelace?' Carmichael asked, wishing to change the subject and move his enquiry along.

'Since we were at Aston University together in the early eighties,' replied Sally. 'Of course she was just plain Caroline Murphy from Wigan then. Her father owned a chip shop behind the railway station and a matter of yards away from his shop was the factory where they made Uncle Joe's Mint Balls. They lived over the shop. I stayed with her once. I have to say that my lasting impression was that it reeked of chip fat and when the wind was blowing in the wrong direction you would get that sickly sweet smell of sugar and liquorice. I don't want to sound a snob, but it was very working class.'

'She's clearly come a long way since then,' commented Carmichael.

'Absolutely,' replied Sally with a mischievous laugh. 'She's jumped two whole levels of the social strata, from working class to aristocracy, without bothering with middle class at all.'

'And you've stayed close friends ever since?' continued Carmichael, although he was now starting to question whether the word friend was really appropriate.

Sally sipped some more coffee. 'Yes, but we are very

different; we often disagree and we don't live in each other's pockets, but we are actually good friends.'

Unless he had known, Carmichael would never have put Sally Crabtree and Caroline Lovelace together as friends. In his eyes they were from totally different worlds. One being well groomed in looks and in her actions, a shallow extrovert with confidence to burn; the other gave the impression of having no interest at all in how she looked and certainly gave the impression of being completely unpretentious.

'What about Tamara Searle?' Carmichael asked. 'Were you close to her?'

'No,' replied Sally with an air of bewilderment. 'We hardly knew each other.'

'Really,' replied Carmichael. 'So why did you give her a reference when she applied to join Sunrise Productions?'

It was clear by her body language that Sally had not expected Carmichael to know this fact. 'I had met her of course,' she responded edgily. 'She was an acquaintance of Mandy's at university and Mandy asked if I would help her to get the job at Sunrise. They thought that my standing as an artist and my relationship with Caroline might help her application. Maybe I was wrong to give her a reference, but I did know her so I don't think I broke any rules.'

'I am sure you didn't,' replied Carmichael. 'However, she was successful and got the position, as did Amanda Buchannan, whom you also recommended for a job at Sunrise.'

Sally quickly regained some of her previous self-confidence. 'With Mandy that was different. I am absolutely guilty as charged in using my relationship with Caroline to get her that job, but I make no apologies for that.'

Carmichael shuffled forward on the sofa and took a sip from his coffee mug. 'So how close were Tamara and Mandy?' he asked.

192

Sally shrugged her shoulders. 'You'd really have to ask Mandy that question,' she replied.

'I did,' said Carmichael.

'And what did she say?' asked Sally.

'She gave me the impression that they were never really close,' replied Carmichael, 'but that doesn't stack up with your niece and Tamara both being at the same university and them both working at the same place and also you being asked by your niece to be Tamara's reference.'

'Young people can be so fickle in their friendships,' replied Sally in an attempt to justify the situation. 'I suspect they may have been reasonably close when they were looking for jobs, but became less close after.'

To a degree Carmichael accepted this, as he knew from first-hand experience with Jemma that there were girls he had thought were her best friends one minute, who then appeared to be sworn enemies the next.

'Maybe you're right,' he replied, 'but out of curiosity who got the job at Sunrise first?'

Sally thought hard before answering. 'I seem to remember that it was Mandy who applied first. I could not be totally sure, but I think it was Mandy. Is that relevant?'

'Probably not,' replied Carmichael. 'I was just interested.'

Sally grabbed another chocolate biscuit from the plate and dunked it into her coffee mug.

'I'm also very interested in your work,' Carmichael commented. 'Would it be possible to have a closer look at some of the pieces you're working on?'

Sally's face lit up. She seemed genuinely thrilled to be asked to show off her work. 'Of course,' she replied with glee. 'Let me give you the two-penny tour.'

With that she stood up and started to walk to the nearest workbench. Carmichael took a quick gulp from his coffee mug before following on behind.

\*   \*   \*   \*

By 3.30 p.m. Paul Cooper was already starting to regret coming back to work so soon. Embarrassingly, his nose continued to dribble and he still ached all over. Before he had left Kirkwood Station, he had despatched three plain-clothed officers to check all the obvious places in the vicinity of Tamara's house where the killer could have dumped her clothes and personal possessions. Once the PCs were on their way he had started to try and set up interviews with the four people on the list Carmichael had given him. Annoyingly, so far, Cooper had only managed to contact two on the phone and only Declan Cashman, the property developer, was available to be interviewed that afternoon. The one stroke of good fortune for Cooper was that Cashman's office was only a short drive from Kirkwood Police Station.

When his beaten-up car arrived outside Cashman's workplace the sky was already starting to look threatening. 'Not more damn snow,' he mumbled to himself.

Cooper parked in the last vacant visitor's space, which was situated right next to a bright-red Ferrari, in the parking bay with the large blue sign which read 'Reserved for MD'. He assumed, correctly as it happened, that the flash car belonged to the man he was there to interview.

His appointment with Declan Cashman was for 3.45 p.m., so Cooper thought he'd spend the few minutes he had trying to contact the McIntyres, who were the only people that he had yet to speak to. Unfortunately their home phone just continued to ring and ring, as it had done on the two previous occasions he had tried to make contact with them that afternoon. Feeling decidedly worse for wear, Cooper placed his mobile phone in his coat pocket then covered his nose with his already soaking handkerchief and gave it one almighty blow.

194

* * * *

Watson's afternoon was faring even worse than Cooper's. He had visited Melanie's house, but her housemates were clueless as to their friend's whereabouts. He had then returned to the offices of The Helpful Angels, but they were of no help whatsoever. He had tried Melanie's mobile number almost every thirty minutes, but she refused to pick up. With no sign of a breakthrough he decided to pay a visit to each of the twelve addresses that The Helpful Angels had given him, which represented Melanie's entire cleaning round. He was sure one of them would be able to help him locate the elusive redhead.

* * * *

In comparison to her male colleagues, Rachel's afternoon was progressing well. She had successfully managed to collect the CCTV tape from the train station which showed the person buying the return ticket to Manchester on Monday evening and, with a little help from the admissions people at Lincoln University, she had obtained a list of the last known addresses of five past students who were known to have shared a house with either Amanda Buchannan or Tamara Searle in their final year at university. So Rachel was hopeful that by the next team briefing she would have made some progress in at least two of her tasks. She had not been so lucky with the third of the chores Carmichael had given her. To her annoyance, the petrol station was unable to provide any CCTV tapes for the 3rd February. This was as a result of an oversight that day by the duty manager, who forgot to switch the system on until 11 a.m., which was forty minutes after the time recorded on the receipt.

At 3.45 p.m. Rachel left the garage and headed back to Kirkwood Station to take a closer look at the tape from the

195

train station and to start making calls to the university housemates of Amanda and Tamara.

\* \* \* \*

Cooper took an instant dislike to Declan Cashman. From their initial handshake when he was ushered into Cashman's office, having waited twenty minutes in reception, to the 'If you'll excuse me now, I'm very busy' which heralded the end of their meeting ten minutes later, there was absolutely nothing Cooper could see in this man that was in any way endearing. It was obvious that he was successful – his office, his clothes, his haughty superior conduct, his condescending tone and the exaggerated mannerisms were designed to tell that story. However, in Cooper's eyes he was without question one of the most annoying people he had met in many months and, given some of the characters Cooper met in his line of work, that was really saying something.

'What a flash git!' mumbled Cooper to himself as he clambered back into his car and fumbled in the glove compartment for a tissue. 'I just hope he's caught this bloody germ from me, that's all I can say.'

\* \* \* \*

Initially Carmichael had very little interest in Sally Crabtree's work, but by the time she had finished showing him around and explaining how she made her sculptures, he was totally absorbed and quite fascinated with what she had to say.

'So you always work the same way?' confirmed Carmichael. 'A sketch or photograph, then you make a miniature out of clay or plasticine, then you make the real thing.'

'Usually,' replied Sally, who was very impressed by her visitor's attentiveness. 'The miniatures are the critical part

196

as that is where you get a feel for the piece and you also start to understand how you will need to construct the final work.'

'What about the piece you gave to Caroline?' Carmichael asked. 'Is that of anyone in particular?'

'That is one of my favourite pieces,' replied Sally. 'I only made fifty and they are now very valuable. I'm told one sold for over £50,000 a few months ago in Japan.'

'It did look very eye-catching, but that's a bit out of my price bracket,' said Carmichael. 'What is it called?'

'It's called *The Friendless Beauty*,' replied Sally sadly. 'I think I've got the miniature here somewhere.' Sally opened up one of the drawers and started delving into the numerous objects that had been recklessly thrown in.

'Ah, here it is,' she said, pulling out the tiny model.

'She is very pretty,' remarked Carmichael. 'Who was your model?'

'The model was my elder sister, Janet, Mandy's mother. She was a beautiful woman but she was troubled and she died tragically when Mandy was small. It's a lovely piece though and, although I say it myself, I caught her just right.'

'The pose that she is in,' continued Carmichael. 'Does it have any significance?'

Sally seemed perplexed by the question. 'No,' she replied. 'It was simply how I remember her, a stunning beauty but often frightened and sad. 'The pose is the most compact way a normal human can be folded. It's designed to show my sister trying to make herself as invisible as possible, which is how she was at times. Why do you ask?'

'Oh, no reason,' replied Carmichael, who took hold of the miniature. 'I was just interested.'

Sally Crabtree looked intently at the miniature in Carmichael's hand. 'Poor Janet,' she muttered.

'Anyway I've taken enough of your time,' said Carmichael. 'I'll make tracks.'

'OK,' replied Sally. 'It's been nice to meet you properly, Inspector Carmichael. Please do come again.'

'Would it be possible for me to borrow this model for a few days?' he asked.

'Of course, just as long as you let me have it back when you're finished,' Sally replied.

Carmichael placed the miniature figure into his pocket and shook his host's hand warmly then made his way back into the hallway.

'If I can be of any further assistance, Inspector, please let me know,' said Sally as she opened the front door.

Carmichael nodded and started to walk through the open doorway. 'Actually I do have a few more questions,' he said. 'First, how did Janet die?'

'She took an overdose of sleeping tablets,' replied Sally. 'It was just a year after I left university.'

Carmichael nodded and then looked up admiringly at the façade of Sally's large house.

'You said you had a few questions,' remarked Sally. 'What was your second one?'

'I was just wondering whether you lived here alone in such a large house,' he said.

Sally smiled. 'Well, I'm not alone here,' she replied. 'Mandy lives here too.'

*   *   *   *

Carmichael had every intention of paying the Lovelaces an unannounced call on his way home from Sally's house. However, he changed his mind once he saw the huge flakes of snow coming down from the heavens and headed straight for home.

Penny was still angry at the way Caroline Lovelace had treated her husband that morning on national TV and she had not tried to conceal her feelings from the numerous people who had called her that afternoon to say that they had seen the show. Carmichael, on the other hand, was largely over the trauma. He had much more to occupy his mind than the vindictive conduct of Caroline Lovelace that morning. So when Carmichael walked into the hallway, he was shocked that his normally calm, measured wife was still so livid about Caroline's behaviour towards him.

'I swear if she was here now I'd slap her smarmy face,' she hollered. 'Who the hell does she think she is?'

'It's not worth getting stressed out about it,' remarked Carmichael coolly. 'It's done now and I'm not going to dwell on it.'

Penny was pleased that he was taking it so well, but wondered whether he was just putting on a brave face.

'I know,' she replied, 'but it was so unfair and so unexpected. You must have felt really awkward.'

'Well,' he replied, trying to pick his next words carefully. 'I was certainly taken by surprise. I didn't see that coming at all. And yes, I did feel very uncomfortable at the time. However, I certainly don't now.'

Penny smiled and gave her husband a massive hug. 'That's the spirit,' she said proudly. 'You just get out there and solve the bloody case and show that cow what a great detective you are.'

'I don't like to correct you, Mrs Carmichael,' said Carmichael, who was still being embraced tightly by his wife. 'But this is not a case. Tamara was her friend, her colleague; her death is not just a case.'

Penny released her grip slightly and kissed her husband passionately on the lips.

'Pompous cow!' she said with a smile. 'I hope she has the manners to say sorry to you when you do uncover the killer.'

'I wouldn't hold your breath, my dear,' replied Carmichael. 'Now that's quite enough of my infamous TV appearance. What's for tea? I'm starving.'

# Chapter 25

**Friday 20<sup>th</sup> February**

Having spent a second night at Mrs Prentice's house, without any word from Clare, Melanie decided that she needed to take the initiative and find her friend. The most obvious place she could think of where Clare might be was with Travis, her elder brother, who lived in Manchester. To be able to contact her there, though, she needed to get her address book, which was where she had written down his telephone number. There was only one problem, her address book was back at her house.

She had no idea whether the police would be watching her house, but she decided that she just had to risk it. If she could get into her house, this would also enable her to collect some clean clothes and her chequebook, which she desperately needed to draw out some cash now that she no longer had her debit card. Melanie tried to be as quiet as she could as she didn't want to wake up Mrs Prentice. She quickly scribbled a note telling the old lady that she would be back around mid-morning and at just after 7 a.m. she crept out of the house and into the cold February morning.

Mrs Prentice was a light sleeper at the best of times and had heard Melanie moving about that morning but had remained in her room. When the front door closed, she carefully peered out of her bedroom window and watched as Melanie carefully made her way through the freshly fallen snow and out of sight. Mrs Prentice was certain that Melanie was not directly involved in the death of Tamara Searle. However, she had been greatly troubled by Melanie's reluctance to speak to the police. The old lady had not had a very good sleep. She had lain awake for most of the night agonising over her dilemma. Mrs Prentice desperately wanted to help her young friend, but she was fearful about where this was all heading. She was sure that the longer Melanie avoided the police, the worse it would be for her when she was finally located. She also wondered whether she herself could be in trouble with the police and charged for harbouring a fugitive. As soon as Melanie was out of sight, Mrs Prentice climbed downstairs and flicked through the yellow pages. Once she'd found the number she needed, she picked up the phone and with a very heavy heart dialled the eleven digits that would connect her with Kirkwood Police Station.

\*   \*   \*   \*

Carmichael was still at home when he received the call from Kirkwood Police Station advising him that an old lady was claiming to have allowed Melanie Dreyfuss to stay with her for the last couple of nights.

'Get hold of Watson and tell him to meet me at her house,' he instructed the duty sergeant, after scribbling down the old lady's address on the back of an envelope.

Having ended the call, he hastily gulped down half of the coffee in his mug and headed for the front door, abandoning the slice of toast that had just popped out of the toaster. He quickly threw on his coat and was out of the door within seconds. Although there had been only a few inches of snowfall that night, the icy snow that lay underneath made the path very slippery. Not wishing to fall, Carmichael carefully negotiated the few steps leading down from his

201

house to the driveway where his snow-covered BMW was parked. Using the sleeve of his coat, he wiped away the thin layer of snow from the side window before opening the door and clambering inside. He started up his engine, put the heater on full blast, gave the windscreen wipers four strokes to clear away the previous evening's snow and headed off to the address he had written down on the envelope.

Once he was on his way, Carmichael made a call to Cooper to find out how he was progressing with the various duties assigned to him the day before. Having discovered that he had still to interview three of the four names on his list, and knowing that Rachel Dalton would almost certainly be more advanced in finishing her tasks, he told Cooper to get Rachel to give him a hand interviewing the people from Caroline Lovelace's party.

'We'll have our next briefing at two this afternoon,' he said to Cooper. 'By then, between you and Rachel, I expect you to have finished all the interviews. Hopefully Marc and I will also have managed to apprehend Melanie Dreyfuss.'

\*   \*   \*   \*

At 8 a.m. Melanie quietly entered the house. She had waited until that time as she knew that both her housemates would have already left for work by then. She could not be totally sure that she had avoided being spotted by the police, but figured that she should be fairly safe as long as she was in and out quickly.

\*   \*   \*   \*

It was Carmichael who arrived at Mrs Prentice's house first. He parked a little way down the lane and waited for Watson to arrive. As he waited, he mulled over in his mind all the clues that he and the team had amassed over the last five days. He enjoyed the challenge of solving complex cases and the deaths of Gerry Poole and Tamara Searle certainly fell into that category. Carmichael prided himself in being able to analyse evidence in a detached and pragmatic way. He always tried hard not to jump to conclusions and, although he did have hunches like everyone else, he believed that he was able to handle these gut feelings and would never allow them to eclipse the way he managed an investigation. In this case, though, that was proving to be a bigger challenge than normal.

By the time Watson's car pulled up next to him, Carmichael had not managed to develop his thoughts too far. He had concluded that there were two key aspects of the case that puzzled him the most and he decided that he needed to unravel these before he could make any real progress. The first was the abundance of coincidences. The two dead people both being invited guests at Caroline Lovelace's party and pretty much all the suspects also being at that party were the main coincidences that bothered him the most. However, the Amanda Buchannan and Tamara Searle relationship also struck him as being strange. He was not convinced that them both being at the same university and then both working at Sunrise Productions was a fluke and he was not convinced that Sally Crabtree had been totally honest with him when he had pressed her on this issue. Then there was the way Tamara's body had been posed, just like the sculpture that Sally Crabtree had created of her dead sister.

The second aspect of the case that perplexed him and needed answering was the apparent absence of any motive for either Tamara's death or for someone to deliberately freeze Poole's body, as Dr Stock believed.

Watson rushed over to Carmichael's car and clambered into the passenger seat.

'How do you want to play this?' he asked his boss.

'Let's get ourselves inside and see if we can find out when she's expecting Miss Dreyfuss to return,' replied Carmichael. 'If it's not too long, we can both wait. If it's going to be ages I'll call for some backup and will leave you to it. I'd like to interview Caroline Lovelace again.'

Watson nodded. 'That's fine with me,' he said.

\*     \*     \*     \*

Melanie was in and out of the house in about fifteen minutes. With a holdall full of clean clothes, her chequebook and her address book she made her way back towards Mrs Prentice's house. Her original plan had been to call Clare's brother from her house, then depending upon what he said, to spend an hour or so that morning trying to hook up with Clare. However, with it being so cold and her bag being so heavy, she decided that her best course of action would be to first get her stuff back to Mrs Prentice's house and to then call Travis Sands from there. As a result, instead of arriving back at the house at around 10.30 a.m. as she had initially expected, she trudged around the corner into Medway Court at just a little after 9 a.m., just as Carmichael was leaving.

Carmichael didn't see her at first, but she saw him and instantly recognised him as the policeman she had seen on the TV the day before and the one that had been at Caroline Lovelace's party.

Melanie tried to make her exit as quietly as she could, but in her haste she slipped on the ice and the thud of her hitting the ground attracted Carmichael's attention.

'Marc, she's here!' he shouted as he ran as fast as he could in her direction.

Watson and the two plain-clothed PCs who had been sent as backup flew out of the front door and joined Carmichael in hot pursuit of Melanie Dreyfuss.

Melanie's heart raced. She was about twenty yards away

from her pursuers but her bag was so heavy she knew they would catch her soon. As she ran, she managed to unzip the top of the holdall. Once she had managed to extract her chequebook and address book which lay on top of her clothes, she dropped the heavy bag and, now being free of its weight, sped off into the distance. Melanie had not been very successful at exams when she was at school but she was the fastest runner in her year and, once the heavy bag had been jettisoned, there was no chance of any of the four policemen catching her.

# Chapter 26

Melanie was smart enough to know that the police wouldn't only be swarming the streets of Newbridge looking for her, but also watching all the main roads out of the village. With no money and her sanctuary at Mrs Prentice's now gone, she decided that her best course of action would be to get to Gerry Poole's house which was only half a mile from Mrs Prentice's. Melanie figured that she would be fairly safe at Poole's house as it would be empty and nobody would expect her to go there. She also thought there may be some food and she might even find some money lying around that she could take. Most importantly, Melanie also knew where Gerry Poole hid his spare key.

\*   \*   \*   \*

After searching in vain for twenty minutes, the four officers regrouped at the front of Mrs Prentice's house in Medway Court.

'She's bloody fast,' exclaimed Watson, who was trying hard to catch his breath.

'What rotten luck,' replied Carmichael, who had abandoned his attempt to apprehend Melanie after running just twenty yards. Having retrieved Melanie's bag, he walked slowly back to the house. 'If only she'd have come back a few minutes earlier or even ten minutes later we would have caught her.'

'So what now?' asked Watson, still gasping for air.

'Get on the phone to the station and get them to put a car on all the exit roads out of the village,' he ordered. 'One of you needs to stay here in case she does double-back, the other two just keep looking. It's bloody cold out here so my guess is that she will try and hide out somewhere.'

'What about you?' Watson asked. 'What are you going to do?'

'I'm going to go and see my best friend, Caroline Lovelace,' he replied as he handed Watson Melanie's holdall. 'I'm then going back to the station for the debriefing with Cooper and Dalton. You don't need to join us, unless you find Miss Dreyfuss before then.'

Watson nodded. 'OK, sir,' he replied. 'I'll keep you up to speed.'

\* \* \* \*

Cooper and Rachel were totally oblivious to the drama unfolding that morning in Newbridge. They had divided between them the remaining names on Carmichael's list. Cooper elected to go to see Euen McIntyre at Kirkwood Academy and then, if he had time, travel over to Liverpool to speak with the GP, Dr Alan Wilson, at his surgery. Rachel was given the task of meeting up with Dr Sarah McIntyre. They knew that whatever happened they needed to be back at the station in Kirkwood at 2 p.m. for Carmichael's next briefing. They agreed that if they could not complete all the interviews in time they would have to finish off what was still left in either the afternoon or that evening.

\* \* \* \*

Cold and scared, Melanie eventually managed to make her way to Gerry Poole's isolated house on the outskirts of

Newbridge. As she crept round the back, Melanie could hear the sirens of the police cars as they headed into the village. She lifted up the glass lid of the crumbling potting frame. As she had expected, she found the spare key under the largest of the three brick-red plant pots.

Having carefully replaced the lid, she proceeded to the back door and let herself in. Although it was quite dark inside the house, she didn't dare turn on the kitchen light in case it alerted her presence to the neighbours.

The first thing she did was to place the address book on the table and dial Travis Sands' number.

'Hello,' replied Travis, who didn't recognise the number that flashed up on the screen of his expensive-looking mobile phone.

'Hello, Travis,' she said. 'It's Melanie, Clare's friend from the Angels. I was wondering if Clare was with you?'

On hearing who was calling him, Travis became more relaxed. He had met Melanie a few times when he'd been over to see Clare and he really fancied her. 'Oh, hi,' he replied trying hard to sound cool. 'She's not here.'

'Did she come to see you on Tuesday like she said she would?' Melanie asked.

'Na,' he replied. 'She's always doing that. She phoned and asked if she could kip down here for a few days but she didn't show.'

'Did you not worry when she didn't turn up?' she asked in amazement.

'No,' replied Travis with surprise. 'She's always doing it.'

'I think she's in big trouble,' continued Melanie. 'I saw her on Monday night and she was really scared. She's got mixed up in something and she said she needed to get herself out of the area for a while. I lent her my debit card to draw out some cash and that's the last I saw of her.'

Travis laughed down the phone. 'You must be out of your mind lending her your debit card. She'll have fleeced you and will be off on a big spending spree. She's done it before.'

'No,' said Melanie firmly. 'I'm sure she wouldn't do that. She was really worried on Monday.'

Travis paused for a few seconds. 'How about I come down there and we could try and find her together,' he said. 'I could be there in a few hours.'

His proposal took Melanie by surprise. She could certainly use someone to help her she thought, but, before she had a chance to answer, Travis made his motives much clearer.

'I could bring down some grass and maybe we could crash out at yours?' he suggested.

'Sod off, Travis,' exclaimed Melanie before hanging up.

\*　\*　\*　\*

It was only a short drive from Newbridge to Caroline Lovelace's house at the posh end of Moulton Bank. Carmichael knew that *The Lovelace Show* was only on air from Monday to Thursday, so he assumed that he might be able to find her at home. If not, maybe her MP husband might be available to answer some questions. So without any appointment he started the short journey. En route, he called Cooper.

'How's it going, Paul?' he asked. 'Have you managed to talk with all the people from the party yet?'

Cooper had just arrived in Liverpool. 'I've spoken to Euen McIntyre,' he said. 'Nice guy and very helpful, but I didn't glean anything much from him. He's only really connected with the Lovelaces and their set through his other half, who works occasionally on the show. Rachel's hoping to speak to her today, so with a bit of luck she'll fair better with his wife.'

'So where are you now?' Carmichael asked.

'I'm in Liverpool,' replied Cooper. 'I'm just about to go in and see Dr Wilson.'

'And how's the bad cold?' enquired Carmichael.

'The man flu you mean,' joked Cooper. 'It's OK. I'm still a bit shivery and my bloody nose won't stop running, but I'm better than I was.'

'Maybe the good Dr Wilson can give you something for it,' remarked Carmichael.

'Maybe,' replied Cooper.

'You'll be at the briefing at two won't you, Paul?' Carmichael enquired.

'Absolutely,' replied Cooper as upbeat as he could.

'OK, I'll let you go,' continued Carmichael, before ending the call.

\* \* \* \*

After her conversation with Travis, Melanie remained in the kitchen to gather her thoughts. She knew Clare was no angel, so it was conceivable that Travis's theory about her doing a runner was true, but Melanie did find that a little hard to accept. She filled up the kettle and searched in the cupboards for some teabags or coffee. Having eventually found a half-filled coffee jar and some sugar in a Tate and Lyle bag, she poured herself a black sugary drink and gazed up at the clock. Amazingly it was still only 10.45 a.m. Melanie stayed in the kitchen for the next fifteen minutes. She could not think where her friend was. Also she could not understand how the police knew she was staying at Mrs Prentice's. As she pondered what her next move should be, she took her phone out of her pocket and flicked through the menu until she found her contact list. When she found Clare's number she pressed dial.

You never know, she might answer, she thought.

The phone rang once in her ear. A few seconds later it rang a second time. This time though it was accompanied by the sound of another mobile, which appeared to be ringing in the next room. Without turning off her phone, Melanie carefully opened the door leading from the kitchen to the lounge and crept through. As soon as the door was open, her nostrils became filled with a pungent smell, the source of which was the cold, lifeless body of Clare Sands, sitting upright in Gerry Poole's armchair.

# Chapter 27

Chief Inspector Hewitt's nightmare of a week continued. He had gone home relatively early the evening before and, with the aid of countless hot drinks and a few more whiskeys than normal, had hoped to wake the next day with his heavy cold under control. Despite having a good night's sleep, his condition that Friday morning had improved very little. To make matters worse, he woke up late and now also had to cope with a sore head, a consequence of the quantity of whisky he had consumed the evening before.

By 10 o'clock he had managed to struggle in his hire car through the snow into the office. Upon his arrival at Kirkwood Station, he incarcerated himself in his office with a pot of tea and some paracetamol tablets and watched a tape of Carmichael's performance on *The Lovelace Show*. He then read the coverage of the interview in the various papers that Angela had brought him. Although a few were reasonably balanced in their treatment of the encounter, the 'red tops' had less than flattering coverage, the worst headline being 'LOVELACE LAMBASTS BUNGLING BOBBY IN TAMARA INQUIRY'.

Having then spent the next thirty minutes fending off calls, first from the Chief Constable's office, then local radio and finally the national TV, he was now thoroughly regretting his decision to get out of bed that morning.

'Get me Carmichael on the phone!' he shouted through to Angela.

Carmichael was already parked on Caroline Lovelace's drive when Angela's call came through.

'Steve,' whispered Angela, so her boss could not hear. 'The Chief wants to talk to you urgently. I should warn you he's watched a tape of yesterday's *Lovelace Show* and he's in a foul mood.'

'OK,' replied Carmichael with more than a hint of despair in his voice. 'Put him through.'

Angela patched Carmichael through to the Chief, but could not help herself from staying on line to listen to their conversation.

As soon as the phone clicked to indicate they were hooked up Hewitt spoke. 'I've seen the tape from yesterday. Have you seen it?'

'No, sir,' replied Carmichael. 'I had it taped at home but chose not to look at it last night.'

'Very wise,' replied Hewitt. 'I can only say that it doesn't paint you in a good light.'

'I expect not,' said Carmichael.

'It's also in most of the national papers today and my phone's been hot all morning with the press and, worse still, the Chief Constable's office too,' continued Hewitt. 'I also had Roy Lovelace on the line last night telling me to take you off the case.'

That word again! thought Carmichael mischievously.

'I hope you supported me, sir,' he responded.

'Of course I did,' replied Hewitt firmly. 'However, you need to start making more progress and be careful in how you deal with the Lovelaces. They are both very influential people and it's perfectly clear that they're just waiting for any opportunity to pounce on you. So make sure you don't put a foot wrong.'

'Be assured I'm fully aware of that, sir,' replied Carmichael.

'I know they can make things difficult for us on this one. However, I've a case to solve and I'll be damned if I change the way I carry out my investigation to satisfy them. As it happens I'm outside their house as we speak and quite honestly there are a number of questions that they need to answer.'

'Surely they're not suspects' said Hewitt, the traces of panic evident in his voice.

'Well, not exactly,' replied Carmichael. 'But their names are entwined in every aspect of this case. They are related to the first corpse. Tamara Searle worked for the same production company as Caroline. The victims were both invited to the dinner party that I attended last Saturday and Tamara's body was found in the exact pose of a famous statue that Caroline's friend had sculpted and given her as a present. I certainly think they need to explain a few of these coincidences.'

Hewitt paused to consider what Carmichael had just told him.

'I fully agree,' he replied. 'But tread carefully. I will give you my full support, but for God's sake try to be more circumspect in the way you move forward on this. There's a limit to how far I'm going to stick my neck out for you. If you go in like a bull in a china shop, you're on your own.'

'I appreciate your support, sir,' replied Carmichael, who was genuinely impressed and surprised how supportive his boss had been already. 'I'll be tactful, I swear.'

'Good,' replied Hewitt. 'Keep me updated, though, as I fear that now the press are against us they won't let up until we crack this one.'

'Thank you, sir, I will,' replied Carmichael who was now well aware of the delicate predicament he found himself in. 'I'm due to have my next debrief with the team at two o'clock. I'll give you a full update after that meeting.'

Even though she knew Clare was dead, Melanie checked her friend's pulse just as she had been taught at Sea Cadets when she was a young girl. She then picked up the handwritten note that had been carefully placed on the small ornate table beside Clare's chair.

It took Melanie only a few seconds to read the note. It was unmistakably in Clare's scruffy handwriting. It was then that Melanie noticed the bags of clothes stacked up behind the armchair. She wondered whether the debit card she had lent her friend on Monday evening was somewhere in the pile. Calmly Melanie started to rummage through the first bag of clothes. It didn't take her very long to conclude that they were not Clare's belongings. There were all manner of items in the bags, from underwear to a mobile phone. It was not until she found a bank statement that she realised the bits and pieces belonged to Tamara Searle. Melanie searched through all the bags to see if she could find her debit card, but she couldn't. She did, however, find Tamara's purse, which still held all her credit cards and over eighty pounds in cash.

She was not sure what she should do next. She didn't want to leave poor Clare in that state and she knew that the police needed to be informed, but she also didn't want to have to give herself up to the police just yet.

Melanie folded up the note and put it in her pocket. She then quietly tidied up the possessions in the bags, so nobody would realise that she had been rifling through them. Having sorted out the bags, Melanie returned to the kitchen and started to hide any trace of her having been there. As she did so she carefully considered her options.

*   *   *   *

Carmichael knocked loudly on the Lovelaces' front door. After waiting a few seconds it was opened by Caroline

Lovelace. By the expression on her face she was certainly shocked to see Carmichael standing on her doorstep.

'I was wondering whether I might have a few moments of your precious time?' he asked in a polite if slightly patronising manner.

'Of course, as long as it's fairly quick,' she replied with her usual air of confidence. 'I've an appointment in precisely forty minutes.'

'That should give me adequate time to conclude my questions,' Carmichael replied with a faint smile. 'May I come inside?'

Caroline gestured for him to come into the hallway.

'Thank you,' said Carmichael. 'Is your husband at home too?'

'He's about somewhere,' responded Caroline flippantly. 'However, he won't be able to talk with you this afternoon. He's very busy.'

Carmichael walked through into the hallway and removed his overcoat.

'Is there anywhere I can leave this?' he asked.

'How rude of me,' replied Caroline. 'I'll take it and hang it up for you.'

Caroline took Carmichael's coat. 'Please follow me, Inspector,' she commanded.

Carmichael followed his host as ordered down the long corridor that divided the house in half. At the far end stood a tall metal hat stand, where Caroline hung up Carmichael's coat. 'Please go through to the conservatory,' said Caroline with a theatrical wave of her arm in the direction of a large stained wooden door. Carmichael again dutifully did as he was told and entered the room.

The conservatory was a magnificent room with a spectacular view of the Lovelaces' well-maintained private grounds. Shrouded in a blanket of snow, the garden fell away sharply behind the property down to a small frozen lake at the end of the grounds. Beyond the garden boundary lay snow-covered fields which stretched for miles. In the far distance, Carmichael could make out the outline of the town of Southport and, if he craned his neck to the right, he could just about make out the unmistakable shape of Blackpool Tower, some sixty miles away.

'What a lovely room!' remarked Carmichael. 'You certainly have a magnificent view.'

For the first time that morning Caroline appeared to relax. 'I'm glad you think so. We do like it here,' she remarked. Then with another grandiloquent motion of her arm, she gestured to Carmichael to sit down. Again Carmichael followed her directive.

'I'd offer you tea but I am in a bit of a rush,' continued Caroline.

Carmichael held up his hand and shook his head. 'I'm absolutely fine,' he replied. 'I realise you're busy so I will not take much of your time, but there are some questions I'd like to ask you.'

Caroline sat down opposite him. 'How can I help you?' she said.

'Well, there are a few things that really puzzle me about the deaths which I am hoping you can help me with,' he said. 'First I'm interested to know about your relationship with some of the people at the party.'

'Anyone in particular?' Caroline asked.

'Why don't we start with Tamara Searle,' replied Carmichael.

'As I told you before, she was a lovely girl,' announced Caroline. 'She was always smiling, she was talented, popular, ambitious and a real asset to the show. It's such a tragedy she was murdered.'

'So you liked her?' Carmichael confirmed.

'Of course!' replied Caroline indignantly. 'Of course I liked her.'

'It's just I was told by someone that you didn't have much time for her,' said Carmichael calmly.

'Who told you that?' replied Caroline angrily.

'I'm sure you will appreciate that I'm not able to share such information with you,' continued Carmichael. 'However, they did take the trouble to tell me how surprised they were by your attitude during the piece on your show yesterday.'

Caroline sank back into her chair and smiled broadly. 'Oh that's it, is it, Inspector?' she said coolly. 'You're still a bit sore about the fact that I made you look a little bit out of your depth on the show. Please don't take it personally. However, you have to admit you asked for it. In my profession, Inspector, you have to be in tune with your public and our viewers will be grieving badly about Tamara's death. For many of our audience, particularly our more elderly ones, she was a member of their family. I just addressed you as they would have wanted me to do. Not because you're bad at your job – I'm sure you're very capable – but because you were insensitive and talked about her as if she was just another case, a statistic. To them she was very real.'

Carmichael waited patiently for Caroline to finish, but chose not to respond to her observations on his style. 'So you would say you and Tamara were very friendly?' he said.

'We weren't best friends, if that's what your informant was insinuating,' replied Caroline. 'We didn't socialise all the time either, but we got on fine and I liked her. In fact, as I think I told you on Wednesday at the studio, she reminded me of myself when I was her age.'

Carmichael nodded. 'Talking about your background,' he continued. 'I understand that you grew up over a chip shop in Wigan. You've come a long way since then?'

It was clear from Caroline's body language and facial expression that she didn't like this reminder of her past.

'I see you've been talking to Sally,' she commented. 'She is fond of telling people about Caroline Murphy and how

218

modest my beginnings were. I'm not embarrassed about my childhood, but I don't shout about it from the rooftops. I'm not like some so-called celebrities who seem to feel that their humble roots made them what they are. I'm proud of my achievements, but all I've accomplished is down to talent and bloody hard work. It has got absolutely nothing to do with my modest upbringing.'

'Marrying an accomplished barrister and MP probably helped too,' remarked Carmichael mischievously.

'When I married Roy I was already doing reasonably well,' replied Caroline. 'I can assure you that my success is not due to my marriage, Inspector.'

'What about your relationship with Sally Crabtree?' Carmichael asked.

'We are old friends from Aston University, as I'm sure Sally told you,' replied Caroline. 'We have been friends for over twenty years.'

Carmichael pulled out the miniature figure from his jacket pocket and placed it on the small coffee table in front of them.

'Did you know her sister, Janet?' he enquired.

'I misjudged you, Inspector,' replied Caroline haughtily. 'You're more thorough than I thought. Yes, I did know Janet and, yes, she and Roy were a couple, but their relationship was over well before I came on the scene.'

It was clear that Caroline thought Sally had said much more to him, a fact which Carmichael was keen to conceal.

'So why on earth do you have a sculpture in your office of your husband's ex-lover, who tragically took her own life and is also your PA's mother?' Carmichael asked. 'I'm sure you can appreciate how strange that appears.'

'Indeed I can,' replied Caroline. 'The answer is simple. It was a present from Sally. I like it and it's valuable.'

Carmichael picked up the miniature and put it back in his jacket pocket. 'So what about the others at the party,' he asked. 'The Cashmans for example. Tell me about them?'

'Declan and Roy have been friends for years,' replied Caroline. 'He's a very successful businessman and has earned millions in the last ten years from property development. He's a go-getter, very driven and has charm in abundance. Emma is very quiet and unassuming, but she does so much for charity. She's a really generous lady and is extremely committed to The Helpful Angels.'

'An unusual couple then?' commented Carmichael.

'Yes, I'd agree,' replied Caroline. 'But they are very close and get on very well.'

'Tell me about The Helpful Angels?' he probed.

'It was Emma's brainchild,' replied Caroline. 'It's an organisation totally focused on helping young women from poor backgrounds to break away from crime and also out of poverty. They do that by taking them out of their normal environment and giving them work that helps them develop and see that there's hope for them.'

'I understand you're also involved with The Angels?' he said.

'In a very modest way,' replied Caroline graciously. 'My name and celebrity status can open doors for them at times with PR and potential clients, but Emma is the driving force.'

'What about the others who were at the party?' Carmichael asked.

'Well, Dr Wilson is another friend of Roy's,' she replied. 'You'd have to speak to Roy about him. The McIntyres are a very successful couple. Sarah has helped me on the show many times. She's a leading light in the world of psychology. She's very accomplished and very clever. I don't know Euen that well but he is very successful in his field too. He's a headmaster of a large school.

'I see,' Carmichael replied. 'So how did you come to choose such an eclectic mix for your party?'

Caroline smiled. 'We select our guests very carefully, Inspector, 'she announced. 'What we try and do is mix up people from our two worlds but try and make sure there's always a balance between the sexes and between singles and couples. Also, we always try to invite some new people along too.'

'That's where Penny and I came in,' confirmed Carmichael.

'Yes, that's correct,' responded Caroline. 'But I also genuinely wanted to ask your wife about the school she works at too.'

'And have you decided whether you will be sending your daughter to the village school?' Carmichael asked.

'On reflection probably not,' replied Caroline. 'No disrespect to your wife or her school, but we will probably send Chelsea to an all-girls boarding school. We think that there may be security issues if we send her to a local school.'

'I see,' replied Carmichael.

Caroline made no attempt to hide the fact that she was looking at her watch.

'I'll only keep you a few more minutes,' Carmichael confirmed. 'I've just a few more questions.'

Caroline frowned. 'I've to be away in about ten minutes so if you could be quick.'

'First, do you know why anyone would wish to kill Tamara?' he asked.

'Absolutely not,' replied Caroline. 'It all seems so pointless.'

'Did she have any enemies?' Carmichael enquired. 'Maybe she had a jealous work rival or an old boyfriend.'

'If she had either it was news to me,' replied Caroline. 'I can't remember her mentioning a boyfriend, but that's not to say she didn't have one.'

'What about Gerry?' continued Carmichael. 'Do you know why anyone would want to kill him?'

'But I thought you said he died of natural causes!' she said with some confusion.

'He died of a heart attack but that may have been brought on by being locked in a freezer,' replied Carmichael.

'What! You think he was frozen alive?' questioned Caroline.

'We're not sure,' replied Carmichael. 'However, it's one line we're following.'

'You'd have to ask Roy,' replied Caroline. 'He was his relative not mine. As I told you before I didn't much care for him, so I never really took the time to find out about his life. I know this sounds very cruel now he's dead, but he was pretty ordinary and quite dull really. He'd also become pathetic and indecisive, two qualities I hate in men.'

'But if you disliked him so much why did you invite him to your party?' asked Carmichael.

'I didn't; it was my husband's idea. So again you'd have to ask my husband,' replied Caroline, who was clearly now getting anxious about the passing time.

'Well, I've just one more question,' announced Carmichael.

'I need you to provide me with a detailed breakdown of your movements from the end of the show on Monday until Tamara's body was discovered on Wednesday morning.'

'Excuse me!' exclaimed Caroline indignantly. 'Do I take it that I am now a murder suspect!'

'I wouldn't put it quite like that,' replied Carmichael calmly. 'But I would like to know anyway. If you would be so good as to come down to the station in the next forty-eight hours with those details, I would be very grateful.'

Although inwardly Carmichael was taking great pleasure in seeing Caroline looking so infuriated, he tried hard to remain calm and not let his gratification show. Having finished the interview, Carmichael stood up and started to walk towards the door. 'If you could also ask your husband to call me as soon as possible,' he said as he passed Caroline his card. 'I will need to interview him too.'

Caroline snatched the card from Carmichael's hand. 'I think you're going to regret crossing Roy and me, Inspector.'

'Maybe so,' replied Carmichael coolly. 'But in the same way you're conscious of the needs of your loving public, Mrs Lovelace, I am very aware of the responsibility I have to the community I work for and I can assure you they would be very unhappy if I didn't investigate every potential avenue.'

Without another word Caroline flung open the door of the conservatory and marched angrily down the corridor. In contrast, Carmichael deliberately took his time. He collected his overcoat from the hat stand and slowly put it on before he followed her. When he eventually reached the front door, Caroline was already there holding it ajar.

'Have a nice day,' he said as he made his exit.

'Your superior will be hearing from us; you can count on that,' she snarled.

'No change there then,' was Carmichael's calm, measured reply. 'Actually there was one other thing. You've mentioned the word "celebrity" a few times today, Mrs Lovelace. Is that how you see yourself?'

Caroline paused before answering. 'There's no reason to pretend anything else,' she replied. 'That's what I am.'

She then slammed the door shut, leaving Carmichael alone to the cold winter elements.

# Chapter 28

Even with her experience as a cleaner, it took Melanie almost an hour to wipe away any evidence of her being at Gerry Poole's house that morning. Once she was comfortable that every trace of her visit had been eradicated, she called for a taxi on her mobile phone.

She was careful to ask the driver to collect her from the corner of the next street, as she realised that once poor Clare's body had been found by the police, the taxi driver could well become a potential witness and she didn't want to be linked to the house. Melanie asked the taxi to arrive in thirty minutes, which would allow her enough time to complete two important tasks.

The first of these was to select a number of items from the house to take with her. Apart from Clare's suicide note, Melanie also decided to take Tamara's purse with the money and credit cards; Tamara's mobile phone; the smallest holdall she could find from on top of Gerry Poole's wardrobe and an unopened packet of biscuits that she found in the kitchen larder. To her surprise and delight, while she was rummaging in the bags of Tamara's possessions, Melanie had discovered that Miss Searle was also a size 10, which enabled her to make use of some of Tamara's clothes. Having had to dump her own clothes earlier when she had been chased by the police, this stroke of luck meant that Melanie would neither have to risk going back to her flat nor waste any of the eighty pounds she had found in the purse on clothes.

Without any hesitation Melanie selected the most practical items of Tamara's clothing she could find. She had no qualms in including Tamara's underwear among the items she took. She expected to be on the run for a good few more days yet and clean underwear would be needed.

Her second job was to key in a lengthy text to Sergeant Watson on her mobile phone. She didn't send it though. She decided that she would only do that once she was well away from Gerry Poole's house.

Melanie quietly slipped out of the house and made her way to Beach Avenue, where she had asked the taxi to pick her up. Fortunately for her the car was already waiting when she arrived, so luckily she didn't have to stand out in the open. She quickly jumped into the back of the taxi and sat as low down as she could in the back seat. Melanie knew that some of the taxis in the village had still to get chip and pin readers installed and wondered whether she could get away with using Tamara's credit card to pay the fare. Her eyes scoured the front for a few moments and to her delight she could not see a reader. She fully expected the taxi driver to refuse to take a payment by card, but she still thought it was worth a try.

'Do you accept credit cards?' she asked in a confident voice, even though her heart was beating so loudly she could almost hear it. 'You see I don't have much cash on me.'

'Yes,' the driver responded, without bothering to turn around. 'But I'm afraid there will be a ten per cent charge added.'

'Oh that's OK,' replied Melanie with a wry smile. 'Can you take me to Kirkwood train station please?'

\* \* \* \*

Carmichael entered the incident room at Kirkwood Police Station to start the debriefing at exactly 2 p.m. He was surprised to see that, in addition to Watson, Cooper and

Rachel Dalton, Chief Inspector Hewitt and the two PCs who had carried out the house-to-house were also in the room.

'I didn't expect to see you, sir,' he commented.

'I thought I should hear the team's progress first hand,' replied Hewitt. 'And I've asked PC Jamieson and PC Morley to join us, as I thought you may need some additional help to bring this case to a swift conclusion.'

'Your support is appreciated,' replied Carmichael, who welcomed the offer of extra resources but was not sure he liked his boss taking such a personal interest. As always, Carmichael wanted to run the show.

'OK, Rachel, why don't you update us first on what you've uncovered,' he said, fully expecting that she would have made good headway on her assigned tasks.

'I've spoken with Caroline's friend Sarah McIntyre this morning,' replied Rachel. 'It's clear that they are very close. Sarah was very complimentary about Caroline. She didn't seem so keen on Roy though. She called him a chauvinist, political fly-by-night at one point when we were talking.'

'Really,' said Carmichael with interest. 'In what context?'

'It was when I asked her about whether they socialised a lot,' continued Rachel, who quickly started referring to her notebook. 'She said they didn't, but that this was really because she didn't like the condescending way Roy treated women and that, in her opinion, his political arguments were not very well thought out.'

'That's very interesting,' replied Carmichael. 'What about Tamara Searle and Gerry Poole. Did she say anything about them?'

'Yes and no,' replied Rachel. 'She said she had never met Gerry Poole. She said she did know Tamara though as she had met her on the set of *The Lovelace Show.*'

'And what did she think of Tamara?' Carmichael asked.

'She described her as talented but very pushy,' replied Rachel. 'She was honest enough to say she didn't like her much, although she did say she was very shocked to hear about her death.'

'So is she a possible murder suspect in your view, DC Dalton?' interjected Hewitt.

Rachel pondered the question for a few moments. 'Well, she says she was at home with her husband on Monday and Tuesday evening. However, I guess they could be in it together.'

'I can confirm that Euen McIntyre also told me they were both at home on Monday and Tuesday evening,' Cooper said.

'Because of their lack of an alibi, they need to stay as possible suspects,' announced Carmichael. 'Although I can't see why they would want to kill Tamara and they don't even seem to have known Gerry Poole at all.' Carmichael wrote their names on the flipchart behind him, then turned back to face Rachel. 'What else did you find out?'

'On the negative side, I was unable to get any tapes from the garage for the third of February,' she said. 'The duty manager forgot to switch the machine on until after eleven, which was forty minutes after the fuel was bought.'

'Damn!' exclaimed Carmichael.

'On a more positive note, I've now had enlarged the best close-up of the person who bought the train ticket to Manchester on Monday evening,' announced Rachel, who at the same time started to pass around copies of the photograph.

'That's not Melanie Dreyfuss,' Watson said.

'No it's not,' confirmed Cooper. 'Do we know who she is?'

'I do,' replied Carmichael, who recognised her as the blonde waitress from the party. 'It's Clare Sands. She works at The Helpful Angels; she's a friend of Melanie's. According to Mrs Cashman, she's also gone missing.'

'She's the main cleaner for Gerry Poole,' added Watson. 'Melanie told us that the other day.'

'According to Roy Lovelace, she was also having an affair with Gerry Poole,' added Carmichael. 'I'm not convinced that's true, though, and so far there's no evidence to support his claim.'

'It may be worth looking at though, boss,' remarked Watson. 'If they were involved, Clare Sands would probably know more about his finances and I think there's more than a fair chance that Sands and Dreyfuss were after his money.'

'I don't know about that,' Carmichael replied. 'However, I fully agree that they have to be suspects.'

Carmichael turned around and, below the names of Sarah and Euen McIntyre, he added the names of Melanie Dreyfuss and Clare Sands to his suspects list.

'We need to apprehend and talk with these two ladies as soon as we can,' announced Hewitt, who clearly had some sympathy for Watson's view. 'They are undoubtedly implicated in some way.'

'I fully agree,' piped up Watson, who was pleased that Hewitt shared his theory about Melanie's involvement.

'So, Marc, how did you get on in Newbridge?' asked Carmichael, trying to move the conversation on. 'Have there been any sightings of Melanie since she absconded earlier today?'

'No,' replied Watson meekly. 'She's just vanished into thin air.'

Carmichael rolled his eyes upwards. 'After this debriefing you three need to get back there and continue the search,' he said, addressing his comments to Watson and the two PCs. 'Did you check out the houses she cleans in the area.'

The three officers all looked decidedly uncomfortable. 'Er, no, not yet,' replied Watson.

'Why the hell not?' said Carmichael, who was starting to get angry. 'I suspect they would be the first places she might look to hide out, particularly if she has a friendly old lady there like Mrs Prentice. Actually Poole's house is in Newbridge; did you look there?'

Watson and the two PCs started to glance at each other. 'Er, no,' replied Watson again. 'Not yet.'

'Well, make it your first call after you've finished here,' replied Carmichael, who felt himself getting close to losing his temper. He took a deep breath before turning again to face Rachel. 'OK, Rachel, is that everything from you?' he asked as calmly as he could.

Rachel's face showed she had some more news that she desperately wanted to share. 'Well, yesterday I spoke to a few old university friends of Tamara Searle and of Amanda Buchannan from Lincoln,' she announced. 'And it would appear that Amanda and Tamara were at first very close friends, but by all accounts Amanda developed a massive crush on Tamara. The friend said that she didn't think anything happened, but at some function in their first year Amanda declared her feelings for Tamara and made a bit of a fool of herself. As a consequence the two didn't socialise much after that.'

'So they're lesbians!' announced Watson.

'No,' replied Rachel. 'The person I spoke to reckoned it was just a crush. At the time, she said, Amanda was just a very innocent and not very worldly eighteen-year-old girl and that, later on at university, Amanda had quite a few heterosexual relationships.'

'What about Tamara though?' asked Cooper astutely.

'Well, according to all the people I spoke to,' continued Rachel 'she didn't have any relationships at all while she was at university, which is strange, as she was very outgoing and a good-looking young woman.'

'That is strange,' concurred Carmichael. 'I'd like you to talk with Amanda Buchannan some more about that Rachel.'

'Now you be very careful, Rachel,' Watson whispered to her. 'Don't get yourself too tarted up in case she takes a shine to you.'

'One last thing,' said Rachel, trying hard to ignore Watson's jibe. 'I've just received the summary of Tamara's incoming and outgoing calls up until Wednesday from her service provider.'

'What does it show?' asked Carmichael.

'It shows her last outgoing call at ten on Monday evening,' replied Rachel. 'But as yet I don't know who the number belongs to. I'll check that as soon as we are finished.'

'I take it that's everything now,' Carmichael enquired of his capable DC.

'Yes,' replied Rachel. 'That's me up to date.'

'OK,' he continued. 'Unless anyone has any objections, I think we need to add Amanda Buchannan's name to our list too.'

Without exception, everyone gathered in the incident room nodded or grunted their agreement.

'What about you, Cooper?' asked Carmichael once he had added the fifth name to the list. 'What progress have you made?'

Cooper smiled. 'I can't match what Rachel has managed to unearth, but I've made some progress.'

'How did you get on trying to find Tamara's personal possessions from her cottage?' Carmichael asked.

'No joy at all,' replied Cooper. 'We have scoured a two-mile area around her house, but have come up with nothing.'

PC Jamieson and PC Morley, who had been given the brunt of this task, glanced knowingly at each other.

'My guess is that the stuff will have been dumped in the skip days ago,' commented Jamieson.

'Maybe,' replied Carmichael. 'However, I still want you to keep looking. Her stuff must have been taken out of her house for a reason, so we need to find it.'

'Agreed,' replied Cooper. 'But Jamieson's right. I think our chances are slim.'

'So what did you discover from the interviews you had with the guests at Caroline's dinner party?' Carmichael asked.

'I interviewed three people from the party,' said Cooper. 'The first was Declan Cashman. He's a real cocky character. I only managed to get a few minutes with him, but I didn't like him much and I think he should be added to your list.'

'Why do you say that?' asked Hewitt.

'First, he knew Poole through his association with Roy Lovelace,' announced Cooper with conviction. 'Secondly, he didn't have a very good alibi for Tuesday evening. He says he was working late alone at the office, but he has no witnesses to corroborate this story.'

'Is there a thirdly?' enquired Carmichael, who expected to hear more.

'Only that he's a smug arse as well,' replied Cooper, before sneezing loudly into his handkerchief.

'Well, I'll add him to the list but, based on what you've said, I think he's an outsider,' commented Carmichael. 'What about Monday afternoon and evening? Did he have an alibi for then?'

'Yes,' replied Cooper, who had managed to compose himself. 'He was with clients all afternoon in Manchester and in the evening they all went to a club. He maintains that he didn't leave the club until two in the morning, which his clients have verified.'

'So if Dr Stock's assumption that Tamara's death happened on Monday is correct, he's in the clear.'

'That's correct,' replied Cooper reluctantly. 'But if it's Tuesday he may be our man.'

Carmichael added the sixth name to the list.

'Who else did you meet up with from the party?' Carmichael asked.

'Euen McIntyre and Dr Alan Wilson,' replied Cooper.

231

'McIntyre hardly knew the Lovelaces and maintained he had never met Poole and, apart from seeing Tamara Searle on TV, had never clapped eyes on her before Saturday. I agree his alibi is weak, so he should perhaps be on our list, but I don't think he's involved.'

'What about Dr Wilson?' Carmichael enquired.

'In my view, he's a non-starter too,' said Cooper. 'He had known Gerry Poole for years, but not well. He appears to be just about the only person any of us have met who had a good word to say about him too, but I'm sure he's not involved in Poole's death or the freezing of his body.'

'Why do you say that?' said Hewitt. 'As a doctor, surely he would be up on the ways to preserve a body, or to induce a heart attack by freezing without leaving a trace.'

'You may be right, sir,' conceded Cooper. 'However, I don't think he's our man.'

'What about Tamara?' enquired Rachel. 'Did he know her before Saturday's dinner party?'

'He maintained not,' replied Cooper.

'I think he needs to go on your list too,' Hewitt said to Carmichael.

'What about an alibi for Monday and Tuesday?' enquired Carmichael.

'To be honest, sir,' replied Cooper sheepishly. 'I forgot to ask.'

'OK,' said Carmichael. 'Until we know more, we need to add him too.'

'So we already have seven names,' announced Hewitt. 'Any more we need to add?'

'We certainly need to add Sally Crabtree,' said Carmichael. 'She knew Gerry Poole and Tamara Searle, she was at the party and I'm still not sure why the pose from her statue was copied by whoever left Tamara on Tuesday night. I really liked her, but she needs to stay firmly on our list in my view.'

Carmichael wrote Sally Crabtree's name under the rest.

'So is that it?' enquired Hewitt. 'Eight suspects.'

'You need to make it ten,' announced Carmichael, who turned and started scribbling again, this time not underneath the other names but right at the top of his list. 'We need to add Caroline and Roy Lovelace. They have to be our main suspects in this case.'

The skin on Hewitt's face became pale. 'You must be joking, Carmichael,' he said loudly. 'Roy Lovelace is an MP and is very well connected with the police. There's no way he would be involved in anything so sordid.'

Carmichael shrugged his shoulders. 'I agree this may not make our jobs that easy, but they have to be prime suspects. They knew both of the dead people well, they organised the party, selected the guests and even chose The Helpful Angels agency to serve the meal. Roy Lovelace has avoided meeting me to be interviewed and you have to admit Caroline has been less than helpful to us so far.'

Hewitt looked decidedly uncomfortable. Theatrically, he pushed back his shirt sleeve to look at his watch. 'I need to be on a conference call,' he announced. 'I'll leave it to you, Inspector, to direct your team. However, come up and see me when you've finished the briefing. We need to discuss the political fallout on this one.'

'Right you are, sir,' replied Carmichael coolly. 'I'll be up with you in about thirty minutes.'

It was not until Hewitt had left and was well out of earshot that anyone spoke. It was Watson who made the first comment. 'I think you may have touched a raw nerve there, sir.'

'Maybe I did,' replied Carmichael. 'But the Lovelaces are genuine suspects and, in spite of their positions, they need to be treated just as we would any other suspect.'

'I fully agree, sir,' replied Watson, 'but my money is still on Melanie Dreyfuss and Clare Sands.'

Carmichael smiled. 'I know and for that reason I want you

to get on with the search for them. Take PC Jamieson and get yourselves back to Newbridge. Check out Poole's house first, but before you go, let me have Melanie's mobile number. I'll call her too. You never know a new voice might encourage her to pick up.'

Watson scribbled down the number on a scrap of paper and handed it to Carmichael, before heading off with PC Jamieson.

'One final thing,' announced Carmichael just before the two officers had managed to get through the door. 'I'd like you two on duty on Saturday. I know it's short notice but we need to get this one cracked and I don't want anyone saying that we weren't committed.'

Both Watson and Jamieson looked less than pleased with the prospect of having to work the next day. 'Don't feel hard done by; I'll be in too and Rachel and Morley will be working on Sunday.'

Watson and Jamieson departed without saying anything more.

Then turning to Rachel, Carmichael said, 'I'd like you and PC Morley to start checking out Tamara's last incoming and outgoing calls. I'm sure they will tell us something. Then when you're done with that, get over and interview Amanda Buchannan again. Put her under some pressure and find out what was really going on between her and Tamara.'

On hearing their instructions, Rachel Dalton and PC Morley got up and left the interview room.

'What about me?' enquired Cooper, still struggling with his cold.

'You can get yourself off home,' replied Carmichael. 'I think you came back too soon. Get some rest over the weekend so that you're a hundred per cent fit on Monday.'

'What about Dr Wilson?' asked Cooper. 'Don't you want me to get back to him and check out his alibi for Monday and Tuesday?'

'No, I'll do that,' replied Carmichael. 'You just get yourself home and get some rest.'

Cooper was surprised, but relieved that he had been excused duties until Monday. He felt totally shattered and was only too happy to be sent home.

Once Cooper had left and he was alone in the interview room, Carmichael started to read through the various lists of facts and theories that the team had unearthed. He then spent a few moments studying the photographs of Tamara Searle and Gerry Poole. He looked again at the miniature figure that he had borrowed from Sally Crabtree, then finally he looked at the ten names he had written on the board. He went through the names in his head one by one. Although he conceded it was possible for the McIntyres, Declan Cashman and Dr Wilson to be implicated in some way, his nose told him that Tamara's killer and the mysterious freezing of Gerry Poole was more likely to be the work of one or more of the others. His instincts pointed him in the direction of Sally Crabtree, Amanda Buchannan or Caroline Lovelace as being the most likely candidates for Tamara's murder. As for Poole, that one really baffled him still, but on balance he felt that Roy Lovelace, Clare Sands or Melanie Dreyfuss were the people most likely to be responsible.

Much as he disliked the thought, he had to agree with Watson on this occasion that finding Melanie Dreyfuss was critical. He was sure that locating Melanie and her friend Clare Sands would prove to be the catalyst to help them solve the case.

Carmichael looked at the eleven digits on the scrap of paper that Watson had handed to him. He then gazed at the clock. 'Hewitt first, then I'll call you,' he mumbled to himself, before putting the paper in his pocket and heading into the corridor.

# Chapter 29

Melanie spread herself out across two seats on the half-empty train as it sped on its way over the Pennines. For the first time in days, she felt a sense of relief that at last she had been able to put some real distance between herself and her pursuers. She knew that there was a good chance the police would soon discover she had left Moulton Bank by train, so she had tried to throw them off the scent by buying a single ticket for Doncaster, even though her intended destination was Huddersfield several stops before.

Melanie had easily managed to hoodwink the taxi driver into allowing her to pay him with Tamara's credit card. She'd had a lot of experience of using stolen credit cards before and she knew that, as long as the driver didn't need a pin number, then she was pretty safe. In her experience the local taxis rarely had the new machines, relying instead upon the ancient swipe technology. This driver was no exception. He didn't even check her signature to see if it matched the one on Tamara Searle's card, which was a shame, she thought, as her copy was quite plausible.

She didn't dare risk using any of her newly acquired cards to buy her train ticket. She knew the ticket office at Moulton Bank wouldn't be so easy to con. So for that payment she had to use twenty-three pounds from Tamara's purse, much to her annoyance.

Melanie looked at the message she had keyed into her mobile before she left Poole's house. She considered sending it, but on further reflection decided that she should wait for another hour or so.

* * * *

When Carmichael arrived outside Hewitt's office, the door was shut. He smiled at Angela. 'Is he going to be long?'

'I don't know,' replied Angela sheepishly. 'It's that Roy Lovelace again. He must have phoned him about three or four times this week already. He sounded very angry when I put him through just now.'

'Really,' replied Carmichael. 'I suspect he may be complaining about me again.'

From what she had already overheard, Angela knew this was true, but didn't want to let on to Carmichael.

'I've just got to make a quick call myself,' said Carmichael. 'I'll come back in ten minutes.'

Carmichael walked out into the corridor and dialled Melanie's mobile number.

Melanie heard the call coming through but, as she didn't recognise the number, she decided not to answer.

'Hello, my name is Inspector Steve Carmichael,' he said into Melanie's answering service. 'I don't know if you remember me but I was at the party at the Lovelace's on Saturday. I saw you and your friend Clare there. I'm responsible for investigating the deaths of Gerry Poole and Tamara Searle. I know you have been talking with Sergeant Watson and I expect you're very nervous about meeting up with us, but I really would like to talk with you. I'm pretty sure you have information that will help us, so please call me back. I can promise you we only want to talk with you. Here's my number.'

Carmichael left his mobile number, hung up and wandered back into Angela's office.

Melanie listened to the message. She remembered

Carmichael not only from the party, but also from his fateful appearance on *The Lovelace Show* and from outside Mrs Prentice's house. She considered her options and decided that, as he was more senior and also more likable, she should send the text to him instead of Watson. She keyed in Carmichael's number and pressed send.

*　*　*　*

Hewitt often looked on edge but, even by his standards, the expression that greeted Carmichael when he entered the office took the emotion of fretfulness to new heights.

'You look uneasy,' said Carmichael foolishly.

'Uneasy!' exclaimed Hewitt in a raised voice. 'I'm absolutely furious. And do you know why?'

'Is it your car still being repaired at the garage?' Carmichael replied even more unwisely.

'No, it's got nothing to do with my damn car. It's because, in spite of my specific orders,' shouted Hewitt, who was sitting upright in his chair and turning purple, 'you went headlong into the Lovelaces and accused them of being implicated in the two deaths. I've just had Roy Lovelace on the line and he's incandescent with rage. He's made it clear that he will be bringing up your clumsy manner with the Superintendent and quite frankly, after everything else this week, I am not going to stick my neck out for you. In fact, I'm going to pre-empt any further embarrassment by taking you off the case.'

'What! You can't do that,' exclaimed Carmichael. 'I've done nothing wrong other than investigate this case … and it *is* just a bloody case … as I would any other investigation. The fact that Mr and Mrs Up-Themselves think they are above the law is no concern of mine. I've no idea if they are guilty of murder but they are prime suspects and should be treated as such.'

'You're so naïve, Carmichael,' Hewitt shouted. 'These people are influential. They need to be managed with tact. You may be right about the fact that they are suspects but you need to manage these types of cases with greater dexterity. You just plough in there and don't seem to give a hoot about the consequences.'

'So I'm off the case just like that?' Carmichael shouted.

'Look,' replied Hewitt, trying hard to calm things down. 'You're a great detective, but in this case you've burned your bridges and it's best I take over and you focus on something else. It is no reflection on you, but I think given the history between you and the Lovelaces a new person at the helm may help smooth the waters.'

'I can't believe what I'm hearing,' replied Carmichael angrily. 'If that is how you manage this station then I quit.'

'Don't be ridiculous!' replied Hewitt. 'You've not been disciplined. I just feel that a new person heading this case up is what is needed, that's all.'

'That's all,' exclaimed Carmichael. 'This is my reputation here. How can I continue to receive the team's respect if they know you don't think enough of me to carry on with the case?'

'Look, I know you're upset,' replied Hewitt as calmly as he could. 'However, I've made my decision. If you chose to quit then that is your choice, but you're off the case.'

'Will that be all, sir?' responded Carmichael, his anger still evident.

'Yes,' replied Hewitt. 'Just go home and talk things over with Penny. I think you've got all this out of perspective. Let's talk again on Monday.'

Carmichael didn't reply. He stormed out of Hewitt's office and slammed the door behind him.

'Pillock!' he muttered under his breath to Angela, as he passed her desk and headed for the corridor. 'That guy's a spineless pillock.'

Carmichael had no intention of hanging around Kirkwood Police Station for a moment longer than necessary. He returned to his office to collect his coat and car keys before heading for the exit. As he passed Watson's desk, he noticed the file on the cattle rustling case they had concluded earlier in the week. Carmichael grabbed the file and put it under his arm. He had been so absorbed in the death of Poole and murder of Tamara Searle that he had not had the opportunity to read through the statements Watson and Cooper had taken from Southwaite and Bradshaw. Now that Hewitt had decided to take him off the case, at least he would have time in abundance to read over all the case notes and everyone's statements. Not that he was in any mood to do so at that particular moment.

# Chapter 30

As soon as Carmichael had left his office, Hewitt phoned through to Angela, his long-suffering secretary.

'Can you patch me through to Chief Superintendent Banks. Then when you've done that, get on to Watson, Cooper and Dalton and advise them that Inspector Carmichael is no longer in charge of the Poole or Searle cases. Tell them that I am heading up these cases now and they need to report any findings they have directly to me.' As usual he didn't wait for Angela's reply.

Ten minutes later when Hewitt had finished his call with the Chief Superintendent and was dialling Roy Lovelace's number, he noticed Carmichael's black BMW speed out of the station car park.

'Mr Lovelace,' he said in as jovial a voice as he could, 'I thought I'd just call to advise you that, with immediate effect, I will be taking over the running of the investigation into the death of your brother-in-law and the murder of Tamara Searle.'

\* \* \* \*

Carmichael's mobile sat in its cradle which was mounted to the dashboard of the car. It was indicating that he had received a text message, but Carmichael was in no mood to read it. He had decided to wait until he got home before contacting his team and letting them know he was off the

241

case. He hoped that by then he would have calmed down enough to disguise how he felt. Carmichael also decided to wait until then before he checked to see who had left him the text.

It was just after 4 p.m. when he left Kirkwood Police Station and, although the narrow country roads were still not totally clear of snow and ice, they were passable. With little traffic about at that time, Carmichael managed to get home in just over thirty-five minutes, which he considered to be a good time to travel the 23.2-mile journey, taking into account the poor driving conditions. As he parked up his car his mobile rang. Carmichael could see from the number on the display that it was Watson.

'Hello, Marc,' said Carmichael as sedately as he could. 'I was just going to call you.'

'I can't believe it,' said Watson. 'What happened?'

'If you're referring to me being taken off the case,' replied Carmichael, 'Hewitt thought it was for the best. I think, after my appearance on *The Lovelace Show*, he had been put under a lot of pressure and, although I'm not at all happy, I can understand why he has taken over.'

'You're taking it remarkably well,' continued Watson. 'I'd be bloody fuming if it was me. Anyway, I just wanted to let you know that I think it stinks and I'm sure the others will too.'

Carmichael was surprised that Watson already knew and quite stunned that he was being so supportive. He rightly assumed that, if Watson knew, then all of the team would now know. Carmichael didn't want to give away his true feelings about Hewitt's decision, but neither was he prepared to pretend that he was happy. 'As I say, Marc, I'm not overjoyed with the decision, but these things happen in life and I'm just going to have to accept it. Anyway the main thing is for you all to demonstrate what a great team you are and crack the case.'

'I haven't spoken to the others yet,' continued Watson. 'However, I'm sure they will be as baffled as I am and, yes, we will make sure we get this one sorted as soon as we can, if only to get Hewitt off our backs and you back at the helm.'

Watson's comments made Carmichael smile. 'How are you doing trying to find Melanie Dreyfuss?'

Watson had not expected to be asked about the case. If he had, he would probably have delayed the call until later as the truth was that, on the way to Newbridge, Watson and PC Jamieson had stopped off at a café for a coffee. It was when they were in the café that Watson had received Angela's call. So, although they had left Kirkwood Police Station over an hour and a half earlier, they had only just arrived in Newbridge when he had made the call to Carmichael.

'We're … we're just outside Poole's house now,' Watson stuttered. 'The traffic was pretty bad with the roads still being a bit difficult in places. We're just about to take a look around to see if she's here or has been here, as you suggested. Then, if she's not here, we'll probably try Mrs Prentice's again or her flat. It's so cold out here that she will need to shelter and, you never know, she may think she's safe to go back to either one of them.'

'OK. Good luck, Marc,' replied Carmichael, who knew full well that the roads were not that bad and guessed that Watson and Jamieson probably made some sort of detour en route. 'I know I'm not on the case anymore and you need to report to Hewitt from now on, but let me know how you're doing.'

'No problem, sir,' replied Watson. 'After Hewitt you'll be the second person to know when we make a breakthrough.'

'Thanks for the call, Marc,' Carmichael said before ending their conversation.

The thirty-five-minute drive and then Watson's call had helped Carmichael put his disappointment into some sort of context. He smiled to himself and, pulling the mobile from its cradle, checked the text message he had received earlier.

\*   \*   \*   \*

It was just starting to get dark by the time Watson and Jamieson eventually arrived at Poole's house. The strong, icy wind blew into their faces as they clambered out of Watson's car and walked towards Poole's ancient, creaky, wrought-iron gate. In the four days that had elapsed since Watson was previously at the house, some contractors had erected huge wooden boards which stood over eight feet high and separated the house from the large, empty field next door. These hoardings acted as excellent shields, protecting the two police officers from the biting wind as they tentatively made their way up the slippery drive.

Watson had no idea whether they would find Melanie within the house but, if she was inside, he was not going to allow her to do a runner as she had done that morning.

'Go round the back,' he whispered to Jamieson. 'I'll give you a minute to get to the kitchen door before I enter. Be ready in case she does try and make a run for it. She's bloody quick, so be on your toes.'

Jamieson nodded and walked towards the rear of the house.

Watson waited out of view beside the front door. He gave Jamieson a few minutes to get into position before he made his entry.

\*   \*   \*   \*

Carmichael read the text message he'd received from Melanie several times before he finally tried calling Watson on his mobile. However, Watson's phone was permanently engaged and for some annoying reason it wouldn't kick into voicemail. After numerous unsuccessful attempts Carmichael decided to switch off his mobile and try again later. He got out of his car and rushed towards the front door of his house, trying hard to get out of the freezing cold wind as quickly as he could.

If he was to believe what was in her message, then the case was even more puzzling than he had previously thought. Even though a little voice at the back of his head kept telling him that Melanie might not be telling the truth, nevertheless her text had ignited his curiosity. However, whether she was telling the truth or not, the reality was that it was no longer for him to decide as he was no longer on the case.

Carmichael certainly didn't want to keep this new piece of information from the team, but his anger with his boss was still strong and he didn't feel inclined to share it directly with Hewitt. He decided that he would call Watson later that evening and tell him what he had been sent and then forward it on to him.

'It's really not my problem,' he muttered to himself as he marched up the drive. 'It's up to Watson and the team to follow it up, not me.'

\* \* \* \*

On the way across the Pennines, Melanie's train had been forced to stop. In the driver's subsequent announcement the passengers were told that this was due to signalling failure. As a result, when the train did finally arrive at Huddersfield railway station, it was almost 5.20 p.m., fifteen minutes late.

The station platform was poorly lit and only partially covered. Melanie was one of only five passengers to get out at this stop and in the half gloom it was easy for the man lurking in the shadows to spot the young woman he had been nervously waiting to meet for the last thirty minutes. As she made her way down the platform, Melanie looked up to the heavens. The patchy clouds above her gave way to large expanses of darkness and she could see quite clearly the

245

shimmering bright stars that peppered the evening sky. It looked quite beautiful but also threatening. It was going to be another bleak cold night, she thought.

Melanie had already walked past the concrete pillar where he had been lying in wait, when he made his move. She didn't notice him rush quickly towards her until his hand forcefully grabbed hold of her left arm.

# Chapter 31

After talking with her father, Jemma Carmichael had every intention of quitting her well-paid job at Jaspers. Her work rota meant that she had not needed to go into work since her mother had paid her the surprise visit on Tuesday. Jemma had written out her resignation letter giving her boss a week's notice and she planned to hand it in that night.

She was very shocked when, at 5.30 that Friday evening, she answered the door to find DC Evans standing on her doorstep.

'Oh, it's you,' exclaimed Jemma with astonishment. 'I thought you said all charges against me were dropped?'

'They are,' replied Evans with a comforting smile. 'Can I come in? It's really cold out here.'

'Yes, of course,' replied Jemma, who stood aside to let him pass. 'Go through into the lounge. It's a bit of a mess, I'm afraid.'

Evans squeezed passed Jemma and went through into the small front room.

'What do you want?' Jemma asked when they were alone.

'A bit of a favour,' replied Evans. 'You can say no if you want, but if you were to agree it would help me enormously.'

'You better sit down then,' Jemma said, pointing to the beaten up sofa.

DC Evans did as he was asked.

'It's like this,' he said in his broad Welsh accent, his piercing brown eyes looking straight at Jemma. 'I want to make you a proposition which I'd like you to consider very carefully.'

\*    \*    \*    \*

When Carmichael had told Penny about being taken off the case, her initial reaction was one of relief. She had still not forgiven Caroline Lovelace for the way she had treated her husband and her first thought was that this would take him out of the firing line. However, as the evening progressed, she could see that Carmichael had been badly hurt by Hewitt's decision and she slowly came to the conclusion that in fact what Hewitt had done was even more unfair and infinitely more brutal than any harm Caroline had managed to inflict on Carmichael on her TV show.

While Robbie and Natalie were still around, Penny tried to keep the mood as friendly and upbeat as she could. She didn't want to give them the slightest idea that either she or Carmichael were in any way upset. As usual, Robbie sloped off to his room after he had consumed his tea and at 10.15 p.m. her youngest finally decided she was too tired to stay up any longer and went to bed. Penny took this as her cue to start to find out what her husband was really thinking.

'So what are you going to do?' she asked, as she slid up close to him on the large living room sofa.

'About the case?' he replied. 'I'm not sure really. I guess I can't do much about it.'

'It seems such a disproportionate step for Hewitt to take,' remarked Penny as she placed her head on his shoulder.

'That's true,' replied Carmichael, 'but Hewitt's paranoid about upsetting Roy Lovelace. I think Lovelace has been at him to take me off the case all week and Hewitt's just not got the bottle to stand up to him.'

'But surely he realises how this leaves you?' enquired Penny.

'I'm not sure he does,' replied Carmichael, 'and if he does he's clearly prepared to sacrifice my feelings if it gets Lovelace off his back.'

Penny grabbed the remote and flicked on the TV.

'I'll make you a cup of coffee,' she said gently. 'Let me just see what they have to say about the weekend's weather first.'

Penny changed the channel so she could catch the North West weather report. As she did and to their astonishment the unmistakeable vision of Chief Inspector Hewitt filled the TV screen.

'So, Chief Inspector,' asked the interviewer. 'Do you think that this latest body found by your officers is in any way linked to the murder of Tamara Searle?'

Hewitt was clearly at the crime scene. He was wearing his thick dark overcoat and behind him it was dark and gloomy. As he answered, Carmichael and Penny could see his breath emanating from his mouth and nostrils.

'It is too early to say for certain and we're not ruling out anything at the moment,' replied Hewitt, as calmly as he could. 'We have been looking for two young women in connection with the death of Tamara Searle and the body we have found this evening is believed to be of one of those young women.'

'Can you confirm the identity of the young woman and also indicate how she died?' asked the reporter.

Hewitt gave a wry smile. 'I'm sure you can appreciate that until we have formally had the body identified I'm unable to say much more. However, I'd like to take this opportunity to ask the public to be on the lookout for a young woman we are keen to talk to. Given the urgency of this request, we are taking the unusual step of naming her as Melanie Dreyfuss. Melanie is in her early twenties. She is approximately five foot six inches tall, is of slim build and has long wavy ginger hair. We believe that she was in the vicinity of the crime scene earlier in the day but hasn't been seen since mid-morning today. It could well be that someone is hiding her in the Newbridge or Moulton Bank area, or she may well have absconded. If anybody knows of Melanie's whereabouts, please contact Kirkwood Police Station immediately.'

The picture on the screen then changed to show the familiar face of the evening newsreader from the local TV station.

'That was Chief Inspector Hewitt who is heading up the hunt for Tamara Searle's killer. The latest body to be found in a house in Newbridge earlier this evening is alleged to be of a young woman called Clare Sands. Although this has yet to be confirmed by the police, we understand that she may have taken her own life.'

Carmichael and Penny looked on in amazement.

'Was Clare Sands a suspect?' Penny asked.

'Yes, she was,' replied Carmichael. 'But, we were nowhere near close enough to be sure and we had about nine other people in the frame too. Actually you met her and Melanie Dreyfuss on Saturday at the Lovelaces. They were the blonde-headed and the red-headed waitresses. I received a text from Melanie earlier today. She said that she and Clare were being set up. My plan was going to be to send it to Marc this evening.'

'So what are you going to do with it now?' Penny asked.

'I'm not sure.' Carmichael replied. 'First off, I'm going to call Watson and find out what's going on. I'll decide then.'

*   *   *   *

Jemma arrived at the club at 10.30 p.m. to start her long shift behind the bar. She was sure her mum and dad wouldn't be happy with the arrangement she had with DC Evans, as it meant her retaining her job at the club, but she needed the money and she felt that, by helping the police, she had a good excuse should either of her parents challenge her. She also thought that DC Evans was really fit, so being his informant was a good excuse to maintain regular contact with him.

* * * *

Carmichael had not switched his mobile on since he had got out of the car, so given the news bulletin it was no surprise to find that he had two voice messages and a new text from Melanie Dreyfuss.

He decided to check his text message first, which read:

> I saw your boss on the telly. So u r not the main man now! What happened? Do you think Clare and I did it like they do?

Carmichael smiled. In truth he was not sure what to think, however, he was impressed at Melanie's perceptiveness and also by her courage.

He scrolled back to reread the longer message she had sent him earlier in the day:

> Hello Inspector. I am not ready to give myself up or to meet with you or any other copper yet! I know what it looks like, but me and Clare have been set up. They have made us look like we killed that weathergirl. They've also now killed Clare and I guess it will be me next if I let them. I'm already out of Newbridge and will be lying low until you find the real killer.

Carmichael then decided to check his voice messages. The first was from Rachel Dalton, which she had left at 4.50 p.m.:

'Hello, sir, it's Rachel. I wanted to call you to see how you were doing. I can't believe they have taken you off the case. I just wanted to say that I think it's crazy. I hope you're OK. I'll see you on Monday.'

251

Carmichael smiled. He was genuinely touched by the message.

The second voice message was from a very excited Sergeant Watson, which he had left at 5.10 p.m.:

'Sir, it's Marc. We've just got into Poole's house as you suggested. Clâre Sands' body is here. She's been dead for a few days at least, I'd say, and all of Tamara Searle's possessions are piled up in the room. I'm just about to call Hewitt, but it looks like suicide to me. It looks like an overdose. There's no sign of Melanie. Anyway call me when you get this as I'd like to brief you before Hewitt arrives.'

Again, Carmichael was moved by the loyalty of his team members. Without any hesitation he dialled Marc's number.

'Watson,' replied Marc.

'Hello, Marc, it's Carmichael. I got your message and have just seen Hewitt on the TV. What's the latest?'

'We've made a big breakthrough,' he replied, the excitement in his voice quite evident. 'Jamieson and I discovered Clare Sands' body at Poole's house.'

'Yes, I know,' interrupted Carmichael. 'I got your voice message and saw Hewitt on TV.'

'The Chief and I are both sure that Clare committed suicide. Dr Stock thinks she may have died on either Monday or Tuesday, so our main theory is that she and probably Melanie killed Tamara Searle, probably at her house. They then took her to the Common in Moulton Bank where they dumped her. They then cleared her house and brought much of it to Poole's as they knew it would be safe here.'

Carmichael didn't think much of this theory. 'But if they did that, why would Clare Sands then kill herself?' he said with clear frustration in his voice. 'Also how did they get Tamara's body to the Common? As far as I know, neither have cars and I'm not sure either of them can even drive.'

'We still have to check a lot of the details out,' replied Watson flippantly. 'However, Chief Inspector Hewitt is telling us to now focus all our efforts on tracking down Melanie Dreyfuss. We are sure she has all the answers.'

'Really?' replied Carmichael, who was still perplexed at how short-sighted Hewitt was being. 'On that account I may be able to help you. Before I was taken off the case I left a message on her mobile and she replied with a text message late this afternoon. I'll forward it on to you to follow up.'

'What did it say?' asked Watson eagerly.

'Just that she and Clare were being set up,' replied Carmichael.

'Well, she would say that, wouldn't she?' retorted Watson dismissively.

'So when you say that you're concentrating on finding Melanie,' continued Carmichael, 'surely this doesn't mean that you and Rachel are going to set aside the main tasks we agreed at the team meeting this afternoon? Rachel's still looking at the last lot of phone calls that Tamara made and she's still going to re-interview Amanda Buchannan, isn't she?'

'I'm not sure what Rachel's instructions are from Chief Inspector Hewitt, but my brief is crystal clear: I'm to pursue Melanie Dreyfuss and nothing else.'

'I know I'm no longer in charge, Marc,' continued Carmichael as calmly as he could. 'However, you really do need to follow other lines of enquiry too. I'm not saying that your main theory is wrong, but it doesn't really stack up that well. We have already identified plenty of other potential suspects, so we need to keep investigating them too.'

'I hear you, sir,' replied Watson glibly. 'But you have to understand my position. Chief Inspector Hewitt has made it clear that he is running the investigation and he has also made it plain to me that I've to focus on finding Melanie Dreyfuss. Maybe Rachel is still being asked to follow up the other leads, but you'd have to ask her.'

'I understand,' remarked Carmichael, who fully got Watson's message. 'I'll send you the text from Melanie and let you get on with it.'

'Thanks, sir,' replied Watson. 'I'm sorry but I will have to go – the Chief is trying to get through to me.'

'OK, Marc,' said Carmichael. 'I'll let you go. Good luck with the case, but please think about what I've said.'

Carmichael ended the call feeling totally despondent. He forwarded Melanie's first text message on to Watson as he had promised, but decided to keep her latest communication to himself.

'Who are you texting?' asked Penny as she entered the room.

'I'm sending Marc a text from Melanie Dreyfuss,' replied Carmichael. 'I've just spoken to him and I can't believe how he and Hewitt are being so blinkered. According to Marc, they're certain that they have cracked the case, but I'm not so sure.'

'Well, it's none of your concern anymore,' remarked Penny. 'Just let them get on with it.'

'Even if I'm sure they're wrong?' said Carmichael with a smile. 'Now you know that's not my style.'

# Chapter 32

**Saturday 21st February**

It was just after 8.15 a.m. when the unmistakeable sound of the newspaper being squeezed through the letter box and then falling with a thud onto the parquet floor woke Carmichael from his deep sleep.

Given all that had happened the previous day, Carmichael was surprised how well he had slept. He had wanted to contact Rachel Dalton the night before, but by the time he had finished talking to Watson it was getting on for 11 p.m. and knowing that she was on duty at the station the next day, he decided to wait until the morning before giving her a call.

He wiped the sleep from his eyes and looked over at Penny who was sound asleep. Not wishing to wake his wife, he gently eased himself out of bed and tiptoed as best he could towards the bedroom door, grabbing his threadbare dressing gown on his way. He sucked in his stomach, slithered between the wall and the partially open door, then sneaked across the landing and as quietly as he could, crept down the stairs. When he reached the hallway at the foot of the staircase he picked up the newspaper and sauntered on, bleary-eyed into the kitchen.

Once inside the kitchen, he stretched, yawned widely, threw the newspaper onto the table and pushed two slices of bread into the toaster. As he started to fill up the kettle, he caught sight of one of the front-page headlines out of the corner of his eye:

## TAMARA'S KILLERS MAY BE WOMEN

The headline swiftly aroused Carmichael from his semi-conscious state. He quickly turned off the gushing tap and, abandoning the kettle on the draining board, started reading the newspaper article.

'Bloody hell,' he muttered to himself as he read that the police were treating Clare Sands as a suspect and were hunting down a second woman, Melanie Dreyfuss, who the paper believed might be an accomplice to the murder. As he turned over the pages to locate page five, where the story continued, Penny wandered into the kitchen and put her arm around her husband's waist.

'Morning,' she said with a yawn. 'What's the kettle doing over there?'

Carmichael didn't hear what she had said as his attention was totally focused on the article.

'Bloody hell,' he said for a second time. 'Hewitt's lost the plot on this one. I'm not sure what he's said to the press, but it's quite clear they think they've cracked it and that Clare Sands and Melanie Dreyfuss are the killers.'

'Maybe he's right,' suggested Penny as she plugged the kettle lead in and turned on the switch. 'Maybe they have cracked it.'

'No chance,' replied Carmichael without taking his eyes from the newspaper text. 'The two women were certainly involved, or they knew something, but they're not the killers. I'm certain of it.'

'Why?' replied Penny.

Carmichael didn't answer. 'I don't believe it,' he exclaimed. 'The papers have not only just practically hung, drawn and quartered Melanie, but to top it all they have got a statement here from the Lovelaces.'

Penny peered over her husband's shoulder at where he was pointing and read the quote out loud:

256

We are both greatly relieved that such rapid progress is being made by Chief Inspector Hewitt and his team in apprehending the individuals who murdered Caroline's colleague and our dear friend Tamara Searle. We would like to thank the police for their hard work in this case.

Penny elected not to continue reading the next line, which went on to remind the reader of Caroline's on-air robust treatment of the officer who had been previously heading up the case, one Inspector Stephen Carmichael. She felt this was something her husband wouldn't want to be reminded of at the moment.

Carmichael pushed the paper away and sat down on one of the wooden kitchen chairs. 'This is unbelievable,' he said. 'They must be bloody mad.'

Two charred slices of bread popped out of the toaster in a plume of thick black smoke, followed a few seconds later by the sound of the fire alarm in the hallway letting off its now familiar shriek.

\* \* \* \*

Rachel Dalton was uneasy when Hewitt had told her to suspend her current lines of investigation and instructed her to focus all her efforts that Saturday morning on tracking down Melanie. She was not convinced that this was what Carmichael would have done but, as everyone else in the station seemed to believe they had found their killers in Sands and Dreyfuss, she didn't feel it was right to push back. She was therefore extremely relieved when at 8.40 a.m. Carmichael called her mobile.

'Hello, sir,' she said. 'Have you heard the latest?'

'Yes,' replied Carmichael. 'I spoke with Marc last night and I saw Hewitt on TV. It's also all over the front page of the paper.'

'I'm not sure it's as clear cut as they are all saying,' announced Rachel. 'They are taking it for granted that Clare Sands committed suicide and are then jumping from that to her and Melanie Dreyfuss being the killers. I understand this is a likely scenario, but it's by no means the only one and, even if it's right, we still don't have enough evidence to prove it.'

Carmichael was relieved that at last someone in the investigation team appeared to be looking rationally at the evidence.

'I agree,' replied Carmichael. 'So why is Hewitt so convinced that Sands and Dreyfuss are the killers? It's really not like him; he's normally very even-handed and objective in cases like this.'

'I don't know,' said Rachel, in a whisper as she had just been joined by PC Morley and she didn't want to let him know whom she was talking to. 'I wasn't at Poole's when they found the body, but I understand that within a short space of time Roy Lovelace had arrived for an update and I think it was as a result of him being there that the press arrived. From what I gather, I think Hewitt was almost ambushed into making a live appearance on the evening news.'

Carmichael sniggered to himself. 'I can't imagine he resisted too long. He's not noted for his shyness when it comes to being interviewed.'

'Maybe you're right,' responded Rachel. 'However, everyone at the station, including Marc, seems quite confident that Sands and Dreyfuss murdered Tamara Searle. So we are all being told to suspend investigating any other lines of enquiry until we have found Melanie.'

'I see,' replied Carmichael. 'What about the summary of the last telephone calls made on Tamara's mobile? I take it you're still looking into them?'

'I will,' said Rachel. 'But I am under strict instructions to help find Melanie. We've just received some photos of Melanie and I'm just about to go with PC Morley to all the train stations in the area and to the bus station in Moulton Bank to see if anyone can recall seeing her yesterday. I'll also try the taxi companies in Moulton Bank and the surrounding villages, as you never know she may have escaped in a cab.'

'OK,' replied Carmichael. 'Good luck! But keep me informed how you do, even if it's by text.'

'I'll have to go, sir,' said Rachel, who could see that PC Morley was looking anxious to get going.

Carmichael put down his mobile on the kitchen table and bit into a slice of thickly buttered burnt cold toast that had been sitting in front of him for the last ten minutes.

'So, what's the plan for today?' Penny asked in the sincere hope that it wouldn't include Carmichael getting himself actively involved in the case he had been removed from the day before.

'I really don't know,' Carmichael responded as he pushed the plate of cremated toast away from him and got up from his chair. 'I'll mull it over while I have a shower and shave.'

He kissed his wife gently on the cheek and ambled off in the direction of the shower room.

*　*　*　*

Rachel Dalton and PC Morley were having a successful morning. Not only had they managed to establish that Melanie had been picked up by a taxi from near Gerry Poole's house the day before, they also discovered that she paid using Tamara Searle's credit card and was dropped outside Moulton Bank train station where she bought a single ticket to Doncaster.

Hewitt was euphoric when he heard the news that the team were onto Melanie's trail.

'Get her photo sent over to our colleagues in Doncaster

and then get over there yourself,' he instructed the young DC. 'Make sure the local police are doing everything they can to track her down.'

*   *   *   *

Carmichael lingered far longer in the shower than he would normally. However, it was Saturday morning, he had nothing else pressing and he wanted to make sure that the decision he was about to make was the right one.

His head told him to leave the case well alone and he knew that this would also be Penny's wish, but his instincts pointed to Hewitt having this one all wrong. So even though he knew it was verging on the arrogant, Carmichael concluded that, unless he personally intervened, there wouldn't only be a real chance of the killer getting away, but also the distinct possibility that a miscarriage of justice would be the outcome of the investigation. Buoyed by this steadfast conviction, he chose to follow his heart and to carry on his own secret investigation into the three mysterious deaths, which he was in no doubt were linked.

Had he still had access to the resources of his trusty team, he would have directed the investigation on several fronts. However, as he didn't have this luxury anymore, and as he dared not implicate the others in his clear flouting of Hewitt's lucid instructions, he decided to focus all his energy on making contact with Melanie before Hewitt and the team caught up with her.

# Chapter 33

It was 11.30 a.m. before Jemma Carmichael stirred that Saturday morning. Had it not been for the piercing screech of her mobile phone telling her she had a new message, she would probably have stayed fast asleep for at least a couple of hours more. Her shift at Jaspers had only ended at 2 a.m. and by the time she had arrived back at her house it was closer to 3 a.m. Feeling totally exhausted, Jemma had sent a very brief text message to the handsome DC Evans before crashing out. It was therefore no surprise to her when she was woken by his text message reply suggesting they should meet up later that day. Through one eye Jemma read the message. She smiled smugly before rolling over to resume her slumbers.

\*    \*    \*    \*

'You must be out of your mind!' exclaimed Penny, when her husband finally broke the news to her that he was going to try and track down Melanie Dreyfuss. 'Why don't you just send Rachel or Marc the second text and forget the case?'

'Because', he replied calmly and deliberately, 'I think she has valuable information that will crack this case and I'm not sure Hewitt will allow the rest of the team to look at any other scenario than the one he seems sure is the truth.'

'But what if he's right?' asked Penny, her exasperation clear in her voice. 'You could end up in real trouble.'

'I know,' replied Carmichael. 'But I simply have to find her first. If I do, I could steal a day or more from the rest of the team and that may be all I need to solve the case.'

Penny shook her head. 'I know I won't get you to change your mind, so I'm not going to say anything more, but I think you're mad.'

Carmichael smiled and gave his wife a hug. 'I think I'm mad too, but I didn't become a detective to just sit and do nothing when I know I can make a difference.'

'So what's your plan?' Penny asked.

'I'm going to call Melanie on her mobile and try and arrange a meeting with her,' he replied. 'If she agrees, then maybe I can help her and solve the case. If she refuses and Hewitt and the team find her first I fear we may never get to the truth.'

'Go on then,' said Penny. 'Make your call, but be careful. If she *is* the killer, I don't want you added to her list of victims. You've still got our bedroom to decorate so make sure you finish that before you get yourself murdered by some crazy serial killer.'

Carmichael smiled. 'As soon as I've cracked the case I'll decorate the bedroom to your precise specifications.'

'I'll hold you to that,' replied Penny, who kissed him before walking out into the kitchen, leaving him to make his call.

\* \* \* \*

Rachel Dalton was desperate to speak with Carmichael to update him on their morning's progress. Unfortunately she was finding it impossible to shake off PC Morley. It was only when they were well on their journey to Doncaster that she finally had the opportunity to make contact and then only by a short text message.

> Have discovered that Melanie left Moulton Bank yesterday, by train. She bought a ticket to Doncaster so we are on our

way there now. Will call you when I get 10 minutes on my own.

'Who's that you're texting?' PC Morley asked as their police car headed at speed down the M62.

'Just my boyfriend,' replied Rachel. 'We are due to go out tonight. I was just telling him I may be late back.'

\* \* \* \*

Carmichael had already left a voice message for Melanie by the time he picked up Rachel's text. His first instinct was to call her to let her know he was also trying to locate Melanie. But after he'd given it some thought, he elected against this. He didn't want to drag poor Rachel into a charge of insubordination. He was prepared to face the consequences himself if it all went pear-shaped, but he would never be able to forgive himself if he hauled such a good officer as Rachel Dalton down with him into the mire.

'Doncaster,' he muttered to himself. 'I wonder who she knows there?'

Had he still been in charge of the case he would have sent an officer over to The Helpful Angels agency to look through Melanie's file to see if she had any links with Doncaster.

'Did you speak to her?' Penny asked as she emerged from the kitchen with a cup of coffee in each hand.

'I left her a voice message,' replied Carmichael. 'The ball's in her court now.'

'So what next?' Penny asked. 'Do we just sit and wait all day on the off-chance this young woman returns your call?'

'Not at all,' replied Carmichael as he took one of the mugs out of his wife's hand. 'We drink our coffee and then I take you down to The Railway for a few sociable drinks and a pub lunch.'

'It's a deal,' replied Penny.

263

# Chapter 34

Robbie Robertson, the larger-than-life landlord of The Railway Tavern, greeted Carmichael and Penny with a huge smile. 'Well, what have we got here! If I'm not mistaken, it's the daytime TV detective,' he shouted light-heartedly from behind the bar.

Carmichael forced a faint smile. 'Hello, Robbie,' he said. 'You saw my fleeting moment of fame on TV then, I take it?'

'Actually no,' replied Robbie. 'But Katie told me you got a right ear-bashing from her ladyship?'

'That's about right,' Carmichael concurred. 'I've not had the bottle to look at the recording yet, but it wasn't my greatest few moments.'

'Anyway, what would you like to drink?' Robbie asked.

'A pint of bitter for me,' replied Carmichael.

'And an orange juice and lemonade for me,' said Penny.

'Take a seat and I'll bring them over,' the landlord replied in his large booming voice.

As was usual on Saturday lunchtime, The Railway Tavern was fairly quiet so Carmichael and Penny had their pick of tables.

'Let's go over there,' said Penny, pointing to a table in the corner which looked out over the fields behind the pub.

No sooner had they sat down when Robbie arrived with a tray of drinks, including his own large pewter tankard of dark mild.

'So the news is that they've found another body,' he said as he plonked himself down on a stool. 'And is it right that you're no longer in charge?'

'Bloody hell,' remarked Carmichael with surprise in his voice. 'I see the bush telegraph's still functioning properly here all right!'

Robbie sniggered. 'This place gets the local news faster than Reuters.'

'Well, your information is correct on both counts,' replied Carmichael. 'They've found another body up at Gerard Poole's house and I've been relieved of my duties on the case.'

'So what's the story then?' Robbie asked. 'Who's in the frame for these murders?'

Carmichael took a sip of his beer. 'You know I can't talk about the case even though I'm no longer in charge. But at the moment, although we have three bodies, only one is a definite murder. The other two are just suspicious deaths.'

'I understand,' replied Robbie.

'Anyway, how's Katie?' Penny asked, trying to move the conversation away to a less sensitive topic.

'She's fine,' said Robbie. 'It's her day off today. She's gone to Kirkwood, shopping.'

'I hear she's soon to be married,' said Penny. 'You must be pleased.'

'Yes,' replied Robbie. 'They've set a date for July next year. I'm not sure I'd have picked a vicar as a son-in-law if I had a choice, but she's very happy and, as vicar's go, Barney Green is about as normal as they come.'

Carmichael was not sure that Barney Green and normal could exist in the same sentence, but said nothing.

'So will they live here after they are married?' Penny asked.

'Well that's the million-dollar question,' replied Robbie with a shrug of his broad shoulders. 'As you know, Katie owns half the pub and my plan was to retire in a few years' time and pass it all over to her. Barney's keen for them to live here and he says he's happy to help out, but he still wants to remain the village vicar. However, I don't think his bishop is that comfortable with their plan, so we will have to see, I suppose.'

'So what else is going on in Moulton Bank and the villages?' asked Carmichael who was getting bored with the conversation.

'Nothing much,' replied Robbie Robertson. 'Other than the three deaths you were investigating, the talk in the bar is usually about what a stuck-up cow Caroline Lovelace was with you. The next most popular subject is the cattle rustlers being caught and Harry Jackson and Melvyn Hitchcock being involved. Then after that not much really, other than the new supermarket that's being built in Newbridge.'

'What new supermarket?' asked Penny.

'Boothroyd's,' replied Robbie. 'It's apparently going to be the biggest food store for miles when it's finished. They started putting the footings down earlier this week.'

'Whereabouts in Newbridge are they building it?' Penny enquired with interest.

'It's sited on a large plot of land on the Moulton Bank road. It's just as you get to the village. Coincidentally, it's actually right next door to Gerard Poole's house.'

'So what's the reaction of the locals to Harry Jackson and Melvyn Hitchcock being implicated in the rustling?' Carmichael asked in an attempt to get the talk away from the new supermarket.

As Carmichael spoke, a new customer entered the lounge and Robbie, seeing the man out of the corner of his eye, got up from his chair to return to the bar.

'A pretty much universal reaction,' he replied as he sauntered across the floor. 'Harry they were not surprised about because he's always been a bit of a bit of a ducker and diver. He's also renowned for being a money-grabbing old bugger. However, we were all very surprised that Melvyn was sucked into the scam. He's a decent bloke and well liked by most around here. Up until now I'd have said he was a straight sort of guy.'

'So a new supermarket,' Penny whispered to Carmichael with interest. 'I wonder if they do home deliveries. That's about the only thing I miss from living in Watford.'

* * * *

It was almost 1 p.m. by the time Jemma Carmichael rolled out of bed. Before heading off to the bathroom she checked DC Evans' text again and sent him back a reply.

What time do you want to meet up? Any time after three is OK with me. Jemma X

Having sent the text message, Jemma left her mobile on the bed and scurried off to start the lengthy process of making herself look suitably presentable for her expected rendezvous with the gorgeous DC Evans.

* * * *

Carmichael had just finished his second pint when his mobile started to vibrate in his pocket. He quickly extracted the phone and looked at the message that appeared on the small screen:

Got your message can meet you this afternoon. Come alone.

'It's from Melanie,' Carmichael whispered excitedly. 'She wants to meet me later this afternoon.'

'Where?' asked Penny.

'I don't know,' replied Carmichael, who was already sending back a reply. 'I'm just trying to find out.'

Carmichael and Penny waited for a few moments before his mobile received their next set of instructions.

Will meet you in an hour near Manchester. You need to set off now and head east along the M62. I'll send you more instructions in 30 minutes.

Carmichael stood up. 'I wish I hadn't drunk that second pint. You may have to drive me.'

'But she says you have to be alone,' replied Penny.

'I know that but I'm not going to drink-drive. If she won't let you come too, then she will have to wait until later this evening to meet up. I'll text her and explain while we are walking home.'

\* \* \* \*

Jemma returned to her bedroom with a bowl of cornflakes in one hand, a chocolate bar in the other and her long brown hair wrapped in a damp towel after her shower. To her delight she had a new text message waiting for her. She eagerly read the message from DC Evans:

I'll pick you up at 5.30 p.m. We can talk over a meal in a nice quiet out of the way pub in the country. Andy.

'Well, Andy, that sounds fine to me,' muttered Jemma to herself as she fired off an affirmative reply.

\* \* \* \*

Within fifteen minutes of receiving the text message from Melanie, Carmichael and Penny were already en route for the M62. Carmichael had sent a text back saying he was being driven by his wife and why, which by text Melanie had accepted. As she drove, the low winter sun reflected sharply off the windows of cars and the snow-covered fields making Penny squint and causing her eyes to become watery. In spite

268

of this hazard, their black BMW made good progress on its way towards Manchester.

As they reached Junction 6 on the M61 Carmichael received another text message from Melanie's mobile:

When you get to Junction 19 on the M62 send me a text. Also let me know the make, colour and registration number of your car.

'This is all very well thought out,' said Carmichael. 'She's obviously planned this meeting thoroughly.'

'So where will we be at Junction 19?' Penny asked.

Carmichael studied the map. 'We'll be on the road to Rochdale as far as I can see.'

'I thought Rachel said Melanie was in Doncaster?' enquired Penny as she accelerated and overtook a lorry that was struggling to maintain a decent speed in the middle lane.

'She did,' replied Carmichael. 'Maybe that's where we'll end up.'

After forty minutes they reached Junction 19 and Carmichael sent the text message to Melanie with the details of his car. Almost immediately he received his next instructions:

Come off the motorway at Junction 22. Take the road towards Oldham and Denshaw. When you come off the motorway send me a text.

It was exactly 3 p.m. when Penny and Carmichael reached Junction 22, which sits remotely at the top of the windswept Pennines. The vast white moorland, with no buildings or trees in sight, looked more like a scene from Greenland than the centre of England. As instructed, Carmichael sent Melanie's mobile another text just as Penny turned right off the motorway over the cattle grid on the Oldham road.

They didn't notice the white Ford Fiesta that had parked up on the bridge over the motorway, monitoring their progress.

As soon as it was clear that the BMW was not being followed, the final text message was sent to Carmichael:

In about 1 mile you will come to a pub on your right. Stop in the car park and wait for your next instructions.

## Chapter 35

Rachel Dalton and PC Morley had found the South Yorkshire Police very helpful and welcoming. By the time the two officers from across the Pennines had arrived, their Yorkshire colleagues had already started circulating Melanie's photograph and had checked the CCTV footage at the train station from the evening before. However, in spite of all their efforts they had drawn a complete blank.

'What now?' asked PC Morley despondently.

'You know, I bet she got off at one of the stations between Moulton Bank and here,' replied Rachel. 'I can only suggest we make our way home via each railway station and see if anyone remembers seeing her getting off yesterday evening.'

'There must be a dozen stations between here and Moulton Bank!' exclaimed Morley. 'That could take us hours.'

Rachel took a deep breath. 'Yes, so the sooner we make a start the better, I'd say.'

\*    \*    \*    \*

Carmichael and Penny's car was the only vehicle in the pub car park high up on the moors. As they waited for their next instructions, they could feel the wind pushing hard against the side of the car and hear it whistling around the hilltops making the whole scene very eerie.

'Do you think they get much business up here?' Penny asked, pointing to the pub.

271

'I doubt it,' he replied. 'Well, certainly not between November and March.'

At that moment the white Fiesta pulled into the car park and came to a rest about ten feet away from their car. It flashed its headlights.

Penny was starting to feel uneasy. 'What now?' she asked.

'Well, if that's Melanie, she's not alone,' he replied. 'If I'm not mistaken there are two people in that car.'

Carmichael was just about to suggest that Penny drove over, when he received a new text message.

Get out of the car and come over to the white car, but on your own. Leave your wife in the car.

Carmichael showed his wife the text message. 'I'll leave you the phone. If it looks like it's all going wrong call Hewitt straight away and tell him what has happened, then get yourself back home.'

'Be careful, Steve,' said Penny anxiously.

Carmichael kissed her full on the lips before clambering out of the car. 'Don't worry, I'm sure it will be fine,' he said just before he shut the car door.

\*    \*    \*    \*

'So where to first?' asked PC Morley.

Rachel looked at the rail journey planner on her laptop. 'Well, it looks like she would have had two options. Either she travelled via Manchester and then Leeds, or she went via Manchester and then Sheffield. They both take about the same time.'

'So which route do we follow?' asked Morley.

Rachel thought for a moment. 'I suggest you take the Sheffield route in the car and I'll take the Leeds route on the train. If we start now, we may be able to meet up in

272

Manchester, and if we've not traced her by then we can stop off at all the stations home from Manchester to Moulton Bank.'

'This could take us hours,' remarked PC Morley.

'I know,' replied Rachel irately. 'If you have a better idea, please feel free to tell me!'

Morley shook his head. 'No, it's just about the only thing we can do I suppose,' he said meekly.

Rachel looked at her watch. 'If you drop me off at Doncaster station, I bet that between us we could get through all the main stations between here and Manchester on both routes, in about three hours. My hunch is that she will have got off somewhere on this side of Manchester, as she won't have had much cash, so she will not have wanted to pay for too much further than she was going. In my view, she's probably smart enough to have got off a reasonable distance before Doncaster too, so it's likely she got off at Sheffield or Leeds or one of the stations between either of them and Manchester.'

PC Morley gazed over his colleague's shoulder. 'Well, there's not much between Manchester and Sheffield, but there are a few largish stations between Leeds and Manchester. So why don't I pick up your route but further down the line, after I've been to Sheffield? We could then maybe meet up at somewhere in between, like Huddersfield.'

Rachel gazed at the route on the screen. 'That sounds a good plan to me,' she said. 'I'll meet you at Huddersfield station. If I'm lucky with the trains, I reckon I can get there in no more than two and a half hours.'

'Me too,' replied Morley. 'And you never know, if you're really lucky you may not be as late as you thought getting back to your boyfriend.'

'Yes,' replied Rachel with a fake smile. 'I'll have to call him when I get on the train to Leeds.'

*   *   *   *

Carmichael made his way over to the white Ford Fiesta. The biting wind blew into his face, stinging his cheeks and making each step that he took a real effort. If this wasn't bad enough, the reflection of the sun's rays off the crisp white snow also made him squint. He bowed his head forward as he walked, which helped block out the bright light but couldn't stop the cold gusts from making his eyes water. With tear drops running freely down the side of his face, Carmichael eventually reached the white car.

'Get in the back!' shouted a man's voice through the partially open driver's window.

Carmichael did as he was told.

Once inside, Carmichael closed the door and looked up at the two occupants of the car. 'It's you!' he said in total surprise. 'What are you doing here?'

*   *   *   *

Penny looked on nervously. She had left the key inserted in the ignition and was ready to follow the white car should it head off with her husband on board. She had also scrolled down on Steve's phone to Chief Inspector Hewitt's number, just in case she needed to speak with him urgently. She kept here eyes fixed on the white car, but even with the sun visor down, she could not block out the sun's bright reflection which greatly impeded her vision of its occupants.

'Be careful, Steve,' she muttered to herself.

*   *   *   *

Sidney Sydes was amused by Carmichael's shocked reaction.

'Nice to see you again, Inspector,' he said with a broad smile. 'I believe you've met my sister.'

Open-mouthed, Carmichael looked across to see first the

shock of orange hair and then the equally broad smile of the young woman in the passenger seat.

'Sister!' Carmichael exclaimed.

'Yes,' replied Sydes. 'You didn't think I came to boring old Moulton Bank for the scenery, did you?'

From the confused expression on Carmichael's face it was clear to Melanie that he needed more information. 'I was born Melanie Dawson,' she explained. 'When Jimmy and Tony were convicted for the murder of that old man I was just four years old.' As she spoke, Melanie looked towards her brother who smiled back at her and was clearly happy for her to tell her tale. 'When they went to prison, Mum and Dad split up. I was really young but I think it was because Dad thought Patrick shouldn't have testified against them, whereas Mum thought he had done the right thing. Anyway Patrick got taken away for his own protection and became Sidney Sydes and our mum and dad divorced. Mum didn't want to stay in the area so we moved away and when I was about nine Mum remarried a man called Ron Dreyfuss, so I changed my name to Dreyfuss too.'

'So have you been in touch for all those years?' Carmichael asked.

'No,' replied Sydes. 'We met when Mum died about three years ago. After the funeral we kept in contact secretly, although we've only managed to meet up once in that time.'

'It was Patrick … sorry I should say Sidney,' continued Melanie 'that encouraged me to find a way out of shoplifting, which is why I joined The Helpful Angels.'

'I see,' replied Carmichael, who was still stunned by what he was learning. 'So your visit to Moulton Bank was to see your sister?' he queried.

'Yes,' replied Sydes. 'However, we didn't manage to get together. First I had really bad flu, then with you and your people coming around all the time to the boat, I didn't want to risk being seen with Melanie.'

275

'I see,' said Carmichael who was still a little lost for words. 'So what are your plans now?'

'First off, to keep one step ahead of your lot,' replied Melanie. 'Just while we find out who really killed Clare and the others.'

Carmichael smiled. 'You may have done a good job so far, but you won't evade the police for much longer. They will find you in the end and my guess is that it will be sooner rather than later … days at the most.'

Melanie's previously happy expression changed to one of serious determination. 'Especially once you tell them that there are two of us now, which no doubt you will do once we've gone.'

Carmichael pondered how he should react before making any comment. 'Look, as you know I'm officially off the case,' he said. 'But I am reasonably confident that neither you nor Clare were responsible for any of the deaths and I'm willing to put my career on the line and do some investigating independently over the next few days to try and get to the bottom of this one.' Carmichael could see from the relieved expressions on their faces that Melanie and Sidney Sydes welcomed this news. 'However, in exchange I've two conditions.'

'Which are?' asked Melanie apprehensively.

'First of all, you tell me everything you know, with nothing held back, and, secondly, you both turn yourselves in to the police within the next twenty-four hours.'

'No deal,' replied Melanie angrily. 'I'm not turning myself in, no way.'

Sydes put his hand on his sister's arm to comfort her, he then turned his head to face Carmichael. 'What if we agreed to turn ourselves in but you gave us a few more days?'

'What are you saying?' exclaimed Melanie. 'These people are convinced that I'm a killer. I don't know why. If I give myself up, they'll put me inside; I know they will.'

Carmichael looked straight into Melanie's eyes. 'They believe you're implicated because you and Clare cleaned Poole's house, you were caterers at the Lovelace's party last Saturday, your purse was found near the body of Tamara Searle, your friend appears to have committed suicide surrounded by Tamara's possessions and because you have absconded. Now I know this doesn't prove guilt and I believe you're innocent, but the longer you're on the run the worse it will get for you.'

'What the hell are you talking about? I've not lost my purse,' retorted Melanie with a puzzled expression on her face. 'It's in my bag.'

With that the feisty redhead riffled through her bag and held out a small red purse.

'Well, on Wednesday, when we found Tamara Searle, we also found a purse with an unused train ticket to Manchester, some cash and your debit card in it,' replied Carmichael. 'We assumed it was yours.'

'That would be Clare's, I suspect,' remarked Melanie. 'I lent her my debit card on Monday evening when I last saw her. She needed some cash to buy a train ticket to see her brother. I lent her the card and told her my pin number.'

'Then you need to tell the police all this,' said her brother sympathetically. 'Look, what if we compromise and say that you'll not say anything to your colleagues on the condition that we promise to hand ourselves in by the end of the day on Monday? That gives you two days to find the real killer and two days for us to spend some time together.'

Carmichael was uneasy about the deal being put to him. He didn't like the thought of Marc and Rachel running around over the weekend wasting valuable time, while all along he was keeping important facts from them. However, he knew that without agreeing there was a strong chance that Melanie and Sydes would scarper taking their valuable information with them.

'It's a deal,' he said reluctantly. 'But, I need to know everything and if you've not handed yourself in by Monday evening I will inform my colleagues that we've met and will do everything I can to help them track you down.'

It was clear from the expression on her face that Melanie was still unsure, but she nodded her agreement before asking submissively, 'So what do you want to know then?'

'Just start at the beginning,' said Carmichael. 'If I don't understand anything or have any questions, I'll interrupt you.'

\* \* \* \*

Across the car park, as Penny waited nervously for her husband to emerge from the white Fiesta, his mobile received a text message from Rachel:

> We believe that Melanie has pulled a fast one and got off the train before Doncaster. PC Morley and I are checking out the stations between Manchester and Doncaster. I'll update you if we find anything.

Penny thought seriously about sending a reply, but after a short period of reflection she decided that Carmichael wouldn't want her to do this. So instead she remained in her seat, motionless with her eyes transfixed on the misted windows of the other car.

# Chapter 36

Melanie swivelled around in her chair to face Carmichael, with her back resting against the glove compartment. 'Like I said in my text yesterday, someone is trying to fit Clare and I up for that weathergirl's death,' she said. 'Them leaving a purse with my debit card in it just proves it.'

'But who would want to do that?' asked Carmichael.

'I've no idea why I've been dragged into all this,' replied Melanie, 'but it's got to be some stuff that Clare got mixed up in.'

'What do you mean?' asked Carmichael.

Melanie looked genuinely confused. 'I'm not sure,' she replied. 'All I know is that she was very worried when I saw her on Monday evening. Actually, she was terrified, so frightened that she planned to hide out at her brother's in Manchester for a while.'

'What was she frightened of?' asked Carmichael, trying hard to coax Melanie to tell him everything she knew.

'I don't know,' she replied. 'All I know is that in the last few weeks she's not been herself. Then at the Lovelace's party last Saturday she was really upset and when I saw her on Monday she was very scared.'

'Start at the beginning, Mel,' said Sydes firmly. 'Tell Inspector Carmichael everything you told me yesterday.'

Melanie nodded and took a deep breath. 'Well, Clare and I both joined The Helpful Angels at about the same time. We became good friends and Mrs Cashman arranged our

279

cleaning shifts so that we covered for each other. Up until about three months ago we would share doing Mr Poole's house. One week Clare would do Mondays and me Thursdays and the next we'd swap over. We did this with other places too. Then Clare said she wanted to do Poole's house every Monday and asked if I'd do another house every Monday. I said yes because it was no bother to me and to be honest I thought nothing of it.'

'But did you not wonder why Clare asked you to change the shifts like that?' asked Carmichael.

'Not really,' replied Melanie with a shrug of her shoulders. 'Knowing Clare there was going to be a good reason, but it was no big deal to me to swap shifts, so I didn't ask any questions.'

'But you would still clean Poole's house on other days?' Carmichael asked.

'We only did Poole's house on Mondays and Thursdays, so yes I'd do the Thursday clean every other week but not the Monday one,' replied Melanie.

Carmichael's thoughts went back to the conversation he had with Roy Lovelace in The Fisheries earlier in the week.

'So what do you think Clare was up to?' Carmichael asked. 'Maybe she was seeing Gerry Poole?'

'No, I'm sure it wasn't anything to do with Poole,' replied Melanie resolutely.

'How are you so sure?' Carmichael enquired.

'Well, first, because he was really not that sort of bloke and, secondly, I couldn't see Clare fancying him,' replied Melanie whose facial expression was one of repulsion at the very thought of such a relationship. 'Anyway,' she continued, 'he was never at home on Mondays. He was occasionally in on Thursdays, but never on a Monday. I did think she was probably using the house to see someone though.'

'You said that in the last few weeks she wasn't herself,'

Carmichael reminded Melanie. 'What do you mean by that?'

'Well, she was moody, not as friendly, and I think looking back she was worried,' replied Melanie.

'Worried about what?' Carmichael asked.

'I've no idea,' replied Melanie. 'She wouldn't say, but I knew something was up.'

'So did you ask her what was wrong?' Carmichael enquired.

'Yes, of course I did!' snapped Melanie. 'But she told me I was looking for things that weren't there and that she was just tired.'

'So what happened at the party last week?' Carmichael asked. 'I saw you and her in the corridor and she was crying. What was the matter with her?'

'I don't know,' replied Melanie. 'She was really upset though. I think someone said something to her. She was going to tell me I think, then you and then that Searle woman both appeared and it seemed to spook her and she shot off to the toilets. It all happened just at the time when we were supposed to serve the coffees, so I couldn't follow her. When I saw her next it was about ten minutes later and she had sorted herself out and looked OK again.'

'So she didn't tell you what had made her so unhappy?' asked Carmichael.

'No, not that night,' replied Melanie. 'She did tell me more though on Monday when I saw her.'

'Really,' said Carmichael, who was starting to feel that at last Melanie's story might be getting somewhere. 'What did she say?'

'Well, I had been thinking about what happened at the party over the rest of the weekend,' said Melanie. 'Then when Mrs Cashman told me I had to do Poole's house on the Monday because Clare had not turned in, I thought I'd go round to see her. Then, of course, I get interviewed by

281

your two detectives and they tell me that Gerry Poole is dead and I started to think that maybe Clare's moodiness and her being upset at the party may be something to do with Poole being found dead. So that evening I went to her flat to talk to her.'

'And what did she tell you?' Carmichael asked.

Melanie looked across at her brother, who nodded to her as a clear sign that she should continue.

'She was terrified,' continued Melanie. 'I've never seen her or anyone else for that matter so scared. She said that she was mixed up in something that was very serious and that she was frightened that she could even get hurt. She told me that she had been seeing someone but wouldn't say who it was. She also said she knew something terrible that she couldn't tell me about, but that, just by her knowing what she knew, she was in danger. It was then that she told me she needed to get away to her brother's while she decided what she could do about the mess she was in.'

'What else did she tell you?' asked Carmichael.

'Only that she had done something really stupid on Saturday evening, that she wished she hadn't done,' replied Melanie. 'She wouldn't say anything more, as she said that, if I knew any more, I might end up in the same trouble she was in.'

'And then you gave her your debit card?' remarked Carmichael.

'Once I knew she was not going to tell me anything else, I told her that, if she was afraid, then she was right to get away,' continued Melanie. 'I asked her when she planned to go to her brother's in Manchester and she said that she wouldn't be able to go for a few days as she had no money for the train ticket. We get paid monthly and our February pay was due in our accounts on Thursday. She said she was broke and would have to wait until then. I thought if she was in as much trouble as she said, she needed to get away that evening or, at the latest, the next morning. So I lent her my debit card and told her my pin number. She was supposed to just draw out enough money for the train fare and drop off my card back at my house before she went, but that was the last I saw of her and my debit card.'

'Why didn't you go with her to draw out the money?' Carmichael asked. 'Surely that would have been easier. You wouldn't have had to leave your card with her either.'

'I wish I had,' replied Melanie sorrowfully. 'I suggested we did that but she wouldn't hear of it. She was sure that if they saw me with her, I could get caught up in whatever mess she was in. She kept saying that she didn't want me being dragged into the mess and once I gave her my card she practically threw me out.'

'She sounds as if she was very frightened,' remarked Carmichael.

'She was absolutely terrified,' replied Melanie. 'And now she's dead, it's clear she was right to be so scared.'

'So was that the last time you saw her?' asked Carmichael.

'It was the last time I saw her alive,' replied Melanie.

Melanie's answer surprised Carmichael. 'So you've seen her dead?' he asked.

'Yes,' said Melanie quietly. 'After you chased me from Mrs Prentice's yesterday, I went to Poole's house. It was the only place I could think to go. When I got there she was dead in the armchair, surrounded by lots of stuff that belonged to Tamara Searle. They made it look like suicide. They even got her to write a suicide note, but I know that she would never kill herself. They made it look like that just to put all the blame on her and me.'

'This suicide note,' asked Carmichael, 'what did it say?'

Melanie smiled. 'You can read it for yourself,' she remarked smugly as she pulled out the note she had taken from beside Clare's body and passed it to Carmichael in the back of the car.

Carmichael took the single sheet of writing paper from Melanie and started to read:

*Dear Mrs Cashman,*
*I'm sorry for what we've done. I didn't mean for it to be like this; it just all got out of control. You have been really good to me and don't deserve this. I know I have to end it and I hope you can forgive us and that our behaviour will not stop you continuing to help other people like me in the future.*
*Clare*

'You say you found this by Clare's dead body?' Carmichael asked firmly.

'Yes,' replied Melanie.

'I take it that this is Clare's handwriting?' continued Carmichael.

'Yes, it's definitely written by her, but she must have been forced to write it,' replied Melanie. 'There's no way she killed anyone and I don't know who she means by "we", although I'm sure your lot will think it's me she's talking about.'

'You shouldn't have taken this,' Carmichael said sternly. 'This is important evidence and the investigation team need to have this. You've really made things so much worse for yourself by taking this away.'

'I told you I should have destroyed it,' snapped Melanie in her brother's direction.

Sidney put his arm around his sister. 'No, you were right to show it to Inspector Carmichael. You've done nothing wrong, so you've nothing to hide.'

Carmichael read the brief note again. 'Why did she address this to Mrs Cashman?' he asked.

Melanie shrugged her shoulders. 'That puzzled me too,' she replied with a frown. 'She did like Mrs Cashman, but I didn't think they were that friendly.'

Carmichael rested his forehead on the palm of his left hand while he thought.

'Look,' he said after a few moments. 'The police need to see this and anything else you've taken from the house. It's one thing keeping our meeting secret and me allowing you forty-eight hours to give yourselves up, but I can't allow such important evidence to be kept from the investigation team. Do you understand what I'm saying?'

Melanie nodded reluctantly and exchanged a sideways glance with her brother. 'You better take these too,' she said sheepishly as she handed over Tamara's mobile phone and the credit cards she had taken from Poole's house. 'I've used the credit card just once but I've not touched the mobile.'

'Is that everything?' Carmichael asked firmly.

'It is,' replied Sydes. 'You have my word on that.'

'Thank you,' replied Carmichael as he placed the letter into one of his jacket pockets and the phone and credit cards in the other.

'What are you going to do now?' Melanie asked, her face showing for the first time her fear at her predicament.

'God knows,' replied Carmichael. 'This has really thrown a spanner in the works.'

'Do you really have to tell the others?' Melanie asked.

'I think you know the answer to that,' replied Carmichael.

'I know,' said Sidney. 'Why don't you just say that I called you and asked you to meet me here. It's almost true. You could say that you had no idea why I wanted to meet you and that when you arrived Melanie was with me and we gave you these things and Melanie told you our side of story. You could then say that we then sped off and you lost us.'

Carmichael didn't like the thought of lying, but hiding such important evidence was not an option and he could not think of a better route out of the muddle he had become embroiled in than the one Sydes had suggested.

'OK,' he replied uneasily. 'I'll give you twenty minutes head start then I'm going to call my colleagues and meet up with them to hand over this evidence. I'll also be giving them a description of your car and the licence plate number too, so if you want that extra time together you better be out of the car within the hour.'

'Thanks a bundle,' remarked Melanie angrily. 'How do you expect us to get away without a car?'

Not for the first time that afternoon, Sidney calmed his sister down. 'It's OK, Mel,' he said. 'We're near enough to several railway stations to dump the car and get away before they have time to trace us.'

Melanie shrugged her shoulders. 'If you say so,' she replied, although it was clear she didn't totally agree.

'Thank you, Inspector,' said Sydes, holding out his right hand. 'I hope you can now see that Melanie is innocent.'

'I hope so for all of our sakes,' replied Carmichael, opening up the car door.

'Remember, I'm just going to give you twenty minutes and then I'll call my colleagues. And I expect you to give yourselves up in forty-eight hours as we agreed.'

'It's a deal,' replied Sydes. 'You have our word.'

Carmichael got out of the car and started to walk slowly towards his BMW, at the far side of the car park. As he walked with the wind whistling around him, Sydes drew the Fiesta up next to him and opened the window.

'There was one other thing,' he said. 'When you came to the boat that first time and I said I hadn't seen anything strange last Saturday, I was not being totally straight with you. At about 4.30 that afternoon I did see three people walking slowly down the towpath towards the boat. They were too far away for me to make them out and I was feeling very ill with flu, so I wasn't really paying too much attention. However, thinking about it, they could have been two people dragging along a dead body I suppose.'

'Were these people big, small, male or female?' asked Carmichael.

'I've absolutely no idea,' replied Sydes. 'All I can remember is that they were walking towards the boat from the bridge, but they never came past the boat, so they must have turned back. Maybe it was two people dumping a body.'

Before Carmichael could ask any more questions, Sydes closed his window and the car sped off onto the main road.

Carmichael made a mental note of the car number plate before continuing to trudge his way back to Penny, waiting in their BMW.

# Chapter 37

Rachel Dalton climbed out of the carriage at Wakefield train station at 4.06 p.m., the first scheduled stop on her protracted journey home. Before arriving she had called ahead to the local Transport Police, who had arranged for two of their officers to be waiting for her when the train came to a halt on Platform 2. Rachel had allocated herself just thirty-five minutes at each of the three stations on her route to Manchester, which she felt would give her an adequate amount of time to hand out photographs of Melanie and to provide enough information to enable the Transport Police to look at the surveillance tapes from Friday evening to try and spot Melanie. At 4.40 p.m., having concluded her business in Wakefield, she boarded the train for the short journey that would take her to Leeds, her next destination.

\* \* \* \*

'Thank God you're all right,' exclaimed Penny as her husband clambered into the passenger seat. 'You seemed to be in their car for ages.'

Carmichael gave out a huge sigh. 'Well, I wasn't expecting that.'

'Expecting what?' asked Penny, who could see from his expression that Carmichael was deep in thought.

'That she would have her brother with her,' replied

Carmichael. 'And he would turn out to be Sydes, the bloke from the narrowboat.'

'What!' exclaimed Penny. 'Wasn't he the one that you were warned off as he was on the witness protection scheme?'

'Yes,' responded Carmichael. 'That's the one.'

'So what did they tell you?' Penny asked.

'Quite a lot,' replied Carmichael. 'And they gave me some evidence too.'

As Carmichael started to recount what he had learned from his meeting with Melanie Dreyfuss and Sidney Sydes, the white Fiesta sped off down the M62. It took the two fugitives the whole of their twenty minutes head start to get onto the M61 and the road north towards Preston, which was enough time for Carmichael to bring Penny up to speed.

As Penny read Clare Sands' suicide note for the second time, Carmichael looked at his watch. 'They've had their twenty minutes,' he said. 'I'm going to call Rachel.'

'I almost forgot,' said Penny, 'Rachel texted while you were in their car.'

\*   \*   \*   \*

When Rachel saw it was Carmichael calling she hurriedly took the call. 'Hello, sir,' she said. 'Did you get my text?'

'Yes,' replied Carmichael. 'So you've given up on Doncaster as Melanie's destination.'

'Yes,' shouted Rachel down the line. 'I'm convinced she got off at one of the stations en route. My guess is that it was either Wakefield or Leeds or Huddersfield. I've just left Wakefield and am due to be in Leeds in about ten minutes.'

'Listen, Rachel,' shouted Carmichael, who was struggling badly to hear her properly. 'I've got some important information that I need to share with you. I've just this minute left Melanie,' he lied. 'She has given me some important evidence that you need. When you get to Leeds,

289

just get yourself on the first train you can to Huddersfield. I'll meet you at the railway station.'

'Did you say you've just met with Melanie?' enquired Rachel, who was struggling to hear her boss over the noise of the train as it sped along the line.

'Yes,' replied Carmichael loudly. 'I'll tell you all about it when I see you. Just get to Huddersfield as quick as you can.'

Carmichael hung up. 'Let me just call into Kirkwood Station to give them the details of Sydes' car. Once I've done that we can get on our way to Huddersfield. It can't be more than thirty minutes away. I'll drive as I think I'll be OK now as it's a good few hours since I had those couple of pints.'

'As long as you are sure!,' replied Penny. 'But what am I going to do?'

'That's easy,' said Carmichael. 'You can copy out Clare's note, then if you can manage it try and take down the numbers of the last calls sent and received on Tamara's mobile. I'll have to give the letter and the mobile to Rachel, but I'd like to get as much information as I can before I hand them over. You never know when it may come in handy.'

\*　\*　\*　\*

Carmichael knew full well that by the time he had got through to the desk sergeant at Kirkwood Police Station, Sidney Sydes and Melanie Dreyfuss would be well on their way to their new hideaway. And just as he had anticipated, the two fugitives had abandoned their car in Preston and were boarding the express train north towards Carlisle by the time the details of the make, colour and licence plate of their car had been circulated.

## Chapter 38

DC Evans arrived at Jemma's house ten minutes early. Surprisingly, this was not an issue for Jemma, who had been ready for twenty minutes.

'I like a man who's punctual,' she said confidently as she shut the front door and made her way towards his car.

'You look very nice this evening,' remarked Evans, who had been taken aback by the self-assured manner of the pretty young student.

'So where are you taking me?' she asked as she glided as gracefully as she could into the passenger seat of his smart red Audi A3.

'My secret,' he replied with a grin. 'It's only about thirty minutes away, but far enough to avoid us bumping into anyone you might know from the club.'

Jemma smiled as she fastened her seat belt. 'I'm in your hands then,' she said playfully.

DC Evans put the car into gear and headed off towards the quiet country pub he had selected for their secret rendezvous.

\* \* \* \*

As Carmichael's black BMW headed down the M62 towards Huddersfield, the only topic of conversation was of that afternoon's meeting and the new information he had gleaned from Melanie and Sydes.

'If you're convinced that she's telling you the truth and that she told you everything,' said Penny carefully, 'then who do you think the murderer is?'

Carmichael shook his head. 'That's the problem: I'm not sure,' he said pensively. 'There's still so much that needs to be investigated and without the team it's going to be a hard slog.'

'So what do we know?' asked Penny.

'Well, for starters,' replied Carmichael, 'it's a very complicated enquiry and, although we should not totally ignore any other possibilities, I'm convinced that the deaths of Poole, Searle and Sands are linked in some way.'

'Why do you say that? asked Penny.

'I don't believe in coincidences. So given the fact that we have three people all dying so close together who are linked through The Helpful Angels, Caroline's dinner party and Sunrise Productions, it suggests to me that they *must* be connected in some way,' he replied. 'In that respect, Hewitt and Marc Watson are correct.'

'So it's just that in your view they've picked on the wrong people in Clare Sands and Melanie Dreyfuss,' Penny confirmed.

'Precisely,' replied Carmichael, who was as always impressed with the structured and detached way his wife was helping him analyse the situation. 'In fact, neither Melanie nor Clare Sands to my knowledge had any connection with Sunrise Productions or Tamara Searle other than meeting her once at the party when they were serving dinner. If that's the case, then why would they kill her? It makes no sense whatsoever.'

'So,' responded Penny carefully. 'If we assume that you're right, then are we also saying that Clare didn't kill herself?'

Carmichael pondered this question for a good few seconds before he responded.

'That's a tricky one to answer without Dr Stock's customary

detailed autopsy,' he replied. 'However, if what Melanie is telling me is true, then you'd have to say she was killed by someone who is trying hard to make it look like suicide.'

'So why would someone do that?' enquired Penny, 'and, if they did, how did they get her to write a suicide note?'

'Good questions,' replied Carmichael thoughtfully, 'but regrettably questions I don't have good answers to as yet.'

\* \* \* \*

Rachel was fortunate to get a connecting train to Huddersfield within minutes of arriving at Leeds railway station. As she settled herself down in the empty carriage, she texted Carmichael to let him know that she expected to get into Huddersfield station at about 5.55 p.m. Rachel was looking forward to seeing the boss again as it had not felt the same with him out of the loop and Hewitt in control. She also wondered what new evidence he had to share with her.

\* \* \* \*

At about the same time that Penny read Rachel's text message to Carmichael, the red Audi carrying Jemma and DC Evans pulled into the large car park of The Unicorn public house, perched high on the windswept hill overlooking the twinkling lights of Halifax down below, just a hundred yards from the M62 junction.

'We should be safe to talk here,' he said to her reassuringly. 'I'm keen to find out how it all went last night and what information you have for me.'

Jemma smiled. 'I hope you allow me to have something to eat first before you start pressing me to hand over the information.'

'Absolutely,' replied Evans. 'And I can assure you the food here is fantastic.

* * * *

Carmichael and Penny had been waiting for forty-five minutes at Huddersfield station when Rachel's train pulled in. Only a handful of passengers got off, so it was no problem spotting Rachel as she hurried down the platform.

'Hello, Mrs Carmichael,' Rachel said with a degree of surprise in her voice. 'I didn't expect to see you here too!'

Carmichael didn't want to waste any time making small talk. He was anxious to discuss the case with Rachel and to get off that draughty platform. 'There's a small bar over there,' he said, pointing in the direction of a cosy-looking pub located next to the station's ticket office. 'Let's go inside and I can explain all to you.'

Without waiting for a reply, Carmichael marched off in the direction of the bar with Rachel and Penny following a few steps behind him.

Once inside, Carmichael found a quiet table and without bothering to order any drinks he told Rachel the story about Sidney Sydes contacting him, just as Sidney had suggested earlier. In truth, Carmichael was not comfortable lying to Rachel, but he saw no alternative other than admitting he had been deliberately disobeying Hewitt's instructions. Fortunately Rachel seemed to buy the tale, which then allowed Carmichael to update her on his meeting with Melanie Dreyfuss and Sidney Sydes earlier that afternoon. Once he had finished, he handed over the three items Melanie had given him. First of all he passed over Tamara's mobile phone and credit cards, and then the suicide note written in Clare Sands' untidy handwriting.

Rachel looked closely at the suicide note. 'Surely this only strengthens the case that Sands was involved,' she contested.

'I agree it may not incriminate Melanie Dreyfuss, but by her own confession it clearly implicates Clare Sands.'

'On the face of it, yes,' agreed Carmichael. 'But, I'm not convinced. It could quite easily have been written under duress.'

'If so why is it addressed to Mrs Cashman?' enquired Rachel. 'Surely the killer would have made her write it without being addressed to anyone, or failing that to a relative of Clare's.'

'I wondered that,' remarked Penny. 'That does seem odd.'

'I don't know,' replied Carmichael in an irritated tone. 'I don't know...Maybe it was Mrs Cashman who made poor Clare write the note.' Carmichael had nothing to support what he had just blurted out; he was simply expressing his frustration at seemingly being unable to convince either of them that Clare Sands was innocent. 'Look, I don't know who it was that made Clare write this note, but I'm absolutely certain this is not as it seems.'

'You may be right, sir,' replied Rachel. 'However, I don't see Chief Inspector Hewitt taking that view when he sees this, do you?'

Carmichael had to agree. 'Yes, I'm afraid from what you and Marc have told me already he seems to have made his mind up on this one,' replied Carmichael.

'But what I don't understand,' interrupted Penny, 'is how such a normally logical person like Chief Inspector Hewitt is so unwilling to look at other alternative scenarios. It doesn't seem to be in character.'

'I think the answer to that is quite simple,' replied Rachel. 'He's under immense pressure from the Chief Super-intendent to resolve this one. I think that is due to all the fuss Roy Lovelace is making.'

'Lovelace does seem to have a lot of influence at a senior level within the force,' confirmed Carmichael. 'And as he and Caroline seem to be making this a personal crusade of theirs, I think Hewitt will be feeling the heat.'

'Then it's up to us to help him solve the case,' replied Penny positively.

Rachel looked uneasy at this suggestion. 'You're right but it will be difficult. With the boss being officially taken off the case and me supposed to be taking instructions from Hewitt, it's going to be tricky to carry out a separate investigation without him knowing.'

'I understand,' replied Carmichael sympathetically. 'I'll try and keep you out of the firing line, but it would help me if you were available to do some minor research for me from the inside, covertly of course.'

Rachel smiled and then looked at her watch. 'I'll help as much as I can,' she replied. 'However, we may have to resume this discussion another time as PC Morley is due to meet me here any minute now, so it may be better if you shoot off so he doesn't see you.'

Carmichael nodded. 'That's fine,' he said. 'I'm going to call Hewitt myself later to let him know I've met Melanie and that you have all the items she gave me. Hopefully I can persuade him to look broader than Melanie and Clare in this case.'

'Good luck with that,' replied Rachel, smiling. 'I think you will be hard pushed to get Chief Inspector Hewitt to change his views, but I hope you succeed.'

Penny and Carmichael only just managed to avoid bumping into PC Morley, who entered the bar a matter of minutes after they had departed.

## Chapter 39

Jemma Carmichael discovered that the food at The Unicorn was as wonderful as DC Evans had promised, certainly a vast improvement on the fare she had been getting used to since she became a student.

'Wow, Andy,' she exclaimed, as she finished the last spoonful of her sticky toffee pudding. 'That was fantastic.'

'Good,' replied Evans with a smirk on his face. 'I'm sure the chef will be pleased.'

'You know him, do you?' remarked Jemma.

'As a matter of fact I do,' replied Evans. 'It's my dad.'

'What!' exclaimed Jemma. 'Is this your pub?'

'Well, my mum and dad's, yes,' he replied.

'But I thought you were Welsh?' said Jemma.

'I am,' replied Evans with a laugh. 'We lived on the Gower Peninsula near Swansea until I was about fourteen. Then we moved here. Did you think Welsh people weren't allowed out of Wales?'

\*  \*  \*  \*

As Carmichael and Penny travelled back home over the Pennines, the temperature dropped sharply. So much so that, by the time they reached the Halifax turning, snow had started to fall and by the time they had descended down into Lancashire it was snowing heavily, making driving conditions extremely difficult.

'I thought we'd seen the back of this,' moaned Carmichael as he concentrated hard on the road ahead.

'Well, they did say on last night's weather report that it would start to clear today,' replied Penny. 'It looks like they got it wrong again.'

Carmichael didn't reply, his thoughts were elsewhere.

\*　　\*　　\*　　\*

Melanie Dreyfuss and Sidney Sydes were detained by the Transport Police at Carlisle railway station at 7.15 p.m. Within twenty minutes the news of their arrest had reached Chief Inspector Hewitt, who was understandably elated, as was Chief Superintendent Banks and the Right Honourable Roy Lovelace, who were swiftly brought up to speed.

\*　　\*　　\*　　\*

It was 7.55 p.m. when Carmichael and Penny arrived home. The snow in Moulton Bank was already lying thick on top of the partially thawed slush from previous falls that week.

Fortunately for Penny, Natalie and Robbie had managed to sort out their own dinners, so, although she herself was hungry, she knew that at the most she would only have to prepare a meal for herself and Steve.

'Do you want something to eat?' she asked her husband.

'I'm not that hungry,' replied Carmichael, grabbing the local weekly paper that had dropped through the door while they were out. 'I'll have something later. I want to call Hewitt and I'd like to just have some time in my office to try and work out what to do next.'

'OK,' replied Penny, who was relieved that she didn't have to cook. 'But please don't be all night up there.'

\*　　\*　　\*　　\*

The snowfall that evening on the top of the Pennines was also heavy. So much so that by the time DC Evans and Jemma had eaten and then concluded their business, it lay over a foot thick.

'There's no chance of me getting you home tonight,' DC Evans concluded. 'I think you'll have to stay over.'

Having not brought any clothes other than what she was wearing, Jemma was not too keen on this idea. However, when she saw the weather outside for herself she could see there was no way they would be able to get back to Leeds in such terrible conditions.

'You can stay in Andy's sister's old room,' announced Mrs Evans from behind the bar, in a very broad Welsh accent. 'She's at uni herself back in South Wales. You're about her size, so I'm sure some of her night things would fit you. Come with me, dear, and we'll take a look.'

Jemma followed Andy's mother upstairs to see what sort of wardrobe his sister had left behind.

\*     \*     \*     \*

Carmichael tried calling Hewitt several times on his mobile, but on each occasion the line was busy. In the end he reluctantly left a short voice message asking his boss to call him urgently. Having left the message, Carmichael then sat back in his comfortable leather chair and gazed out of the window at the wintry scene outside, while he tried to fathom out what he should do next.

\*     \*     \*     \*

Travis Sands marched purposefully through the deep crisp snow. It was 8.15 p.m. and, although the narrow lane was dark and badly lit, this didn't bother Travis. He was also totally oblivious to the biting cold wind that tried its best to push him over and to the thick snowflakes that swirled around him, settling for a moment on his head and shoulders before quickly melting away. Clad in faded, torn jeans, training shoes and a thin hooded jacket, his clothing was totally unsuited to the severe conditions on that cold February evening. However, this didn't seem to worry the angry young man who had just had the harrowing experience of identifying the cold lifeless body of his little sister. Not even the five-foot wooden gate that blocked his path as he reached his destination could slow him down. Without breaking stride, Travis vaulted effortlessly over this minor barrier and into the thick white layer of virgin snow that covered the driveway beyond. As he hit the ground he glanced up to the twinkling lights of the imposing residence that lay just fifty yards away up the steep slippery slope. Inside, his intended quarry monitored the CCTV pictures of the young man as he strode rapidly towards the house.

\*   \*   \*   \*

It was fortunate that Carmichael had no knowledge of the arrests which had been made that evening in Carlisle, or the major fracas occurring less than two miles from where he sat. It was also probably lucky for Carmichael that Hewitt had decided not to return his message that evening, even though he had picked it up within a matter of minutes of it arriving. And it was certainly advantageous that Carmichael knew nothing of the way his eldest daughter had been recruited as a police informant for a drugs operation at a Leeds club and had spent the evening supplying the police with information which could put her own safety at risk.

Had Carmichael been aware of any one of these situations, it is unlikely he would have been in the right frame of mind to spend the next five hours in his study thinking about the three deaths.

In those valuable uninterrupted hours Carmichael finally managed to collect his thoughts properly. In his blissful ignorance of all that was going on outside, he considered carefully the evidence at his disposal. At long last he now also had time to look at the case notes and statements of the cattle rustlers that he had hastily taken from the station the day before. And, importantly, he also had time to study the article by Norfolk George on the front page of the local paper.

It was 1.45 a.m. when Steve Carmichael finally called it a night. By the time he turned off the light in his attic study he was totally convinced that he had at last started to unravel the mystery of why Gerard Poole had been frozen then dumped beside the canal towpath, the seemingly motiveless murder of Tamara Searle and the unexplained death of Clare Sands.

# Chapter 40

**Sunday 22<sup>nd</sup> February**

It was the deafening din of the snowplough as it grinded its way up the road directly outside her bedroom window that caused Jemma to wake up so early and so abruptly. For a second or two Jemma panicked as she tried to remember where she was. However, as soon as she did, her anxiety quickly subsided and she was able to relax. In spite of the small fragments of light breaking through the gaps in the curtains, the room was still quite dark and Jemma could not work out what time it was. Through half-shut sleepy eyes, she peered at her watch which she had rested on the small bedside cabinet the night before. Even though Jemma was still tired and even though the hands on her wristwatch were very slender, she was just about able to work out that it was either 6.35 a.m., or if the hands were the other way round 7.30 a.m. Whichever way it was, it was still much too early to get up, Jemma concluded. She pulled hard on the thick duvet until it covered her ears and then, still clutching the bedding tightly, rolled over to face away from the bedside cabinet. Safe and warm in her cocoon, with her thoughts only for the handsome Andy Evans, she tried desperately to get back off to sleep.

\*　\*　\*　\*

Carmichael woke up in an ebullient mood. He checked the time on the illuminated face of his large alarm clock and, seeing that it was 7.45 a.m., leaped out of bed like an excited child on Christmas morning and, without any consideration, turned on his bedside light and walked quickly over to the curtains before pulling them wide open.

'What time is it?' enquired his poor tired wife who had been in a deep sleep just seconds earlier.

'It's seven forty-five,' replied Carmichael chirpily. 'You need to get up as it may take us a bit of time to get to church this morning. It looks like it snowed a little more last night.'

'Don't you think we should give it a miss again this week?' replied Penny wearily. 'If the weather's bad, we'll struggle to get up Ambient Hill.'

'It's not as bad as all that,' Carmichael responded. 'We'll be fine as long as we set off a bit earlier. Anyway, I need to talk to someone urgently and I know he'll be at church.'

Penny gazed out from under the duvet with a look of disbelief at how lively her husband was that morning. 'Why are you so bloody cheerful?' she asked. 'And who do you have to talk to who's so important?'

'You'll see,' replied Carmichael with the glow of anticipation etched over his face. 'I'll have a shower first. Do you want some tea?'

Before Penny could make any reply, Carmichael was already on his way down the landing.

'Three sugars in mine,' she shouted to her husband, before burrowing herself back under the covers.

*  *  *  *

No sooner had Carmichael come out of the shower than the phone in the hall started to ring.

'Who the hell is that at this hour on a Sunday morning?' he

303

muttered as he hastily wrapped himself in a large white bath sheet and made his way along the hall to pick up the receiver.

'Hello,' he said in an enquiring way.

'Good morning, Inspector,' came the all too familiar tone of Chief Inspector Hewitt. 'I hope I didn't wake you?'

'No,' replied Carmichael, who had been thrown a little off guard by the call from his boss at such an early hour. 'I was just in the shower.'

'I got your voice message,' continued Hewitt, 'and I also want to bring you up to speed on some developments which you need to be aware of. Is there any chance of you coming into the station today?'

'I'm sorry, sir,' replied Carmichael eagerly. 'Are you saying I'm back on the case?'

There was a few seconds pause before Hewitt replied. 'No, not exactly,' he said nervously. 'I will still be heading up the enquiries on the deaths of Poole, Searle and Sands, but there has been a development last night which I'd like you and Cooper to look into. It's related to the case, but is very separate.'

'What development is that?' Carmichael enquired.

'There was an unpleasant incident yesterday evening at the house of Declan and Emma Cashman,' replied Hewitt. 'Travis Sands, Clare's older brother, tried to break in. Fortunately nobody was hurt and he's now in custody, but if they hadn't got CCTV fitted, and had we not responded as quickly as we did, it could have got really nasty.'

'What was Clare's brother doing at the Cashmans' house?' Carmichael asked.

'He's yet to tell us,' replied Hewitt. 'He was in such a rage that it took four officers to restrain him and I shudder to think what he would have done had we not responded so quickly. We think he was trying to attack Emma Cashman but we're not sure and he's not saying anything. I'd like you to try and fathom that one out.'

'I see,' replied Carmichael, who was intrigued by this new development, but disappointed that Hewitt seemed only to want to use him for such a minor chore, when there was so much real policing that needed to be done. 'I'm just about to go to church with Penny. I'll come in after the service.'

'That's marvellous,' replied Hewitt, the relief clear and palpable in his voice. 'Can you speak to Cooper?'

'Yes,' replied Carmichael. 'I'll call him right away.'

'Good,' replied Hewitt.

'Has Rachel updated you on my meeting with Melanie and Sydes?' Carmichael enquired.

'Yes, she has,' replied Hewitt with the air of disapproval. 'I have to say that I'm very dissatisfied with you meeting Dreyfuss on your own like that. I'm told that the meeting was not of your initiation, but you're off the case, Inspector, and you need to allow me and the rest of the team to pursue our enquiries without the fear of you undermining our efforts. Is that clear?'

'Perfectly,' replied Carmichael angrily. 'However, I feel that I wouldn't be doing my duty if I didn't say to you here and now that if you're still certain Melanie Dreyfuss and Clare Sands murdered Tamara Searle then I think you're making a massive mistake. For sure they are in some way mixed up in all this, but neither of them killed Tamara Searle in my view. I also don't think they had anything to do with dumping Poole's body that Saturday and, although I've not seen Stock's report into Clare Sands' death, I would be amazed if that turns out to be suicide.'

'I can assure you, Inspector, that we are still keeping an open mind in this case,' snapped Hewitt angrily. 'However, Dreyfuss and Sands are our prime suspects and Sands' suicide note, which Dreyfuss deliberately removed from the scene, in my view only supports our supposition in this one.'

Carmichael thought for a few moments about sharing his thoughts and the conclusions of his long deliberations the night before, but he quickly decided against this. There was no way, that Hewitt was about to change his mind without cast-iron undisputable evidence. Carmichael took a deep breath to calm himself down.

'I'll come into the station as soon as I can,' he said in a composed and deliberate manner. 'However, I don't agree with the assumption you're making about Melanie Dreyfuss. After speaking with her yesterday, I am convinced she's innocent. There are probably five or six others I would put above her as prime suspects.'

To Carmichael's surprise, Hewitt didn't come back at him straight away. He fully expected Hewitt to outrank him with a flippant comment and abruptly end the call there and then, but he didn't. Instead Hewitt calmly but smugly replied. 'Well, I will know more in the course of the morning. I forgot to mention that Miss Dreyfuss and her brother were apprehended last night in Carlisle. We have them here in custody and Marc Watson and I will be interviewing them as soon as I've finished this call.'

This news hit Carmichael like a bolt of lightning. He had not expected Melanie and Sidney Sydes to be captured so quickly. His heart sank as he realised that time was now no longer on his side. 'I see' was all he could initially muster in reply, the jubilant mood he had woken with now deserting him completely. 'Maybe once you've spoken to her, you will start to see where I'm coming from,' he continued, although he had little confidence that Hewitt would look further than his blinkered hypothesis.

'Anyway, I must go now,' said Hewitt, who was clearly revelling in the fact that his deliberate bombshell had so obviously unbalanced Carmichael. 'I'll see you later once you have been to church.'

Wrapped only in the large white towel, Carmichael

wandered into the living room and flopped down onto the sofa. 'Bugger!' he said out loud.

\* \* \* \*

DC Evans finally dropped Jemma off outside her house at 9.30 a.m.

'Are you sure that it's Harvey Liddle, the bouncer at Jaspers, who's the person supplying the drugs?' he asked her.

'Absolutely,' replied Jemma with total assurance. 'I saw him with my own eyes hand over something to a customer. I'm sure it was a wrap of drugs and two of the girls I know there who use drugs confirmed he was their supplier.'

'OK,' said Evans with a smile. 'You've been great. I'll take it from here, but thank you so much for your help.'

'Do you want to come in for coffee?' Jemma asked, desperately hoping he would say yes.

'Er, no,' replied Evans who looked at his wristwatch. 'I really should be heading off to the station to write up my report.'

'Will I see you again?' asked Jemma, who was starting to get the impression that she was no longer of any value to DC Evans.

'I think it's probably safest all round if we aren't seen together,' replied Evans with no emotion in his voice. 'It would be dangerous for you if Liddle or any of his cronies knew you were my informant, so I think it's in your best interests if we don't meet again. Also, my advice to you is to quit the club as soon as you can. It's not a place for a decent young lady like you.'

'Is that right?' replied Jemma irritably. 'Well, that's my decision and, as I told my mother, I'll quit when I feel like quitting and not before. Anyway, what about us?'

'What do you mean us?' replied Evans quizzically. 'There's no us. There never was and never will be.'

307

As she had been saying the words, Jemma knew it was a mistake, but she could not stop them coming out of her mouth. She now felt totally stupid and utterly embarrassed. Red-faced, but without a second glance back, she clambered out of the car and slammed the door shut. As Jemma marched up the steps that led to her front door, DC Evans shrugged his shoulders, chuckled to himself, then after checking his rear-view mirror sped off.

In her distraught state it took Jemma a few moments to find then extract her front door key from all the clutter in her bag. However, once she was safely inside, Jemma stormed up the wooden stairs into her room and with the door shut behind her, fell onto the bed sobbing into her pillow. The love affair that was only ever in her head was now over.

DC Evans parked his red Audi a few streets away and keyed eleven digits into his mobile phone.

'Hello, Harvey,' he said threateningly. 'It's your old pal Andy Evans. I'm reliably informed that you're up to your old tricks again. I thought we had an agreement that when you sell that muck on my patch, I get a slice. You wouldn't be trying to go back on your word, would you?'

## Chapter 41

It came as no surprise to Penny to discover the church less than half full when Barney Green started the service. The mile journey from the village up Ambient Hill to the church was quite a climb on a good day, but with the current snow and ice it was much tougher. So much so that almost anyone who had a reasonable distance to travel had taken the sensible option and stayed at home that morning.

Penny's 'I told you so' look was ignored by Carmichael, who once inside the church, spent the first five minutes scouring the congregation to try and find Norfolk George, the main feature reporter on *The Observer*, the local paper which served the villages in and around the Moulton Bank area. After a few anxious moments, Carmichael spotted his man, who was sitting near the front.

'Who are you looking for?' asked Penny, who was starting to get irritated at her husband's furtive behaviour.

'Norfolk George,' whispered Carmichael. 'He's over there. I need to talk to him.'

'What about?' enquired Penny, just as Barney Green grabbed his guitar and started strumming.

'I'll tell you later,' whispered Carmichael, as the choir started to sing.

\* \* \* \*

Having taken Carmichael's call earlier that morning, Sergeant Cooper arrived at the station a little after 8.30 a.m. He had spent the whole of Saturday in bed trying to shake off his flu-like symptoms and to his relief that short rest appeared to have done the trick. He was feeling considerably better than he had felt for many days. Cooper spent thirty minutes familiarising himself with the case notes on the incident at the Cashman's, then having also talked at some length on the phone with the sergeant on duty at the time, he entered the interview room and started to question Travis Sands.

\* \* \* \*

As soon as Barney Green had ended the service, Carmichael shot out of the pew like an Olympic sprinter. Penny could not remember the last time she had seen him move so fast. He certainly was never that sprightly if she required him to help her in the garden or with the household chores.

Outside the church the sun had at last broken through the grey clouds and was shining so brightly that the snow, at long last, was starting to thaw.

Norfolk George ambled out of the church and, after shaking hands with the vicar, started to make his way down the path towards the main road.

Norfolk George was not his real name, but was the nickname he had been given thirty years earlier when his parents moved the family from Ipswich when George's father's firm asked him to relocate to head up their North West branch. The young George, who was just nine years old at the time, had such a strong and unusual accent that it became an obvious trait for the rest of the children in his class to comment upon. In those early days, when one of those children had asked their parents what accent it was, they had been incorrectly told it was a Norfolk accent. So

310

from that day forward the boy from Ipswich in Suffolk became Norfolk George to everyone, a nickname he grew to like so much that he had even adopted it as his pen name when he later started at *The Observer*.

'George,' Carmichael shouted, 'can I have a few minutes of your time?'

Norfolk George didn't reply, but smiled broadly and waited while Carmichael walked briskly over to join him.

Penny correctly assumed that Carmichael wouldn't want her earwigging in on his conversation, so she remained where she was and started a conversation with Mrs Hunter, the always talkative wife of the village pharmacist.

After about ten minutes, Carmichael thanked Norfolk George for his help and walked back over to rescue his wife who had been and was still being talked at by Mrs Hunter, with no obvious pause to allow her to escape or even make any more of a contribution to the discussion than to say 'Yes' or 'No' or, at suitable junctures, 'Really?' or 'Is that right?'

Penny was therefore much relieved when Carmichael grabbed her arm and said, 'I'm sorry to break up your conversation, but it's really important that we go now. I've got a couple of urgent meetings that I need to attend. I hope you don't mind, Mrs Hunter?'

As Carmichael marched them both down the path, Penny kept a tight hold of her husband's arm. 'What's the hurry?' she asked. 'What did Norfolk George tell you?'

'Put it this way,' Carmichael replied excitedly, 'I now know why Gerry Poole was frozen and, from what George told me, I'm fairly sure I know who did it, too. I just need to talk to a few more people to be certain and to have enough proof to charge them.'

# Chapter 42

Carmichael spent the short car journey back home from church enthusiastically explaining to Penny what he had unearthed the night before and how his discussion with Norfolk George had been so valuable. Penny listened intently. She had always found it hard to understand how someone who found it impossible to fix anything mechanical and who still had to ask the children to help him record a TV programme could so expertly solve complicated cases. She was always genuinely impressed by her husband's powers of deduction and felt that his theory in this case was very plausible, especially given what Norfolk George had just told him.

'So what are you going to do now?' she asked eagerly as their car approached the house.

'I really need to get down to the station to see how Cooper's doing with Travis Sands and I'm also curious to find out how Hewitt's interview is progressing with Melanie Dreyfuss, but before I do I'm going to talk with Vivek Gupta, one of our cattle rustlers, and then drop in to see the Cashmans.'

'Do you want me to do anything?' asked Penny, even though she had no idea what help she could possibly give her husband.

'Actually,' replied Carmichael, 'you could do one thing for me. Can you call Rachel and ask her if she's checked out those numbers that we took off Tamara's mobile. I'd really like to find out who they belong to. If she has, can you ask her to call me and let me know what she's found?'

'I assume Rachel's mobile number's in the book?' replied Penny, referring to the tatty old address book that was located in the drawer by the telephone.

'I'm fairly certain it is,' replied Carmichael, although the truth was that he had no idea if it was there or not.

* * * *

As Penny was taking off her warm, thick overcoat, she was greeted by Natalie, who sauntered past her, still in her pyjamas, with a bowl of cornflakes in one hand and the Sunday paper in the other.

'Hi, Mum,' she said casually. 'Did you enjoy the service?'

'It was OK,' Penny mumbled back. 'Anyway don't you think it's time you got dressed?'

'In a minute,' replied Natalie. 'It's Sunday, so there's no rush.'

For a few seconds Penny started to question the wisdom of having got her children out of attending church. They would at least be up and dressed if they'd gone to the service, she thought.

'Oh, Jemma called,' announced Natalie loudly. 'She asked if you'd call her back.'

'Fine,' replied Penny, who had by then hung her coat up and had started to look through the address book to try and find Rachel's number. 'I'll do that later as I've a few things I need to do first.'

'She sounded quite upset,' continued Natalie. 'I think you might want to call her soon.'

'Upset?' said Penny. 'Did she say what she was upset about?'

Natalie shrugged her shoulders and walked off into the living room. 'She didn't say,' she replied.

313

The first person Carmichael wanted to speak to was Vivek Gupta.

The short telephone conversation with the self-confessed cattle rustler provided the information he wanted, so much so that Carmichael was now absolutely certain that he knew who was responsible for the dumping of Gerry Poole's body eight days earlier.

Buoyed by this and with more than a little self-satisfaction, Carmichael made his way to the Cashmans' house to commence the task given to him that morning by Chief Inspector Hewitt.

Carmichael parked outside the grand driveway that led up to the Cashmans' even grander house. He got out of the car and opened up their heavy wooden gate. Once back in the car, he slowly made his way up the long slippery driveway. Carmichael was really looking forward to this meeting.

It was Emma Cashman who answered the front door.

'Good morning, Mrs Cashman,' Carmichael said with a smile. 'May I come in to talk to you and your husband?'

Emma Cashman looked pale and tired, as if she had hardly slept. 'I'm afraid my husband's not here,' she said quietly. 'He's gone to see his brother in Hull. I don't expect him back until very late this evening.'

'I see,' replied Carmichael who was disappointed that he wouldn't have an opportunity to talk to Declan as well as his wife.'

'I assume you're here to talk about that madman who tried to break in last night?' asked Emma Cashman.

'Yes,' replied Carmichael. 'That mainly, but I've some other issues I'd like to discuss with you too.'

Emma Cashman pulled the door open wide and ushered Carmichael in.

*　*　*　*

Jemma poured out her heart to her mother over the phone. She explained how she had agreed to stay on at work to help DC Evans, how the bad weather had forced her to stay over at his parents' pub and how she had made a fool of herself a few hours earlier. Penny listened intently, interrupting only occasionally when she felt compelled to prompt her daughter to elaborate her story.

'Well, I don't think it's as bad as you think,' was the conclusion Penny gave when Jemma eventually finished and asked what her mother thought. 'You were certainly foolish going back to the club in my view, especially after you told your father you'd be quitting that job. However, I wouldn't worry about DC Evans. You'll probably never see him again, so just forget about it.'

By the silence Penny could feel her daughter was still not sufficiently reassured.

'I know,' continued Penny assertively. 'Why don't you just phone the club today and tell them you're leaving immediately. They can send you the money they owe you by cheque.'

'I doubt they will,' replied Jemma. 'I'm supposed to give four weeks' notice so they'll probably refuse to pay me for everything I've earned so far this month.'

'Rubbish,' replied Penny. 'And if they do we'll just take them to court.'

'OK,' replied Jemma with little enthusiasm, 'but I'll call in and hand in my notice this afternoon. I'm not due to be working tonight but I'd rather tell them face to face, so I'll call in at about five thirty, which is when the staff start to arrive.'

Penny wasn't that keen on her daughter even setting foot in the club, but she accepted this as a compromise. 'As long as you don't let them talk you into staying, then OK,' she replied.

*  *  *  *

The inside of the Cashmans' house matched perfectly the opulence of the imposing exterior. It had clearly been designed to provide the owners with large, open living spaces, with few obvious signs of when one room ended and the next began. It was beautifully decorated throughout in light colours, fitted with sumptuous, thick carpets and expensive furniture with luxurious chairs and soft, inviting sofas dotted all around.

'You have a lovely house, Mrs Cashman,' remarked Carmichael.

'Thank you,' Emma Cashman replied as she gestured to Carmichael to be seated. 'I certainly want to press charges against that lunatic,' she continued, even before Carmichael's bottom had made contact with the soft, orange sofa. 'He would have killed us I'm sure if your colleagues hadn't arrived so swiftly.'

'So I've been told,' responded Carmichael calmly. 'He's currently being interviewed by one of my sergeants, however, what I'd like to get from you is a full account of what happened.' As he spoke, Carmichael took out his pocket book and a pen to take some notes.

'I've already made a statement,' replied Emma Cashman fractiously. 'Your colleagues took it last night.'

'I know,' replied Carmichael with smile, 'but I'd really like to hear it from you.'

'Very well,' responded Emma Cashman, who was clearly not that keen to retell the tale. 'The first we knew was at about eight fifteen when we saw this figure on our CCTV screen marching up the drive. He was a scruffy-looking man whom we'd never seen before. Although it was very cold outside and it was snowing, he was dressed totally inappropriately, but it didn't seem to bother him; he just kept ploughing on up the drive at a hellish rate of speed. We

316

knew he was trouble so we refused to open the door when he rang the bell. When we told him to go away he started swearing really badly and hammering on the door. It was then we called the police, and fortunately they arrived and took him away before he managed to get in.'

'So you never found out why he'd come to see you or why he was so angry?' Carmichael asked.

'He was shouting but we could not make any sense of what he was saying,' replied Emma Cashman. 'I suspect he was drunk.'

'Did you know he was Clare Sands' brother?' Carmichael asked.

'Not at first,' replied Emma Cashman. 'It was only later when we were making our statement that we were told who he was.'

'Yes, he had just that afternoon had the painful duty of identifying his little sister's body, I understand,' continued Carmichael. 'So I'm sure you can appreciate that he may not have been himself last night.'

'I do understand that,' replied Emma Cashman. 'However, it's no excuse to start terrorising us in that way.'

'That's what is troubling me,' continued Carmichael. 'I keep wondering why someone who had just experienced such a trauma would then be so eager to visit you and your husband, especially as the weather was so bad. And why he was so angry with you. Can you explain that?'

Emma Cashman blushed and, like a child being scolded, her eyes looked downwards, unwilling to catch Carmichael's stare. 'You'd have to ask him that,' she replied nervously and with little conviction.

'I expect my sergeant is doing that right now,' replied Carmichael. 'What's more, I also expect he is being told that Travis Sands came to your house to confront you or more likely your husband whom he suspected of having something to do with his sister's death.'

'Well, if he did, then he's mistaken,' replied Emma Cashman, her eyes having once more returned their glare in Carmichael's direction. 'We had nothing to do with her death.'

'But your husband was having an affair with Clare Sands, wasn't he?' Carmichael asked with assured confidence. 'You knew that at Caroline Lovelace's party, didn't you?'

'What rubbish!' replied Emma Cashman dismissively. 'Declan and I are happily married. The suggestion that he was having an affair with Clare Sands is totally ridiculous.'

'Oh really?' replied Carmichael, his certainty in his facts undiminished. 'Then why did you confront Clare at the party and tell her to stay away from him? That's why she became so upset. You had marked her card. What exactly did you say to her, Mrs Cashman?'

Emma Cashman squirmed in her chair. 'This is all nonsense,' she exclaimed. 'I'd like you to leave.'

Carmichael remained seated. 'You can deny it all you like, but I know it's true and sooner or later you and your husband will have to come clean, as his relationship with Clare and your confrontation with her that evening are central to everything that has been going on here.'

Carmichael could see that Emma Cashman was uncomfortable. She fidgeted nervously and, however hard she tried, she could not retain eye contact with him for more than a few seconds at any one time. 'Whether you like it or not, Mrs Cashman, the truth here will need to come out, so do yourself and your husband a favour and start being honest with us, as if you don't it will only get worse for you both.'

'You're wrong,' insisted Emma Cashman. 'Declan was not having an affair with Clare.'

'I'm not wrong, Mrs Cashman,' Carmichael said firmly. 'In fact, the person who found Clare's body found a note next to it addressed to you. I believe Clare was planning to post it to you before leaving town.' Carmichael removed from his pocket the handwritten copy that Penny had made the day before, and handed it to Emma Cashman.

Ashen-faced, Emma Cashman carefully read the note. After a few moments she handed it back to Carmichael.

'I think that note was found by the person who murdered Clare and then left by them to try and make us think it wasn't an apology to you for the affair she was having with your husband but her suicide note.'

'I'd like you to leave now,' she said quietly.

'I've just about finished,' replied Carmichael. 'I just have one last question to ask you. Does your husband drive a red Ferrari?'

Emma nodded. 'Yes, he does,' she replied.

Carmichael stood up and made his way to the front door. After taking his overcoat down from the antique-looking coat stand, he then handed Emma Cashman his business card.

'When you do come to your senses give me a call,' he said before walking out into the cold.

With tears trickling down her cheeks, Emma Cashman watched Carmichael's car slowly descend the driveway. She stared guiltily for a few moments at Carmichael's card, before thrusting it into the small pocket in her beige woollen cardigan. Then, shutting the front door behind her, she walked back into the house to consider her options.

# Chapter 43

It was just after noon when Carmichael parked his car in his usual spot and marched confidently into Kirkwood Police Station. Although it was still fairly cold outside, the sun had managed to shine through the clouds for most of the morning and had made great inroads in melting the snow and ice on the pavements and rooftops.

Carmichael was in a positive mood. Having spoken to Emma Cashman and studied her guilty expression as she tried to deny her husband's affair with Clare Sands, he was now totally convinced that he not only knew how Gerard Poole died, but also why his body had been frozen. More importantly, he also knew who had been responsible for this seemingly bizarre act and had enough proof to now challenge them. He was not yet one hundred per cent sure who had killed Tamara Searle and could not yet explain Clare Sands' death, but he was sure that these deaths were linked to Poole's death, so he felt confident that once he started delving more into the strange death of Gerry Poole, the details of the other deaths would start to become much clearer. First, though, he would have to convince Hewitt to allow him back onto the team, a mission that Carmichael knew wouldn't be easy but one he had confidence in achieving. He was sure that if he could get his boss to listen to his theory, he would be reinstated.

As Carmichael made his way along the corridor his mobile rang. It was Rachel Dalton.

'Hello, sir,' said Rachel. 'Your wife called me earlier and asked me to call you.'

'Oh yes,' replied Carmichael excitedly, although he spoke in a whisper so that nobody else in the station would pick up on the fact that he was talking to Rachel. 'Did you trace the last calls and texts from Tamara Searle's mobile phone?'

'Yes, I did,' replied Rachel with more than a small degree of enthusiasm in her voice. 'The last text message she made was on Tuesday morning at ten past eight to Tony Yerbovic, telling him that she wouldn't be in work that day. Other than that she had sent just one text message in the previous twenty-four hours. That was at ten thirty on Monday evening.'

'Who was that to?' Carmichael asked eagerly.

'It was to Clare Sands' mobile,' replied Rachel.

'And what did that text say?' Carmichael asked.

'It said meet me at Poole's house at seven thirty in the morning. I've some good news for you,' replied Rachel.

Carmichael pondered this latest piece of news. 'And that was all you found on her phone?' he enquired with disappointment.

'I'm afraid so,' replied Rachel. 'The only other activity was a missed call at two on Monday afternoon.'

'Who was that from?' enquired Carmichael.

'It was made from a phone in one of the Sunrise Production offices,' replied Rachel. 'It could have been anyone who worked there.'

'Yes, it could,' said Carmichael, 'but I imagine it can only have come from one of three people.'

'Who?' enquired Rachel eagerly.

'Either Caroline Lovelace, Amanda Buchannan of Tony Yerbovic,' he replied. 'But I'm not sure which once.'

*   *   *   *

After spending two hours questioning Melanie Dreyfuss that morning, Chief Inspector Hewitt ended the interview in a confused and gloomy mood. As he and Watson sauntered slowly down the corridor, he saw Carmichael walking towards them.

'Good morning, sir,' said Carmichael cheerfully. 'How did the interview go?'

'Why don't you both come up to my office in thirty minutes,' replied Hewitt despondently. 'Bring Cooper too. We can discuss the case there and also find out what Clare Sands' brother was playing at last night at the Cashmans'.'

'Do I take it that I'm back on the case, then?' asked Carmichael. 'And do I take it from the expressions on your faces that you're no longer as sure about Melanie Dreyfuss's guilt as you were before?'

'We can talk about it all in my office,' growled Hewitt moodily, 'but yes, you're back on the case.'

Carmichael waited until Hewitt's forlorn figure disappeared from view before clapping his hands together in delight. 'Normal service resumed, Marc,' he announced with unbridled glee.

'Glad to have you back, sir,' said Watson

'Thanks, Marc,' replied Carmichael. 'Do I take it that Melanie is not now your number-one, well, only suspect?'

'Not after we interviewed her this morning,' replied Watson sheepishly. 'She was very convincing and, although we think she is involved, she couldn't have got Tamara Searle to the Common without someone helping her, and, as neither she nor Clare Sands could drive, then there would have needed to be a third accomplice, and we don't buy that one. Also, we can't think of a motive for either of the deaths.'

'I'm pleased that at last a semblance of sanity has broken out here,' replied Carmichael, who was enjoying every second of his restored authority. 'Now let's get back to some serious structured policing and drop all these wild hunches.

Get hold of Rachel Dalton on her mobile and tell her to get herself down here right away. I'm now starting to understand what's been going on and, once Rachel gets here and Cooper's finished interviewing Travis Sands, I'll bring you all up to speed on what I think happened.'

# Chapter 44

Within half an hour, Carmichael, Cooper, Watson and Rachel Dalton had all gathered together in the incident room at Kirkwood Station. Cooper, who was now feeling and looking more like his old self, was asked by Carmichael to spend a few minutes updating the team on his interview with Travis Sands.

'Well, there's not much to say,' began Cooper. 'Sands confirmed his intention was to assault Declan Cashman. This is because his sister had told him weeks before that she had been seeing Cashman for the past three months and that he was going to leave his wife for her. He put two and two together and, although he had no real evidence, decided that Cashman was the reason his sister took her life.'

'Well, he's correct in part,' replied Carmichael. 'Declan and Clare *were* having an affair but I believe that Clare was murdered and Cashman has got to be a prime suspect.'

'Dr Stock has today confirmed that in his opinion Clare didn't commit suicide,' announced Watson. 'She had marks on her wrists that indicated she had been tied up and she had received a blow to her head which, Stock reckons, would have rendered her unconscious.'

'So what's Dr Stock saying?' asked Carmichael, who was determined to get clarity from Watson on this issue.

'He believes that Clare was knocked out, tied up, then, in a very woozy state, given a full bottle of paracetamol washed down with vodka.'

Carmichael looked at his watch. 'We need to get up to Hewitt's office,' he remarked. 'I'll update you all on what I think happened when we're up there.'

Once inside Hewitt's office, the now fully restored officer leading the inquiry took great pleasure in enlightening his four colleagues with a meticulously detailed account of what he believed had taken place and how he had come to his conclusions.

'If I hadn't had the time to go to the pub on Saturday or to read up on the statements from the cattle rustling case or see my local newspaper headline, I may never have fathomed this one out,' said Carmichael. 'However, I did have time and what I learned from my local pub landlord was that there's to be a new supermarket built next to Poole's house on land that, I discovered from my conversation with the newspaper reporter, was owned previously by Roy Lovelace and Gerry Poole. I also discovered from my reporter friend Norfolk George that the architect and developer for the work was none other than our friend Declan Cashman.'

'So do you think Lovelace killed Poole because he wouldn't sell the land?' asked Rachel

'No,' replied Carmichael. 'However, I want you to speak with the solicitor who handled the sale to find out when the deeds were signed and who witnessed Poole's signature. My guess is that the attempt to make Poole's death seem like it was later is something to do with the sale of the land.'

'We will still need more evidence than this if we are to convict Roy Lovelace of fraud, and we have nothing to link in Declan other than an alleged affair with Clare Sands,' said Watson.

'That's where the cattle rustlers come in,' replied Carmichael gleefully. 'When I was reading through the statement, Vivek Gupta indicated that he had been forced to swerve and damaged his tyre and axle by two flash sporty cars that were speeding down the country lane.'

'That's right,' agreed Rachel, who remembered taking the statement. 'One was a new, blue Jaguar XF and the other was a red Ferrari.'

'So who do we know who had a blue Jaguar XF and who has a red Ferrari?' Carmichael asked.

'Well, Poole's car that we found under the canal bridge was a blue XF,' said Watson.

'Yes, and Cashman has a red Ferrari,' added Cooper.

'Precisely,' replied Carmichael, his smugness starting to become unbearable. 'And it would have been about ten or twenty minutes before the time that Sydes said he saw the men walking down the canal towpath.'

'It all ties in,' remarked Hewitt. 'I think we've enough to arrest them both. We should do it simultaneously though. I don't want either one of them to get away.'

'I agree,' replied Carmichael. 'But that may have to wait until the morning as I know Cashman is away and is not expected back until quite late tonight.'

It was clear to everyone in Hewitt's office that the Chief was still feeling embarrassed and foolish at having taken Carmichael off the case and at having so quickly, so publicly and, as it turned out, so mistakenly concluded that Clare Sands and Melanie Dreyfuss were the culprits. In spite of this, Hewitt swallowed his pride and gave the action plan that Carmichael then outlined his full support.

'Is everybody clear about what they need to be doing?' Hewitt said as they ended the meeting.

'Yes, sir,' came back the enthusiastic synchronised reply from his team.

\*   \*   \*   \*

Jemma Carmichael had spent no more than five minutes scribbling out her notice. If the truth was known, she still felt unhappy at having to quit such a well-paid job, but she knew

326

it was the right decision and now just wanted to be shot of the club and any future contact with DC Evans.

It was normally only a twenty-minute walk from her house to the club, but, with there still being snow and ice around, Jemma decided to leave a little earlier to allow herself plenty of time to get there as the evening staff arrived. To give her some moral support, she had asked Lizzie and Alex, a couple of her housemates, if they would go with her which they happily agreed to do. The sun had been out for most of the afternoon so much of the snow and ice had already melted and their walk to the club took no longer than usual. As they walked, Jemma had confided to her friends about her undercover work with DC Evans. She also confirmed that she had spent the night snowed in at his parents' pub in Halifax. She decided to skip the embarrassing episode outside their house when he had dropped her back, and robustly dismissed any suggestion by her friends that there was any attraction at all between her and the good-looking Welsh DC.

The walk to the club took the three girls past rows and rows of stone-built Victorian terraced houses, which in their day would probably have been quite striking homes for well-to-do middle-class Yorkshire folk. However, following many decades of neglect these houses were no longer as impressive as they had once been and, save a handful of exceptions, looked badly in need of maintenance. In the main they had been converted into flats that were then rented out to students or the unending flow of immigrants who had settled in Leeds from every corner of the earth.

As they neared Jaspers, Jemma noticed down one of the side streets the unmistakable bright red Audi belonging to DC Evans. With the car having tinted windows, she could not make out whether he was inside or not. She had no desire to be spotted by him so she hid behind one of her friends and strode on quickly.

To her surprise and great relief, the club manager was very understanding and amenable. Not only did he accept her false arrest the week before as being the reason for her resigning, he also agreed she could leave straight away and, more surprisingly, paid her what was owed in full out of the till.

'Result!' Jemma exclaimed when they were back outside once more. 'I can't believe how nice he was.'

Merrily, the three girls headed off in the direction of The Oakhouse, a well-known pub popular with students just five minutes' walk away.

'Celebration time,' shouted Jemma, waving her clenched fistful of money in the air.

Even though it was still only 5.45 p.m., The Oakhouse was full of students, most of whom were watching the live football match on Sky TV.

'The first round's on me,' announced Jemma to her friends as they pushed their way through the crowd and arrived at the bar.

As she waited for her drinks to arrive, Jemma noticed the familiar face of DC Evans sitting in the corner. He sat alone with a small glass of Coke on his table. He was clearly uninterested in the game on TV and seemed to be waiting for someone. Jemma nudged her friend Lizzie. 'That's DC Evans over there,' she whispered in her friend's ear. 'I wonder why he's in here?'

'He's drop-dead gorgeous,' replied Lizzie. 'Shall we go over?'

'No,' replied Jemma, who felt uneasy at seeing DC Evans in such close proximity. 'Let's just see who he's waiting for.'

The three friends paid for their drinks but remained at the bar. Frightened that she might be spotted by DC Evans, Jemma turned her face away from his direction and for the next few minutes relied upon her two friends to provide a commentary on what he was doing, although this amounted to not very much. However, after a while Lizzie grabbed Jemma's arm. 'He's been joined by someone,' she exclaimed.

Jemma turned slowly around to take a peek at DC Evans' new companion, fully expecting it to be a good-looking woman.

'My God, it's Harvey Liddle,' she shrieked.

'Who?' replied Alex.

'He's the bouncer at the club,' replied Jemma. 'He's the person supplying the drugs.'

'So do you think he is going to arrest him?' asked Lizzie.

'I've no idea,' replied Jemma.

'Let's get closer,' said Alex

'You must be joking – they'll both recognise me,' replied Jemma.

'But they won't recognise us,' said Lizzie. 'You go off to the other side of the bar out of sight. He's never met Alex or me, so we can sit at that table next to him and he won't bat an eyelid. What do you say, Alex?'

'I'm game,' Alex eagerly replied and, before Jemma had a chance to protest, her friends were already making their way over to the table next to DC Evans and Harvey Liddle.

Jemma had no intention of being seen by either man, so she moved quickly away to the other side of the pub, well out of sight.

\*     \*     \*     \*

It was also 5.45 p.m. when Carmichael finally left Kirkwood Station. By then the warm sun had already melted away most of the snow and his 23.2-mile journey home took him just thirty-two minutes, which was very close to his best ever time. He was in an ecstatic mood. He was delighted to be back in charge and very pleased that his carefully constructed plan of action was now in place. Carmichael was looking forward to successfully concluding the investigation. There were just two small issues nagging him. The first of these his wife would be easily able to resolve; for an answer to the other he knew he would need to look elsewhere.

*   *   *   *

Jemma sat on her own nursing her Bacardi Breezer for almost half an hour before she was rejoined by her two friends.

'You can come out of hiding, Jemma,' said Lizzie with a laugh. 'They've both gone.'

'So what did they talk about?' asked Jemma impatiently.

'It was difficult to make out all they said,' replied Alex. 'However, that policeman of yours was very aggressive towards the other man.'

'What do you mean?' enquired Jemma.

'He was really having a go at him,' interjected Lizzie. 'At one point he said if he tried to cut him out again he'd regret it.'

'Really!' exclaimed Jemma, who was stunned by what she was hearing. 'It sounds like he's part of the whole drug thing at Jaspers.'

'There's no doubt,' said Alex. 'We even saw some money change hands at the table.'

'Really!' exclaimed Jemma again, before her hand engulfed her mouth.

'Look,' said Lizzie, who showed her friend a fuzzy picture on her mobile with Alex's face at one side and, behind, DC Evans clearly placing a thick white envelope into the inside pocket of his jacket, with Harvey Liddle looking on.

'What should we do?' asked Alex.

'I'm not sure but, whatever you do, don't erase that picture, Lizzie,' said Jemma. 'In fact, send it on to Alice and me, so we have backups. I think right now we need some more drink and in the morning I think I need to talk with Dad.'

\*    \*    \*    \*

As soon as he stepped through the front door, Penny could see that Steve was excited and she knew it would only be as a result of some development in the case. However, she and her husband followed their rule not to discuss Carmichael's cases in front of the children. It was almost 10.30 p.m. before Robbie and Natalie finally headed off to their bedrooms, by which time Carmichael had closeted himself away in his office to make some urgent calls to ensure that his plan of action for the next day was still on course.

The first opportunity Penny had to find out from her husband where he was with the case was just before midnight, when he finally came to bed.

'Well,' she said impatiently, 'what went on today?'

Carmichael spent the next thirty minutes enthusiastically explaining to Penny exactly what had happened since he had dropped her off that morning. Penny was still trying to get her head around what her husband had just told her, when he asked her to cast her mind back to the party and try to recall how her conversation had gone with Caroline Lovelace regarding the school.

'It was very brief,' replied Penny. 'I can't remember exactly what we said but the conversation could only have lasted a few minutes at the most.'

Carmichael yawned. 'Just as I thought,' he said wearily, as his tired head hit the pillow.

# Chapter 45

**Monday 23rd February**

Carmichael was already awake when his alarm went off at 5.00 a.m. Within twenty minutes he had showered, shaved and was starting the engine of his black BMW. It had been a very mild night and most of the snow had now melted away, which was just what Carmichael wanted.

Six thirty a.m. was the time they had agreed to make the arrests. Cooper and Watson had been tasked with leading the team to apprehend Declan Cashman, while Rachel Dalton, Hewitt and Carmichael were simultaneously going to make the arrest of Roy Lovelace.

Confident that these were the two people who were not only responsible for delaying the discovery of Gerry Poole's body, but also quite likely to have been involved in the murders of Tamara Searle and Clare Sands, Carmichael was in a very cheerful mood as his beloved car sped along the tiny Lancashire country lanes. His joyful frame of mind, however, was quickly shattered when he received the call from Watson.

Carmichael listened in total dismay. 'Is it suicide?' he enquired as he brought his car to a halt just out of sight of the Lovelace's imposing Victorian house.

'Looks like it,' replied Watson, who had been first on the scene when the milkman had reported finding Emma Cashman's body in the fume-filled car parked inside her garage.

'Could she have been murdered?' asked Carmichael.

'I suppose she could,' replied Watson. 'We'll have to wait and see what Dr Stock and the SOCOs say after they've finished examining the scene.'

'We need to find Declan Cashman,' said Carmichael. 'Search the house and grounds, and get his description circulated quickly. We need to apprehend him before we find anyone else dead.'

'Will do, sir,' replied Watson.

Carmichael was no longer in a happy mood. 'We should have moved in last night,' he cursed as he met up with Hewitt, Dalton and the three uniformed policemen.

'That was Watson. They've just found Emma Cashman dead in her car. It looks like she may have killed herself.'

'What about her husband?' asked Hewitt.

Carmichael shook his head. 'They've not located him yet,' he replied. 'My guess is that he's long gone by now.'

'OK,' said Hewitt. 'We'll have to leave Watson and Cooper to sort that loose end. We need to get in and arrest Cashman's partner in crime.'

'That's assuming he's not done a runner too,' remarked Rachel.

Hewitt and Carmichael looked anxiously at each other.

'The only way to find out, Rachel, is for us to get in there,' said Carmichael, who half expected Rachel to be right.

'Come on, everyone,' ordered Hewitt. 'Let's get on with it.'

\* \* \* \*

Roy Lovelace had heard the police cars arrive outside his house, so was already putting on his dressing gown when they started thumping on his front door. As was often the case, Caroline had left to get to the studio of Sunrise Productions a couple of hours earlier.

'Hold on, hold on!' he shouted down the hallway as he made his way as fast as he could to the front door.

It took Lovelace a few moments to undo the two Yale locks and open the door. 'What's the panic?' he said as at last the door opened wide.

Hewitt stepped forward and personally made the arrest, much to the surprise of Roy Lovelace. 'I assume I can get dressed and call my wife and my solicitor before you take me away,' he said once he had regained some of his composure.

'You can get dressed,' replied Carmichael, before his boss had an opportunity to respond. 'And you will be allowed to make one call when you get to the station, but not before.'

Carmichael then gestured to the burly uniformed officer stood next to him. 'Go with Mr Lovelace while he gets dressed,' he ordered. 'Don't let him out of your sight and he's to make no phone calls.'

The officer nodded and with his right hand clamped tightly around Lovelace's left arm he marched his prisoner upstairs.

'It's a shame her ladyship's not here,' Carmichael whispered to Rachel. 'I'd love to have seen the look on her self-righteous face.'

*  *  *  *

Declan Cashman's red Ferrari was spotted by the traffic police on the A14 heading towards Cambridge at just after 7 a.m. By 7.30 a.m. Watson and Cooper were already on their way south to bring him back to Lancashire.

*  *  *  *

Roy Lovelace and his solicitor were sitting calmly in the interview room of Kirkwood Police Station when Carmichael and Dalton entered the room. Carmichael looked up at the large clock on the wall and turned on the tape. 'It's Monday the twenty-third of February. The time is nine thirty-five. Inspector Carmichael and DC Dalton are conducting an interview with the Right Honourable Roy Lovelace. Mr Lovelace's solicitor, Rex Mansfield, is also present.'

Carmichael sat down facing Roy Lovelace. Rachel Dalton sat next to her boss, her arms resting upon the desk in front of her.

'Mr Lovelace,' said Carmichael, in a composed and controlled manner. 'You have been arrested this morning in connection with the forgery of your brother-in-law Gerry Poole's signature. We believe you did this in an attempt to complete the sale of land you jointly owned in order that you could profit from its subsequent sale for the construction of the new supermarket in Newbridge.'

'This is preposterous,' said Roy Lovelace in his familiar booming voice. 'What proof have you got to support this ridiculous allegation?'

Carmichael smiled. 'To save us all a lot of time, let me tell you what I think happened. I think that all this is about a quick but healthy profit from the sale of the fields next to Gerry Poole's house. This was land that your father left jointly to you and your sister. I believe that you and your great friend Declan Cashman saw an opportunity to sell that land for a massive price for the development of Boothroyd's new supermarket. How am I doing so far?'

'It's all pure fantasy,' replied Lovelace. 'Gerry signed the land away before he died.'

Carmichael ignored Lovelace's protest. 'My guess is that this was all concocted between you and Cashman well before your sister passed away and I suspect that by using your extensive connections the pair of you managed to get Boothroyd's the planning permission they needed as part of the deal. All would have gone fine except that your sister died before it could all be completed. Once she had gone, the ownership of her half of the land passed to Gerry Poole, who for whatever reason was not keen to sell.'

'All this is exactly what you said earlier, Inspector,' announced Mansfield. 'It's simply a guess.'

'OK, just bear with me,' replied Carmichael confidently. 'When we met for lunch in The Fisheries, you said to me that Gerry wanted to sell as he needed the money and that he had signed the title away before he died. That wasn't true, was it, Mr Lovelace? We checked Gerry's finances and he was very comfortably off. He didn't need the cash at all. I think it was you who needed the cash and I think Gerry didn't want to sell. It may well be that you finally persuaded him to sign but I think he died before you'd managed to get him to put pen to paper. Isn't that the truth?'

Carmichael glared at Roy Lovelace as he awaited an answer.

'Rubbish!' replied Lovelace. 'Gerry wanted to sell and signed days before he died. Ask the solicitor who managed the transaction.'

'We did,' replied Carmichael with confidence. 'DC Dalton tracked him down at his house yesterday and he confirmed that he had received the signed authority to proceed well before Gerry Poole's body was found. In fact, it was received about ten days before Poole was found. However, he also confirmed that he had not personally witnessed the signature and when we checked who the signature *was* witnessed by we found it was your friend Declan Cashman. We also took the signature to a handwriting expert who checked it against other genuine signatures of Gerry Poole and he is quite convinced that the signature is not authentic.'

'Well, you'd have to talk with Declan about that, but as far as I am concerned it's absolutely genuine,' replied Lovelace bombastically.

'Oh, we will be asking Mr Cashman all about it,' replied

Carmichael with a broad smile on his face. 'In fact, my officers will be doing that very soon. They will also be talking to him about how you and he hid Gerry Poole's body in a freezer, probably Gerry's own freezer, for several weeks while you sorted out this fraud. Then we will put it to him that, after you had forged the signature, you both took Poole's body out of the freezer to try and thaw it out before leaving it by the canal on Saturday the thirteenth of February. To throw us off the scent you then filled up Gerry's freezer with various items you'd bought. That would explain why it was so tidy when we looked in it. That was a mistake as, in my experience, most freezers are pretty messy places. With regard to the date you picked to dump the body, I suspect you chose that day very carefully and to help with the conspiracy you even persuaded your wife to invite Penny and me to your party, knowing full well that one of your invited guests wouldn't arrive. That was very clever.'

'This is just pure fantasy,' interrupted Lovelace.

'What did you tell her was the reason you wanted us there, Mr Lovelace? Was it something to do with your involvement on one of the police committees? Was I being secretly vetted by you to see if I was up to some big appointment you were working on?'

Roy Lovelace was starting to look uncomfortable, but was in no mood to admit to any of Carmichael's accusations.

'The excuse being given to us was that your wife wanted to know about the school my wife worked at, but Caroline was not interested in my wife's school,' said Carmichael firmly. 'She spent no more than a few seconds talking about it. No, I think you made up some cock-and-bull story to your wife too, in order that she agreed to invite us to the party.

'You have absolutely no proof of any of this nonsense,' Lovelace shouted angrily.

'Oh, but I do,' replied Carmichael with an even more confident air. 'First, we have a statement from a witness who confirms he saw Declan Cashman's distinctive red sports car and Gerry Poole's blue Jaguar driving near the canal on the evening the body was dumped.'

'Who is this witness?' Lovelace sneered.

'He's a gentleman called Mr Gupta,' replied Carmichael. 'He remembers seeing the cars as they were driving so quickly and so badly that they forced him to swerve and caused his transit van to hit the curb and break its axle.'

'This is all rubbish,' fumed Lovelace, who proceeded to fold his arms and slump back into his chair.

'But there's more, gentlemen,' continued Carmichael who was now in full flow and thoroughly enjoying himself. 'Then we have an eyewitness who saw two men dragging another man down the towpath at around five on the same day. The descriptions of the two men fit you and Declan Cashman perfectly. One was a tall thin man and the other a shorter rather rotund man. I think that's you and your friend Declan.'

'That's not evidence,' replied Lovelace angrily. 'You're just fishing.'

'Then let's just put the fraud aside for a moment and turn to the more serious matter of the deaths of Tamara Searle and Clare Sands,' said Carmichael. 'I think the murders are related and I believe that they are linked to the death of Gerry Poole.'

'Come on then, Inspector,' retorted Lovelace sarcastically as he leaned forward with his arms open. 'Let's hear your Mickey Mouse story about how Declan and I killed them too.'

'This is not Mickey Mouse, Mr Lovelace, but to save everyone's time I'll tell you how this whole tragic episode came to happen.'

Roy Lovelace slumped back in his chair again as he waited for Carmichael to explain his theory.

'We need to start about three months ago,' explained Carmichael. 'It was about then that Declan Cashman started

338

an affair with Clare Sands. I reckon it was not that easy for them to meet up without being noticed. However, they got around this by meeting every Monday at Gerry Poole's house. The Helpful Angels would clean the house every Monday and every Thursday. For some reason, on Mondays whoever cleaned the house would never see Gerry Poole, so I suspect Clare hit upon the idea of them meeting at the house each Monday. She spoke with Melanie Dreyfuss, who was the only other person who ever did Mondays at Poole's, and they agreed that from then on Clare would do the cleaning every Monday. I suspect that for several weeks they then met there without any problems. Then one Monday, about a month or so ago, Clare arrived to find that Gerry Poole was dead. In her panic she called Declan and told him. I can't believe she had any idea of the problem that the death of Poole would cause you and Declan with respect to the sale of the field, but I imagine that Declan told her to go and that he would handle things from there. I think Declan would have tried to make sure she was out of the way before he and you came over to try and work out what you should do. But I expect that she did see something, maybe she saw you arriving at the house, or maybe she looked in the freezer at some time later. Whatever she knew or saw, she was uneasy, and on the night of the party she made a big mistake, one that would ultimately cost her life and the life of Tamara Searle.'

'Utter fantasy,' remarked Lovelace.

Carmichael ignored Lovelace's latest outburst and carried on with his story.

'During the party I think something happened which made Emma Cashman realise something was going on between the two of them. I spoke with Emma Cashman yesterday and, although she denied it, I'm now convinced that's what happened. Then one of the Cashmans must have said something to Clare. I suspect it was Emma, but whoever it was it made her very upset and, to try and compose herself, she went into the bathroom. Unfortunately for her, at that time Tamara Searle also went into the bathroom. I suspect that during her genuine efforts to comfort the young waitress, Clare must have confided what she had seen at Poole's house that Monday. It's hard to say what she said, but it would have been enough for Tamara to realise that the information was potential dynamite.

'Being a clever and resourceful young lady, Tamara probably then tried to use this information to blackmail you and Declan, which is when you or Declan realised that both she and Clare had to go. I think you killed Tamara on the Monday evening at her flat. You then set about tidying up. Having killed Tamara you placed her naked body and her possessions in one of your cars and drove them first to Poole's flat, where you hid them.'

'Total rot!' shouted Lovelace. 'You're just clutching at straws.'

'I think not,' replied Carmichael. 'I would imagine that poor Tamara's body remained all night scrunched up in the boot. I think you contacted Clare by text on Tamara's phone on Monday evening and lured her to Poole's house on the Tuesday morning. Once she was there, you killed her too and tried to make it look like suicide. Then, on Tuesday morning, you texted Tamara's work on her mobile to say she wouldn't be in that day.'

'This is just farcical,' shouted Lovelace. 'You have no evidence at all to support this half-baked story.'

Carmichael ignored this outburst and continued.

'It must have been a real stroke of luck for you to find the letter that Clare had written to Emma Cashman. I suspect it was in her bag, the same bag that contained her purse which you would later leave on the Common, along with Tamara's body and Melanie Dreyfuss's debit card. Who had the idea to use the letter as a suicide note, Mr Lovelace, you or Declan?'

340

Roy Lovelace remained slumped back in his chair with his arms folded. 'This is total rubbish, Carmichael. You have got nothing to connect me or Declan with those deaths. You're just making yourself look an even bigger fool.'

'Very well, Mr Lovelace,' said Carmichael, who stood up out of the chair. 'We'll leave it there for now, but I strongly suggest you have a serious discussion with your solicitor. Maybe you can persuade him to be more cooperative with us, Mr Mansfield.'

Rex Mansfield looked perplexed at Carmichael's request. 'I think you will find it's my job to protect my client from bogus accusations and false charges, Inspector Carmichael. Which, I have to say, is pretty much all we have heard so far this morning.'

'Interview suspended at ten a.m.,' said Carmichael just before he turned off the recording equipment.

'Come on, Rachel,' he said as he headed for the door. 'Let's give these gentlemen a few hours to think about things. In the interim, let's see what Declan Cashman has to say for himself.'

'So you've arrested Declan too,' remarked Lovelace.

'Oh yes,' replied Carmichael, who was now at the door. 'I suspect that by the time we come back he'll already be trying to do some sort of deal with us to save his skin. That's what you normally find in these circumstances.'

Carmichael didn't bother to look back at Roy Lovelace before leaving the room. If he had, he would have seen that his prisoner was starting to look anxious and become quite agitated.

\* \* \* \*

It was just after 10.30 a.m. when Cooper and Watson arrived at Huntingdon Police Station. As their car pulled into the car park, Cooper called Carmichael on his mobile to get some final instructions.

341

'We've just arrived, sir,' announced Cooper. 'Do you want us to inform Cashman that his wife is dead?'

'No,' replied Carmichael. 'Just bring him back as quickly as you can.'

'How did your interview go with Roy Lovelace?' Cooper asked.

'He's not admitting to anything as yet,' replied Carmichael. 'But that's what I expected. We've left him to stew for a few hours. I'm hoping he'll start to cooperate a bit more once he's had time to think.'

Cooper looked at his watch. 'My guess is that we could be back at the station by three if the traffic is OK.'

'That's good, Paul,' replied Carmichael. 'I'll see you then.'

Cooper was just about to end the call when Carmichael shouted down the line.

'One last thing,' he said. 'Make sure you don't have any news on the radio when you're driving back here. I expect once it gets out that we've arrested Lovelace it will be wall-to-wall coverage, and I don't want Cashman to hear anything other than what we tell him.'

'Right you are, sir,' replied Cooper.

'But if he says anything in the car that you feel is important let me know immediately,' Carmichael insisted before turning off his mobile.

'Back there you mentioned that the two men whom Sydes saw by the canal matched the description of Lovelace and Cashman,' remarked Rachel. 'I didn't know Sidney Sydes had given you such a detailed account of the men?'

'Rachel, let's go and have a coffee,' said Carmichael with a smile and a wink. 'I think I need a break.'

Rachel nodded to indicate she got the message, before dutifully following her boss as he bounced up the stairwell to the first-floor canteen.

\* \* \* \*

Jemma Carmichael had spent the whole of the previous night tossing and turning as she considered what she should do about DC Evans and Harvey Liddle. The report that Lizzie and Alex had given her and the photographic evidence could only point to Evans taking a bribe. After so much heart searching that her head ached, she decided that she needed to talk with her dad.

'Dad,' she said timidly down the line. 'It's Jemma.'

\* \* \* \*

Carmichael had just sat down in the canteen with a cup of coffee in front of him when the call came in.

'Oh, hi darling, how are you?' he replied, his attention not totally on the incoming call as he saw the all-too-familiar face of Caroline Lovelace on the large TV screen. He put his hand over the receiver.

'Turn the sound up, Rachel,' he ordered. 'Jemma, I will have to call you back,' he said before switching off his mobile.

Having spent ages plucking up the courage to talk to her father, Jemma was now totally deflated at having been so unceremoniously cut off. She threw her mobile down on the chair and slumped onto her bed.

Rachel did as she was instructed and the crowded canteen hushed to listen to what Caroline Lovelace had to say.

'After I left home this morning, Roy, my husband, was abruptly woken in his bed by police and he has been taken to Kirkwood Police Station. I've just learned from our solicitor that he, along with a friend of ours, has been accused of the murder of Tamara Searle and is also being questioned about other incidents. Under the circumstances, I don't feel able to take part in today's *Lovelace Show*. However, I want everyone to know that these allegations brought against my husband are totally without foundation and that we will be strenuously

343

defending his good name and reputation. I am sure that you all appreciate how distraught I am at this time and be assured that I will be back on air tomorrow. Thank you all for your understanding.'

The camera remained on Caroline's anxious-looking face for a further fifteen seconds before it eventually cut away to the local regional news desk.

'She looked ready for a battle,' remarked Rachel.

'She certainly did,' replied Carmichael.

'What do we do now?' Rachel asked.

Carmichael thought for a few moments, 'I want to wait for Cooper and Watson to get here with Cashman before we interview Roy Lovelace again. In the interim I'm going to go over to Cashman's house to see if I can get a feel for what happened there this morning. On the way I'll call in to see Dr Stock. Knowing him, I'm sure he'll already have found something interesting for us. He's normally pretty good like that.'

'What shall I do, sir?' Rachel asked.

'You stay here and make sure, if Caroline Lovelace arrives, she's not allowed to see her husband. Apart from his brief, he's to remain totally isolated from the outside world until I've spoken to him again. That also includes access to the radio, newspapers or the TV.'

'Right you are, sir,' replied Rachel, who having finished her coffee, left her boss alone to his thoughts.

# Chapter 46

'So you're back on the case, Carmichael,' announced Dr Stock in his normal laid-back, rather patronising style. 'I should have guessed. There are always twice as many bodies when you're in charge.'

'You can cut out the sarcasm, Stock,' replied Carmichael. 'Just tell me what you have got for me?'

'I've got a woman in her mid to late thirties,' continued Stock in his usual monotone voice. 'She was found in her night attire and clearly died from inhalation of carbon monoxide and the assortment of all the other nasty gases a car exhaust pumps out. If you want a list of their full names, I can tell you them.'

'No, that won't be necessary, Doctor,' replied Carmichael, who was keen for Stock to get the point. 'Can you say when she died and can you say whether this was suicide or murder?'

'Two good questions, Inspector,' replied Stock. 'I would say to the first that she died between six and six thirty this morning. With regards to your second question, I suspect she was unconscious before she started to inhale the deadly brew.'

'So it was murder then?' replied Carmichael.

'Well, unless she hit herself on the head, I'd say definitely murder,' confirmed Stock.

'Are you sure she couldn't have died before six?' asked Carmichael.

Stock carefully considered the question. 'Possibly five forty-five but certainly no earlier,' he replied. 'Why do you ask?'

'I ask because I've two main suspects for the murders. One of them I arrested myself in his pyjamas at his home this morning, at six thirty. As his home is thirty minutes' drive away from the scene I need to know if he could have done it.'

'I think he would have been pushing it,' replied Stock. 'However, I suppose it *is* possible.'

'I'm not sure,' replied Carmichael pensively. 'There were officers outside already when I got there so I struggle to see how he could have managed to kill her and then get back home without being detected.'

Stock nodded as if to concur. 'I assume you checked for the most obvious indicator?' he asked.

'The most obvious indicator,' Carmichael repeated, the curiosity clear in his voice. 'And that would be what?'

'The temperature of the car engine,' replied Stock. 'Had he driven for thirty minutes the engine would stay warm for several hours.'

The forlorn expression on Carmichael's face answered Stock's question.

'Anyway, what about your other suspect?' enquired Stock.

'He was spotted in his car at seven about one hundred and forty miles away,' replied Carmichael.

Stock thought for a few seconds. 'If your driver was able to maintain an average speed of one hundred and twelve miles per hour he could just about have done it.'

Carmichael shrugged his shoulders. 'He does drive a Ferrari, but I suspect that travelling at an average speed of one hundred and twelve miles per hour would have got him nicked by the traffic police well before he got to Birmingham.'

Stock smiled. 'I'm sure you're right. But going back to your first chap, I suppose it is possible he's your man, but he would have to have been quite nimble on his feet.'

Try as hard as he could, Carmichael could not envisage the portly Roy Lovelace being able to carry out the crime and get back home and into bed so quickly.

'Do you know if anyone checked the CCTV tapes at the Cashman house?' Carmichael asked.

'Not to my knowledge, Inspector,' replied Stock. 'She was found in the car in the garage, which is not attached to the house. I've been totally preoccupied with the body. You'd need to ask the SOCOs back at the house about any other evidence.'

'I will,' said Carmichael, who shook Stock's hand and then dashed out of the pathology lab and quickly got into his car.

\* \* \* \*

When midday arrived and her dad had not returned her call, Jemma decided to take matters into her own hands. Nervously she dialled the number on her mobile. It rang for a few seconds before being answered.

'Hello, it's me, Jemma Carmichael,' she said in as confident a voice as she could manage. 'I need to meet you this afternoon, it's urgent.'

\* \* \* \*

As Carmichael's car sped along the winding country lane he thought about the conversation he had just had with Stock. He was really angry with himself for not checking the temperature of Lovelace's car engine that morning. This was such a basic error on his part and he knew that it was too late and the engine would be stone cold by now. He consoled himself to some extent by figuring that, if Stock was right about his times, which, knowing Stock was pretty much a certainty, it was highly likely that neither Roy Lovelace nor

347

Declan Cashman could have been responsible for killing Emma Cashman that morning.

Carmichael was now even more desperate to see the CCTV tapes from the Cashman's house. He was totally convinced the identity of the murderer of Emma Cashman would be on those tapes.

*   *   *   *

After she had left Carmichael in the station canteen, Rachel had headed straight down to the custody sergeant and made him aware of Carmichael's clear instructions about Lovelace having no contact with the outside world.

'Well, that's easy while he's alone,' replied the custody sergeant. 'But I assume his solicitor's got a mobile, so when he's with his brief he could borrow his mobile to call out.'

Rachel's heart raced. 'Bugger!' she cried as she dashed down towards the interview room where they had earlier left Roy Lovelace and Rex Mansfield alone.

*   *   *   *

The journey back up the M6 for Watson and Cooper seemed even longer than the trip down. Without the distraction of the radio, every mile seemed like ten and, even though the traffic flow was good, the time dragged by at a miserably slow rate. Cooper had driven down, so it was Watson's turn to drive back, which left poor Cooper confined to the back seat handcuffed to Declan Cashman who, in his agitated state, did nothing but wriggle and fidget.

'You're making a massive mistake,' Cashman said as they headed up the M6 toll road. 'I've absolutely nothing to do with any murders.'

Cooper could see that his prisoner was starting to get flustered but remained silent and continued to show a total lack of interest in Cashman's attempt to engage him in conversation.

'If that Searle woman's death is linked to the sale of the land, then Roy must have done that on his own,' continued Cashman, who was now starting to look very nervous.

Cooper at last turned to face Cashman. This acknowledgement seemed to calm Cashman a little, but it was clear to Cooper that the detainee was getting himself into quite a disturbed state.

'Marc,' he shouted forward. 'Why don't you stop the car at the next services. It might help us all if we stretched our legs for while.'

'OK,' replied Watson. 'I think there's one about fifteen miles ahead.'

'You need to calm yourself down, Mr Cashman,' said Cooper. 'I can assure you that if you come clean and tell us everything, then it will help you no end when the case comes to trial. So my advice to you is to stop denying everything and start telling us the whole undiluted truth, with no omissions.'

\*　\*　\*　\*

When Jemma told Lizzie and Alex that she was planning to confront DC Evans with their evidence, they were horrified.

'You must be out of your mind!' exclaimed Alex. 'We either forget the whole thing or report him – there's no other option.'

'I agree,' said Lizzie. 'Anyway I thought you were going to talk to your dad?'

'I tried,' replied Jemma. 'But he didn't have time to talk to me and he's not called me back.'

'So where have you arranged to meet him?' Alex enquired.

'At The White Lion pub across the road from the uni,' replied Jemma.

'I said I'd meet him there at six thirty this evening. I wish I hadn't, but I feel like I've got to go through with it now.'

Lizzie looked at her watch. 'That gives us just under seven hours. It will be tight but it should be enough time.'

'Time to do what?' asked Jemma.

'Time to catch him once and for all,' replied Lizzie. 'Now here's the plan ...'

\*   \*   \*   \*

It was 11.45 a.m. when Steve Carmichael's car finally arrived at Declan and Emma Cashman's house.

There were still plenty of SOCOs milling around, looking for clues. Although most were in the garage and outside the house, a few had started to look inside the Cashmans' impressive home.

Carmichael had no concern in what they were doing; he was only interested in looking at the CCTV tapes. As he strode with resolve towards the front door his mobile rang.

'Hi, sir, it's Watson here,' came the muffled voice. 'We have stopped at a service station on the M6 toll road. We should get to the station in under two hours.'

'OK,' replied Carmichael. 'Has he said anything to you?'

Watson turned to look back at the ashen face of Declan Cashman who was now sitting silently and despondently in the back of the car handcuffed to Cooper, some twenty yards away. 'He denied everything at first,' replied Watson excitedly. 'But now he's given us chapter and verse on the mystery of Poole's death.'

'So what's he saying?' enquired Carmichael.

'It was exactly as you said,' replied Watson. 'Roy Lovelace and he had been trying to persuade Poole to sell for months. According to Cashman, Poole eventually agreed but, before he could sign the documents, Poole died. He has also admitted to having an affair with Clare Sands, and you were right too about them spending Mondays together at Poole's house.'

'So they put the body in the freezer, forged Poole's signature and then thawed Poole's body and dumped it by the canal just before the party,' said Carmichael, who was delighted that his theory was correct.'

'Yes,' replied Watson. 'And you were also right that your invitation to the party was their way of getting you to believe that Poole had just gone missing. According to Cashman that was Roy Lovelace's idea. He apparently told his wife that he was vetting you as a potential candidate for a secret police operation. That's how he got his wife to invite you.'

'Cunning buggers!' replied Carmichael.

'Yes, that's what we thought,' said Watson.

'So what about the receipt that was in Poole's trouser pocket?' Carmichael asked.

'That was just an old receipt Cashman had on him when they dumped the body,' replied Watson. 'Cashman maintains that was just a spur-of-the-moment thing they did to try and reinforce the story about Poole being alive when he signed away the deeds.'

'So what else is he saying?' asked Carmichael.

'He's also confirmed that his wife did twig that he and Clare were having an affair, and that she had confronted Clare about it at the party,' replied Watson. 'He categorically denies having anything to do with the death of Tamara Searle and he says that he wasn't planning to leave his wife for Clare Sands, but he does seem genuinely upset about Clare's death.'

'What about the evening they dumped Poole's body?' continued Carmichael. 'Does he recall almost running the van the Guptas were using to steal the livestock off the road?'

'Yes,' replied Watson eagerly. 'He confirms that too. He was driving his Ferrari and Roy Lovelace was driving Gerry Poole's Jaguar with Poole slumped in the back seat under a rug. He says they were running late and were travelling quickly. They almost hit the van and he remembers seeing the vehicle swerve and hit the curb. I guess that's when it knackered its axle.'

Carmichael was ecstatic. 'That's brilliant, Marc,' he said enthusiastically. 'Get him back up here as quick as you can and take a full statement.'

'OK, sir,' responded Watson, who was equally excited. 'But what about his wife? Do we tell him she is dead now, or wait until he is back at Kirkwood Station?'

Carmichael thought for a few seconds. 'No, tell him now. To be honest, I'm not sure about him being involved in the murders. I think he's probably telling you the truth. It's most likely that neither he nor Roy Lovelace is the murderer, so you should tell him.'

'So who *is* the murderer then, sir, if it's not them?' Watson asked with surprise.

'That's what I'm hoping to find out,' replied Carmichael. 'If all goes to plan, I'll know very soon.'

## Chapter 47

Carmichael's heart pounded as he walked down the hallway to the small room at the rear of the house where the Cashman's CCTV monitor was installed. Although it was possible that Roy Lovelace could have murdered Emma that morning, Carmichael could not visualise such an aging, unfit and portly man being agile enough to commit the murder of Emma Cashman and then get back to his house and into his pyjamas so quickly. He dismissed Declan Cashman as a suspect, mainly due to the fact that he had been apprehended so far from the house that it was totally inconceivable that he could have carried out the murder and got so far away in the time, even in his Ferrari. Also, he knew that Cashman was no fool and would have known he would be caught on his own CCTV footage. So if Cashman had committed the murder, Carmichael assumed he would have certainly disabled the system first. Although Carmichael knew that, even discounting Declan Cashman and Roy Lovelace, there were several other potential candidates for the murder of Emma Cashman, he had a strong feeling who her assassin was and was sure the tape would expose Caroline Lovelace as the killer.

\* \* \* \*

After over two hours alone together in the interview room, Rex Mansfield, Roy Lovelace's brief, emerged and announced to the duty sergeant that his client was now prepared to not only make a full admission to fraud, but also to the murders of Tamara Searle, Clare Sands and Emma Cashman. In the absence of Inspector Carmichael, a jubilant Chief Inspector Hewitt accompanied Rachel Dalton into the interview room to listen to Roy Lovelace's unexpected confession.

\* \* \* \*

Carmichael sank back in the chair. His worst fear had become reality. The CCTV system had been switched off and there were no tapes anywhere, not in the system and not on any of the shelves, nor in any of the drawers.

'Damn it!' he cursed.

\* \* \* \*

It took less than half an hour for Roy Lovelace to provide his verbal confession to Rachel Dalton and Chief Inspector Hewitt. The two officers were completely amazed to hear that his story was almost word for word identical to the story that Carmichael had deduced and outlined to them the day before. The only deviation was that Lovelace maintained he alone had murdered Tamara Searle and Clare Sands and that Declan Cashman was only involved in the fraud. This was not in line with Carmichael's theory the day before when he had suspected Declan Cashman to be involved in the murders, too. And, of course, at that time Emma Cashman was still alive.

'So why did you kill Tamara Searle?' Hewitt asked.

'Because she was trying to blackmail me,' replied Lovelace. 'She spoke with Clare Sands at the party who told her that Gerry Poole had died weeks earlier and that Declan and I had hidden the body. Tamara was an ambitious girl and she told me that she wanted me to use my influence with Caroline and the production studio to get her a role as a presenter. If I didn't, she would sell the story to the papers. I couldn't let her do that.'

'And presumably you killed Clare to tidy up the loose ends?' remarked Rachel.

'Yes,' replied Lovelace. 'She was the only person left other than Declan and I that knew what had happened, so I couldn't risk her doing the same thing as Tamara. It was a stroke of luck finding the letter she had written to Emma in her bag. I realised immediately that it could be mistaken for a suicide note. Then, by planting her purse where I left Tamara's body, I thought it would be assumed that Clare killed Tamara and then killed herself. I also thought it would help keep Declan off the scent too.'

'How do you mean?' enquired Hewitt, who was struggling to contain his exhilaration at getting such a full confession.

'Because if he thought Clare had killed Tamara and then killed herself, he wouldn't make the link between what we had done with Gerry Poole and the murders.'

'So why did you clean Tamara's flat so thoroughly?' Rachel asked. 'And why did you then take her belongings to Poole's house?'

Lovelace shrugged his shoulders. 'To implicate Clare Sands, of course,' he replied, as if it was obvious. 'I cleaned Tamara's flat to get rid of any evidence of my being there. I also thought *you* would think that that was the sort of thing a person who cleaned would do.'

'It must have taken you hours to do all that on your own?' remarked Rachel, who was starting to have some doubts about Lovelace's story.

'It did,' replied Lovelace, although he appeared not that keen to elaborate any further.

'So why did you dump Tamara's body on the Common, like that?' asked Rachel. 'And why was she naked?'

Lovelace considered the question for few moments before replying.

'I had taken her clothes off at her flat already,' he said. 'I thought that would make it more difficult for you to discover where and when she died. I then wrapped her body in a blanket and carried her down to the car. As you know, Tamara was quite tall and the only way I could carry her and also fit her in the boot was to fold her up in a foetal-like position. I forgot to mention I was driving Caroline's tiny Peugeot that evening, as my car was in the garage, so it was a very tight fit.'

Rachel was still not convinced that what she was hearing was the whole truth, but she could not think why Lovelace would make up the story as he would clearly not benefit from putting all the guilt on himself. Also, his explanations were so good that it was almost impossible to accept that he could have made it all up.

'So when did you kill Tamara Searle?' she asked.

'I killed Tamara on the Monday evening and, when I went to dump her body the following night, she had already started to get quite stiff. It took me ages to decide where to leave her and when I did it was really difficult to carry her across the Common. However, I managed it. I left her sitting upright as I thought that may confuse the police and cause you to go off in all sorts of strange directions. It was also really cold that night and I did hope that the body would be frozen by the time it was found, which again might throw you all off the scent.'

Lovelace looked intently at his two inquisitors before continuing. 'I left Clare's purse so you would think she had been there and then I used a branch to rub out my tracks in the snow as best I could.'

'So why did you kill Emma Cashman this morning,' asked Rachel.

For the first time Roy Lovelace didn't appear to be as assured.

356

'At four this morning Declan called me to say that he was doing a runner, stupid sod,' responded Lovelace. 'He'd apparently had an argument with Emma last night and she'd told him that she knew all about his affair with Clare; she had also had a discussion with Inspector Carmichael and she had become suspicious about Declan's involvement in the deaths. She was going to call your Inspector Carmichael this morning to come and talk to him again. Although I don't think Declan thought I had anything to do with the murders, he was sure his wife was now going to help implicate him in the land sale. To be honest, I'm not sure how much she knew, but I decided I couldn't risk it, so I drove down to the house at five and…well, you know the rest.'

Rachel was about to ask Lovelace to be more specific about Emma Cashman's death when Hewitt decided to intervene.

'Is that everything?' said Hewitt, who was clearly excited and appeared to bring the interview to a close.

'Yes,' replied Lovelace. 'Can I now see my wife?'

Hewitt shook his head.

'Before you can see Caroline we will need a written statement from you, Mr Lovelace,' said Hewitt, who then nodded to Rachel to instruct her to end the interview.

'Once I've done that, can I then see Caroline?' Lovelace asked as the two police officers made their way to the door.

'I see no reason why not,' replied Hewitt. 'But you can see her only after we have your full written confession.'

# Chapter 48

'I wish you had waited for me before you interviewed Lovelace. This doesn't seem right,' remarked Carmichael angrily, after reading Roy Lovelace's confession in Hewitt's office that afternoon. 'I can buy that Declan Cashman and Roy Lovelace were the only people involved in the fraud. I can also buy that Declan Cashman was not involved at all in the murders. What I don't buy is that Roy Lovelace single-handedly murdered Tamara Searle, Clare Sands and Emma Cashman. I don't see how he could have tidied up her flat so thoroughly on his own and I can't see him being able to carry her body on his own and dump it in the middle of the Common.'

'But that's what he's saying,' replied Hewitt, 'and it does all make a compelling story.'

'And also,' continued Carmichael, 'I don't feel that he would have thought to text Yerbovic on her mobile to say that she was ill on Tuesday morning. I suspect he wouldn't have even known Yerbovic was her boss and I definitely can't see him being cunning enough to use the letter in Clare's bag as a possible suicide note. It also doesn't explain who it was that called Tamara's mobile from Sunrise Productions on the Monday afternoon. That couldn't have been Roy Lovelace.'

'Well, he has written it all in his statement and I'm completely satisfied that we have the right man and we should close the case. What's more, you need to be congratulating yourself on a job well done, Inspector. If it had not been for your tenacity in all this, we may well have never solved the case. You should be proud and ecstatic, not downhearted.'

'I know how it looks,' replied Carmichael pensively. 'And I am confident that when they come to court Declan Cashman and Roy Lovelace will get what they deserve. However, my view is that Caroline Lovelace is the real murderer. I think it was she whom Tamara was blackmailing, not Roy. I'm sure her husband would have helped her tidy things up, which is why his story is so vivid and persuasive, but I think it was Caroline who called Tamara from Sunrise Productions and it was she who killed Tamara. I think she also killed Clare and she definitely killed Emma Cashman. I want to go back in with Roy Lovelace again and double-check his confession'

'Stop right there, Inspector,' said Hewitt in a raised voice. 'I think you're letting your uncomfortable experience on her show the other week cloud your judgement. We have no evidence at all to link Caroline Lovelace to the deaths. Her husband has admitted that he's the killer. I am satisfied with this, as is the rest of the team, and you need to draw a line under this whole episode.'

'I think you're wrong, sir, and if only I could find those damn CCTV tapes,' mumbled Carmichael to himself. 'That would prove her guilt, but I suspect she's already destroyed them.'

\* \* \* \*

At 6:30 p.m on the dot, DC Evans walked into The White Lion. Apart from a few students playing pool and a handful of the university's rugby team at the bar, the place was fairly empty. Evans therefore had no problem spotting Jemma sitting alone with a half-full glass on the table in front of her. He smiled and walked over to where she was sitting.

'So what's so important?' he asked as he sat down beside her.

'This,' replied Jemma, as she showed him the picture on

her mobile phone of him taking the package from Harvey Liddle.

'I don't understand,' he replied. 'What's this?'

'It's you taking money from the person responsible for pushing drugs at the club,' snapped Jemma angrily. 'You used me!'

'That's nonsense, Jemma,' replied Evans with a smile. 'This is not what it looks.'

'What is it then?' Jemma demanded.

'It's police business,' replied Evans. 'It is nothing to do with you, so just leave it, Jemma.'

'No, I won't leave it,' said Jemma in a raised voice. 'It's a bung, isn't it? You're taking money off a drug pusher to turn a blind eye.'

Evans' demeanour changed following Jemma's bluntness, from the amiable young man she had grown to fancy to a different person, a serious aggressive individual with a dark, frightening look in his eyes.

'Listen to me, you stupid little fool,' he said, pushing his face within an inch of hers. 'This is nothing to do with you. The people I'm dealing with here are not the sort of people who mess around. My advice to you is to shut your mouth and forget you saw anything. If you don't, I can promise you that you'll regret it.'

'You don't frighten me,' replied Jemma, who was trembling all over. 'I'm going to your superiors and I'm going to tell them what you're up to.'

Evans snatched the phone out of Jemma's hand and smashed it on the table.

'I don't think so,' he snarled. 'Without this you've got nothing. I'll just tell them that you're making it all up because I wouldn't take you out.'

'Well, I don't think so,' remarked one of the burly rugby players who had sidled over to where Jemma and Evans were sitting. 'We have plenty of copies of that picture.'

'Also, we have a camera set up over there in the corner,' said Jemma, pointing to the lens sticking out of the sports bag on the bar.

'And we have microphones attached to the table you're sitting at and hidden behind Jemma's jacket,' said the second heavily built young man.

'All in all, we have enough evidence here to show your superiors what a crook you are,' said the first man. 'In fact, we are now going to make a citizen's arrest.'

Evans tried to stand up, but was quickly wrestled back down to his seat by two of Jemma's muscular friends. Realising he was not going to escape, Evans remained quietly in his seat looking very apprehensive.

'Great plan, Lizzie,' said Jemma, who had left the table to join her friend at the bar. 'I can't wait to tell my dad.'

'I knew sharing a house with half the university rugby team and doing media and broadcasting as a degree would one day come in handy,' she replied with a smile.

'Yes,' said Jemma. 'Never again will you hear me say that a Media Studies degree is useless!'

# Chapter 49

Carmichael stared down from his first-floor office window onto the main entrance at the front of the Kirkwood Police Station. It was 7.15 p.m. and, although he and the team now had more than enough evidence to prosecute Declan Cashman for fraud and Roy Lovelace for fraud and the three murders, Carmichael was feeling far from elated.

The story of The Right Honourable Member for Mid-Lancashire being arrested for murder was national news and the street outside the station had dozens of reporters and TV camera crews waiting for a glimpse of anyone associated with the case or for a chance to pick up any small titbit of information so they could share it with the world.

As he looked out into the dark February evening, Caroline Lovelace stepped out of Kirkwood Police Station and, without making any comment to the waiting media, was ushered into a large black car which then sped away into the night.

Carmichael didn't hear Rachel Dalton enter the room. It was not until she handed him a mug of steaming coffee that he realised he had company.

'I suppose we should all feel pleased with ourselves,' he said without bothering to look at her. 'But to be totally honest with you, Rachel, I feel we've been cheated. That smug, self-righteous cow is going to get away with this, you know, and there's sod all we can do about it.'

'I know,' replied Rachel, 'but at least we've well and truly

362

got Roy Lovelace and Declan Cashman. They won't get off with this and, given that only a few days ago poor Melanie Dreyfuss was our main target, you've at least managed to get the case back on track.'

Carmichael took a sip of coffee. 'I suppose you're right,' he replied.

Rachel turned as if to leave.

'What I don't get', said Carmichael, 'is how Roy Lovelace knew enough about Emma Cashman's death to be able to give such a plausible written confession? I'm certain that this morning he wasn't even aware that she'd died. We didn't mention her death when we arrested him or in this morning's interview.'

Rachel shuffled nervously and cleared her throat. 'I've not had time to talk to you about this,' she said sheepishly, 'but I think Rex Mansfield may have allowed Roy to talk to Caroline earlier today on his mobile.'

'What!' exclaimed Carmichael. 'I thought I told you that he was to speak to nobody.'

'I know, sir,' replied Rachel, 'but when I got back to the interview room after I left you in the canteen, Mansfield was outside the room and when I went in Lovelace was using Mansfield's phone. I took it off him right away but I suspect it was Caroline he was talking to.'

'What a complete cock-up!' muttered Carmichael, the frustration palpable in his voice.

'I'm sorry, sir,' replied Rachel, who was clearly devastated about what had happened.

Carmichael looked up at her pale, worried face. 'It's not your fault, Rachel,' he said. 'I should have insisted that Mansfield hand over his phone before we left the interview room, just like I should have had the intelligence to check the temperature of Lovelace's car engine this morning when we arrested him. I'm afraid I must take the blame for both of these mistakes, not you.'

Rachel was clearly relieved that her boss wasn't angry with her, but at the same time felt sorry for him.

'Get yourself off home, Rachel,' announced Carmichael. 'You need a good night's rest as we've both got a heap of paperwork to do in the morning.'

Rachel smiled. 'Good night, sir,' she said as she made her way to the door.

'Good night, Rachel,' replied Carmichael, as he picked up the small miniature he had borrowed from Sally Crabtree from his desk, before turning to stare out of the window once more.

\* \* \* \*

Amanda Buchannan scurried down the hallway of her auntie's house to open the front door.

'Oh, it's you,' she said with surprise when she realised it was Inspector Carmichael.

'I'm sorry to call at such a late hour,' said Carmichael. 'I was just wondering whether I could talk with you and your aunt.'

'Well, my auntie's out I'm afraid,' she replied. 'She's round at Caroline's house doing her "best friend in your hour of need" routine.'

'That's a shame,' replied Carmichael. 'I wanted to return this to her.'

With that he pulled out the small miniature from his coat pocket and handed it to Amanda. 'I understand this is of your mother,' he said. 'She was very beautiful.'

Amanda gently took the small sculpture from out of Carmichael's hand. 'Yes, she was,' she replied.

'May I come in, Amanda?' Carmichael asked. 'There are a few loose ends from the case and I was hoping you could help me tie them up?'

'Of course,' replied Amanda, who stood aside to allow Carmichael to enter.

Once inside, Carmichael was ushered into the front room.

'How can I help you?' Amanda asked.

'As you're aware, earlier today we charged Roy Lovelace with the murder of Tamara Searle,' said Carmichael.

'Yes, I know,' replied Amanda.

'There are, however, a few things about the case that are still perplexing me,' he continued. 'First of all is Tamara's house.'

'What was so confusing about that?' Amanda asked.

'Well, it didn't look as most homes look,' replied Carmichael. 'There were no personal items in the house, which almost made it look like she didn't live there.'

'Really?' said Amanda.

'Then there's the fact that your aunt gave her a reference,' continued Carmichael. 'Even though she says that she hardly knew her.'

Amanda didn't reply at first, but after a few seconds forced a smile, 'Well, I suppose it's not going to make any difference now if I tell you.'

'Tell me what?' replied Carmichael.

'The truth is', began Amanda nervously, 'that Tamara spent most of her time here with Aunt Sally and me. Tamara and I were very close at university and when we graduated we decided it would be nice to try and work together.'

'But why keep it such a big secret?' enquired Carmichael.

'That was not our intention at first,' continued Amanda. 'However, Tamara was very ambitious and she thought it might help her cause if Caroline didn't know that she was so close to her PA.'

'I see,' replied Carmichael. 'So the plan was for you to use your close working relationship with Caroline to provide Tamara with snippets of information she could then use to assist her climb up the greasy pole at Sunrise Productions.'

'It wasn't quite that bad,' remarked Amanda defensively. 'However, the gist of what you're saying is correct.'

'And I take it Tamara stayed here a fair bit then?' Carmichael asked.

'Yes,' replied Amanda. 'We have our own shared living room upstairs and Tamara and I shared a bedroom.'

Carmichael's eyebrows became raised.

'No, it was nothing like that,' Amanda said firmly. 'We weren't lovers; we were just really good friends.'

'I believe you,' replied Carmichael. 'But why didn't you tell me this after Tamara's death?'

'I did think about it,' replied Amanda. 'However, it was a private matter between me and Tamara, and I didn't think it was important.'

'It would have been much better if you had let me decide whether it was relevant or not,' remarked Carmichael.

Amanda nodded. 'Yes, I realise that now.'

'I'm sorry about Tamara,' continued Carmichael. 'It must be a difficult time for you right now.'

'It is,' replied Amanda. 'But I've decided that I need to look forward not backwards and my aunty has been great as always.'

'So are you comforted by the fact that we have arrested Roy Lovelace for Tamara's murder?' Carmichael asked.

Amanda gave a wry smile. 'Yes, of course I am,' she said, her eyes focused on the small miniature sculpture that she had taken from Carmichael at the front door. 'Especially as I'm sure that Roy Lovelace was also the person responsible for my mother's death. However, his arrest won't bring Tamara or my mother back.'

'I understand,' Carmichael replied.

Following a pause of a few seconds Carmichael continued. 'So what's your relationship like with Caroline Lovelace?' he asked.

Amanda looked back at Carmichael. 'It's totally businesslike,' she replied. 'I admire her professionalism and her abilities in front of the camera, but that's it. Away from the camera she's not a nice person and, to be frank, I don't like her much at all.'

'So will you continue working for her now that Tamara's dead?' Carmichael asked.

'For sure,' replied Amanda. 'I have my ambitions too, Inspector, and, whether I like it or not, they will be best served by staying close to Caroline Lovelace, at least for the immediate future.'

'So you also fancy being in front of the camera?' Carmichael asked with a note of surprise in his voice.

'Why not?' replied Amanda. 'You never know what fate has in store for you.'

Carmichael looked at his watch then got up out of his seat. 'It's late and I've taken enough of your time,' he said. 'Please give my regards to your aunt.'

Amanda stood up and shook his hand. 'I will,' she said, before escorting her guest to the door.

*   *   *   *

Although it was getting late and he was tired, Carmichael was in no great rush to get home that evening. He felt frustrated, but the simple truth was that he didn't have the evidence he so desperately needed to enable him to add Caroline Lovelace's name to that of her husband's as the murderer of Tamara Searle, Clare Sands and Emma Cashman. When he arrived back in Moulton Bank, he made a short detour to the Railway Arms for a quick drink with his friend Robbie Robertson and by the time Carmichael did eventually arrive home it was almost 10:30 p.m.

'You're really late,' remarked Penny as she greeted him with a peck on the cheek. 'You look like you could use a drink.'

Carmichael smiled. 'Yes, I could murder a large whisky,' he said, omitting to tell her he had already had a small one in the pub.

Ten minutes later Carmichael had kicked off his shoes and, with glass in hand, he and Penny sat together on the sofa in their living room.

'I made a few stupid errors today, Pen,' he said. 'And as a result that snotty, stuck-up cow, Caroline Lovelace, will almost certainly get away with the murders. I can't prove it but I'm as certain as I can be that it's her who carried out the murders and, although her husband was involved and helped her dispose of the bodies, I'm convinced that she's our killer.'

'So why is he taking all the blame?' asked Penny.

'God knows,' replied Carmichael. 'He's clearly totally obsessed with her and is willing to take full responsibility and allow her to walk free.'

Penny thought for a few moments before nudging her husband in the ribs. 'Would you do that for me?' she asked.

'No bloody chance,' he replied without a moment's hesitation.

'So is there no possibility of you being able to charge her too?' Penny enquired.

'Only if Roy Lovelace decides to change his tune,' replied Carmichael. 'And I think that's unlikely. The only other possibility would be if we found the CCTV tapes that were missing from the Cashmans' house this morning.'

'And is there much chance of you doing that?' asked Penny.

'Not really,' replied Carmichael. 'I'm pretty sure her ladyship took them and she's probably already disposed of them by now.'

'You never know,' said Penny. 'She may get her comeuppance – that often happens.'

'Not you too!' exclaimed Carmichael. 'You're the second person I've talked to this evening that seems to place their trust blindly in fate.'

# Chapter 50

**Six Months Later**

It was a red-hot August day when the case against Declan Cashman and Roy Lovelace was concluded. Before passing sentence on the two accused, Judge Percival Walker-Wells paid tribute to Inspector Carmichael and his team, whom he described as being meticulous and conscientious. He also praised their haste in bringing the two offenders to task.

'The court owes you, Inspector Carmichael, an enormous amount of gratitude for the way you tenaciously pursued the defendants in spite of much opposition towards you as a result of the high profile of one of them and also as a consequence of the popularity of Tamara Searle in the media. Your dogged resolve to get to the bottom of this complex case does you and your constabulary great credit.'

As the courtroom emptied and those who had attended the trial filed out into the warm summer sunshine, Carmichael could not help thinking how different the weather was to that freezing wintry week when the murders had all taken place.

As he left the courtroom he bumped into Melanie Dreyfuss and Sidney Sydes.

'Hello,' he said. 'What are you two up to?'

Melanie laughed. 'We've decided to emigrate and start afresh in New Zealand.'

'Yes,' interjected Sydes. 'There's nothing for us here so we thought we'd give it a shot.'

Carmichael smiled broadly and shook them both by the hand. 'I really hope it works out for you both over there.'

As he watched brother and sister walk away, Carmichael was joined by Hewitt dressed in his shiny well-pressed uniform. As they descended the courtroom steps together, Hewitt put a fatherly arm across Carmichael's shoulder. 'Well done, Inspector,' he said with genuine feeling in his voice. 'I would just like to echo the judge's words: you did a great job.'

'Thank you, Sir,' replied Carmichael. 'I really appreciated what he said and your support too. In a way it was a good result. I'm pleased that Lovelace got life; he deserved it and I'm also pleased that Declan Cashman got a custodial sentence too. I think two years for his part in the fraud was fair. However, I'm still annoyed and angry that the person I know was the real perpetrator of these murders is still free. She's lucky her husband is so loyal and is prepared to take the can for her actions.'

Hewitt shrugged his shoulders. 'You may well be right, Steve,' he said. 'However, we have nothing on her and with her husband's confession and no evidence to link her to the murders, we're powerless.'

'I know,' replied Carmichael, who over the last six months had not only come to terms with this injustice, but also with the painful realisation that he was unable to do any more. 'Roy Lovelace must be feeling pretty foolish, though, given that his dear wife has now sold up and moved house and she didn't even bother to attend one single day of the trial.'

'Yes,' replied Hewitt. 'She's still doing her daily talk show too, and I hear that her ratings have never been higher.'

'I've not watched it,' replied Carmichael. 'But I'm told it's now not just her show. Isn't it now called *The Lovelace and Buchannan Show*, with her old PA now a co-presenter with equal billing.

'Is that right?' replied Hewitt.

'Yes, my daughter Jemma says Amanda Buchannan is actually very good, but, as I say, I haven't bothered watching it myself,' replied Carmichael.

'And how is your daughter?' Hewitt asked. 'Has she landed back on earth after all the media attention following that business with the DC in Leeds she helped bring to justice?'

'Just about!' Carmichael replied with a laugh. 'I wasn't happy with her at the time, but now the dust has settled I'm actually very proud of what she did.'

'You damn well should be, Carmichael,' replied Hewitt. 'She's clearly a chip off the old block!'

Carmichael smiled broadly; he hadn't thought of it in those terms but certainly enjoyed hearing Hewitt's flattering comparison.

\* \* \* \*

Sally Crabtree burst into Caroline Lovelace's dressing room.

'Have you heard the verdict, Caroline?' she asked with not a hint of sympathy in her voice.

'No, I haven't,' replied Caroline meekly.

'He got life,' Sally announced without any thought of how her abruptness would be received by Caroline. 'It's no surprise given the charges.'

'I see,' said Caroline, her voice no longer exuding its customary self-assurance. 'Poor Roy.'

Although Sally could see quite clearly that Caroline was distressed, she was in no mood to show her any sign of compassion.

'I was wondering about tomorrow's show,' continued Sally. 'I think it might be good if Amanda did the main interview with the Home Secretary.'

'Oh you do, do you?' replied Caroline with indignation. 'I think we should leave it as it is with me doing that interview.

371

The production team may feel that this is a bridge too far for Amanda at the moment.'

'I don't think so,' retorted Sally confidently. 'I'm sure she can cope and I know that, as long as she has your full support, the production team will agree to anything. And as long as Amanda and I have our own separate copies of those CCTV tapes that she found in your locker, I think we can be assured of not only your undying support, but also that she and I can both sleep safely in our beds without any fear of mishap to either one of us. Isn't that right, my dear, old friend?'